RIO GRANDE RUBICON

We were talking on an open satellite link, speaking in Malay. I was pretty rusty because, fighting in Yucatan, just speaking English was enough to confuse any comm-circuit eavesdroppers.

"Gran," I said to Corbin, "no way I can bring the division back to the States. That would be illegal, bang, dead. You *know* that."

"I'll take responsibility. I am to be impeached on trumped-up charges in the House, followed by a criminal trial, probably for treason. Pollock is finally going to do away with me. He thinks."

"We are going to invade the continental United States, without securing a strategic nuclear capability or even heavy air support? That could be suicide, you know."

"Yes ... but then, the country has no opposition in the field, and no standing army since '98. We can walk ashore."

THOMAS T. THOMAS

FIRST CITIZEN

BAEN BOOKS

FIRST CITIZEN

Copyright © 1987 by Thomas T. Thomas

A Baen Books Original

Baen Publishing Enterprises
260 Fifth Avenue
New York, N.Y. 10001

First printing, December 1987

ISBN: 0-671-65368-7

Cover art by David Mattingly

Printed in the United States of America

Distributed by
SIMON & SCHUSTER
1230 Avenue of the Americas
New York, N.Y. 10020

For Rob

The world according to Quantum Mechanics:
Anything can happen at least once. Therefore,
given infinite time and space, the impossible
happens regularly. . . . Change is the only constant.

And according to Granville James Corbin:
Reality is what you make of it.

Recent Amendments to The Constitution of the United States

ARTICLE XXVIII

(Sent to the States June 20, 1992, by the 102nd Congress; ratified October 3, 1997.)

Section 1

The fourth section of the fourteenth article of amendment to the Constitution of the United States is hereby repealed. The Federal government shall incur no debts nor make any promises of repayment of debts to any person, party or nation.

Section 2

All debts of the Federal government in existence at the time this article may be ratified are hereby repudiated.

Section 3

This article shall be inoperative unless it shall have been ratified as an amendment to the Constitution by the legislatures of three-fourths of the several States within seven years of its submission to the States by the Congress.

ARTICLE XXIX

(Sent to the States June 20, 1992, by the 102nd Congress; ratified April 10, 1998.)

Section 1

Article I, Section 8 and the sixteenth article of amend-

ment to the Constitution of the United States are
hereby amended to revoke the power of the Congress to lay and collect taxes (including general income taxes), duties, imposts, and excises, to pay the
debts and provide for the common defense and general welfare of the United States.

Section 2

The Congress shall levy no general taxes nor disburse
the proceeds from any duties, imposts, or excises for
purposes other than those in support of the activities
from which the duties, imposts, or excises were
collected.

Commentary by G. J. Corbin:

In 1997 the U.S. government was a debtor to the
tune of $18.2 trillion, an amount more than six times
the country's gross national product. The country's
balance of trade was twelve to one against.

For almost two decades, various administrations
had wrestled with Federal deficits and the growing
national debt. Self-imposed budget restraint and legally imposed spending cuts both had failed to curb
the people's appetite—exercised through Congress—
for a free lunch. No one had the courage to raise
taxes to the levels needed to fund the government:
That would have had the same effect on the faltering
economy as a stone tied to a sackful of bravely swimming kittens.

Of course, when these amendments were proposed, debate raged furiously across the country.
Half the electorate and most of the media's opinion
leaders claimed it would impoverish the elderly and
disadvantaged, imperil the national defense and destroy the American Way of Life. The other half claimed
that a prime rate of thirty-five percent and inflation
at 300 percent were well launched toward those ends.

When the amendments were finally ratified, the Federal Government adopted, in place of taxation and deficit spending, a fee-for-service system. Licenses and fees supported those judicial and regulatory functions without which society would have foundered. The administrators of these functions no longer petitioned for their budgets before some congressional appropriations committee. Instead, they paid costs and salaries out of income, like any business. And they sent a percentage—a profit—upward to General Funds.

High tariffs and a system of limited monopolies protected the country's markets, igniting a wave of price-pull inflation that, for a while, felt like prosperity.

Postal and police services were farmed out to the commercial express and security firms which had already appropriated these markets among all but the very poorest users.

The military establishment was broken and turned over to public subscription and private contracting. The former supported a core of government-employed strategic planners, diplomacists and operators of the nuclear arsenal. The latter supplied weapons, materiel and a mixed body of volunteer regiments and mercenary troops.

The rest of the government—the masses of career bureaucrats and clients of the welfare state—were abandoned like the blackened carcass of a beached whale. And with time they were absorbed into the general prosperity, as rind and blubber are absorbed by the tide, the salt and the sand.

For a while in 1997 the U.S. government was a debtor, ten years later it had become the richest organization in human history, with liquid resources exceeding those of any emperor, tsar or pope.

ARTICLE XXX

(Sent to the States April 14, 2003, by the 108th Congress; ratified September 30, 2003.)

Section 1

Article II, Section 1 and the twentieth article of amendment to the Constitution of the United States are hereby amended to provide expeditiously for the succession of the President, in the event that both the President and the Vice President are simultaneously removed from office, die, resign, or otherwise become unable to discharge the responsibilities of their respective offices. In such case, the Speaker of the House of Representatives shall assume the powers, duties, and prerogatives of the executive branch and retain them until such time as a special election may be called to fill the vacated offices.

Commentary to G. J. Corbin:

This surprisingly simple piece of legislation was proposed and swiftly passed after the Hundred Lost Days, which began December 19, 2002. On the surface, it is merely a clarification of procedures that are addressed—but not entirely resolved—in earlier constitutional amendments.

The Thirtieth Amendment is hardly the sort of sweeping reform that one would expect to come out of the power brokering and confusion of those three months. It is at best a firecracker compared to the big gun of the Emergency Powers Act, which ended the Hundred Days. However, this amendment—not the Act—was the foundation upon which House Speaker George McCanlis assumed the power of the executive. And he did not let go for a long time.

Twenty years after this insidiously flawed legislation was ratified, legal scholars would note that "Speaker" is an exact translation of the Latin word *dictator*.

Chapter 1

Granville James Corbin: Head Fakes

[Transcript from the Library of Congress Video History Series, "Famous Americans" Section, Catalog No. 540-3222-00-2025A, N$42.95]

I was born at Whistling Winds, North Dakota.

At least that's what the official histories will say. Actually, the event occurred within eight miles of the place—straight up. We were at 39,000 feet at the time, my mother and I, on a polar flight from Los Angeles to London. She was more than seven months pregnant, looked six, and claimed only five—although what fun she thought she could have in London while seven months pregnant, I don't know. But she was, after all, Jennifer Corbin, nee Scoffield, of the Houston Scoffields, and a more self-determined woman did not breathe.

I did once visit Whistling Winds, in a professional capacity some fifty years later, during the Civil War. It reminded me of a false-front set for a small western town. Half a dozen single-story buildings stood along the main road. Only the old United States Post Office had any stone or brickwork on it, the rest were gray wood that might years ago have been painted brown or blue. Everything seemed temporary, made for show and, if you opened a door and stepped through, you'd be standing in dead prairie grass with the wind blowing in your ears. Everything looked like it would blow away across the flats. Except the grain elevators: They leaned over the cluster of buildings like a piece of mountain landscape.

The residents, all six of them, were gray people, too. Wheat farmers, they had long ago been edged out by agri-business strategies, expensive technology and the better rainfall in other, kinder States. If they had heard my claim of de facto citizenship, they would have been impressed not at all, no matter who I was.

There is a story, still told by my enemies, that Mother's labor was so long and terrible I had to be delivered by caesarian section. That an obliging doctor on board was forced to operate using only morphine, a scalpel and a packet of 00 sutures from his black bag. The experience was supposed to have crippled Mother, destroying even her capacity to have sexual relations, and thereby embittering my father toward me before I was actually born.

What did my younger sister ever make of these tales?

In some versions, the doctor orders the pilot to divert to Winnipeg, and I am cut away from the womb there. In others, he delays the operation until the plane is over the Irish Sea on final descent for Heathrow.

All are lies. I was delivered promptly into the hands of flight attendant Kimberly Johnson, of Fort Wayne. She was a cheerful girl who, so Mother claims, had a practical nursing license and kept her head at all times.

However, because I was two months premature and below the average birth weight, my first visit to London was spent "in hospital," as the natives say. But otherwise I suffered no ill effects: no congenital weaknesses, neither limp, nor palsy, nor slurred speech, nor mental retardation, nor fondness for exotic sexual prosthetics—no matter what my enemies may claim.

Was Father on that London flight? Of course not.

Let's see, the year was 1970, so he would have been in the United Arab Emirates, tidying up reserve estimates. Peter Corbin was senior geologist with Petramin Oil and claimed to know, personally, where more crude

was buried than the Japanese could buy in any six good
years.

The year before I was born, he had been in
transit between Palembang and Prudhoe Bay. Mother had
absolutely refused to relocate with him to Indonesia. And
the closest she would come to the North Slope was Val-
dez, where she believed she could pass the winter in a
detached house with central heating and clean sheets.
After six months of looking at black ice and listening to the
wind, Jennifer put her high heel down and insisted on
living forevermore in the Lower Forty-Eight and occasionally in Europe, because she could afford to. Let Peter
chase around the heathen world taking core samples where
he may.

It's a wonder I was ever conceived.

However, life was almost normal when I was a boy. And
that's odd, considering those were the years of the great
Arab oil embargo and the first energy crisis.

When I was old enough to participate in the confusion
of moving, packing my own toys and helping label the
book cartons with my crayons, we moved to Marblehead,
Massachusetts. I must have been about five, because I
wasn't in school then, just the next best thing to an Animal
Farm penitentiary, called pre-school. Why is it that all
teachers of very young children seem to be latent social-
ists? That political outlook must make it easier, morally, to
quash their individual and creative energies.

My first memories of Marblehead are of the statue,
down on the green grass along the seawall, of the bronze
fisherman at the wheel in a rain-slicked sou'wester and
oilskins, in memory of those who go down to the sea in
ships. Peter, my father, was mostly off at sea himself,
sailing around the Georges Bank on a research ship, dropping charges and scaring the cod. I always associated him
with the bronze man.

We lived in a gray-shingled saltbox set on a half-acre of
wooded land. Some of the lot was lawn on a layer of black
topsoil, and some was the original coastal pines growing
out of their own duff and sand. The house had real plaster

walls, not just gypsum board—as I discovered by knocking a few holes with a hammer. So it must have been a real, one-of-a-kind historical place and not some real estate agent's twenty-at-a-time subdivision. But I was too young to understand the difference then.

The backyard, where the pine needles were inches thick, had blueberry bushes growing like weeds. That was my only taste of fruit discovered by my own hands and tested for ripeness with my own tongue: those blueberries and the wild, once-a-season, solitary, sour strawberry that would grow in the lawn. All my other fruits and jams came out of a can, a jar, or a waxpaper-lined bin at the grocery store.

My hands and the points of my knees were always dirty with pine pitch, grass stains, loam, chalk dust, and grease from the wheels of, first, my little red wagon and, later, a bicycle. I always had a scrape or a cut somewhere on my hands and shins, and every summer my face and arms were puffed by mosquito bites or poison ivy. How durable and flexible we were as children; how stiff and brittle we become as adults.

The school at Marblehead quickly taught me to keep my first name a secret. Who wants to go around as Granny-Fanny all the time? So I went as Jay and sometimes James. For some reason never Jim, except to those who didn't know me at all and were trying to be familiar.

It would take me thirty years to learn the psychological advantages of letting people use a mildly embarrassing nickname. It lets them think they own a piece of you, and that binds them to you.

The school also taught me how to fight. Or, anyway, how *not* to fight. Little Granny got his Fanny pushed out of shape once too often by the childish taunts and lashed out with his tiny clenched fists. A fair, brown-haired boy, named Gordy Somebody-or-other, got in the way of my first, ill-timed swing and went down with a smear of blood in his nose. He probably deserved it, having been at the front of the circle calling names. He may even have started the whole thing.

First lesson: It doesn't matter who starts a fight, just who finishes it.

That incident also taught me about crowd psychology. I was preoccupied with the satisfying *snap* his head had made going back—and with the good feeling of standing over an enemy whom I had personally brought low—when the first counter blow caught the small of my back. I could feel the sickening shock of it in my kidneys and almost threw up. Then the circle closed over me in a wave of mittened hands, corduroy jacket sleeves, and scuffed Keds.

Second lesson: A crowd decides, with its own logic and in its own quick time, who wins and who loses. The crowd is the voice of history, and its version is official. I suffered a black eye, a split lower lip, and two red stars on my conduct card for fighting on school grounds. After that, I kept my name and my hands to myself.

At the age of eleven I nearly died, and took my sister Clarice with me, all on a childish conceit.

We had gone sailing one Sunday afternoon in a rented pram. That's an eight-foot open boat with a single dacron sail, just right for children puddling around the marina docks. We'd gotten this crazy idea, mostly mine, I guess, that we were going to sail off to Georges Bank and visit Father. Our imaginations put this mythical place about two miles beyond the town breakwater, just out of sight over the horizon. We happen to have picked the day of that summer's worst storm, but then, children do not listen to the Marine Band's weather channel.

The black clouds came up fast from the south as we rounded the tip of the breakwater. A water-smart child would have turned back immediately, but we were land-lubbers at heart. I had pretty easily learned how to make the boat turn this way and that, and had figured out that we had to keep the bladelike centerboard down in the water by hooking our feet under the seats and leaning way out over the high side. That was enough success; so I thought we could sail the little boat anywhere, even into the coming black rain.

Of course, I had not considered the wind and how it might be a lot stronger at sea, with no houses or trees to break its force. The first squall bent the aluminum tube of the mast sideways, like a soda straw crimped on the edge of a glass tumbler. It also flipped the boat so hard that Clary and I were catapulted out and about ten feet downwind.

Right there I did the first brilliant thing in my life: I figured out that we should stay with the boat. Even when it was upside down, had a bent mast and was drifting out to sea. Even when the shore looked close and we were both good swimmers.

I towed Clary back to the overturned pram, boosted her up and clamped her hands around the stubby keel. Clary is normally a pretty tough lady, but that day she was gritting her teeth and rolling her eyes like a bad trip on O-dyne. She was also beginning to freeze in that cold water, being a lot smaller than I was.

The waves were like long-fingered ghosts pulling at our legs, pushing at our arms and chests. While the wind sang in our ears, the waves chanted: "Come with me . . . go with us . . ."

Clary must have heard that song, too. Out of her throat came a tiny whimper, "No-oo."

Then I started talking to her, talking around my chattering teeth and shuddering lungs, about holding on and how soon somebody—Mother, Father, the man who rented us the boat and wanted it back—would certainly be looking for us, even with the rain and wind and all.

For six hours it went on like that. We held on while the storm passed and the water smoothed and the golden light of a summer evening broke over the shoreline, some miles away. Clary sobbed quietly with fright and the cold, and I gabbled about holding on and rescue coming soon.

Toward the end, when the cold was really beginning to get to me, so that my fingers and feet were like amputated stumps, my body stopped shivering and went hard inside. A white flame burned deep inside my chest. I thought it was my soul. Its light was without a flicker, like the cold white flash, edged with all colors, that I had once seen deep inside Mother's wedding diamond. I knew then that it would take a lot more than fifty-degree water and a summer rainstorm to put out that flame.

I talked to Clary about the white flame and told her she

had one inside her, too. The way she screwed up her face with concentration showed she was trying to believe it and not doing very well. I fanned that little fire with words until she admitted that, yes, she had one too.

It was almost eight o'clock and getting dark when the police patrol boat from the Town Dock found us. An old man in oilskins—not my father—pulled us off the turtled hull of the pram and wrapped us in blankets. He looked like the fisherman's statue come alive.

Mother was waiting on the dock and publicly cried over her draggled, shriveled babies for ten minutes. However, in our station wagon on the drive home she straightened and set her mouth.

"You've made a spectacle of yourself," she said to me. The tears in her eyes turned into a gleam of contempt.

"I just—"

"Please don't tell me what you were doing in that silly little boat. I don't want to know. Clearly, you were careless and got in over your head—although I can't imagine where you thought you could sail a boat like that. You not only risked your own life but your sister's as well."

"Momma," Clary started, "he was just—"

"I meant it when I said don't tell me."

Mother took a breath, as if to begin again. "You are a Scoffield. And a Corbin. It's your responsibility, James, to set an example for those about you. Live so that they can see how it should be done. Not so they have to come along and pull you and your sister out of the water. That's a weakness.

"Now, you'll never do a thing like that again, will you?"

"No, Momma," we chorused.

There was more, but I forget most of it. What stood out was Mother's absolute belief in *politesse oblige*. Her family, her social set were destined to civilize the crawling masses who were not fortunate enough to be Scoffields. Or Corbins. As Clary and I grew up, the simple lessons of right and wrong were too obvious for Mother. Instead she taught us to distinguish grandeur from *gaucherie,* seemly behavior from eccentric bombast, *beaux gestes* from rude gaffes, and personal freedom from plodding conformity.

Of course, it *was* remarkably stupid of me to try sailing an open pram out to the Georges Bank. If she had known that was my plan, Mother would have whinnied that high laugh of hers and called me an utter fool. Thanks to Clary it remained a secret between us until we were all too old to care. But I never forgot.

Somehow, in the excitement of finding and bringing us children back to port, all the grownups forgot that I had broken the rule of the boat rental place about staying in the harbor. Everyone, that is, except the owner. He tried to sue my family for the loss of the pram. Father in turn sued him for negligence in renting to obvious minors. The matter dragged listlessly through our respective lawyer's offices until the family moved to California.

For political or environmental or some other unreal reason, the oil never came in on the Bank. So Father was off to the other side of the country. Mother went happily because she remembered trips to California—Santa Monica and the LA Basin—as a girl and she thought the Monterey coast would be almost as nice.

It was nicer.

Jennifer Corbin settled into the art galleries of Carmel the way a tent caterpillar settles into an apple orchard. Father sailed the offshore fault system, dropping charges and scaring the people.

We lived in a mock adobe house—gunnite shot through chicken wire and troweled until it looked half-melted, like cake frosting on a hot day—in Asilomar. That house had two and a half tons of glass sliding in doors and windows, all on ball bearings, and an acre of ultra-white carpeting you couldn't walk on but had to keep to the clear plastic runners. I didn't spend much time there.

Asilomar was west of the action, and I don't remember how I got around. Too young to drive and but-nobody rode what buses there were. I hitched a ride with friends or clean-looking strangers, I guess. Most of the time it didn't lead to trouble. And when it did, I could handle it.

My place was Cannery Row, fifty years after Steinbeck, when the canneries were gone except as building shells. And in these, like bold hermit crabs in weathered surroundings, were established the latest designer bars, the tourist galleries, the street artists, the rock bands, and the pushers. It was like a permanent, genteel carnival. Just perfect for a boy turned thirteen who could think this slice of plastique was adult life.

And then, for two weeks every summer Mother retreated to Copenhagen; for two weeks in winter, to Venice and Florence. Clary and I ate ice cream in our hotel, picked up Danish and Italian from the local television, and never asked about the giggles and thumps coming through the wall from Mother's room. All thirteen-year-olds are hardened realists. I told Clary that Mother was playing adult games in there. I suppose she was.

The taste for drama, like the taste for love, has come and gone with most boys by the time they reach thirteen. It died especially fast for boys coming of young age in mid-'80s America, when drama was lighted with phosphor images of kung fu fists and hurtling cars, when love was sticky with rock video, zip-tab cola, and pinches of coke. I remember being a coldly rational child, too old for my years. I parceled out my emotions and my flights of fancy the way a miser parts with gold.

For example, we used to play football, shirts versus skins, in a narrow park with an inconvenient pathway—a strip of bare, packed dirt—running right across the widest part of the field. The game was supposed to be touch football, but everyone got to tackling when the runners kept ignoring the two-hand fanny slap and no one called them on it. I watched as one of my teammates, a skin, took a tackle on the edge of this dirt, rolled, and came up with a red patch looking like shiny paint across his shoulders. It proved his manhood, presumably.

Two plays later I had the ball and found myself bearing down on the same edge of path with one shirt just a stride and a half behind me and two more closing from the grass side. No slap on the rear was going to satisfy them, and flying face-first across that dirt was going to hurt enormously. And for what? A scratch game of football, the teams chosen and their loyalty bonded with the casual point of a finger.

So I stepped out of bounds deliberately and, to keep the man behind from tackling me anyway, got down on one knee.

"Coward!" yelled the first side blocker.

"Faggot wimp," tossed in the second.

The one behind punched my shoulder as he ran by.

It was just a friendly game.

Given no strong directions, a poor boy will function as the economists' Rational Man. That is, he will capitalize on his opportunities according to his nature—engaging either in dealing and light-finger if he's a talker or strong-arm and territorial warfare if he's a doer. A rich boy with no direction, however, will go precisely nowhere. And that's where I was headed.

That summer I was hanging around a locksmith's shop, going on calls with him, doing some cleanup, nothing he was actually paying me for. The training he gave me in return—just letting me watch, examine his tools and occasionally try my touch—was probably a breach of his code of ethics and illegal to boot. He thought I was just a clean-cut kid from Asilomar, and I thought I was going to be an international jewel thief.

That was the summer, too, that I started karate—another facet of my secret agent self. Just about everyone in my class at school took a six-week course in quote self-defense unquote. Some of us followed it up with a short-lived enrollment at Kan's down on the mall. But I stayed with it four years, in the end becoming a part-time, unpaid teacher for Sensei Kan.

Karate is the ultimate bore. You practice each move—which itself is made up of smaller, more precise moves of muscle and tendon—over and over until your arm or leg glides like a programmed robot. Then you combine the moves into sequences, and the sequences into extended imaginary fights, the *kata*s. It's more like ballet than fighting.

Don't think that, because I could put up with all this minutiae, I was obsessed with karate. No, it was just part of my tender self-image. Mastering finicky details like keeping my wrists straight and my feet parallel in a step-and-punch seemed like little enough to pay for my internal fantasies.

I never gave myself one hundred percent to anything. Not to any discipline, any ideal, any art, any person, any love. It was all just a friendly game, remember? And none of it mattered more than my personal integrity and my own sweet hide. That distancing, that distinction between myself and the world around me, was the secret of my strength in the years to come.

You may not like that. You don't have to. This is my life we're talking about here.

Sensei Kan was a tiny man, all muscle. He taught about one class in four himself, the rest going to senior students while he walked the *dojo* floor, observing, correcting tiny flaws, encouraging. Of course, he taught the advanced course in the evening for brown belts and above. To me he was just this presence, a small smiling shadow, until I earned brown—in about three years—and was invited to join those evening classes.

What I remember most about Sensei Kan was his movements. They were so fluid, like water over a stone. Sensei seemed like a middle-aged man to us—at least forty—and although he was Korean he spoke perfect English without an accent. He wore a belt, a black one with red Chinese writing down the end. The school brochure claimed him to be an eighth degree in karate and a fourth in judo, but Kan never talked about his belt. Only about his teachers and their lessons.

He ran a tight class and made you sweat, which was okay, but we thought he was a little heavy on the bow-and-smile, respect-for-all-living-things crap. Or we called it crap.

Once two boys went out on the floor to settle a grudge in full-focus sparring and started throwing for-real kicks without the padding. Sensei Kan was on the other side of the *dojo,* sitting cross-legged with his back to them, watching a *kata* group go through their exercises. In two seconds he crossed the distance to the sparring square in a white blur and waded into the middle of a murderous bridge-kick and back-hand exchange. He tripped both of the angry boys onto their asses as if they were just standing around. And for the next free period he lectured the whole class about how we were brothers upon the Way and should have no animosities among us. And we all thought: yah-yah, yack-yack.

The first time Kan sparred with me, I believed it was because he had seen how really good my feet were. I had practiced a roundhouse and back-kick combination until I could lift a flowerpot off a six-foot wall and crunch it before it hit the ground. I was puffed up, touchy about my skills, a real brat.

It was his head fake that caught me.

We were sparring in the warmup before class. I was in a modified straddle stance, Kan in a tight side stance with his hands cocked at the ready.

"Don't look at me," Sensei whispered—for the second time. Being new to the advanced section, I didn't know that two warnings were Kan's limit. In the next instant, the young-old man's eyes locked with mine and his head started to unscrew.

The eyes never lost their focus, just panned left, out across the floor with the same seeing-but-not-alive gaze that a department store dummy has. Sensei's head was held as level as a white china teacup. I watched, fascinated, as the cords of his neck twisted and overlapped, until the chin was pointing back over his shoulder. It was the same smooth, sinuous flow that a snake makes in the sand.

Sensei's arched foot was suddenly tucked under the lapels of my white *gi* jacket. The wind went out of my chest like cream poured out of a pitcher. The clacking in my ears was my own knees striking the hardwood floor.

Putting it together later, in afterimage, I saw how the head fake had blended into a shoulder fake, a body fake and a 360-degree roundhouse kick that had caught me in the solar plexus.

Perfect.

But the admiration came after; right then, the problem was oxygen.

With gentle hands Sensei supported me under the arms and forced my head forward to help me breathe.

"You believe me when I tell you not to look at your opponent?" Sensei asked with a lilt that I heard as a smile. "You aren't fast enough yet to look at him. Look past his shoulder. Use your peripheral field to see *movement*. Not eyes. Not hands. Not feet . . . Movement."

When I could stand, still hunched over, the young-old man walked me to a sideline bench and sat me down, directing my weight and balance as easily as pushing a cart.

"You are quick," Sensei squinted at me with those Asian eyes that belied the English voice. "Good coordination. Good moves. When you learn to see without looking, you will be as fast as your body promises."

Right at that minute, with the ache in my chest still blossoming like a gong tone, I began to realize something. The sensei had just called me a brown-belt asshole, a pizza-breath kid, and not such hot shit after all. Hell, he had *shown* me that. And it hadn't hurt, not inside, as a rebuke from any other adult would. From Sensei Kan, I could accept it.

Then the sensei had said something nice about me. Not extravagant praise, but an acceptance, an honest appraisal. As if I were a horse we were both admiring but didn't particularly plan to ride or buy. It was just true and no reflection on either of us.

With the gong fading now, I had put a few of the pieces of my cocky, sixteen-year-old life together. I still held a handful of puzzle parts with tabs and hollows, colors and shapes that in no way fit together. But I had made a start.

Chapter 2
Granville James Corbin: Personal Kill

The year I made brown belt at Sensei Kan's karate studio was also the year I met Alice Wycliffe and lost my heart.

A number of rapes had scared the women at the high school, and everyone was thinking self-defense again. Alice came into the *dojo* with two of her girl friends. They were all from the cheerleading squad, but alongside them Alice was like a gold sovereign tossed in with two old nickels.

They all had pretty faces but, compared to Alice's, the others were out of focus, with a nose too long or a chin too short. They all had slender legs, tight asses and jutting breasts but, compared to hers, the other two were lumps and bumps, fat calves and calloused elbows. They all had clean, layered blonde hair, but Alice's made the other girls' seem like old bird's nests.

Today I can still remember what she looked like.

Sensei let the girls observe a class, and they walked along the edge of the oak-plank practice floor with their leather pumps making tappity-tap sounds, like a team of horses on cobblestones. Everyone else in the room was barefoot.

Seeing this absolutely beautiful girl from across the room, I suddenly felt foolish. The white cotton *gi*, even when it's freshly washed and pressed, is a loose-fitting pair of pajamas, like something worn by a walk-on from *Lord Jim* or *Gunga Din*, with sagging knees, short coat, loppy lapels.

The belt ties just under your navel, above the second *chakra*, which is your sex. The loose ends flap around your groin. And all I was wearing under this baggy suit was a jockstrap with a nut cup. We'd been working hard, I was sweating, the cotton was sticking to my ass, and it was definitely two days too long since I'd had the whole rig washed.

And here came the most beautiful girl in our high school, probably the most beautiful on the Monterey Peninsula, maybe in the State of California, into the *dojo* where I happened to be class leader that day. Sensei Kan brought the girls over toward me and, with his twinkle, introduced them.

Alice actually put out her hand, a slender, clean hand with four beautifully shaped fingers and even a nice-looking thumb. She was standing close enough that I could smell her scent, something-lemon, which meant she was close enough to smell me, overworked-horse.

Mother once told me that as a baby I was a knockout. But all babies have the same sweet-Buddha face: rounded cheeks and forehead, clear eyes, gentle smile—at least when they are sleeping well.

With the years, however, I got to watch in the mirror as my face changed to the contours of a painted wooden puppet, something crafted in Europe for the sophisticated New York art market. My blue eyes had pinched up, I thought, above ruddy apple cheeks. My chin and nose had sharpened—one like the point of a ballerina's toe slipper, the other like a knife blade. My lips and mouth grew wide and worked constantly between a rubbery smile and a bowed pout of anger. I had red hair that thickened and curled until, under some lights and all summer long, it looked like a clown's string wig.

As my voice and vocabulary developed, my brat self began to come out with flashes of wit, malice and occasional wisdom that Mother and Father heard with uneasy tolerance. For many of the things I mouthed, they could probably find no root in themselves. Like any boy, I was full of cheap enthusiasms and echoes of my environment. And that—abetted by the Cannery Row scene and with fantasies of being an international jewel thief, secret agent, kung fu master swirling in my head—wasn't exactly *their* environment. I also read a ton of books and watched people . . . judged people, if I remember rightly. I was a brat, really self-centered. But I've since learned to live with myself.

"How do you do?" said the future Salinas Valley Lettuce Queen, lightly pressing the fingers of the grinning puppet who smelled like a horse.

"Okay, 'n' you?" I mumbled.

The two other girls giggled, Alice smiled faintly, and Sensei Kan nodded and adroitly wheeled them away across the floor. Right then I could have killed him—if I'd had a hand grenade and room to throw it.

For the rest of the hour they stood on the sidelines watching the class, talking among themselves, and occasionally pointing and giggling. At me, or so I believed.

It turned out that the other girls thought karate was too much like work and decided to take the mace course instead. Alice, however, had found something graceful and meaningful in the movements. She bought a *gi*, signed up for the beginners' eight-week course, and I taught her.

For two months I gave that girl personal attention. I held her beautiful feet straight while she practiced stances, steadied her hips while she kicked, braced her shoulders as she punched. In sparring, I even let her kick me—hard—in the stomach. And I only occasionally peeked between her lapels. Because the *gi* jacket tends to fall open in a side kick, most girls wore a tee-shirt under it, but Alice always wore an iridescent leotard with an interesting neckline.

No one was more patient with her, no one more loyal and devoted. She smiled, nodded at everything I said, and still learned nada, zip, zero. Alice was graceful, all right, and worked hard, but she had absolutely no spatial sense, no timing. She also confused left and right. She must have made cheerleader on her smile alone.

And yes, for those first two months I thought about asking her out for a date. But every time my internal ear could hear her saying no, she had to wash her hair, study for a test, catch up on her letter writing, et cetera—just like every girl I had ever wanted.

I was still a virgin at sixteen, at least as far as girls were concerned. Boys didn't count. I had played my share of grab-ass in the showers, had explored my section of the sand hills, and made the obligatory jokes about it. All the time we were also talking about girls and how to get to them. Whatever we boys might do, it wasn't "balling." The official thing was Doing It With a Girl.

After two months of positioning Alice's feet, fists and elbows during class, I finally got up the nerve to ask the future runner-up Miss California for a date. Right away she let me take her to Fleur de Lis on Cannery Row and later, in her father's car, let me manipulate her limbs in other ways.

During the year and a half that we went around together, Allie showed me that girls worry just as much about impressing boys as boys do about girls. Sometimes more so. It's just that boys are like weasels in their curiosity and their pleasure, being wired directly. Girls are more like kittens or butterflies, being wired obliquely.

Alice also taught me that a beautiful girl needs love and companionship, just as much as a plain one. Often more so. You see, a heartbreaker like Alice, even if she's never done a thing, soon gets a reputation among the boys: She is at once a whore and unattainable. A whore because sex is all they can think about when they see her. Unattainable because they are intimidated by her and by the others they are sure compete for her attentions. A truly beautiful and sexy woman frustrates—and so angers—the average man, who usually thinks himself homely and unworthy.

After a couple of months of straightening her feet and uncrooking her wrists on the twist punches, I was seeing Allie as just another goofball white belt who had a long way to go before she'd be any good at karate, if ever. Then I could love her: she had become a definite person, not just a beautiful face and body in the abstract.

I soon discovered that Allie also had a head, as well as a cutting sense of humor. With her, boys and boyish conceits were all presumed to be just a little absurd. So when I told her about becoming an international jewel thief, she just laughed.

"You'd be caught in two minutes, Jay. You're too basically honest, aren't you, to creep into people's houses and take their things? Besides, if you were *really* interested in becoming a jewel thief, you'd study gems, not locks, because you don't know a thing about diamonds or emeralds. You don't know much about being a thief, either, because nobody locks up her jewels with a *pad*lock, f'gosh sakes. It's either a safe with a combination, or a bank vault. So you'd have to study dynamite and demolition. Risky, dear. . . Study business or law instead. With your wits and quick mouth, you'd be good at them."

And then she would show me what else a mouth was good for. That was a nice summer.

Mother hated Allie.

"She's just a little tramp who wants to get you into her pants, James. I'm not saying she doesn't have good taste. But you have to have the good sense, and the self-restraint, to put a trollop like her in perspective. She's not really up to the level of a Scoffield, or a Corbin, is she?"

"Well, Mother . . ."

"You want to find a woman with whom you can share your life, your ideals. You're still . . . *pure* . . . aren't you, James?"

"Yes, Mother." That was the least of the lies I told her.

What was school—my high school, not the Sensei's *dojo*—like?

The Sixties doctrine of "relevance" still held the neck of education in steel fangs. Irrelevant courses like ancient history, dead languages like Latin and Standard English, and arcane sciences like physics were dropped from the curriculum as quietly as corpses slipped over the rail of a plague ship. Nothing that did not prepare the student for the "real world" was permitted to survive. We were to be indoctrinated in the ways of work and play and politics of

what, so our teachers thought, would be the twenty-first
century. We took courses, complete with lesson plans and
outside readings, in computer games theory, cryogenic
medicine, situational ethics, Swahili culture, and economic
feminism. The soft sciences had hardly escaped the relevance craze; these were downright mushy.

Teaching was out, *process* was in. We held study groups.
We did independent research. We "immersed." We assembled "postulate outlines" of clippings from the news
magazines—that was for a hist-soch course. We played
with half a megabuck worth of cameras and editing equipment as part of an "appreciation of video" course.

We touched the fashionable high points and learned
nothing deep. But the twentieth century was a screwup
anyway. Going deep into it was like scuba-diving in a pot
of boiling pasta: tangled, slimy and, ultimately, you come
up covered with burns.

I liked languages. Learning a new one was like dressing
up in costumes. So before my senior year I had pinches
and puffs of French, Bantu, Russian, Japanese, Thai, and
Turkish to go along with the Danish and Italian. I learned
enough on the oral-aural method to conjugate a few verbs,
put together simple sentences and imagine myself a coun-
tryman. But I usually bombed out when we got into
translations of milksop versions from the national literature. Translating always seemed mechanical to me: pick
up the next word, look it up in the dictionary, fit it into
the syntax. Coding and decoding. Today we have specialists who do that—dull ones.

It was not until my second year at Berkeley that I was
introduced to a language that was no longer spoken and not
relevant to a war-torn country. I took two semesters of
Latin grammar because my major was, loosely, pre-law
and my advisor was a disorganized romantic who filed my
cards too late the previous semester to get me into "Le-
ninism and the African Enlightenment" or some equally
solemn three-credit sophomore seminar.

For fifteen weeks I struggled through the declensions of
agricola and *gladium*. I learned verb forms and tenses that

slithered and scraped like rusty armor. Latin is a language that's bolted and hinged like a machine, and to my ear—which was comfortable with the syntax and phrasing of "We was down to the drive-in"—it sounded hard and brittle, like a roach in a pie tin.

That was the first semester. In the second we began translating Caesar and that was worse. I knew as much about Gaius Julius Caesar as any high school boy: Bald man. First of the Roman emperors. Stabbed by a ring of fellow senators twenty-one times in 44 B.C. Or was forty-four times in 21 B.C.? Anyway, I had once heard "Beware the Ides of March" and always confused it with income tax time.

After three chapters of Caesar's kindling-dry prose, I was ready to stab him myself. "At the sounding of the trumpet, we marched forth four days and met the Belgae. . . ." Poor Belgae! To be run over by the Roman mowing machine. March, fight, camp, march. That's all Caesar wrote. For a great general, he came across as a stuffed shirt, a cunning diplomatist and a steel-hearted surgeon when it came to letting blood. It wasn't until much later that I would read his life with more interest and understanding.

Absent from all the languages we sampled in school was Spanish. It wasn't something we studied because it came at us from the air, off the street, on certain bands of the AM dial, and over the counters of every dimestore in town. Spanish was the second language of California and, if you didn't have at least a lick of it, you were blind and deaf to half of what was going on. For a gringo, I could work my way along *poco a poco* in conversation and with signs and notices. That helped a lot when we took the AirCav into Yucatan.

Hispanics were never a problem with me. They are survivors. Whether it's the religion, the Indian blood, or the years of making do on their own and never leaning on the government—because no government ever truly belongs to them—they get by, raise kids, raise corn, walk slowly into the years and through the generations. They don't go crazy in the head, eat their children, worship cats, and blow the price of a BMW 733 up their noses. Or not many of them do. Indian and Spanish ancestors alike, they were done with all that big government, the bureaucracy, the terror, the Inquisition, *auto-da-fe*, and blood sacrifice on a carved stone . . . All of that happened to them hundreds of years ago, and now they've outgrown it. Survivors.

So it was sad that my first personal kill, the first man— boy, actually—that I took out with my own hands, was a Hispanic.

That was one evening about six months after Allie and I had started going together. We were hanging on the edges of the crowd at The Whaling Station, down on the Row, getting beer from anybody who would order two extra, taking hits off whatever was passing around and listening to the band, which was off key, off the beat and off the top of the charts.

It was a Thursday night, October, and the sun had gone down early behind a rack of clouds that could be sea fog but might be the cutting edge of the first winter rains.

The Hispanic boys were five, making a knot in the crowd and moving against it, tough and brittle. They had Fifties-style combed-forward haircuts, tight black jeans and long-sleeved nylon-satin shirts in solid fluorescent colors, citron, garnet, and amethyst, all looking like Bernahhhdo out of *West Side Story.* They definitely did not blend into a down-jacketed, suede and bluejean crowd that in about three hours was going to scatter toward the Seventeen Mile Drive, Carmel and points south.

Like iron filings to a magnet, the five of them circled and then settled around Alice, who was a bright spot of golden hair and white leather jacket in the darkness of the bar.

Cooing, chirpy voices caressed the air around her, giving her "Hey, chickie!" and "Wanna good time?" and other slightly lewd suggestions. All with heavy-lidded smiles. They were giving her one-finger touches, light brushes that were a cross between homage and dog-pawing, while cutting me deftly back into the shadows of elbows and shoulders. At first Allie was laughing with it, because it was all friendly, and then she started looking my way with a frightened lift of the eyebrows.

"Come on, Al, time to go," I said, reaching in through their circle and extracting Allie almost faster than her feet could move. The five boys could see I was annoyed, not taking it friendly. And perhaps I used a few words and hand gestures that someone who was less buzzed with beer and pot, more sure of himself, and not so touchily proud of his beautiful lady might have avoided.

Anyway, the circle came with us until we were all standing out on the street. The wind was kicking fretfully at papers in the corners between buildings and flagging Allie's hair. The boys' hands went, slowly, casually, into jeans pockets and hung there. Suddenly I didn't want to know what was in those pockets.

It was bad luck that her car was parked up the Row, away from the wharf, at the dark end where the asphalt breaks up in sand and weeds and rusted railroad tracks. As Allie and I headed up there, the circle of five followed like a dog pack, making growly, barking noises. The fun had quickly faded and a waspy, crawly, serious note had come on. The hands never left their high slash pockets. In the glances I took over my shoulder, I could see that the pressure of palms against hips was making them swagger like girls.

Flankers were moving out fast. In another ten paces they would have us surrounded again. My beer buzz was clearing up fast.

"Can you keep one of them busy?" I asked quietly, out of the side of my mouth.

Allie had stuck with the karate course at Kan's, but she was still only a green belt and had been talking for two weeks now of maybe dropping out. Tonight she was wearing skintight jeans and gray leather boots with four-inch stiletto heels. That made her just about helpless, unless she flopped on her back and shot up with those street-diggers. Accurately. Once.

"I—I'll try."

"Better stay behind me," I decided.

Except there wasn't any behind. Before I could get my back to a car or something and limit the field of battle, they were around us in the center of the street. No taunting or standoff now, the first punch was coming in low at six o'clock in the ring even before the other boys were fully in position. I blocked it with a back-fist and countered with a hip rotation and mulekick to the groin that missed by inches and hammered his thighbone. If I had wanted to break out of the circle, I could have walked through him like a door. But that would have left Allie inside and vulnerable. So I spun in line one-eighty degrees and put the second kick high into the throat of the man at twelve o'clock. The bright-colored shirts were making their positions easy to spot in the shadows. Still, the kick skittered up his breastbone and thunked under his chin. Neither man went down and that was a bad sign. Three o'clock and nine came in to pin my arms. Where was the fifth man? I bumped Allie out of the way with my hip and snaked my arms up to escape the pin, then swung them right back down for simultaneous double-fists to the groin. Where was the fifth man? The move caught one of the boys low in the stomach, no help. But the other was hit square in the nuts and he cried out. That cry was a signal to my battle circuits and I flipped over to full attack. As he doubled over I brought my left knee up into his face and both hands down in a cross-chop across the back of his neck. Bone snapped like a bundle of dry twigs. Where was the fifth man? A hot point dug into my back, just above the kidneys, from the twelve o'clock side. I was turning before I knew it, and a line of pain stitched across to my shoulder blade as the knife tried to settle in but slipped past. Was that the fifth man? My turn was led by a cross-arm block that bulled aside his knife arm. That opened him up and my counter punch went three inches into his solar plexus. The second alternate went into his throat. The third into the center of his forehead. And the fourth fanned the air because he was already down. The last beat in the series was a stab I took under the left armpit, straight in with a five-inch blade, and *that* was the fifth man. I could feel liquid metal begin to fill my lung and knew that in three seconds I would be bubbling and spraying blood. But I wouldn't die for a couple, three minutes and before then the fight would be over. The idiot pulled his knife out of me, probably thinking he wanted to have it for another stab and not knowing that as long as it was in my side he had a handle that could take me anywhere. I lifted into a sidekick that pulled all sorts of bloody strings under my ribs and put the edge of my foot squarely in his throat. He just about flipped over backwards. And that broke the circle.

The count was two down and three wobbling when they scattered, one of them dragging the boy who took the three punches. That left me, standing tall and bleeding; Allie, with a face as white as her leather coat; and the man with the broken neck.

Sometimes you can just walk away from a mess like that. Not always, but sometimes.

His name was Emilio Lopez. They guessed that later from a tattoo and a steel ID bracelet. He was an undocumented alien, or the child of such, and didn't have a scrap of paper on him. He wasn't a citizen, anyway, and no one came forward to press charges.

I was an Anglo from a good home, under eighteen, and only a brown belt at the time. It was a fight with knives and there was the honor of a white girl to protect. So, in the flashing red and blue lights of ambulances and patrol cars, the Monterey police wrote it up as self-defense while the medics packed the hole under my arm.

They bundled me off to the emergency ward. The resident on duty probed and stitched, then confirmed that it was a muscle wound and the knife had turned on a rib. Meanwhile the patrolmen finished up their paperwork and then told Allie and me to get our butts out to "Asshole-mar," which is what they called our part of town, and to stay there.

When we pulled into the driveway at the mock-adobe, it was dark. Both my parents were at sea, Father on the *Petramin Explorer II* and mother on the good ship *Cutty Sark,* which she had begun to sail with regularly. Allie took her wounded warrior upstairs, undressed him and made gentle, tender love with her mouth.

As I say, sometimes you can walk away from it. Afterwards, I always felt it was a sign of how sick our country, our culture had become that a man could be killed on the streets and, because he did not have a piece of paper or powerful friends, the incident would close like that. It did not even make the front section of the paper, which was a miracle in a small tourist town like Monterey, and no one ever followed up with my parents.

A man had been stomped like a cockroach and the stomper had driven home the same night. It was to happen a lot in the closing years of the last century.

But Sensei Kan wasn't part of that century. He was straight out of sixteenth-century Japan or wherever they practiced *bushido,* chivalry, honor. When I was healed enough to return to the *dojo,* he called me up in front of the whole class, stood me at attention and took off my brown belt. Then he tied on a white one with his own hands.

"You may think that to kill a man in battle makes you a warrior," he said in a way that bounced off the oak floor and echoed in corners of the room. Anyone could tell he was furious.

"If you have so little control of yourself, of your art, that you kill your opponent when you should disable and discourage him, then you must start over at the beginning."

"But," I blustered, "there were five of them!" The note of injured protest in my voice was mixed with pride.

"Then it is very lucky that your clumsiness did not kill more!"

"But—"

"Please be silent. Take your place at the back of the class."

No one met my eyes as I walked past the rows of students, not even Allie. She dropped out a few days later, unable to bear my humility. To her, I was a hero who had been wounded defending her.

I thought about dropping out, too. But the next day

Sensei had cooled off and treated me just as before. So I decided to stay. What with the ripped muscles, the stitches and the loss of body tone with being laid up, it took me six months to work back to brown belt. By the time I graduated from high school and left for college, I'd earned a first-degree black belt and learned twelve of the thirteen *katas* in our style.

Sensei Kan always said the belt didn't matter, but just then it was the most important thing in my life.

they had never seen as go back to what they had known and rejected.

At the end of the valley, the only thing to do was climb the Barren Mountains, the Tehachapis. Today those hills are good only to fly over and look down into, dreaming what it would be like to crash and have to walk out of them. Beyond the mountains, my people crossed the rolling sandy desert, the Mojave, with its dry lakes and praying cactus plants. The desert was worse than the mountains. Finally they came to the Big Red, now the Colorado, the river of swelling, muddy waters which so blinded the fish that they leapt into our baskets.

There my people camped and, unlike any of the bands before them, they sent out scouts, pathfinders. They were smart redskins.

Six months, a year later these young men came back and said that all beyond was the stony deserts of Sonora. The news just about broke the spirit of the squaws and boy children, but the older men conferred solemnly among themselves. Then the traveling chiefs put aside their skins and laces and went off to fish. The camp chiefs sat down to meditate their circles in correct proportion with the Sun and the Earth, and they sent the women to see what grew nearby and was it good to eat.

So my people, the Mohave, settled beside the river. They were still there twenty-five thousand years later when I was born. Except they were on different land, a poorer piece that was mostly sand, granted to them by the white man for no reason they could understand.

The valley that had been ours was now crowded with casinos, condominiums, trailer parks and snowbird nests. Flashing neon by night and glaring aluminum siding by day. All straight lines, hard edges, fast words and brassy music. Money. Dams and power stations and taco stands and gas stations. The white man's world hurts the eyes and nose and ears.

The river was still there, too, but it was a poorer river. Instead of rolling on to the ocean, the Big Red was so throttled by the white man's dams that it wandered off and died in Mexican sand before it could reach the Sea of Cortez. So it lost its true purpose as a river.

I was not born in a sagebrush wickiup covered with skins and standing as part of a circle, which is the proper birthing place for any native American child. I came forth into a frame house, with no paint on its splintering boards, standing in a white man's straight line along the road. My mother told me all this, as I was too busy at the time to notice and understand.

It was being born in a straight line, like the whites, that caused all the trouble. I have lived sixty years too long. When Quetzalcoatl the Serpent came for me in the Bay of Campeche, even though he had to fly a hundred miles across the waters, I resisted like the white man. Now I am lost and have no true place to go.

Of course, it does not help that my father was not an Indian. He was a Hell's Angel on a run. His tribe had turned up one day on the reservation, half drunk and looking for peyote buttons, which we did not have. His name was Red, so he must have been Irish. All he owned was a chrome and steel Harley-Davidson with a turquoise-blue teardrop gas tank. That and his greasy denims. He and his companions lived like Apaches: just a horse for travel, a pair of leggings for the brush, and an attitude. My father was a white Indian.

He may have come from Las Vegas or Los Angeles, I never found out. When I was tall enough for my thumb to be seen above the roadway, and smart enough to figure that staying on the reservation was no good unless I could learn to farm sand and eat it, I went to both places. But I never saw or heard about a Hell's Angel named Red.

You might think that all tribes are rich, now that coal and oil and other precious things have been found under the sad scrublands the White Father deeded to us in perpetuity. The Navaho are rich, yes, if they can sell their mineral rights at a good price, or finance the machinery to dig the coal themselves—and not get taken by the white lawyers and moneymen.

The Chinook are not so rich, having exclusive rights to the salmon on the Columbia—so long as they take the fish

themselves with techniques that are more picturesque
than profitable.

The white law is sometimes clumsy. Here and there it
lets a native American make off with something of value,
just as here and there a crack in the pavement lets a tough
weed, a thistle, grow up to the sunlight. But it is still the
white law.

What I learned in Las Vegas, and improved on later in
Los Angeles, was how to find things that people wanted.
Cigarettes, loose change, tape decks, contraband—there
was usually a way. The most valuable lesson for a twelve-
year-old scrounger was the *margin*: the more people wanted
something, the greater is the risk of obtaining it, so the
higher the price must be. Hubcaps are easy to get, but
nobody wants them.

The first corollary to the rule of margin is: dodging and
hiding. You never tell anyone, no matter how strong or
mean he is, what you have in your pockets. You never tell
precisely where you got anything. You never tell your real
name.

What else did I learn between Las Vegas and Los Angeles? How to pick anything that grows, fast enough so that I
could afford to eat. How to walk a horse slow enough to
keep from crippling him—that was as stable boy at the
racetrack. How to bus dishes fast enough to keep the
Mexican mamas who owned those storefront eateries from
taking a nick out of my ear.

I learned that a native American, whose people have
been buried in this land twenty-five thousand years, has
the same economic value as a guy with squishy sneakers
who is still shitting jalapeño seeds that grew in Chihuahua.

That does not mean I wanted to keep America for the
tribes. Nothing is funnier than those intertribal community houses and their unity nights, when everyone sits
around drinking 7-Up and pretending that the next brave
over did not used to eat human flesh. And those tribal
songs, sung high in the nose. Like some kind of Red
Rotary . . . No, I did not want to keep the Mexicans out,
but I wanted everything they were getting and a big slice
of what the whites had.

And I got it.

I was bussing tables at Tacqueria Tuya just off Olvera Street, when a beanpole of an Anglo with a droopy moustache came in carrying an attache, a Samsonite with many miles on its gray hide.

This Anglo had been in the shop a couple of times before, doing some kind of deal with Eduardo, the other busboy in the place. But today he had called in sick and there was just me, doing the job for both of us.

Before Beanpole found either Eduardo or a table, he found me and his eyes lit up.

"Hey, you're a friend of the Rico kid, aintcha? I seen you around with him. He said you're an okay guy, you know?"

"Yeah?"

"Look, I have to get this out to Topanga Canyon Drive right away." He shoved the case at me, exposing a length of dirty wrist.

"Try the mail," I shrugged.

"No, I need someone to take it."

"Long way. It will cost you."

"I'll pay a hundred."

"Unnh." I looked at the wrist again.

"One twenty-five."

"Okay."

"Paid at the end . . ."

"Well." Pause, two, three. "Okay."

A fool's errand, with only disappointment at the other end, right? But remember the margin. Nobody pays a stranger that much, first offer, for a simple put-and-take job, even if the guy receiving is a bet to dicker or welsh. So the case was either valuable or dangerous. It was also locked.

I took the case, grabbed my coat, and went straight to the airport. Out of the money in my pocket, $132 as this was the day after payday, I bought a one-way ticket to the farthest place that money would buy. Turned out to be Seattle, with nine dollars' change.

The nine dollars bought me an inland bus ticket, fifty miles to a place called Skykomish. From where I walked to the edge of town, uphill into the woods, and behind a tree. Then I broke the locks off the case with a rock. Messed it up badly.

If there was nothing inside but some papers, I was going to be out my good suit, a change of skivvies, and a good pair of boots that I had left back in my room in Los Angeles.

There were three plastic lunch bags, each hefting about four pounds. Pure white powder. The side of me that pushed brooms said Beanpole might just be sending confectioner's sugar to his aged mom. The side of me that hated pushing brooms said that, at current rates, twelve pounds of pure Colombian snoot music was worth more than half a megabuck. Of course, cocaine is shipped a lot purer now than it was then. And, if the bags contained heroin, then grade and cut were even bigger question marks, but the street value was still in the tens or hundreds of kilobucks.

I did not go back to Los Angeles for fifteen years.

The money—the powder turned out to be almost 100 percent cocaine—I used to set myself up in a service industry. Teenage prostitution. That may shock you but, hell, I was a teenager myself. Invested wisely in girls and contacts, the money was sure to take me on a long ride. If I avoided conspicuous consumption and the notice it would bring. And if I kept out of the risky front lines of the business.

The money took me right up to the day the draft started breathing heavily on me. As I was young and tough, evading or buying my way out did not appeal. This drunken Indian enlisted.

I told them I wanted to fly. Somewhere in the back of my head was the idea that, as a pilot, I could do small-parcel runs to deserted airstrips and double or triple what had been in the Samsonite case. A big piece of that half meg was still buried, and one day that would buy a plane. But I goofed and enlisted in the Army.

How was I to know the ground pounders of that time—although the rules changed later—were not permitted to fly fixed-wing aircraft? They flew helicopters, and the training for them is not even an introduction to airplanes.

You may never have stood in a field as a Bell HU-1 Iroquois, or any other chopper for that matter, flies over. The thud-thud of the rotors is like a direction-finder: when the noise is at its loudest, the helicopter is coming right at you. It took the Pentagon thirty years to figure that this makes the helicopter a bad carrier for sneaking up on ground troops.

It took me thirty seconds to figure it would be useless for smuggling. But by that time the papers were signed and my butt belonged to the government for three years.

I spent two of them in Nicaragua.

If, twenty-five thousand years ago, the Mohave had not stopped beside the river to fish, then I might have been on the other side, a Chorotega fighting with the Sandinistas. But the fishing was good that day, so I wore jungle green and flew the whip in a four-bird vee formation dropping Rangers and beer all over that country.

Did I ever see the famous *Escuadra de Muerte* in action? No, few outside the Squad itself ever did—and lived. So were the stories about them all wrong? Well, did all the Sioux take coup on Custer? Only the first three hundred!

The white establishment thinks good soldiers do not skin people. Only savages do that, right? Was it not the British and their bounty who taught the native Americans to take scalps? Did not the blond boys of the Seventh Cavalry mutilate red-skinned women and children? Were not *ears* the favorite souvenir of Vietnam? Please do not talk to me about savages.

Every time I brought my shudderbucket across the ridges of *Cordillera Dariense* and the *Isabella*, I navigated by white cairns of boiled skulls. And we were flying at a thousand feet.

Once, in Muy-Muy Viejo, a corporal tried to sell me a wallet he claimed was made of human skin. It was a dark brown, darker than me. The proof, he said, was the lumpy knot of a bellybutton on the inside flap. It might have been a pucker scar in cowhide. But I do not know enough about animal anatomy: Does a cow even *have* a navel? Is a monkey's navel as big as a man's . . . a child's? This one seemed fully grown. I did not buy the wallet.

We got a lot of flying in the final attack on Managua. The lakes north and east of the city blocked our line of advance, so we airlifted everything. You cannot appreciate the power of a CH-54 Skycrane's dual turbines until you see it pick up an M-60A3 tank like a gull making off with a sweetbun.

When it was over, the official policy toward the city was as old as Rome. Some of the tools were new, though. They shot every tenth civilian by the numbers, man, woman, or child. They dynamited every structure left standing and sent us—even technicians and warrant officers like me—over the ground with picks and sledge hammers to knock the bricks apart and break up the concrete chunks. "Nothing bigger than your boot" was the order. Later I saw tee-shirts with that motto. We even smashed up the roads. Then they flew some of our helicopters across the city with spraying gear. They never told us what the chemical was, but the pilots had to wear moonsuits. The Apaches—helicopters, that is—flying that mission they burned in a big pile.

Today, fifty years later, in the stony field where Managua stood, not a bush, not a weed, not a blade of grass grows. Birds avoid the area. Lizards and snakes turn around and crawl away. Poisoned sand.

I do not claim to understand that war. We acted like we really hated the Sandinistas. And we had some reason to, after the radiological dusting they gave the Big Pine Eight maneuvers in Honduras. But the air was thick with hype all during the police action. The officers routinely handed out the most unbelievable atrocity stories about the Sandinistas. They came from loose-leaf binders of computer printout that looked to have been ground out in Arlington.

The brass repeated the hate phrases so routinely that all the venom was sucked out of the words. How many times can you hear "motherfuckin mestizo" and "spittle-lickin spic" without suddenly finding them warm and comfortable? The words were too literary, too alliterative, not to have been invented by some general's press agent. And when half your troopers are already Hispanic-surnamed . . .

All I know is, the mosquitos were enough reason to kill everybody and get out of there.

After demobilization I thought of going back for the rest of that half meg. But what was there to do with it, right then, except get myself killed? Teen prostitution had just about been choked off by the Mothers and Others. And the Feds were freelancing pretty heavily in the drug traffic. Nobody protects turf harder than a bureaucrat who has stepped over the fence. The loose side was overpopulated by straight types with a mean streak, so I went over to the straight side. For a time.

My only marketable skill was piloting choppers, so I decided to sell that. The highest bidder was Petramin Oil. They started me flying the supply circuit to their Mexican rigs in the Bay of Campeche. That was good experience for the war we fought two decades later. But after only six months Petramin Air Services switched me to Saudi Arabia to haul executive ass.

The Saudis are racists. And sexists. And about every other *ist* you can think of, except Communist. They were trying, at the time, to create a pure Sunnite-Wahabi society. Other brands of Arab were welcome to visit the Kingdom, round trip to the sacred mosques of Mecca, drop their cash and go. Other semi-acceptable peoples—Anglos, Orientals and Mohave Indians—needed a good reason to enter, were required to set up separate accommodations in isolated cantonments, and had their exit visas pre-stamped. The rest of the Third World and certain select peoples—Jews and Iranians—had their mail returned at the border and were rudely ejected from the few consulates the Saudis maintained abroad.

The local laws were a bramble thicket with long thorns everywhere: too much amputation of hands and heads. Not the kind of place to run a stable of young girls or deal in cocaine. Boys maybe, if they were good Arabs and said their Koran or whatever while being reamed.

So I planned to live quietly, fly where they told me, and leave on June 15, 1995, like it said on my visa.

The very first run was trouble.

To start with, the night before I had partied in the

Petramin Compound. Our host was a ground mechanic
claiming to be the only American in the Middle East who
knew how to mix an authentic Long Island iced tea—and
the only man in Saudi Arabia with the right booze to do it.
He must have had six hundred dollars' worth of contraband alcohol. And even then he was using an off-brand
Iranian vodka and a rum distilled in the Seychelles that
had the flavor and consistency of JP-4.

The trouble with Long Island iced tea is, it does not
look or taste like liquor. It tastes just like a tall, cold glass
of iced tea, which is exactly what my throat wanted after
five days of walking around in the hot sun getting my
papers signed and my eyeballs scorched by more white
plaster and concrete than they ever wanted to look at
again in my life.

I was slurping up my third glass and smacking my lips in
appreciation when the first glass took effect. Like a hypo-
dermic full of curare while malefic spirits play tippy-tap on
your skull with little silver hammers.

My first coherent thought was for the glass and a half
that was still in my system and waiting to pounce. If I
moved fast, if I could move at all, I would get to the pad,
fire up a chopper, and stick my head up among the blades
as a merciful alternative to what was surely coming. I
briefly considered asking someone for a gun to shoot myself with, but my mouth would not work.

The ground mechanic thought I was asking for another
hit, so he handed it over and even helped me tip it back.
Kind soul.

It was one hungover brave that showed up at the pad on
the outskirts of Riyadh the next morning, squinting at
sun-blazed stones and sand with hurt-filled eyes.

I warmed up one of the new Bell Counter 101s with the
blue Petramin shield on its side panels. The ship had a
single turbine with a split transmission that drove two
disks side-by-side and counter-rotating. The design was
supposed to neutralize torque and make the ship easier to
handle. Actually, it was designed merely to fascinate arm-
chair pilots in procurement departments at Houston.

The Mixmaster, which is what the real pilots called it,

flew like a spooked horse in a field full of gopher holes. And those blades meshing right over my head, with maybe the clutch on one of those trannies drifting out of sync by a half-rev or so . . . I had a lot to think about while going over the console.

The copilot was a Saudi-subsidized trainee, Prince Abd el Feisel Something, a grinning, slick-skinned kid who could care less about driving a helicopter. He had papers, but I did not trust them, being written in Arabic. It was obvious from the linen and gold that he made three times the take-home I did and was sitting in the cockpit only because the Royal Family currently thought some of the poor-relation princes should be fully employed. He was holding a Louis L'Amour paperback and looking out the window. No help there.

Our passenger was late. We were expecting an executive type, listed as an associate in the Law Department, Houston office. "Granville J. Corbin" sounded silver-haired, about sixty, fighting a paunch with Saturday and Sunday tennis sets. He would be wearing a deep tan that extended to the vee at his neck and mid-thigh, where the tennis whites started. He would probably talk like a New Englander with a corncob up his nose. He would be out to inspect the oil fields because, after forty years in the business, one must—just once—see where the stuff comes out of the ground.

So when the Citation IV taxied over toward the pad and popped the hatch on a baby lawyer with more elbows than stomach, I was set up for my first surprise.

He was not a bad-looking kid. Hair red-blond and curly, a strong nose, for a white man, twinkling eyes that missed very little, a grim-smiling mouth that turned up at the corners, like a recurve bow. It was hard to read anything from that mouth except an honorary good will that might not go deeper than his teeth.

"Hi, are you Petramin?" he asked above the whine of the Counter's turbine. He rested his overnighter on the lip of the passenger door.

"Right here. You Corbin?"

"Call me Jay." He slung the bag through and put a hand

forward between my seat and the copilot's. It was an awkward grip, so I shook lefthanded. An offsides handshake like that is supposed to be bad luck. I guess it was, on that trip.

He plopped into the bucket behind me then, pulled the door shut and fumbled with the lap and shoulder belts.

While I was adjusting for takeoff, a woman came running from the Citation, or possibly just from that side of the runway—I did not see, being too busy staring at gauges right then. But when I looked up, staring at her was more rewarding.

She was the reason the Saudis veil their women. A heavy fall of black-black hair bounced around her shoulders. Her eyes were arched and outlined like something out of an Egyptian tomb. She had painted her mouth the bold red that goes so well with olive coloring—not the peach and pink that washes out on an Eastern woman. Very un-Saudi, she was wearing high heels that made her calves stand out and a gray wool mini-suit that made everything else stand out.

Our copilot, Feisel, seemed to share my assessment of this bobbling *houri*. Before I could move, he was out of the right-hand seat and opening the door. That was lousy protocol, as I was technically captain of the ship and we were airworthy if not actually in the air at the time. I turned toward him and was about to raise my voice to object when he put a gun barrel in my right ear.

In the second before he ordered my eyes front I caught, through the side-plex of the cockpit, a last glimpse of the girl. She was still running but had pulled a stubby weapon out of her suit jacket and now held it in a professional double-handed grip. It had to be a big weapon—an Ingram MAC-10 or an Uzi automatic pistol—to look that huge at a distance of fifteen feet or so. Something with punch, anyway. I realized that her silhouette had been too good to be true.

"Clear with Air Control and take off," she said as she scrambled through the doorway and pushed past the baby lawyer, Corbin. "Fly east-southeast, one-twenty degrees."

"But our flight plan says north."

"We have *changed* your flight plan. You will take us to Juwara. In the Sultanate of Oman."

Her English was perfect, lilting and accentless. The weapon she held was really some kind of derringer sawed from the action of a double-barreled shotgun. It would mess up the cockpit badly if she fired it.

But I knew the map. "Juwara is over eight hundred miles from here," I said carefully. "That is beyond the operational range of this helicopter. There is nothing to the southeast within our range, except the Rub' al Khali. The Great Sandy Desert."

"Fly!" She glanced at Feisel. "You will pilot us, or we will fly ourselves."

I shrugged, picked up the collective and twisted on the throttle. It was going to be a long flight into nowhere.

Chapter 4

Granville James Corbin: Seeds of Vendetta

By the time I graduated from high school, life in the mock-adobe at Asilomar was getting pretty raggedy.

That summer Mother was admitted to the Drylands Farm, a kind of resort up north in the Napa Valley. She referred to her stay as "a rest." Father called it "dehydration." Drylands catered to nonviolent alcoholics and drug abusers.

Mother wrote to me faithfully, once a week to start with, mostly about the fog in the hills, the afternoon heat, and the prospects for the wine, uh, grape harvest. Over the years, she faded into a husky voice that whispered from slightly scented letters scrawled in thin blue ink. For some reason she had a fixation on caterpillars and the birds that ate them. She rarely wrote about butterflies.

That August, as I packed to leave for the University of California at Berkeley, my father was reassigned to the Pacific—Indonesia or Malaysia. Oil at eight dollars a barrel, down from forty-two a year earlier, had knocked the Oil Patch on its tailbone. Petramin was no better off than anyone else. Father's staff had been cut back to just one man, him, so he was off to taste the drilling mud in Sumatra or wherever.

During the preparations for departure, he sold the mock-adobe right out from under Mother and me. He would be gone for three years, Father said, and to save the high cost

of transoceanic air fare, he planned to take his leaves in
Sydney and Hong Kong. So he, too, turned into paper for
me: a checkbook and a handful of polaroid snaps, some of
them decorated with strange, dusky women.

Berkeley may once have been the western world's center of dissent and anti-fascist, anti-imperialist rhetoric. But
by the time I arrived the careerists and academics were
back in control. The Associated Students were again selling book covers illustrated with a winking, grinning hu-
manoid California Bear. The political shouters at Sather
Gate were replaced by skateboarders and falafel stands.
The coffee houses of South Side, with their beansprout
crêpes and guerrilla theater, gave way to the nouveau-
cuisine delicatessens of North Side's gourmet ghetto, serving open-face sandwiches of prosciutto and fig jam on
seven-grain bread. Radical action was out. Gelato was in.

It was at Berkeley that I first crossed paths with Gordon
Pollock.

He was a beautiful young man, tall and well-muscled,
with a headful of curly brown hair and with heavy, sleepy
eyelids over smoky hazel eyes that missed nothing. He
was an athlete, an aesthete, a scholar, a natural attraction.
People pooled around him. In three years he would be
class president, associate editor of the campus paper, *The
Daily Californian*, and captain of the gymnastics team.

His father was something in the current Washington
Administration, a dollar-a-year man who floated between
the Department of Energy and the defense industry. He
later became ambassador to Egypt and died in the Matrûh
massacre that took out Hosni Mubarak and half his general
staff.

The younger Pollock and I first shared a class in my
freshman year, a survey course in astronomy which satisfied a pesky science requirement in my pre-law curriculum. One sweet spring afternoon, in a roomful of restless
young bodies, I heard his high, slightly mocking voice
drift down from the rows of seats behind me.

"Corbin is wrong, sir. Johann Kepler enlarged upon the
works of Nicolaus Copernicus, and not the other way

around. You see, Copernicus had been dead twenty-eight years when Kepler was born."

The professor smiled up at Pollock. Most people who saw and heard him in those days smiled with a kind of inner appreciation, as if gratified to have so perfect a being on the face of this humble Earth.

"You're right, Mr. Pollock. Of course. Thank you for correcting the error."

Right then I hated Pollock. I glanced over my shoulder and caught him looking down at me. It was not the cheerful face of a fellow scholar happy to have resolved a doubtful question on the side of truth. It was the intent, gleaming stare of a cat that has just mangled a bird.

From that day forward, I marked him. As he rose in the campus politics and athletics, I kept track and took mental notes. Where others saw a young Adonis, the grace of youth, the beauty of such obvious talent, I remembered that gleaming stare of malice. I knew something about Gordon Pollock that others did not: Beneath his smooth pelt there was a were-cat, a fiddlestring madness, and it sometimes needed to lash out. Gordon Pollock was my summertime, Sunday psychology exercise. I collected him the way other people kept odd facts about Napoleon or Ramses II.

But it was not until two years later that we would really clash.

I can't say my years at U.C. Berkeley were very well spent. There was too much to see and do in San Francisco— which seemed to be Cannery Row writ large—to keep me hunched over a book at midnight. And I was openly a creature of pleasure.

In my first Halloween parade, I dressed as a chimney sweep, a ragged urchin boy in top hat, tails, and soot. The costume fitted my mood—abandoned by the breakup in Asilomar. Everyone loved it.

The San Francisco scene was probably a bad place for an adolescent boy. Adults would worry about the risks of violence done to my person, but it never worried me because I had a black belt and could kill with either hand. Venereal infections and AIDS—which had by then reached the sexually active hetero population—were not much of a concern because, as a young stud, I could be fussy about things like condoms. Everyone humored me.

More affecting than death and disease was the terrible loneliness. San Francisco was a city of lost souls. Every man and woman, in the bars and coffee houses, on the street at dusk and after dark, searched your face with that hopeful and haunted look, asking: "Are you the one? Are you my true love?"

Being young and superior, I could take or give, walk or stay. I owed the bars and the street nothing but a good time. On my terms. But for others, the narrow boundaries of the city defined their whole world. They were trapped. It was this creepy loneliness that, regular as the tides, drove me back across the Bay to the pot parties, beer bashes, and golden, bare girls of Berkeley.

Although Pollock and I were both pre-law, we didn't share another course until my junior year. That was not unusual at a university as large as Cal, with hundreds of students in the same major. The two of us might pass in the computerized list of standings but not meet in the flesh for years. In truth, I had almost forgotten about him. Better we had remained strangers forever.

The course we shared was political economy, a seminar in current problems. Professor Ballenger took us all over late-twentieth-century economics: the Federal deficit as negative investment, the social functions of defense spending, entitlements as an economic lever—ah?—the idea of "entitlements" may need some explaining now. . . .

You see, the laws at the time guaranteed State and Federal payments, usually in perpetuity, to arbitrarily selected classes of people such as the aged, the "unemployed," veterans, farmers, mothers of unsupported children, and others who fell outside a narrow spectrum that had been pre-defined as economically able-bodied. These people were said to be "entitled" to these "transfer payments," which were thought to redistribute the country's wealth along "equitable" lines. At one point the monies involved were as much as forty percent of all Federal disbursements, incredible as that may seem.

Many people at the time argued that the economy depended on these transfer payments and the consumer spending they made possible, that to dispossess the holders of entitlements would have destroyed the American manufacturing and marketing base. Of course, they ignored the damage this negative investment was causing in the capital markets. And they missed the most important characteristic of money: It is inherently non-fluid. No matter how fast you pump it, some always sticks to the sides of the pipe and the hands of the pump-turners. It's much more efficient for the recipient to obtain money directly, through work or stealth.

Anyway, Professor Ballenger covered all of this with a certain grim wit. After fifteen weeks of discussion, he announced that our only grade would be from the final exam, which would be in essay form, three hours, on a topic of his choosing. A chorus of groans met this news.

When the day came, the professor's topic was: "Define the constitutional implications and restraints upon a repudiation of the national debt."

As luck would have it, I was exceptionally well prepared on this question. Actually, it was not a matter of luck but astute guesswork. Proposals for a repudiation were even then in the air, and Ballenger had mentioned them repeatedly, and favorably, in class. He also had spent an inordinate amount of time on the negative side of a $5-trillion debt, which is where it hovered that year. Any child, or a resident of any one of a half dozen Latin American countries, could see the drift of his thoughts. So I came to the final armed with four or five constitutional sections penciled in my mind and at least three arguments for and against the repudiation. As a contingency. The whole preparation took me fifteen minutes. Really.

In the wrapup seminar, where a professor usually returned the exam papers and discussed them, Ballenger presided with the face of the thunder god. All the happy, malevolent wit had withered away. He told us not even to look at the papers he had handed back. We were all a bunch of time-serving ninnies who would one day find out how ignorant we were, how incapable of any coherent thought that had not been spoon-fed down our slender throats. We would certainly find this out in law school—if any of us ever were accepted—and met some *real* professors. All of us, that is, but one. Mr. Corbin. Mr. Granville James Corbin, to be specific, whose final essay was exemplary, whose reasoning was exquisite, whose facts were extraordinary. This paragon, Mr. Corbin, should stand up and take a bow so that all the lesser mortals in the room could see what a truly adept legal mind was fashioned from . . . except . . .

"Except even in the case of Mr. Corbin do I have my doubts," the ginger beard and lion's mane of hair that Ballenger combed back from his forehead shook sadly.

"Sir?" I quavered from the second row—the last row in a tiny seminar room filled with sixteen undergraduate bodies.

"Do you want to explain to me why," Ballenger rumbled, "with your normal classroom discussion bordering on the moronic, you were able to prepare a nearly brilliant response to my left-fielded question?"

"Sir, it seemed obvious—"

"Of course it seemed obvious, Mr. Corbin. You were in my office last Tuesday, were you not? You will no doubt have noticed that the exam questions were stacked on the *right* side of my center desk drawer, the one with the small padlock on it, the padlock that has been *missing* since Tuesday. But perhaps you can be so astute as to tell me why you restacked those papers on the *left* side?"

"Sir, sir. *I* restacked? Are you accusing me of—"

"Your own essay accuses you. As does your classmate." Ballenger shifted his focus. "Mr. Pollock?"

"Yes, Professor?" came that mocking voice, so at ease with this monstrous, this nightmare confrontation.

"Would you tell us all what you reported to me Wednesday morning, before the final?"

"I saw Jay Corbin at the door of your office, sir."

This was a patent lie. I had indeed gone to Ballenger's office, to discuss a theoretical point with him, and had arrived some minutes after his scheduled office hours.

Then I went away. If Pollock had been around to see me, I would certainly have seen him.

"Yes, yes," Ballenger fluttered. "But was he entering or leaving?"

"He appeared to be—" Pollock paused, as if to be certain-sure. "Leaving, sir."

"Thank you, Mr. Pollock." Ballenger turned his scowl to me. "Your next meeting with me, Mr. Corbin, will be in the dean's office, the day after tomorrow. You will be asked to show cause why he should not have you expelled."

I was terribly offended by Professor Ballenger's insinuations. Not just this accusation that I had cheated on the exam, that was bad enough. But it was doubly insulting that he thought I was so inept a thief as to misplace the padlock *and* forget which side of the drawer the questions had come from.

At a guess, either Ballenger had lost the lock himself, shuffled the papers, and then grown wildly paranoid, or the real cheater had known the exam question beforehand and *still* bungled his essay as badly as everyone else. Irrelevant either way—the professor still wanted my scalp.

In the end it never came to a formal expulsion, which would have gone on my record. They offered me the choice of resigning from the university or undergoing their formal procedure. Since the case against me consisted of several sets of words against mine, I chose the path of least resistance and fled with my transcript. I passed every subject with honors that semester, except political economy. There I got a simple "fail."

The next semester I enrolled again at Berkeley—but at the Alternative University, a nonprofit, semi-accredited institution in West Berkeley on Fifth Street. It was on the site of the old Urban Commune, a decrepit Victorian where the residents of fifteen years past had baked their human wastes for compost and slaughtered cagefuls of rabbits for protein.

The curriculum when I went there was a little more practical. Course names were just camouflage to keep the State inspectors happy. "Political economics" at this university meant how to write a Health and Human Services grant proposal, conduct direct-mail fund raising, and launder proceeds from volume deals in alternative pharmaceuticals. "Chemical engineering" introduced us to fifteen types of liquid and solid explosives that could be made from ingredients found in the local supermarket and hardware store. "English literature" was a straight how-to in propaganda. "Music appreciation" taught the finer points of automatic weapons. We studied beginning Arabic—*wahid, ithnain, thelatha, arbe'a* and "Where is the water closet?"—in order to sensitize us to the political struggles of the Palestinians.

My great love in those months was Mandy Holton, one of the teachers. Through all the scatter and the chatter of the Commune, she moved silently, gracefully, like a tigress among the monkey tribes.

I never saw Mandy wear anything but the same faded jeans—the sort that went white in the seat with wear and washing—an Army fatigues jacket over a rib-knit gray sweater, and waffle-stomper track shoes with white socks. She was utterly unconcerned about appearances. Her dark-blonde hair was chopped off just below her ears and, although it was always clean, she never brushed or fussed with it.

She was double-jointed, had to be, the way she could sit on the floor in full lotus for hours at a stretch. Other people got restless, shifted, fidgeted. But Mandy, absorbed in the lessons, forgot her body entirely.

There was a time, about four hours one Sunday afternoon, when I would have picked up an AK-47 and followed her anywhere. It was a rainy afternoon, and we were shut up in Mandy's room on the third floor of the Commune house. She was in a sharing mood, and I was hanging around, moth to the flame. I had brought a bottle of not too young zinfandel, and she broke into her stash of seedless stuff—hash oil for some twisted cigarettes.

Mandy rolled her wine around in a plain tumbler and talked about capitalism. The zinfandel got her on the subject of the wine country and the Napa Valley lifestyle, which she detested.

". . . all the white pig and the super rish—*rish*—rich,"

she slurred, high on my wine, then giggled. "But never mind. Some day, when we've taken the Syshtem apart, put it back together the way the people want it, I'm gonna have a place of my own—our own—up there. F'rall our friends. Place to get wasted. Swing all the *facistas* right at the gate. You'll see . . ."

And after we were floating off the floor, quiet for twenty minutes or so, Mandy just said "Oh, shit!" and unrolled her sleeping bag. It wasn't some musty old green Army bag, but one made out of red nylon, slick as satin, with a gray plastic zipper that didn't cut if it got in the way.

While I was still contemplating the bag's sexy fabric, Mandy was peeling off her jeans and a pair of green nylon panties. "Come on!" she crooned, trying to work my belt buckle around my waist. Then I had a chance to find out if she was really double-jointed.

She was.

I left her wrapped in that red satin and sleeping like a baby. The last pull in the wine bottle wiped my throat out with acid and musk. I wrapped my pea coat around me and went walking in the rain.

Doing sex with Mandy, I had imagined, would be some kind of political anthem or maybe an impersonal tumble. Instead, she was sweet, and a little clingy, not to mention good fun, and almost certainly a virgin. Walking along with the big, slow droplets hitting my face, I began to wonder what my responsibilities to her were—a new thought for the brat. No way to tell until we saw each other again, I thought . . .

But soon good sense, or my sense of humor, reasserted itself. Mandy would always be a person who fit into her lifestyle, her doctrine, her opinions, and her capabilities like a ballerina fits her leotards. There were no rough edges, no seams, no gaps for the Bourgeois Bandit, Jay Corbin, to fit into. Her completeness was frightening—and I would do best to keep my distance.

She must have had the same thoughts. Because when we did meet, the following Tuesday, the cadre leader was back in place, wearing her white-seated jeans and her seamless rhetoric.

A few weeks later I graduated from the Alternative University. There was no formal ceremony, no valediction; you just learned as much as you could absorb and then drifted on. But the subterfuges of the curriculum committee made the credits earned there mostly transferrable. By that time my head was settled and a mean streak of careerism had surfaced: I believed more than ever that law should be my career.

So I wrote to my father, who wrote to an Old Boy in the Petramin legal section, who wrote on my behalf to an Old Boy in the Harvard admissions office. My Berkeley records were still good, and they passed off the semesters at the Commune as a spell of "social conscience," construing it to my credit.

Boston is much like San Francisco, except warmer in the summer. Both of them were old working-class towns which had, in the closing years of the twentieth century, grown self-conscious of their history. They had tried to preserve it through commercial developments that sandblasted the brick faces of their factories, installed modern glass and air conditioning, and rented charming cubbies to bakeshops, brasseries, and boutiques in the hope of depriving tourists of their dollars.

But the similarities went deeper.

Both Boston and San Francisco were the hubs of their geographic areas—New England and Northern California, respectively. Both had cashed in early on the Information Society with high-tech colonies near to but not right within the city—Route 128 and Silicon Valley, respectively. Both had long been centers for the ultimate information flow, money—in the form of insurance and banking, respectively. Both prided themselves on regional foods—Maine lobster and Indian pudding, Dungeness crab and sourdough bread, respectively.

It was the similarities, the consciousness of their own sophistication and tradition, that made these regions natural allies in the war twenty-five years later.

A San Franciscan, transplanted to Boston and broadminded enough to overlook superficial differences like winter snow and the catarrhal speech pattern, would claim native status within six months. I did it in three, but then my childhood on Massachusetts' North Shore gave me a running start.

For me, coming to Harvard was like coming home. The brickwork and the small-paned windows of the Yard, the winter-barren trees of Cambridge, the smell of old book-bindings and steam heat, the summer boating on the Charles . . . after the politics, pot and saucepan chemistry of the Commune, it was like being reborn in a dream of scholarship. For those three years I worked like a demon, searching precedents, analyzing cases, drafting and then redrafting briefs, submitting to the *Review* and finally getting published.

The law seemed like *kumite*, the delicate, feather-touch sparring of the Sensei's karate school. For every attack there was a blocking move, and a counter move to the block, until your head buzzed with endless permutations of if-he-does-this-then-I-do-that, like a chess master mentally playing out three games in his mind before moving even one piece.

I thought the law was elegant and beautiful, the highest application of human mind to human, social problems of rights, injury and ownership.

Ironically, the proposed Twenty-eighth and Twenty-ninth Amendments to the United States' Constitution—the same subjects that had brought me low in Ballenger's class—were the hot topics during almost my whole time at Harvard Law School. We debated endlessly, and smilingly, the enabling legislation, the text of the amendments, the course of the ratifications, the implications. And, like everyone else, we totally underestimated, by at least a thousand percent, the social and financial impacts if these acts were ever ratified.

When we are young, the political and economic events of the day pass us by too quickly. We have no background of experience to say *this* assassination will be pivotal in the balance of power, *that* law will set the course of all that follows. Because of the course these amendments would set for *me* and *my* fortunes, I should have fixed them with my whole attention.

What I had missed was the trend toward "market forces" that had grown in the United States over the past dozen years. Almost every industry had undergone a course of deregulation: banking, airlines, trucking, energy. They had shown what economic efficiencies—and havoc—could follow when a free market replaced modified central planning.

I had also missed the deficit pressures of the Nicaraguan war. Like Vietnam before it, this war was fought on the margin—financed with promises and with bulges in the national debt and Consumer Price Index, instead of with direct taxation, which would have entailed some kind of popular referendum.

Also, I could not foresee the crash program the Federal government would undertake in the mid-Nineties to build new central station power plants. A decade of high interest rates and optimistically low projections of load growth had all but shut down the private utilities' building programs. The incidents at the Three Mile Island and Chernobyl reactors had put a bad odor on the nuclear option—both for the energy companies that would invest in it and for the public that would watch them. The shouting about acid rain in Canada and our own New England States made coal a sour alternative. Oil or gas cost too much and the sun didn't always shine on solar power. So all the utilities stopped building new plants and assured themselves that, when the crunch came, they could buy excess power from each other.

Within three years, the Federal Energy Regulatory Commission would be commanding extraordinary powers to begin building single-design, site-licensed nuclear power plants in the 550-megawatt class. A nation that was facing evening brownouts and two Black Days a week would applaud the effort and never ask what it was costing. It would cost plenty.

However, I precede myself.

At the time I was in Harvard Law School, the Twenty-eighth and Twenty-ninth Amendments seemed a radical, blue-sky approach to the minor economic problem of the Federal deficit. Just as the Eighteenth Amendment's ban on making and selling liquor seemed a radical approach to the minor social problem of public drunkenness. The only people who could debate the amendments seriously were the nuts: the Radical Republicans, the Supply-Siders, the "Clean Slaters" and Deregulationists. Just as the minority Prohibitionists had pushed for the Volstead Act. Their social agendas were so well displayed that the rest of us dismissed them—and those agendas remained effectively hidden.

But we wouldn't find that out until the amendments were ratified five years later and the great experiment had begun.

One of the best things about Harvard was that Gordon Pollock and the crippling envy he represented were at least three thousand miles away.

In 1994 I graduated seventh in my class. Neither Mother nor Father could attend the ceremonies, but a senior counsel from Petramin's legal section had come up to take an honorary doctorate of law. He applauded my diploma with the rest of them and then took me to dinner. Within three days I would report in at the Houston home office, begin studying for the Texas bar, and start earning my way as a *bona fide* attorney.

I was a kid with a lot of potential, and I knew it.
Veritas.

Gordon Pollock: On Reflection,

Twenty-Five Years Later

He was guilty, guilty, guilty! How many times do I have to say that?

All right, so now he has become a big man: wheels and deals in resources and energy, singlehandedly wins the war in Mexico, welds together the bickering, raggle-taggle TENMAC coalition in the West. Agreed to all of the above.

But he is not that clean and shiny, no sir. Beneath that bright eye and enameled smile is a corruption as sour and deep as a pus-filled abscess. One day he will break and it will all come seeping out.

I tell you I saw him sneaking off around the corner from Ballenger's office. Saw him! He had the exam questions in his hands. It was for a class in economic history, or some such. Ballenger was the professor. They ran him out of Berkeley for cheating.

Of course the record says he quit voluntarily. That was the deal they made, they always make. But he had an expulsion order hot on his heels. I *know* that.

The point is simply this: His record was excellent. His grades were top notch. Wish I had as good. He was liked and respected. So what was the point in cheating on a God-damned *essay* question? Unless he was and is, at heart, a corrupt soul. Unless he is so crooked he will make three lefthand turns where one right will do.

And the further point is: You must not believe his easy explanations on this insurance resolution. He is an attorney, like the rest of us. So why would he cut his own throat and ours and all of his profession's unless he could take monstrous profit from it?

And still further: He has ambitions. He wants nothing less than to steal this country. After he has done away with you and me, the Constitution, and the fellow behind the tree. He has it all plotted out in his mind. Step by fiendish, fanatical step. We can stop him now, here, or we will have to stop him later. And then it will take a war!

You are still not listening. I tell you, you must not trust the man!

Chapter 5

Granville James Corbin: Rub' Al Khali

Our helicopter took off from Riyadh with a clatter of rotor blades. Otherwise it was quiet.

The situation had caught me off guard. No, that's not right. It was my own swelled head. I had come to the pad thinking that the company was treating its newest Harvard acquisition with the proper respect. Two Saudi pilots— though one turned out to be native American—had been detailed to chauffeur me on a private tour of the northern oil fields. And then this incredibly full-bodied Arabian stewardess, sans veil, was coming over to tuck me in.

The price of oil had been inching back up toward thirty dollars a barrel, so Petramin was starting to flex its fiscal muscles again. Sending the American brass and top staffers out to the field on orientation trips was part of the company's good-times consumption pattern. "Visiting the money," our senior counsel in Houston had called my trip which, he'd hinted, would spotlight me as an important player in the organization.

It's a wonder my head fit through the helicopter's sliding door. I was so smug that I forgot to avert my gaze politely when the stewardess lifted one long, nylon-smooth leg over the door's sill. My eyes took a bite out of her exposed thigh. Then I saw her sawed-off shotgun.

The social dynamic in the cabin changed immediately. She and the American pilot argued briefly about destinations, which I could follow only from the maps I'd seen pinned to the wall in the airfield's office. The Saudi pilot seemed to be backing her; so the American shrugged and lifted off with a clatter.

And by that time, my moment had passed. If I had been more alert, watching her hands instead of her legs—and if I hadn't already buckled my lap and shoulder belts—I might have broken her wrist, on the hand holding the scatter gun, with a flying side kick while she was busy climbing aboard. Or taken her with a straight kick to the throat: she wouldn't have had time to bring her weapon to bear and fire if she were busy strangling.

But the little conference up front ended too quickly, and we were fifteen feet in the air before I woke up and remembered all those good karate moves. By then she was settled in and ready, and a single shot from her would have blown out both pilots and the nose of the aircraft. But for the rest of the flight my eyes never stopped measuring distances, angles of fire, the tension in her hands, the focus of her attention. My hand never strayed far from the quick release on the seat harness.

I wasn't too worried about the Saudi pilot, who was displaying a NATO-issue Beretta 9mm automatic pistol. If he tried to get a shot at me, moving, from between the cockpit seats, he only had about a one-in-ten chance of hitting something vital in my anatomy. Of course, he had about nine-in-ten of drilling the turbine engine, which was aft of the bulkhead behind us. But if that happened, I imagined they could autorotate down to some kind of landing.

Still, the situation was frozen up right then, a bad time to move. So I decided to lie back and enjoy the inevitable.

"Do you want to tell me what's going on?" I asked, keeping my voice on the line between adult casual and kid smartass.

The woman looked at me for, it seemed, the first time. Her eyes were wide-set, deep, a liquid-black that in other circumstances I could stare into for hours. They showed a flash of nameless recognition—that same instant of sexual understanding that sometimes passes between strangers in a waiting room or on a bus. Then the veil of private purposes, other aims, fell across her eyes.

"We are kidnapping you, Mr. Corbin." Her English was perfect, slight British accent, education and polite society hinted in the tone and syntax.

"Really? What for—money? You'll find my family doesn't have all that much, and the company will probably care more about getting their helicopter back than saving me. They paid more for it." I thought I was lying smoothly; later I found out what a helicopter can cost.

"Not money," she said. No trace of a smile at my humor. Her grip on the scatter gun never varied. "This is an act of terror directed against the fanatical regime that has seized my country and seeks to return it to a state of feudal peonage. They slaughter our youths and squander our national wealth in a futile war against Marxist—"

"What country are you—?"

"Persia."

"And you seek to restore Queen Farah Diba?" My years among the books of Harvard hadn't shut out *all* of the current world situation. I could guess that this reverse tide of imperialism had already fired debates, revisionism and schisms back at the Commune—if it was still in business.

"Of course," she said. "Our aim is a return to the course of modernism and enlightenment begun by her husband, the late Shah."

"I see. And taking an *American* hostage is going to bring the ayatollists to their senses? I'm hardly a bargaining chip. They'll pay you a bounty for my dead hide!"

"Why do you Americans always think of money?" Her mouth curved around in an ugly bow. "It is not ransom we propose, but cooperation. Your company holds contracts, through third parties, for twenty-eight percent of Persia's oil production. If Petramin refused to take delivery, even for a week, the backup would exceed the Ministry's storage capacity anywhere along the line. As you may be aware, the last four attacks at Kharg Island were targeted on tank groups and pumpage. A slowdown in the take will strangle the oil fields. They will have to cap wells and lose pressure. It will take the Ministry months to recover."

"Do you really believe Petramin would manage an oil field just for me?"

"You are a senior official, are you not?" Even as she said it, her eyes clouded. It must have been obvious even to a terrorist that I was still a green kid in my twenties. Maybe they mature early in the Middle East. "Anyway, your company will cooperate," she said, "when we begin sending pieces of you to your family."

"And you call yourselves modernists?"

"Terrorist pressure is a very modern concept. If we were truly barbarians, we would be offering you the hollow consolations of martyrdom and an easy way to Paradise."

"Yes, well, I do appreciate that."

I turned away from her and stared out the window. My attention focused on the small of my back, where the gun still pointed.

The helicopter had crossed the outskirts—or at least the narrow fringes—of the Saudi capital, Riyadh, some minutes ago. The last tended terraces and lines of palms around cloistered villas had given way to the near desert. The land rippling below us was gray rock and gravel, with here and there a clump of scrub that showed dusty green. If you looked long enough, you could begin to pick out the dry watercourses, deep S-curves cut in the gravel where desert storms had poured out a rush of water. Every five years or so.

Luckily, I had come dressed for a field trip: khaki shirt, denims, gray-suede Italian climbing boots. I tried to picture myself walking out of that countryside in a wool three-piece and wingtips—looking something like a new ad video for men's cologne. Except for the sweatstains.

The woman's position, *theirs* if she represented any real organization, was incredibly weak. She had thought she was kidnapping an American *beegweeg*, someone she could trade for concessions, but she ended up with a small fish, really, a nobody and no use to her. It said so on my traveling papers: No deposit, no return. In about five minutes she was going to figure out that her winning strategy was to shoot me and the American pilot, dump

the chopper and set us all ablaze . . . . To fight again
another day.

My winning strategy was to keep her talking, to find a
way to strengthen her bargaining position, and so my
prospects for continued breathing.

"What's your name?" I said quietly—or tried to. Actually, I was still facing the window and, even in the insu-
lated cabin, the clatter of rotor blades tended to drown out
whispers; so I had to shout it.

"That is not important."

I turned and looked at her, a long measuring stare
straight in the eyes.

"Of course it's important. We're about to fly out into the
Great Sandy." I jerked my head toward the even, brown
horizon ahead of the aircraft. "That makes us traveling
companions. People who must depend on each other in a
land of thirst and cold and blowing dust. That land can kill
us all, no matter who is holding the guns. . . . Now, what
is your name?"

She seemed to wilt for a moment. "Sybil Zahedi."

"And where do you come from, Sybil? You obviously
haven't been home to—Persia—in many years."

"London, and before that Cairo."

"Educated there?"

"In London, yes."

The gunman in the front seat was watching this closely.

"And you?" I said to him.

"Feisel Ibn Mehakim."

"Are you something royal?"

He actually smiled. "No, my father is a sheikh. One day I
may be sheikh, too—if I survive this adventure."

"But you're not Persian?"

"Only a sympathizer."

"And the man who's doing the flying?"

The American glanced back at me. "Billy Birdsong. I
work for the company, same as you."

"So you're not in on all of this?"

"Just caught in the crossfire. I fly the bird for Petramin,
but nobody will have any tears if they get a piece of my
finger in the mail."

"All right. Where are you from, Billy?"

"California."

"Hey, so am I. You know the Bay Area?"

"Too rich for me, Boss. I come from down near Needles."

"High desert man?"

"No, just Injun."

I marked him for about two notches less hostile than the
people wielding the guns. No way to tell, yet, how he
would jump if an opportunity came along.

"You said we were going to Oman, Miss Zahedi? And
that's a long flight, Billy says, over eight hundred miles.
What's that in time—about eight or nine hours?"

"Yes." Her gun drifted. Hesitation.

"Do you have a refueling stop planned along the way?"

"Why do you ask all these questions?"

"My life depends on your good planning. We're traveling companions, remember?"

"Wrong. You are my hostage."

At a nudge from Feisel's gun, Birdsong veered off on a
long arc to the south. I looked out along our original
course and saw the squared-off edges of rooftops in the
heat haze. Jabrin, it had to be, according to my memory of
the map. In the landscape below us, rock and sand turned
to pure sand, and the sand built into the standing lines of
dunes, regular as waves of the ocean. This sea of sand, the
Rub' al Khali, was fully as large as the Black Sea or the
Caspian.

"Do you think I'm trying to escape? Into that?"

"You ask questions. . . . And you are not afraid. That is
bad in a hostage."

"Hey! I'm an American, remember? Tourists want to
see everything there is to—"

"Shut up!"

Her hand whitened on the grip of her gun. I could see
that the rough-sawed edge of the walnut grip was dark
with sweat, even though the cabin was air-conditioned
cool. I shut up.

The sand below went on and on. So did the pulse beat
of the rotors. My mind drifted and, after a minute or an
hour, my chin slid forward and my eyes closed.

I was awakened by a change in the pitch of the engine. We were dropping past, then circling back toward, a cluster of blocky houses in a thin grove of date palms that hid a flash of open water, with the dunes all around like hills. That would be Abaila, the one permanent settlement the map showed in the northern or Ar Rimal quadrant of the desert.

A welcoming committee waited for us on the only flat place, west of the date palms. About fifteen men and women in green fatigues stood in a well-spaced semicircle with Uzi submachine guns at parade rest. They squinted but didn't flinch when the rotor wash kicked up a blast of dust and sand.

Sybil Zahedi was first out of the ship, followed by me, Birdsong and Feisel. Sybil spoke a little *abracadabra-kush-kush*—which I assumed was Farsi—to a yard-wide, hard-bitten man with a graying moustache, a scar across his chin like a bad weld, and two pistols stuck in his web belt. He nodded, and Sybil walked off alone toward the buildings. At a word from him, the team moved on Birdsong and me, separating us, handcuffing us, and walking us off in different directions—me toward the buildings, him toward the open desert.

"Hey, uh, wait a minute." I twisted in their grip to look over my shoulder, back at Birdsong. "Where are you taking him?"

Shrugs. Blank looks.

"No. No, this isn't right." I stopped my feet, but their hands just swept me along. "No! Stop this! Miss Zahedi!" She was ahead of us by fifty yards. "Sybil!"

She turned, waited for us to catch up.

"Where are they taking the pilot, Birdsong?"

"To dispose of him."

"Wha—? Why?"

"He said himself he is of no use to us." She tipped one shoulder in a shrug. "No one would grieve for him."

"Yes, well, but, ah, think of what that will do to your bargaining position with Petramin."

"Our bargaining position?"

"If you have already killed one of your two hostages—not for effect, but just on a technicality—before you even start negotiating, they're going to figure you for a loose bunch of amateurs. Lightweights. Unstable. Unpredictable. Unable, probably, to close a deal."

I watched her eyes change as she heard this, from a cynical squint to an offended glare to a cunning glint. She finally nodded and said a few words to the man nearest. He raised his Uzi in the air and fired a measured burst, then whooped something and raced off toward the other party.

Sybil turned and started trudging on toward the buildings.

The others brought Birdsong up and took us both to a tiny hut, made of whitewashed clay—or maybe concrete, I meant to find out which—like the rest of the settlement. It was a storage room, twenty feet on a side, with just the one door of rough boards, no windows. A quartet of horizontal slits, six inches wide, were cut below the roof for ventilation. And it still smelled as if the Arabs had stored camel dung in there.

Without a word, Birdsong and I prowled this gloomy cell—he moving left and I right—tapping the walls, scuffing the rammed-dirt floor, fingering the edges of the vent slits. I felt around the door hinges and the bolts of the hasp, trying to judge the effect of a straight heel-kick on the dry wood. Three kicks, maybe four, would pop the door right off its hinges. Then we could rush out and overcome half a dozen guards who were holding machine guns. . . . I needed a new idea.

The room was empty except for fourteen one-gallon cans stacked in a corner, the labels all alike. I couldn't figure out the Arabic scribble-squig on them; my command of the language was just first-grade conversational.

"What they got?" Birdsong asked.

"Paint. . . . Pink paint," I said, seeing the dried stuff around the edge of one lid.

"Hey! You can read Arabic?"

"No."

That left him puzzled, but my mind was working too fast

to explain. Now if I only had a cigarette lighter, we could burn the paint, call for the guards, and when they rushed in . . . I still needed a new idea.

Birdsong faced me in the dark middle of the room. "Hey, tell me . . . what was all that, out at the landing site? First they split us up, then put us together. What happened?"

What should I say to him? "Conflicting orders . . . For the torchbearers of the new Shahdom of Iran, these people do not exactly have the details worked out."

"Bad news for us."

"Not necessarily . . . You remember that little piece of paper you signed, before coming into the country?"

"Which one? I signed about sixty of them."

"The one that legally acknowledged International Travel Order 6263."

"Oh, yeah, the Dead Meat Clause. Some of the pilots were joking about that one."

"What's the joke?"

"Just that declaring political hostages legally dead did not apply to George." He caught my blank stare. "He is one of the company's pilots—and also our nickname for the automatic control on an airplane. . . ." I was still blank. Birdsong waved it away. "Professional joke. But why is that order *not* bad news? These people will kill us if they cannot bargain."

"But they obviously don't know that. Or don't believe it. The situation gives us an opening."

"To do what?"

"Don't know yet. I'm working on it. How long does it take to refuel that chopper?"

"Not long. But no more flying today."

"Why not?"

He pulled a hand out of his jumper pocket, cupping half a dozen fuses in his palm. "Technical difficulties."

"You don't think Feisel will spot what's wrong?"

"Him? That one is ballast. Never flown before."

"How do you know?"

"Any co-pilot knows to keep his hands off the stick and

his feet off the rudder bars when he is not actually flying. Feisel screws around. Had to fight him for the controls all the way out here. I will disable my bird before leaving it with a guy who thinks four hours of watching qualifies him."

Birdsong walked over to the far wall, put his back to it, and sank down to the floor. I began to wonder if he knew how close he had come to taking those fuses into a desert grave. He was a sensible man; he probably did know.

The Iranians were going to leave us overnight, apparently. I settled in against the other wall and, in the dark, Birdsong and I talked. At least we tried to, but our backgrounds were too different. Places, foods, women, tech stuff, company politics, the price of oil. The topics rose and fizzled out almost immediately. We ended up dozing in the cold.

Come the feeble light of dawn, with my muscles in knots and a taste like sour slime in my mouth, I felt mean enough to begin poking our captors.

"Hey! Hey, out there!" I shouted, pounded on the door, kicked it for the noise value. "Up the Shah! Down with Khomeini!"

Birdsong roused and squinted at me.

The guards were right outside. They slammed the door open and leveled their burp guns.

"I want to talk to Sybil Zahedi!"

They just stared at me.

I tried some of my halting, phrase-book Arabic: *"Laish hel intidhar? Wain Zahedi?"* [Why are we waiting? Where is Zahedi?] And when they still didn't move: *"Mumkin tesa'idny?"* [Will please you help me?] Finally, with my hands I pantomimed breasts, hips, ass—then talk-talk with my fingers.

The one on the left got the message and smiled. He jerked his gun to show I was to come out.

He took me to a two-story house down by the shallow pond at the center of the oasis. The building had generator power, air conditioning, moisture seals on the doors, windows that faced out on green plants. And it didn't smell of camels. Sybil was sitting at a small table, smoking, drinking coffee out of a tiny cup and looking out at the water. Even with all this luxury, she appeared to have spent a night no better than mine.

The guard pushed me through the door, then stammered an *abracadabra* explanation of why he had brought me. Sybil looked up at me with tired eyes.

"What is it that you want?" She took a drag on her cigarette.

"To keep you from making a mistake."

"Your companion has sabotaged the helicopter. We cannot move or call for help. Do *you* know what he did?"

"No, but I can find out—and convince him to fix it—if you will listen to me."

She motioned the guard to move closer. I felt the muzzle of his machine pistol brush my kidneys. My hands were not bound and this bumpkin had actually brought his weapon inside my range. Well, well, karate hero . . . But not now.

"Just for two minutes?" I pleaded.

"All right. What mistake am I making?"

"You must have guessed by now that Birdsong and I are no prizes. He's just a pilot, one of a dozen on staff out here. I'm a very junior attorney, not even passed the bar yet. I've been with the company less than three months."

"What you are saying is not likely to prolong your life."

"I know. And I want to live. I want to help *you* do that. You see, I know all the Petramin officials here in the Kingdom, know where they're staying, their itineraries, their plans. I can take you to them, help you capture someone important, someone Petramin will really care about getting back."

"Are you such a coward that you would do this to your own people?"

"I don't want to be killed."

"You will write all of this down."

"No, I'd have to go with you."

Her eyes darkened. She started to signal the guard.

"I'm not sure of the place names! But I'd recognize

them, and I could identify the men for you. So there would be no mistake!"

That stopped her.

"We would need the helicopter," she said slowly, working it out.

"I promise you, Birdsong can fix it."

"But the Security forces will be looking for it, of course. They would shoot us down."

"Not if we camouflaged it."

"How?"

"With paint."

"There is paint here?"

"Yes, in our cell."

"We could do it. . . ." While she came to a decision, I shut up. Hell, I held my breath. "Yes . . . You will fly with us back to the north. The others hold Birdsong here as a hostage to your honor—if you have any."

"Of course I do!"

"That remains to be seen."

When I told him, Birdsong wasn't happy about it. Not about Feisel doing the flying. Nor about painting over his chopper's Petramin colors, which were an overall midnight-ice blue with orange striping. Very snappy. He was even more unhappy about using a water-based paint that had mostly gone over to gummy glue. Especially using *pink* water-based paint.

"You think this is going to be inconspicuous?" He whispered to me an hour later, still angry, as we went about the job.

Birdsong took another swipe with his rag, leaving a smear of pink with streaks of dark blue underneath. In the hot sun, the gluey coat dried almost before he ended the stroke. We were using rags because there had been paint in the cell but no brushes. He was whispering because the guard on our work detail, which included two of the terrorist band and us, was giving orders in broken English punctuated with clouds of Arabic and Farsi, and we couldn't tell how much more English he might understand.

"I didn't say that," I hissed back at him. "Just that it won't look like the same helicopter we took off in."

"Sure, man. And do you know how many 101 Mixmasters there *are* in Saudi Arabia? Three counting this one. All flown by Petramin. Ten seconds after we take off, the Saudi police are going to be telling each other, 'Look for the *pink* one.' "

"Shhh! And it's only pink up close. You know how camouflage colors work. Get this out in the desert, against the sand, in the bright sunlight, and it will look more . . . beige."

"Pink—hey, watch it!" He was shouting at one of the work party, a boy about thirteen, who was dribbling paint into the intake screens over the engine cowling. "No, stop! Hey, tell him if he clogs them up the engine will flame out. Tell him just to leave them blue."

I waved at the head guard and pointed. "*La el-loun! La!*" [No color! No!]

"No?" he asked.

"No. *Muharrick neffath. El-mirwaha 'atlana.*" [It's a jet engine. The airvent will jam.]

"Ahh." He nodded pleasantly and cuffed the boy for his stupidity.

"Color its feet, please?" The guard pointed down at the landing skids, half-buried in the sand.

"No, better not."

"Ahh, not. And wings?"

"Wings?" I asked.

"*Jinah?*" He pointed up at the clusters of rotor blades.

"*La!* No, no."

"Hookay." More smiles. He went about the plane, telling the others exactly how he wanted it painted, reinforcing his orders by banging on the fuselage with the muzzle of his gun.

I turned sideways to Birdsong and spoke out of the corner of my mouth. "Did you get the fuses back aboard?"

"Sure," he whispered. "Made it look like they had been jarred from their brackets and spilled out when I pulled the access. Feisel thinks I am a mechanical genius. . . . Now, what is your plan?"

"Fly back to Riyadh for bigger Petramin fish."

"Do you know any?"

"Not really."

"Then what point . . . ?"

"The idea is to get us separated from this crowd of disciplined and heavily armed crazies. Then we work it out from there."

"Are you going to get us killed?"

"Maybe. But it beats getting our brains summarily blown out when Princess Zahedi discovers that Petramin conforms to Travel Order 6263."

"Hunh!"

The head guard came around and smiled again. "No talk."

His submachine gun was strapped casually over his shoulder, the barrel level and pointing toward us.

I could see that he had somehow managed to pack the muzzle tightly with clay or sand. The other guards' weapons were twenty yards away, leaning against the building. . . . What a temptation!

Looking him straight in the eye, I said, *"Feeh atal."* [There's something wrong.] I reached slowly but smoothly for the barrel of his gun.

"Ish? Gif!" [What? Stop!] The man started to pull back on the weapon, and I tipped the muzzle up so he could see. "Ahh!" he exclaimed. *"Shukren jezeelen!"* [Thank you very much!] His face, which had clouded up, was all smiles again.

I began to think Birdsong and I might have a chance.

Four hours later, when the aircraft was properly painted a smeary pink with faint blue stripes, we were ready to go.

Then Sybil had a big fight with her lieutenant, Scar Face, who was hearing about our plan for the first time. Their fight worked to my advantage, because his opposition forced her to argue *for* the idea, which closed her mind to any rational assessment of the risks. They screamed Farsi at each other in the main avenue between the houses of Abaila, while the rest of their force looked the other way and toed the dirt.

Finally, at midafternoon, Sybil herded Feisel and me

into the helicopter. She was holding an Uzi in a rigid, angry grip. It would have been a perfect time to hit her, except for the dozen people standing around with their own machine guns.

It took fifteen seconds to find out that Feisel was a worse pilot than Birdsong had described. He flunked the start-up sequence three times, and on the last try even Sybil was telling him which switches to try. The engine roared to life just once, and then the plane bucked three feet into the air, stalled and dropped with a bang.

"Out! Out!" Sybil screamed, pointing her gun more at Feisel than at me. We all climbed out of the cabin.

"You stay here, you worthless Wahabi weasel!" She pointed the gun at Birdsong and at Scar Face. "Get in! Get in!"

We all quickly climbed back aboard. Birdsong settled into the pilot's left-side seat, Scar Face on the right. Sybil and I in the back. The same relative positions as yesterday. Except that Scar Face, caught by surprise, did not have a weapon, at least showing, although there could be a pistol holstered under his fatigue blouse. And Sybil, instead of her sawed-off scatter gun, had the big, two-handed, awkward Uzi. Better and better.

Birdsong wound up the engine and we lifted off fast, with a head-snapping bounce. *That* was the time to hit them.

In one motion my left hand went out to pin the barrel of the machine gun while I rolled my hips toward Sybil, bringing my right leg up and over, cocking my knee to clear the backs of the front seats, arching my foot and then releasing all that muscle tension and kinetic motion into a point on her forehead. Her head struck the rear bulkhead with a thunk that could be heard above the rotors. Continuing my body twist, I flipped over almost onto my stomach, catching myself and pushing up with my right hand against the seat cushions. Bracing a foot somewhere on Sybil's neck and shoulder, I dove forward over the back of Scar Face's seat, drawing in my left fist and then pistoning it, with my whole moving weight behind it, into his quickly turning face. His body recoiled into the control stick and the instrument panel.

By this time Birdsong had the helicopter about thirty feet in the air and moving forward. He had instinctively pulled back on the stick when I erupted in the cabin, and that motion saved us from nosing in when Scar Face's body pushed the stick forward.

"Fly!" I screamed at Birdsong.

My hands scrambled across the front of Scar Face's fatigues, trying to haul him off the controls and also to kill him. The blow had just barely stunned him; he was blindly fighting me and working his hands under his blouse to get that holstered pistol. I would have climbed into the front with him, except my belt buckle had caught against the seat's back frame. I was stretched across the length of the cabin and could feel Sybil stirring down near my feet.

Sensei Kan had always warned us about head shots. The face is full of small bones and teeth, he'd say; they cost your opponent nothing in losing them except pain, but these sharp little bones damage your hands when you strike against them. The skull, fragile as a porcelain vase, is still well protected by cushioning layers of muscle, cartilage and hair. Also, a blow to the head is too variable: the same force that will kill one man may not even distract another. Better to go for the body structure, the joints and the nerves, Kan would say.

I would have, Sensei, I really would have, if human bodies sitting in a confined space offered any better—more *structural*—targets. So here I was, caught on my stomach between two half-stunned terrorists who still had their guns.

The other thing Kan had always said was: When you run out of options in the middle of a fight, don't stop moving.

And my internal battle computer said that, based on elapsed time alone, Sybil needed to be hit again. I slid down off the seat back, twisted to face her, and let fly with a one-two-three-four-five series of straight punches to the base of her throat. I then snatched the Uzi from her loose fingers and whirled to see what Scar Face was doing.

He was crouching behind the seat cushion, exposing

just the top of his head, two eyes, and the muzzle of the biggest pistol I had ever seen. Clearly he was afraid: The whites of his eyes showed all around as he tracked my movements. His gun jerked right and left trying to get a bead on me without hitting Sybil. I pulled the Uzi's trigger and unloaded a full clip through the back of his seat. The roar drowned out all the noise of rotor wash and engine. The inside of the windshield fogged up with star cracks and blood.

Chapter 6

Billy Birdsong: Dolabella

I was braced for the impact when the big terrorist's body—what was left of it—threw the control stick forward for the second time. With my right hand I took a squishy grip on the tatters of his uniform and dragged him off it. The pieces slumped on the floor.

One glance across the right-side instrument panel showed what Corbin's swarm of bullets had done. Most of the engine readouts were shot up, but the turbine sounded steady—for now. The electronic navigation gear was gone, but the digital compass on my side still worked—or seemed to. The radio had evaporated. So had nonessentials like the switches for landing and running lights, the gauges for altimeter, airspeed and fuel pressure. The important stuff, circuits for the controls and the hydraulics, was on my side, so at least we were still flying upright.

I did not know that baby lawyers could fight with their hands. Nor that Corbin was going to start the minute we lifted off. But once he was launched, I tried to help with a few gyrations that would keep the two terrorists off balance.

My big worry had been the crowd on the landing pad behind us. The bucking of the ship, while Corbin was flying around in the back seat, was going to be noticed on the ground. It would look exactly like the trouble it was. Those people had weapons—and would be firing them into our engine. What a bullet or two does to a

71

high-revving turbine looks like an explosion in a knife factory. Therefore at the first lull in the fighting, while Corbin was trying to climb into the front seat, I cracked on the power and got us a stretch of sand and a big hunk of altitude.

After Corbin had wasted the man with the woman Zahedi's burp gun, I just took a compass heading for Riyadh and held the ship at 5,000 feet and what sounded like eighty-five percent power.

"You about done?" I asked after a minute.

"Yeah . . ."

"What about the woman?"

"Her breathing is hitching pretty badly. I think I cracked her sternum."

"She going to live?"

"For now."

"What about you?"

"Bruises. Can you fly us out of here?"

"Well . . ." I gave the proposition serious thought. "Jabrin is one hundred and seventy-five miles northwest of us. Northwest, at about the same distance, is 'Arada. At least two hours' flying either direction. We can land anywhere, once, if we have to. But after that, we will never get off again without instruments. Now, the engine *sounds* all right, but with a turbine you have to watch your gas temps, and I got nothing to watch with. The flight manual says not to fly with two or more instruments showing faulty readings." I pointed to what was left of the panel. "And my contract says I can refuse to fly this ship on the grounds of airworthiness. But, unless you want to circle back to the oasis and try to explain this . . ."

"No thanks."

"Thought not. So . . . Can we fly? We have to."

"I wonder what kind of reception we'll get from the Saudi Security Police?" Corbin mused.

"They will welcome us as heroes, of course."

"Hmmm."

"Why not? We foiled a kidnapping of American citizens, by agents of a foreign power operating inside the Kingdom. The Saudis are so paranoid they will shit their jellabas when they find out about it."

"I think they already know," Corbin said. When I kept quiet, thinking about that, he went on. "Well, work it out. The Ayatollah's Boy Army is already entrenched in Kuwait and operating freely in the Neutral Zone. The Saudis don't dare attack directly, or the rolling wave comes right on into the Kingdom. Right across their oil fields . . . The other option is to hit the Shi'ites economically. Sybil's plan."

"Kind of farfetched . . . What does she say about it?"

There was a pause from the back seat.

"I don't think she can talk."

"Well, then . . ."

"Feisel wasn't one of them," Corbin said suddenly. "He was a Wahabi and son of a sheikh. And he couldn't fly worth a damn, as you said. And that's the only thing Sybil wanted from him. So he must have been some kind of Security plant, to keep tabs on the group certainly—possibly to help them."

"Sounds reasonable, I guess . . . But what does that mean for us? I mean, do we really want to surrender at Jabrin? The government might just fly our asses back out to those people. We could fly to 'Arada, which is over the border in the Emirates. Would they be in on the plot?"

"No, but they'd count the bodies in here and then hold us until the proper Saudi authorities could sort the matter out. Can you make it all the way to the Petramin Compound in Riyadh?"

"You mean, without being spotted? In a bright pink helicopter? Dripping blood out of a smashed-up nose bubble?"

"The Saudi Air Force isn't that thick in the sky."

"But those people back at Abaila certainly have radios to warn them with."

"Right . . . What about ditching short of some town and walking in?"

"All right," I said. "My instruments include a compass and a wristwatch. I have no accurate topo maps of this area. And, anyway, all they would show is rolling dunes.

So, you tell me when you think we are 'short of' some place, then we find out how far we have to walk."

"Ouch!"

"Exactly."

"I guess, then, we fly to Jabrin and trust our luck with that famous Arab hospitality," Corbin said. "And there's just a chance that, seeing we've gotten free, they won't have the balls to send us back. They might just play us straight and sacrifice the whole group at Abaila."

"Think so?"

"Nah!"

But that is exactly what the Security Police did. When we brought the Mixmaster shuddering and groaning into a sideways landing at the Jabrin airstrip, the first people to reach the craft were uniformed police. So they may have had some kind of tipoff.

But they came with their sidearms holstered—until they saw the busted plexiglass and bloody tatters hanging off the nose of our bird. Then they all pulled their guns and sank down on one knee to get steady aim.

We climbed out with our hands up. Corbin talked to the nearest man and the man's pistol for three minutes in that halting, grade-school Arabic he used. I wondered if his phrasebook had words like "terrorist" and "submachine gun."

I was left watching their hands and faces. When I saw both relax, I started to bring my hands down. From there, things happened fast.

Corbin led them back across the runway toward the hangers, walking quickly. He was using the command stride he would perfect later, during the war: hands always in motion, pointing, gesturing, emphasizing, and always in beat with the tempo his feet set. He had a way of looking at the man on his right and talking to the one on his left, wrapping them all in the scope of his thoughts. I do not understand how, but he still held the burp gun that had killed the big terrorist—and the Security men let him carry it.

An ambulance, a converted Cadillac with a truck body welded onto the back and all painted white with red crosses, rolled past us, out to the shot-up helicopter to take Sybil off. I would not see her for another three weeks, and then under much different circumstances.

There were a few shaky moments when we were brought to the colonel in charge of the post. From something Corbin said in that strangled Arabic, the colonel must have assumed I was one of the terrorists. They separated us, leveled their sidearms at me, and brought out the handcuffs.

Jay talked fast then, pausing only to find the right words. The policemen hesitated and looked at their colonel. He finally said two words and I was released.

Inside of half an hour, the entire force was being mustered. They were breaking out riot guns and grenades, warming up helicopters and light airplanes.

I took Corbin aside and asked what was going on.

"We're going back."

"They are returning us to—?"

"No, no. Colonel Museddes thinks he can catch the whole group on the ground before they call in support from Oman or the Emirates."

"You sure of that?"

Corbin shrugged. "We can stay here . . . if we want."

"No way. Count me in. Besides—you may need a pilot."

So we flew back to Abaila. On the first pass, they blanketed the oasis with tear gas canisters. Anyone who came out peacefully, they bound and held for evacuation on a big troopship they had whistled down from Riyadh. The rest they went in after, wearing gas masks and flak vests, and took by force.

I was standing next to Corbin, watching the fun from upwind by the lead helicopter. Then I looked around and he was gone, just a shadow among the swirling gases. When he came back, he was toting a police-issue Ingram and claimed to have bagged four.

"Did you see Feisel?" I asked.

"Nope!" Corbin gave me a big clown smile. "He's either in hiding or being hid."

"Should we tell someone about him?"

"Who would you tell?" He slung the empty assault gun into the nearest bird. "And anyway, why spoil his game?"

In Riyadh, where the Security forces dropped us off the next day, we were met by the senior Petramin official and the American consul. They wanted us to leave the country immediately. However, the Saudis moved in smoothly and said we had to stay for the trial, to give evidence against the terrorists. It was an official diplomatic suggestion that our corporate bosses could not ignore.

In the meantime, we were put on administrative duty. Which meant Corbin and I did paperwork and kept to the compound.

I understood nothing of the trial. Robed judges and prosecutors droned in musical Arabic. Sybil and a dozen of her lieutenants were seated in a fenced area, like the dock in British courts. She had a neck brace and a head bandage that covered most of her beautiful black hair. Her eyes were puffy. Corbin and I were interrogated through translators. We told the kidnapping story at least three different ways and nobody noticed. Sybil never looked at us and hardly seemed to follow what was going on.

Then it was over and the verdict was in: death for them all. I thought this would be like an American court, where the death penalty is just a distant threat and they would have a dozen years or so of legal footwork. But no, the next day the Saudi government invited us back.

One of the city squares had been cleared of traffic and market carts. A scaffolding had been set up from folding risers, like you might see at a rock concert. Fifty or a hundred thousand people were ranged around this platform, waiting noisily. Corbin and I had box seats, with some other Petramin people. Very big people.

At noon they led out a dozen figures, dressed in simple white pullover gowns, like they issue in hospitals. From a distance of three hundred feet, I could not recognize them. Then I saw the one on the near end had long, black hair. They had removed Sybil's brace and bandages.

One by one, with Sybil last, they were brought forward and their heads laid on a block. A man in classic Bedouin robes swung a great, two-handed, silver-shining sword to cut those heads off. With each swing a mist of blood flew out over the crowd, and the crowd screamed cheers.

Corbin explained to me how big an event this was, a chance for the Saudis to strike back at the Shi'ite threat hovering along their northern borders. The entire country was watching these executions on television. He pointed to a nearby camera, which panned across our box every thirty seconds or so. We were celebrities.

But wait, I said, it was all wrong. The terrorists had been on the royalists' side, the Saudi side, against the Ayatollah, right?

And Corbin said, no, that is not the way it had come out at the trial. The translators had freeformed their own story out of our testimony, and not one of the English-speaking judges had contradicted them.

All the time he told me this, Corbin never took his eyes off the sword and the flying blood. Beside us, I could hear one of the other Petramin people being sick down near his shoes.

Finally it was Sybil Zahedi's turn. She walked toward the block, and I could see her lips moving. I thought she might be saying a prayer, but no, she was shouting something to the crowd, to the man who was going to kill her, to us sitting a hundred yards away. What she might have been saying was lost in the animal howl of the aroused crowd. It was like watching a silent movie. Two men pushed her down, her mouth still working, and the third cut quickly.

Jay Corbin did not even flinch. I know because I had my eyes on him.

Then we were allowed to leave the country. We became a nine days' wonder back in the States. Corbin was interviewed on at least four video talk shows and I had two radio spots when they could not get him. There was a ceremony at the White House with the vice president giving us the Medal of Freedom. Finally, Petramin paid us a nice severance and left us on the street. . . . That seemed to be another suggestion from the Saudis.

After a brace of years I had had my fill of taxi flying for rich corporoids or hauling the beer around in a jungle war.

So I headed west, unfroze the rest of my stash and set up in the business I knew best, selling kiddy ass, loosely basing myself in Carson City, Nevada. My front was talent scout and booking agent for a fictitious Chicago modeling school. You see, the prettiest girls—and boys—never feel very secure and need to test themselves against the plastic faces they see every day on video and in the magazines.

Let me tell you: All of Nevada is not the same. A misinterpretation of local statutes for which, in Vegas, they would give you steep bail and a dozen continuances, in Carson City they do not even bother taking through the desk sergeant. They take a hank of tow rope out of their Jeeps and look around for a lamp post. Confronted with such an angry crowd during my first month back in the business, I had to walk through three citizens to find a stretch of pavement with running room. Even now I look over my shoulder anytime I get ten miles this side of the State border.

So, about six months after separation from the oil company I was in Portland, with no forwarding address that anyone knew, when I got a call from Corbin.

"You used to be in the service, in Nicaragua, didn't you?" he asked right off.

"How did you know I was in Nicco?" My voice dropped about an octave.

"Your Petramin records, of course. Do you know anything about—conditions there?"

"You mean today?"

"No, at the end of the war, just before we blew Managua away."

"I saw the American side of it."

"Any reactions?"

"Yeah, palefaces should not be allowed to wage a war. They know scoot about etiquette and taking coup."

"Uh—right. Look, can you—could you come down to San Francisco and help us with a case we're putting together?"

"What kind of case?"

"A prosecution. We're taking one of the colonels apart over the war."

"What he do?"

"Killed a lot of people."

"Hell, we all did that."

"Yeah, but this one got caught."

"When do you want me?"

Inside of two days, Corbin said, and he gave me an address. So I went down to help him prosecute Colonel Donald L. Beyer, the Butcher of Boaco. And after that I never left his side—Corbin's, that is.

The address he gave me was on lower Montgomery Street, three entire floors of an elegant old granite-faced building that was only six floors tall, a luxury low-rise in that soaring part of the city. The name, in gold letters raised half an inch, was Knox, Schnock, Hughes & Thayer, Attorneys. Corbin was listed, in a gold-colored decal on the building directory, third from the end among the junior associates.

"They hired me mostly on the wave of publicity, I think," he said as he led me back through the shelves of law books to his cubicle. It was a work station built out of chest-high fabric partitions; it contained a data terminal and three square feet of desk space. There were just the two chairs.

"You need a pilot in here?" I grinned.

Corbin shook his head. "Tell me about Managua, the last days . . . And by the way, you aren't still on active reserves, are you?"

"Nope, I got clean of that shit."

"You didn't sign anything with the government—"

"Only about a million forms."

"But nothing which promised you would not reveal what you saw on duty in Central America?" he prompted.

"Does not matter. I will not be sworn in a court of law," I said firmly.

"Why not?"

"My reasons." Who could know what charges were still pending against me in California from the old days? I had three bail bondsmen on my payroll at one time, from all over the West."

"All right . . . We can find others to testify. Just tell me what you saw."

I told him.

Although I had not been personally involved in the house searches that followed the seige of Managua, I knew enough troops who were. There was not much hand-to-hand fighting, because by that time the population was out of ammunition, long out of food and water, and completely out of spirit. The Marines rounded up ghosts, pale-eyed children, old women, young boys with rust-pitted weapons and bloated bellies.

Of course I had heard rumors about genosquads, but I never met anyone who had served on one. The camps they set up on the east of the city at Jinotepe, Masaya and Tipitapa were just that—refugee and resettlement camps. No executions, no gas chambers, no fiendish experiments, no cremations, no ashes to scatter. But those stories reflect the temper of the times.

I saw the special sapper units go through the city, using professional demolition techniques. Five satchels of plastique, strategically placed, and a fifteen-story apartment block would come straight down like the earth had opened beneath it. For the shack rows on the city edges and the cottages of the middle-class suburbs, they fitted 'dozer blades on M-60 battle tanks and drove diagonal lines across the landscape. The rest we soldiers broke up with picks and crowbars, as I have explained.

Looting? What could the average infantryman want in one of those places? A five-year-old transistor radio? Hand-made clothing? Cracked dishes? A dimestore cherrywood Madonna? The CIA teams had gone through the government buildings, and staff officers had gone through the hotels and official residences. The rest was a thousand times poorer than an East Los Angeles garage sale.

Yes, I saw the dusters at work. That was one of the assignments of the 452nd Airborne, although I never flew one. Yes, moonsuits and breather gear were the uniform of the day. But no, they never did explain what the stuff was, except that one day the ground in Managua showed plenty of black soil and green plants, and the next it was blowing dust and brown stems. The lakeshore was three feet deep in dead fish for a week.

Yes, I did know some of the pilots—names if not serial numbers—who flew the duster flights. Yes, I could probably contact two or three without any trouble; some of them kept in touch through the battalion newsletter.

Then it was my turn to ask him the questions.

"Why do you want to know all this? Just history now."

"We are trying to find out, through various sources, who it was that gave the orders for the dusting of Managua," Corbin said.

"Came from the President, right?"

"No, not according to any published source. The highest authority we can locate is this Colonel Donald Beyer. He was in charge of 'Special Operations.'"

"Who is 'we,' exactly?" I asked.

"This law firm."

"But why are you involved? If there was something wrong with the orders, if this Beyer exceeded his authority, then it would be a military matter, a court-martial."

"Not necessarily. This is a civil case, a class action suit brought for damages on behalf of the soldiers who were exposed to this unknown 'dust' you describe."

"How many of these soldiers are there?"

"We don't know that yet."

"Come again?"

"The firm is—ah—prospecting right now."

"You mean you are peeking inside the ambulance to see if there is a case for you."

"Indelicately, yes." Corbin smiled that wide, clown smile he had.

"And you want me to help you find pilots who can testify about the dust."

"Or exhibit symptoms that may be related to its use."

"All right."

"We can make the effort worth your while. . . ," He eyed me steadily. "Do you want to name a sum?"

"I will have to think about it."

In the end, I agreed to work with them. Over the next eight months I helped him and the other lawyers question veterans from the Nicaragua campaign, about four hundred of them. How much help I was, who can say? Three

obvious bullshitters—men who never left the States on
active duty, although to hear them tell it they cleaned out
Managua singlehanded—were eliminated on my say-so in
half an hour. But Corbin and his paralegals would probably have weeded them in twice that time themselves.
Sometimes I could corroborate a man's testimony, sometimes just correct a few town names.

Corbin himself was as distant and cool as a judge, although he must have wanted the case against Beyer pretty
badly. Still, he would have blown it if he had gotten into
the spirit of their stories, adding and embellishing. He had
to hold off and explore whatever doubts came to him. He
had to think like Beyer's defense attorneys, who would
surely raise those doubts themselves. And Corbin could
do it every time—think through the evidence and testimony rationally and coolly—all but once.

That was over a young soldier, he must have been
fifteen when he went to Nicco, because he could not have
been more than eighteen when he came into the KSH&T
offices. He had blond hair in fine curls, doe eyes just like a
girl's, and a beautiful mouth. To me, he was just another
immature kid, at most a PFC with a worm's-eye view of
the action. But when he walked into the office that first
day, I thought I could hear Corbin draw breath from
across the room. Jay believed everything this Harry Schisser
had to say. And once, when I corrected the little darling
about a landing zone—he had been just a wrench jockey, a
ground mechanic, after all—Corbin cut across me in his
defense. Corbin took him to dinner, and afterwards he was
talking about the little jerk as some kind of star witness.
The boy sat at his right hand like a poodle.

The big surprise came when I had to call Corbin's office
to change the timing on an appointment. The call might
have been picked up by his secretarial pool or an answer-
ing machine. It might even have been picked up by Corbin
himself. But the voice on the other end was little Harry's.
And when he knew who was calling I swear his voice
changed from his normal demure to sassy-brassy bold, like
he had aced me out or something.

For that alone I was ready to render him for parts. But

the heavy stuff came down three days later, when I found
him in Jay's apartment, alone, in a silk bathrobe mono-
grammed with the familiar GJC, holding a pillowcase half-
full of silverware, desk accessories, and some crystal. I
worked out the contents later, but right then all I could
see was some sharp-angled bulges that did not look like
feathers.

"Hey! I can explain!" Harry protested.

I threw him across the living room.

Up against the book case, he tried to take a stance,
digging his toes into the thick carpeting.

Before he could plant it I kicked him twice, once in the
balls and again higher, in the solar plexus. Neither was a
crippling blow—just a light snap with my instep, a lion
tamer.

Harry screamed like a woman and went down clutching
himself. He curled up on the floor like an infant, or some
kind of wounded snake.

I bent down and put my mouth close to his trembling
ear. "Now listen to me, fellah. I am going to turn my back
for three minutes. You are going to get up, take off that
stupid bathrobe, put everything back where you found it,
get your clothes on, pass a little inspection—with all your
pockets turned out—and then get out of here. Go find
yourself a bus back to wherever you came from. Can you
remember all that, hey?"

He nodded, blinking back tears.

"Very good, soldier. Now march!" I nudged him with
my shoe.

Harry moved. And none of us ever saw him again.
When he did not show at the law offices, there was not a
word from Corbin, even though I was listening for it. The
case went on without our "star witness."

I soon figured out that Jay Corbin had a blind spot for
beauty. He reacted strongly to people with pretty faces
and bodies, because he thought his own were not. He fell
for people who were self-centered, because that sort of
self-absorption sometimes passes for confidence, which the
young Corbin sometimes lacked. So he would close his
eyes while the love of the moment climbed up on his or

her pedestal. Corbin was always looking for a state of grace and beauty that was perfect and permanent. He never found it.

He had another weakness that I discovered during the investigations for the Beyer case. We were locking up the papers and tapes after a long day of depositions. Corbin was rolling on about the latest testimony.

". . . clearly had the authority to order suppression of the Nicaraguan civilian population," he was saying, "but not the destruction of public property. And if that compound *was* dioxin based, as those medical officers claim, then we have at least a violation of OAS environmental principles if not of the Contadora Con-con-con . . . vention . . . of eigh-eigh-eigh . . . ty-nine . . ."

Corbin's voice stuttered out like an engine running down, dying at last in a hiccup. I looked across the work table after a minute, to see if he had just lost his train of thought. His face was a blank, his jaw hanging down toward the knot in his tie. He had half-risen from his chair, then he threw it over backwards as he flopped down.

It took me perhaps four seconds to get around the cubicle, and by that time the seizure was in full flood. I got my billfold out and jammed it into his mouth—I still have it today, with a perfect set of Jay Corbin's canines and bicuspids cut into the leather.

His head, elbows and heels were all bouncing in different rhythms on the carpet. To keep him from busting his skull, I grabbed him around the shoulders in a kind of wrestler's pin and held his head up. Since then I have read that holding him like this was most dangerous, because it put pressure on his back muscles and could have injured his spine. I should have just put something soft under his head.

The spasms went on for about five minutes, and in that time he wetted himself. Eventually he went limp and stayed that way, almost a natural sleep, for about an hour. It took most of that time to clean him up, blotting his trousers with a paper towel as much as possible, then I just sat over him, watching and waiting.

When his eyes opened and focused, he looked at me with a great frown.

"Did I forget what I was saying?"

"Yes."

"Then the—uh—*grand mal?*"

"Yes."

"How long?"

"A few minutes."

"Not getting any worse," he said, mostly to himself.

He started to sit up, discovered the damp stain in his pants. For an instant his face broke up like he was going to cry. Then his mouth firmed and he stood up, leaning heavily against a chair.

"Are there medicines—?" I asked slowly.

"There might be, if I were stupid enough to tell anyone about this."

"Why not?"

"Because epileptics get dumped on. I could lose my job, my driver's license, my freedom . . . People would be watching me, waiting for me to flop over. It's a misunderstood sickness and I will not have it."

"Hunh!"

"Hunh! Right, Chief!" he spat the words at me. "Hunh!"

"I did not mean—"

He stared at me for an uncomfortably long time. "Can you keep this secret? Can I *trust* you?" His eyes bored into me and there was no weakness, no pleading in them.

"Yes, Jay, of course."

"There isn't any 'of course' about this. No matter what happens, no matter who asks, can you keep your mouth shut?"

"What if you die?"

"The seizures are messy and debilitating but not lethal. Can you keep shut about them?"

"Yes."

"Good."

With that he turned and walked stiffly out of the workroom, back straight, limping slightly from a pulled muscle in his calf.

It took us six months to prepare the case on Beyer; a

year more to get venue, go through discovery, pull a jury; two weeks of argument and two weeks of deliberations. And in all that time I never saw another seizure. So they must have been pretty rare.

How did the Beyer case go? He was convicted of unauthorized use of dioxin compounds that endangered the lives of the soldiers assigned to him. The award was six hundred million, of which Knox, Schnock, Hughes & Thayer would keep forty percent—if and when. Because the case was on contingency, nothing would be paid until the appeals process was completed; and that was still pending three years later when Corbin disappeared into the mountains of Japan.

Of course, Corbin got his regular salary—maybe a hundred thou a year with all sorts of options. And I was paid, all told, about twenty-five thousand for my time. It kept me in room and firewater.

Those were rocky times, what with inflation heating up again and the transition to an "information economy" all over but the shouting. The only ones making out were the lawyers, it seemed, and even then Corbin barely had enough to get married on.

Oh, yes. A couple of months after our Harry split for Kansas City, Jay introduced me to his newest lady, Anne Caheris. She was a practical young woman with smiling gray eyes, a straight jaw, and a father in the U.S. Congress. I do not think she had any money of her own, and Daddy still owed bundles from his last three campaigns. So she had to be the only woman Jay Corbin married for love.

He should have quit while he was ahead.

Chapter 7

Jay Corbin: Good For Nothing

Anne Caheris never lied to me. She said she wanted three things from our marriage—money, security, and children. So long as I could provide the first two and promise the third, she stayed with me.

I suppose Anne cared so much about money because of her father. William Caheris was living proof that not all politicians are crooks. He ran for the House three times and never was less than a hundred thousand in debt. He was a fine man and I respected him, but he never did figure out how to make a living by serving his country.

To her credit, Anne never asked me to help him out. What was ours was his, and she was just thankful that inheritances didn't work the other way.

So long as I stayed with Knox, Schnock, Hughes & Thayer we had everything a young couple in San Francisco could want: a six-room apartment on the north side of Nob Hill with a view of the Gate; a Porsche 979 Eierförmig under valet parking; catered brunches, with confections from Just Desserts; morels in brandy six nights a week if we wanted them.

We were so flush and fat, I could even afford to finance my own dip into politics, running on the '96 ballot for the city's Board of Supervisors. The voting was at-large, with four candidates for three seats.

That winter and spring I went in succession to the

Chinese New Year and ate smoked duck, to the Saint
Patrick's parade and drank green beer, to the Cherry
Blossom Festival and sucked teriyaki chicken off a stick,
and to Cinco de Mayo and packed away giant burritos. I
gained fifteen pounds and shook half a million hands. I
spoke at the Commonwealth Club on the Beyer case,
which we were winning at the time. I bought time on
Sunday morning radio talk shows and dittoed Beyer.

The issues of the day were a downtown sports arena
(again!), children's housing rights, and the city's control of
certain strips bordering the Golden Gate National Recre-
ation Area. My issues were pass the salsa and get the man
who poisoned Lake Managua.

I lost by a 4,000-vote margin—and ended up with $35,000
in campaign debts. Anne just curled her lip, then went
into the bathroom and locked the door for a while.

The Beyer case eventually went to the Supreme Court;
of course, it was long out of my hands by then. They
overturned everything on the specious grounds that chain-
of-command decisions were not subject to challenge in the
civil courts. Piffle!

Did I hate Donald Beyer? Not at all.

He was a sad man, balding, pot-bellied, hesitating on
the edge of growing old. A staff man with twenty-five
years, more a bureaucrat than a soldier. I remember thinking once that this was a man who somewhere had a good
woman who loved him, children who honored him, grand-
children perhaps who searched his pockets for candies
when he came to visit. Hardly a butcher who, for the love
of mayhem, would poison a thousand square miles of lake
and massacre a city of half a million people. But that was
our story, supported by accounts that we or anyone could
recover from eyewitness sources and public documents.
So we went after him full throttle. And all for nothing.

That spring of 1996, while I was minding my cases and
eating my way through the municipal campaign, we had
an unfortunate accident in the firm. It happened on April
first, which used to be known as April Fool's Day.

I had gone down to the mail cubby for the ten o'clock

delivery, expecting an express package. The mail clerk, Hubie, told me that all the "non-mail" items were in a bin under the table. He was a loose-jawed kid with zits and bad posture. What Hubie was really telling me was, if I wanted to get my package before the regular delivery, I could root around under his knees. His infuriating insolence probably saved my eyesight, if not my life.

While I was hunkered down, with Hubie bumping packages around and slapping papers on the tabletop over my head, a thin *bang!* thumped up there, like a cherry bomb going off. My head jerked up and hit the underside of the table. Something hit the small of my back and bounced away—turned out to be Hubie's left hand. Still on my knees with my head down, I caught a glimpse under my elbow of Hubie backing up fast to the far wall of the cubby. The wall was one of those fabric-covered "office system" partitions, and it held him up for half a second, then crashed over into the next cubicle, where one of the word processors worked. In the instant before he went over, I could see two bloody stumps and a mask of blood. Then just his sneakers kicking among the fallen panels.

It was a letter bomb, of course.

People were running up. Someone brought over a fire extinguisher and began shooting cold clouds of carbon dioxide around, although nothing was visibly burning. From the way their jaws were working, everyone seemed to be shouting but the sounds came out dim and far away, like a riot at street level heard from the thirtieth floor. The honk of the CO_2 nozzle seemed to me only a soothing *whoosh*. So my ears were partly deafened by the blast. I sat there, watching it all, trying to tune in my hearing like a weak radio signal.

Hughes, one of the for-real senior partners, tried to get the FBI to come in that same day and comb the area for clues. What he got was the SFPD bomb squad, dressed in canvas smocks over steel-mesh body armor. When they found out that the bomb was *post facto* instead of *ante*, they drank our coffee and scarfed down a dozen pastries from the hospitality center, flirted with the receptionists, and left taking as souvenirs every Xeroxed postal reg and personal notice from the partitions around the mail cubby. So they made sure any surface which might harbor traces of bomb packaging or wire shavings was effectively cleaned.

In the meantime, someone had thoughtfully scrubbed the soot-blackened table top where the bomb had gone off. So, if the FBI ever did come, all they had to go on was an interview with the receptionist, a heavily hormoned lady who "remembered this really weird thing, you know, about the guy who delivered the morning mail."

"What weird thing, Miss?"

"Well, he wasn't the regular guy. He was a lot better looking."

"Better looking in what way?"

"Well, he wore his uniform sort of, tighter. With these good pecs and, like, nice buns hanging out of his jacket. It was to drool."

"Right, Miss. Could you describe his face?"

"Yeah . . . He had one."

"Thank you, Miss."

It is not unusual for a prestigious San Francisco law firm to attract a certain amount of hostile, possibly radical-fringe attention. This may not have been the first letter bomb that Knox, Schnock, Hughes & Thayer had ever received.

Except that same morning two of our junior partners, Hills and Pettigrew, were carpooling to work as usual when their BMW 775si was boxed at an intersection in the classic wishbone formation. Between a garbage truck and a Muni bus, the soft-sided sedan didn't stand a chance. One dead on the scene, the other three days in a coma and expiring in intensive care. Later the traffic report alleged negligence on the part of the truck driver.

No big thing. Happens all the time.

On that April 1's lunch hour one of our paralegals was leaving the building and got mugged in broad daylight. Except "mugging" is when some villain sticks a lethal implement, a knife or a gun, in your face and asks for money. This incident was along the lines of a Victorian-era "bug picking": Someone sandbagged the girl from behind, ripped the purse from her limp arm, and ran down the street.

For dessert that evening the elevator in our building parted a cable at the second floor, sending it to the basement fast and putting five people in the hospital with three broken legs and a mass of bruises.

Lawyer Day.

It was never an officially declared holiday. How could it be, considering the number of lawyers who controlled Congress and the State legislatures? It was never sanctioned, never even mentioned by the American Bar Association. Lawyer Day did not even start as a folk tradition, although it quickly became one.

It started as a statistical glitch. One so minor that not even the media or the hottest trendalizers spotted it in the presumptive first year. I was getting inklings, however.

The next year, 1997, Lawyer Day was still just a statistical thing, like having all your bad luck in a single day. One of our junior partners involved in a minor fender-bender ended up with a .38 slug in his brain. Two associates eating in the local taco palace went home early with stomach cramps and succumbed before morning. Four letter bombs. Five unrelated muggings.

On April 1, 1998, the media casters were beginning to comment on the incidents, noting that almost every news story that day involved someone related to the law—a justice, judge, counselor, or clerk. For myself, I recall a graffito spray-painted on a brick wall three weeks before the date:

LAWYER DAY—

FRAG EM, SCRAG EM

AND BAG EM

However, I had resigned from Knox, Schnock, Hughes & Thayer by May of '97, the year before that. I didn't need a bazooka shell through my picture window to tell me that the legal business had suddenly become life threatening. Somewhere, someone—probably a whole lot of someones—was fingering lawyers. Maybe it *was* only one day a year, but the odds seemed to be stacked against surviving it. And anyway, by that time I had seen a chance to make a bundle on the deal of a lifetime.

"You're going to what!?"

I could see Anne wasn't happy with the idea but I tried to explain anyway: "Put solar cells on roofing tiles. Sell them, along with power converters and battery sets, to homeowners who need a new roof."

"Why?"

I couldn't believe how dense the girl could be. "Ever hear of the energy crisis?" I asked facetiously. By that time the Power Gap was into its second year. We had brownouts coming every other day and our district in San Francisco was on rolling outages.

"Each one of these tiles generates about a watt of power," I went on. "A patch twenty feet by fifty would put out a kilowatt, which is about as much as the average household uses at any one time. And on foggy days or at night you run off the batteries, or take a trickle from the electric company. Otherwise, you're free of them. Nobody owns the sun."

Anne's face clouded up. "Did you think of this yourself, or is someone selling you on the idea?"

"It's ninety percent mine. Ten percent from this fellow, Michael Braden, who came into the law firm today trying to get out from under a shipment of amorphous silicon cells Nippon Kagai sent him two months early, by mistake, with 120-day delayed billing. By the time his invoices come in, what with the current inflation rate, the cells will have cost him more than twice what he'd agreed to. If we can divert them to this roofing tile project, we can keep them in bond for that time and dodge the price rise."

"Is this just some sort of import scam, then?"

"No, no. It's legitimate, Anne. We incorporated Solar Tile, Inc. this afternoon, right after lunch."

"Who's going to supply the roofing tiles, the electrical equipment, the crews to do installation?"

"We're working out the details. I've already talked to Birdsong about organizing the crews. He's good with the men."

"Who's going to supply the *money?*"

"We'll issue our first stock Friday under the Security and Exchange Commission's new XPD guidelines. As for working capital, I thought that . . . um . . . ah . . ."

"Ye-ya-esss?" she drawled.

"Money's not a problem," I protested.

But really, it was *the* problem—or so I thought right then. The Fed was squeezing the capital markets from one side, while Treasury double-dipped to keep the deficit going. Braden and I would be lucky to raise our working funds at thirty-nine percent, through legitimate channels. That didn't scare us, of course, because 285-percent inflation would eat up the interest costs in three and a half months' time. The problem would be attracting venture capitalists under any circumstances. And then getting the business running fast enough; otherwise that same inflation would turn our capital into chickenfeed before we could even get it spent. That's what XPDs were all about.

"I thought we could use our savings . . ."

That money wasn't cash in a savings account, of course. The inflation rate was miles ahead of any bank's passbook rate. No, we had about $300,000 in money market instruments, mostly overnight certificates, that were managed by the SAFENET Fund and guaranteed us an annual percentage rate equal to at least 299 percent. That kept our nest egg just ahead of the gobble machine, but we were not exactly liquid: The fund wanted thirty days' notice on any withdrawals.

"Think again, buster," Anne snapped. "I'm not about to live under a bridge with you after you've blown those bucks on some freaking solar power scheme."

"Well, maybe something else will turn up. . . ."

In those days I found it prudent to retreat before Anne's dedicated stare.

Braden and I did find a source of capital, five hundred thousand worth, but it had a long string. The venturists wanted us to "protect their liability," which meant submitting our plans to formal risk analysis and arbitrage before the Insurance Commission. Which meant we had to put together all the details I had so airily dismissed to

Anne—source of materials, electrical equipment, roofing crews, power system sizing, tile substrate designs, marketing plans, accounting systems, contractor licenses and bonding, et blinding cetera—before we were cleared to see one penny.

"Oh, you're not done by a long shot," said Elton Weems, the risk analyst the commission had assigned to our filing. "What about an environmental impact report?"

Braden and I looked at each other. Michael was a big man, with shoulders fairly bursting out of the lapels of his suit jacket. When he shifted uncomfortably in his chair, its legs creaked.

"Why would we need one?" I asked.

"Weh-yell now, you *are* proposing a major modification in the way people do roofing, aren't you? We'd have to consider how that might impact on the atmosphere. For instance, is the new roof more or less reflective than existing systems? Do you use any special chemicals in applying the roofs? Will the material deteriorate and deposit any chemicals into the atmosphere? All these things have to be studied."

"Can you tell me where in the Code of Federal Regulations or statutes of the State of California this is required?" I asked politely.

"Now, Counselor," Weems smiled. It was like a nervous tic with him. "You know risk analysis doesn't work that way. We must presume that if there shall have been a failure or litigable damages, the test of law will be those investigations or other protective measures which you *might* have undertaken, not merely those you were required by law to undertake."

"But you're talking about materials tests needing *years* to complete. Perhaps if we showed that similar substances— terra-cotta tiles and silicon cells, to be exact—have long been used in building and in power systems with no ill effects?"

"Used together?"

"Sometimes."

"And with what glue or bonding agent?"

"Ummm . . ."

"You see?" Weems put up his hands—and smiled. "There are imponderables here."

Braden leaned forward. "Roofing mastic!" he barked in exasperation.

"Have you tested it in your particular application?" Weems simpered.

I thought Mike was going to hit him.

"No, we haven't," I cut across.

"Well, then your filing can hardly be said to be complete, can it? I'm afraid it will be impossible to make an accurate assessment until you provide more complete data." Weems sat back.

Clearly, with the way inflation was going, by the time we complied with the Insurance Commission's testing and reports, that half a mill in financing wouldn't buy us a photocopier to make the necessary submittals in sextuplicate.

Braden and I parted company in the lobby of the commission's building in Sacramento. I never found out what he eventually did with that shipment of solar cells. Ate them, I guess.

"Your problem," Birdsong told me, when I explained why the deal fell through, "is trying to start a legit business just before the tide turns."

"What tide, Billy?"

"All energy is circular," he said with that Indian sangfroid of his. "There are easy times, cycling into hard times. In the easy times, all the energy is flowing your way. Banks, the stock market, the government are all flooding with cheap money and pushing opportunities at you. You have to be stupid not to make a buck. In hard times, it is all ebbing away and everybody has a reason why not—why you can not get a loan, a license, a permit, a share of the market. Nobody can make money right *before* the turn. Either at the end of a flood, when the opportunities are pretty much used up by the suckers who just fall into them, or at the end of an ebb, when the noes have been said so often that nobody can hear yes.

"The time to make money," he said, "is *during* the change, at the point of maximum instability. Then the suckers get shook out and the opportunities are there for only the smart ones to see."

"Why, Chief," I said, "you're a natural-born doctor of economics. And a poet to boot. How come you never made any money?"

"Who said I never did?" he answered, looking at me darkly. Birdsong hated being called "Chief"—which I only did because the project had fallen through and I was mad at everybody.

For a while I thought about going back to the law, but by then I had another idea—setting up as a color consultant. When Braden and I had needed a marketing brochure for Solar Tile, Inc., a slick young designer from one of the China Basin firms was sent to us on call to dummy up the graphics. Looking over his shoulder, I discovered that printer's ink came in only a short range of primary colors, but each ink maker's system mixed them differently to generate the thousands of hues a customer might want. And each printer, of which there were hundreds in the San Francisco area alone, had his own way of combining screens of those primary colors as an alternate way to make those same hues. And each color showed up slightly differently on the many different paper stocks—coated, uncoated, matte finish, textured and laid, off white, near white, antique white—all of which were available from the dozen or so paper houses. It took an expert to make an accurate color match, and then only with the right sample books.

And that was just in printing.

For brand-name firms, which often had to coordinate brochures, films, videos, uniforms, truck and sign paints, neons, crockery in the executive dining room, carpets in the headquarters lobby, et blinking cetera, matching colors to the company identity could be a nightmare.

Unless they called in the color consultant, who had all the right sample books. And getting those books was just a matter of talking to the manufacturers' reps.

It took me a month to make the contacts; rent office space; paint, paper, carpet, and light that office in purples and bronze-tone greens; get an Insurance Commission ruling that, no, the damages proceeding from an error in color matching were not liable to exceed my bond of $2 million, of which I had to put up one percent; and waving my rainbow business card, make a series of cold calls on my catalog of Fortune 1000 customers.

It took me two months to discover that most of the world is just color blind enough, or budget-minded enough, not to notice that the uniforms of their counter clerks are two shades off the paint on the wall signs behind the counter.

And I was fast running out of excess spendable.

"Thank God you didn't get your hands on our money!" Anne said, after the collapse of Solar Tile, Inc. and then the color consulting.

"Yeah, we might have made something of it."

"No, Jay, not you. You're just not the entrepreneurial type. You would never make it, outside a big company like Petramin or the law firm. You need a structure to operate in, and to protect you from your impulses."

That's how she saw our marriage. Some kind of shell that would strap me down and protect me from my impulses.

What Anne Corbin, nee Caheris, didn't realize was that for the last thirteen months I had been exercising those impulses pretty thoroughly. San Francisco is an exciting town: All sorts of young, brainy, sophisticated women come to find work and romance. Too late, they discover that the ratio of themselves to the single, unattached men who also vibrate AC is about the same as the ratio of sparrows to jays at your average country bird feeder. Is it any wonder that the jays are bandits? When I got tired of Anne, I could take my pick of the young professional women wandering up from the Financial District. I always ate for free.

Toward the end Anne began to suspect. She had to. A trace of perfume, a mismatched phone reference, an expense account that didn't tally. I never was too careful, and she never was that dumb.

But it wasn't my peccadillos that finished the marriage.

While I was waltzing around with the venture capitalists and the Insurance Commission, Anne was racking up a tidy fortune. How, I never knew. She had her own money with a team of brokers and never tried for the Big Kill, which was my own personal strategy. She just played for twenty thou here and fifty thou there. You would think that inflation and taxes would eat that for breakfast, but no. Her accounts kept sopping up money and expanding faster than the economic quicksand could gobble them down.

The end came when there was one of those periodic blowouts in the financial market: insider trading, stolen secrets, a few smiling faces, and the rest losers. Anne sat on the edge of the bed and chewed her nails.

"What's wrong?" I asked her.

"You don't want to know."

"But you're my wife, Anne." I sat beside her, put an arm around her shoulders. "Your trouble is mine. That's what a marriage means, doesn't it?"

"All right." She took a deep breath. "One of the brokerages where I have money, Anderson Durandy-Coopertine, went under investigation today. The SEC is going to be opening accounts and naming names, under the new Daylight Laws. . . ."

"And your name—?"

"Our name."

"But I never . . ."

"Most of the accounts were in my married name."

"But did you *do* anything?"

"That doesn't matter, does it? I—we—profited from the results of ADC's trading. The SEC is very clear about implied consent."

"But I never saw a penny."

"The law is clear about marriages, too." She held me in a level gaze.

If I had been faster or smarter then, I would have filed a divorce on her the next day. A man in my position, trying to make his way as an entrepreneur in a fast-changing world, could not afford the stain of scandal. A reputation for looseness with money and secrets repelled the venturists, at least when they saw it in someone they were about to trust with money and secrets. I felt my life, and my wife, had to be above suspicion.

But I wasn't fast or smart, then.

Anne grabbed the Porsche and the nest egg from our fund manager—which must have involved forging my signature on the release alongside hers—and disappeared. It was, I suppose, simply those three things she had wanted. We never had a great deal of money. After Lawyer Day and the enterprising schemes, we didn't have any security. And there were no little Corbins coming along. So she tried to provide the money and security for herself. What she did for children, I never learned.

Of all my wives, Anne was the one I loved the best. She understood me. She certainly wasn't afraid of me. She could accept me as a unique and self-sufficient person, not as some imaginary "husband" or "lover" acting out her dialogues on the screen of her mind. But when the marriage wasn't giving her what she needed, she knew when to leave. Anne was a realist. And, I believe, she was the person most like me I've ever met.

Six months later she surfaced with a Mexican divorce decree *in absentia*, which I certainly could have broken in any Stateside court she cared to name. Except by that time I was out of the country getting my head regrooved.

"Martin Luther:" Twelve Points

The following text, written in felt tip on onionskin, was found nailed to the oak-panel doors of Knox, Schnock, Hughes & Thayer's offices in San Francisco:

"Twelve things they don't teach you at Harvard Law:

"1. A lawyer is someone paid to lie in support of a particular point of view. Sorting out the truth with a lawyer is like sorting balloons with a pitchfork.

"2. Politics is the pursuit of law by other means.

"3. Truth and 'reasonableness' are always negotiable.

"4. Advantage is everything. The strength of your position is more important than the accuracy of your facts.

"5. Precedent is everything. A crackpot statute or a vague judicial decision is more useful than an army of verifiable facts.

"6. A certain compromise is better than an uncertain victory. Thirty percent of nothing is still nothing.

"7. Keep meticulous personal records. Even on a contingency case, you charge by the hour.

"8. 'Other people's money' is a term *invented* by a lawyer.

"9. Just because a person is guilty doesn't mean he's not entitled to a strong defense. The guiltiest people need the best lawyers—and usually can pay for them.

"10. Someone is always responsible for an 'act of God.'

"11. Don't trust the short words. The longer the words you use—and the *more* words—the more elbow room you'll have for shifting your meaning(s) in the face of adversity.

"12. Don't trust a jury, even one you've picked yourself and paid for. People can be obstinately open minded."

Lady Anne Meers: Sunrise, Sunset

Yes, I was married to James Corbin—except he was "Jay" then—for about eighteen months in the mid-Nineties. God, it was so *long* ago. We were just children, really. Spoiled children.

The times were too good. And too bad, if you know what I mean. You could have made it if you were a saint: lots of material for practicing your sainthood on. Or if you were a devil: ditto. There was a lot of money floating around, and nice things to buy, and loose people looking for a charge. But not many ideals. You had to bring those with you or you were fresh out of luck.

Which was Jay, saint or devil? I think he wanted to be both and got pulled two ways. He couldn't be crooked enough to make a good devil, and he saw too many possibilities to make a saint. Still, Jay had a keen awareness that he was Somebody. He didn't know who, not yet. But he had reached that disagreeable stage where he was sure the sun rose in his navel and set in his arse.

That made living with him difficult. I'll tell you, and I don't care how politically important he's become, with how many armies to back him up, Jay Corbin is the most selfish man in the world.

Sure, he has that "friend to all the world" smile, that blank check of responsibility for everyone he touched, that well-known code of honor. But it's all to serve his ego, you see. Watch closely: If a deal, an agreement, a treaty, a marriage—anything—won't work his way, it just doesn't exist for him.

You remember that about Jay Corbin, or he'll bite you every time.

Chapter 8

Jay Corbin: The 13th Kata

"Why do you come here?" Master Takusan Matsu asked.

"I wanted to find you, to study with you," I answered. "I want to learn the thirteenth *kata*. I need it in order to advance in rank."

The Master spoke clear English, almost without accent. I had been afraid we would have to talk through the Tourist Ministry translator, a smiling young dolt who, in bringing me up the mountain, had told me more about his impressions of America—gained mostly from "terrevision" and rock videos—than he did about his beautiful countryside.

We had driven the rental car, an old Toyota Coronet, from the steaming cities and the crowded suburbs around Nagoya into the spine of mountains that runs down the back of the big island, Honshu. When the road to Hakusan National Park ran out above the public campgrounds and the cluster of country inns, we walked up a narrow, rocky path. The gripper soles of my Pivettas were doing an excellent job, but the translator's city shoes were giving him grief.

Five hundred feet above the end of the road, we came to a clearing in the pines. Set into it were a spring, a circle of stone-and-thatchwork cottages, and a theater stage—or it might have been an oak-planked boxing ring without ropes. The clearing was arranged so that for most of the day sunlight focused on the stage's well-sanded floorboards.

"Why do you come here?" the Master asked again.

"I want to finish my training. I learned everything I could from Sensei Kan, but it's not enough, not complete. I know I'm missing something essential, something deep. There *has* to be something more. And I hope you can provide it."

Takusan Matsu had taught my old teacher, Sensei Kan from the shopping mall *dojo* in Monterey. Matsu was the master of our style: more than forty years ago he had blended the karate teachings of *his* masters into a single discipline of mind and body. Kan had learned it from him and I had learned from Kan.

In Monterey, we had heard stories of how a Japanese karate master was tested. First he was supposed to perform forty-eight hours of continuous movement, doing *katas*, calisthenics, sparring, running, jumping—just no sitting still. Then he was to stand at the center of a free-for-all battle with fifty other black belts; against each of them Matsu had to score two points, landing technical, almost-touching death blows on his opponents, while he himself absorbed no more than one blow from all of them together. . . . Or those were the tales we heard.

The legend of this man had grown to the point that we all believed he was a hundred and ten years old. That he drank boiling water without blistering his throat. That he could shinny backwards up a rope like a monkey, leading with his feet and pushing with his hands while his bald head hung toward the hard ground. That he could deliver ten death blows in half a second. That he worshipped wood spirits and believed they inhabited modern technology such as telephones and carried messages along the wire. Some kind of spook, he was supposed to be.

He looked remarkably normal here, and not a day over sixty-five. He was wearing gray sweatpants with a red stripe on the side, a yellow nylon windbreaker with a tee-shirt underneath, and Nike running shoes with white ribbed sweatsocks. No silk robes, not even a karate *gi*. Matsu had the sleepy, hooded eyes of an old turtle. He looked at you by looking past you. The movements of his hands, his jaw, his feet were as precise and slow as a turtle's. I was asking myself if this was a mistake, someone other than our legendary master?

The coterie of dedicated and slightly vindictive young disciples I had imagined would surround him was nowhere to be seen. Just one dull-eyed boy who broomed the theater stage.

"Why do you come here?" the Master asked again, mildly.

"My whole world has collapsed. I want you to tell me what has gone wrong and how to put it right."

And that finally was the truth. What Anne took when she flew to Mexico, both in love and money, was nothing compared to what the Twenty-eighth Amendment had done to my security and my fortunes, not to mention the rest of the country's. Some call it the Repudiation Amendment; to others it's the Debtors' Delight.

For half a dozen years we had debated the effects of a repudiation of the national debt. The economists were about evenly divided—between forecasts of gloom over money markets that would be dashed by a landslide of worthless Federal paper, and joy at the prospect of money markets that would no longer be sucked dry by an impoverished government able to commandeer capital at need and pay for it in promissory scrip. The politicians talked on both sides of the question, confident that in the battle for ratification their party could fight the good fight and retire in righteous defeat—that is, that nothing would happen. The media trumpeted every opinion, trembling and exulting by turns. Sensible people were certain that, like most momentous questions, the Federal deficit and the national debt would remain unresolved for their lifetime. We lawyers merely rubbed our hands, knowing there would be pay work for us no matter how the question fell out.

And when West Virginia finally voted to ratify and seal the three-fourths majority, with the Twenty-ninth Amendment—repeal of the power to tax—not far behind, the U.S. economy just fell apart. Anyone with a stake in the government was going to suffer: holders of "Savings Bonds" (what a joke!) would see their assets vanish in a cloud of shredded paper; contractors for defense and large civil works would watch their stocks plummet. In the weeks while West Virginia debated, the smart money moved out of these and hundreds of other areas. The banks grew fat on parked cash, then crashed when the Federal Reserve folded up like a magician's cabinet. When the banks fell, the economic structure of the country went into free fall.

Today, we refer to that time as the Money Warp. Like a wrinkle in the fabric of space-time, this was a wrinkle in the fabric of the national economy. It was similar to the convulsions of the mid-'70s, when the price of oil rose almost a thousand percent, dislocating every market, the cost of every product, and twisting the tail of the dollar itself. Except, on a logarithmic scale, this warp was a hundred times worse.

I wasn't exactly with the smart money, having delayed until the morning after ratification to show up at my bank. And I only decided to go after the automatic tellers, those "magic money machines," all went closed on us. However, I was smart enough to go down about half an hour before opening time—so I could join a line stretching around the corner and down the block.

When I finally got inside, the managers were manning a single window. What remained in my personal account was something over $5,000, but these fellows were only offering ten cents on the dollar, take it or leave it. A man in a cream silk suit, three places ahead of me, had tried to counter this proposition with a small automatic he'd had tucked under his arm. And he was suddenly looking down four barrels of two shotguns, held by his friendly bankers.

Outside on the street, adult men and women were standing like wide-eyed children, wondering how a law that was supposed to be so good for the country could hurt so much. Blink, blink.

Truth was, it would take another two or three years for the economy of the United States and the rest of the world to absorb these shocks and settle into a pattern. The edges were hazy, the direction scattered, but the pay-as-you-go society we have now was then abuilding under the stimulus of a tax-free economy. The power of Enterprise was picking up the reins that Debt and Inflation had dropped. But the whole scenario would take time to shake out.

For myself, suddenly pauperized and alone, a proven failure at almost anything I had tried, this was a good time to absent myself. It had long been in my mind to go back to studying karate, to pick up that last *kata* and to sharpen my skills, which admittedly had been getting rusty in the law library and in the Porsche-sushi-swingle world of San Francisco in the Nineties. So I grabbed my last $500 and the stub end of my credit to buy a one-way ticket to Japan, cabin class on a jumbo jet.

The Master took his time about deciding. He left me standing in the sun on the edge of that clearing, the sweat dripping down my ribs under the Pendleton wool shirt. My feet, inside those Italian boots, were squishy with the heat and with fatigue.

Old Turtle looked at me, seeing my entire life, my worth and my future, pass somewhere in the shivering pine boughs behind my head.

"What can you pay me?" he asked at last.

"Well, I have some money, not much of course. The thing I have most of is time, and I can give you all of it."

"You will pay with more than time." He nodded, up and down, grimly, like an old turtle.

"Surely, if that's what you want . . ."

"You can stay," he said.

"And will you teach me?"

"You can stay."

So, under those conditions, I dismissed my Tourist Ministry translator and stayed.

The rest of the day was some kind of Zen test.

The Master went into the middle cottage and remained inside. I was left in the sandy center of the clearing below the edge of the stage. I tried to talk to the boy who was cleaning it, but he just shook his head. I walked around and pretended to study the framework underpinning the stage, the stonework of the cottages, the technique of their thatching. I walked the outside perimeter of the cottages, noting the location of paths leading presumably to outlying buildings. After that circuit, I tried to climb up on the stage but the boy stopped me. So I took off my boots and socks and ran through a few *kata*s in the sand. My muscles were stiff from traveling, the day was getting hot, and from that middle house I could feel the master's eyes watching, judging me. I took off my sticky shirt and did one more half-hearted phrase from the fifth *kata*.

Then I just stopped moving, sat down in the shade and waited. The air cooled me. The sand slowly, slowly crunched aside under my buttocks and made a comfortable seat. The sound of water running into the pool below the spring soothed my ear. The dapple pattern of light and shade under the trees soothed my eyes. The sun walked around the edge of the clearing. The wind inspected the thatchwork of the cottages. The light did *kata*s in the sand. Time cleared my head.

I thought I was becoming wise.

Toward the end of the afternoon, the boy came over and led me down the path to a tiny adjacent clearing with a latrine trench dug across it. I relieved myself clumsily, with him watching, and started back up the trail.

The boy barked something. When I turned back, he was pantomiming with a shovel: fill trench, chop brush, dig new trench.

"Have fun, fella," I said and turned away.

"Bark!" and he was thrusting the shovel at me. Then he stuck it in the ground between us, folded his arms across his chest, and mimicked the master's turtle smile.

This was what he'd meant by "pay with more than time." So Jay Corbin, the black belt who had already killed two men in battle and foiled a Shi'ite terrorist plot, the sparkling young lawyer who had prosecuted the Butcher of Boaco, the swinger from San Francisco, picked up a shovel from an illiterate Japanese peasant boy and dug latrines.

Late in the afternoon I went back to the circle of cottages. The Master was still invisible inside his house and there was no sign of dinner. As I was to learn later, he and his disciples followed the rule of the Buddhist orders, rarely eating after eleven in the morning. Now I know why they were all so thin.

I spent the night curled in the sand behind one of the buildings. They seemed to be empty, and the doors were only sliding paper screens, not even latched. I might have gone in and made myself at home, except the Master was still watching me, I felt, testing me. The sand was cold and the night air heavy with dew. I was wretched.

With the dawn a line of men came into the clearing. Their ages were anywhere between twenty and fifty. All were dressed simply: loose pants and shirts, thongs on their feet, an occasional headband. They clustered briefly on the sandy area, and I could see them kicking off their sandals and pulling karate belts—all black—from their pockets. Then they mounted the stage and stood in even lines.

I was struck most by the negatives. They had no fancy uniforms, no patches, badges or stripes of rank. They wore no padding, no neoprene-foam body armor, no Ace bandages. They didn't roughhouse or tease one another but were quiet and respectful, like a troop of veteran infantry.

From the house where he had retired the afternoon before, the Master stepped forward. He was dressed as before, except now he wore a uniform belt—a red one.

"*Hajime,*" called one of the front-row students when he saw Matsu.

The Master walked across the sand slowly, casually, then he leapt onto the stage in one standing bound. No running steps, no swinging arms, just a straight levitation of about four and a half feet. He landed without a sound. Any lingering doubts I might have entertained about this old man vanished with that one catlike movement.

And what was I doing at this time, the foreign visitor who could "stay"? I was standing in the gap between two cottages, still rubbing the sleep out of my eyes, and feeling like a ball of dirty laundry.

Sensei Matsu blinked once in my direction and said, just loudly enough to carry across the clearing, "*Hajime.*"

That was the call to attention, and I was losing a mountain of face by making the teacher take special notice of me.

I pulled off my boots, sprinted across the sand, and scrambled up on the stage, taking a place at the back of the lefthand line. As far from the front position of rank and prestige as I could get. I didn't have a belt to wear, except the wide leather one in my jeans.

The next hour was calisthenics and basic exercises: straight punches, kicks, arm blocks, two-, three-, and five-move combos. All cadences were called by the Master, who stood off to one side and watched the front row. I knew most of these moves from my first days at Kan's in Monterey. The unfamiliar combos I picked up by watching the man next to me. All monkey pattern. We practiced twist punches until the muscles in my forearms knotted and my wrist bones stuck out sideways.

The Master's critical attention never got farther back than the third row, and I didn't know whether to be insulted or relieved. It had been about ten years since I had performed these beginning exercises—or at least done them this fast in group drill. I was stiff and slow and awkward. Just like a white belt.

However, in this school there were no white belts. At Kan's school in the shopping center, we had always known where we stood: white belts advanced to yellow, yellow to green, green to brown, brown to black, each rank bringing the student more prestige. And black belt was very big time for us. None of us at Kan's paused to consider that the black belt itself is ranked into ten degrees of which, among the masters, the first degree signifies a raw beginner, barely able to control his art. None of us ever stayed that long. Here, in the clearing at Hakusan, everyone was a black belt with years of experience. A society of equals, with some more equal than others. As a first-degree myself, I felt very green.

After a too-short break, the class went on to group *katas*. Each man moved through the routines in place, the whole formation moving back and forth like a school of fish turning and flashing in the sun. I could follow them through the twelve *katas*, then dropped out on the thirteenth, the one I had come to learn.

After two hours of group exercise, the morning finished with *kumite*, or sparring. The students knelt along the edges of the stage; the Master pointed to two at random;

they rose, bowed, went through a flurry of almost-touching-but-not-quite kicks and punches; the Master pointed at the winner; they sat down. Each fight took about eight seconds. When my turn came, I went into my foot position or "stance," put my hands up on guard, absorbed three feather-touch blows, and sat down the loser. The whole process was very dry and formal, with no anger or pride, nothing like a real fight.

Those first twenty-four hours in the mountain *dojo* set my pattern for the days to follow: work out in the early morning with the students who came up the trail; eat a midday meal of rice, which I learned to cook for them all, with chicken or fish or some other light meat that they brought as a present to the school; then do physical labor under the direction of the boy, Suru. He seemed to be the school janitor, or Takusan Matsu's nephew perhaps, because I never saw him work out with the class.

Suru showed me one of the cottages I could live in. Unlike the other neat houses in the clearing, it was a wreck. The thatching of the roof had rotted, letting in the rain to melt the paper partitions and curl the plank floors. I was to make it whole again.

He showed me how to thatch, by doing the least part of each operation. There are about fifteen steps—cutting the reeds at a tiny pond about three miles away, spreading them to dry in the sun, clearing the old straw from the framework of the roof, repairing or replacing rotted stringers, binding the new reeds into sheaves, anchoring the tops to the stringers, tying down the splayed ends, shaping the eaves—and these steps are repeated endlessly. The job took me almost a month, and that was at the beginning of the rainy season. But the work was satisfying: Each night I had a few more square feet of protected space to lie down in, and it was all by my own labor.

When the roof was done, Suru brought sanding blocks and showed me how to work the floor. In another three weeks I had created a surface as smooth and white as a lady's skin. I expected that he would show me how to make the paper screens next, but those were brought up by the students one morning. They moved around the tiny

cottage, laughing and friendly, asking what arrangement of
rooms I wanted, trying the different-size screens here and
there, then nailing down the tracks for them.

I had a home, my first since the breakup in San Francisco. Then, after all my work, it was time to cover the
latrine again and dig a new one. Suru showed me where.

When the rains came, he oiled the wooden practice
stage to protect it. We rigged an army-surplus parachute
in the trees to cover it like a tent and went on with the
lessons.

It took the Master two months to work his way back to
the last row of the class, back to me. All he did was look at
my feet and shake his head.

That afternoon after the meal, and as the other students
were leaving, one of them came up to me. He was from
the third row, a man in his forties with a receding hairline
and a crewcut. He bowed once to me and said, stiffly,
"Foot ex-ur-cise-ah?"

This phrase turned out to be the only English he knew,
and I suspected the Master had taught him to say it this
morning, as a way of introduction.

I bowed in return and the man, Shizuka, led me back to
the stage. There he demonstrated a complicated pattern of
steps—no punches or kicks, just a flow of stances that
square-danced around the platform. From the feet-parallel
of the forward stance, to the reverse-tee of the crane, to
the feet-at-right-angles of the straddle, to the feet-turned-in
of the side stance, position followed position until Shizuka
was back facing me.

Then he gestured toward the open space: I was to
repeat the pattern. Of course, I had spent more time
admiring his grace than memorizing the steps in order, so
I could only start out, falter after the first crane, and stop.

Still smiling, he shook his head and proceeded again
with the pattern, catching up to me and taking me through
step and turn and step. Twice over he did this, then stood
off to one side and watched. After I had made five complete run-throughs without losing my place, he began to
criticize individual stances and misaligned feet. Shizuka
did this silently by darting forward, slapping lightly at the

knee, ankle, or instep that was out of place. If I did not
understand what was wrong, he would demonstrate the
correct posture, bouncing once in place to show how it
was set.

After three hours on the same pattern, I could dance it
in my sleep. At one point I did drift off, and Shizuka was
on me like a hawk. He gently cuffed the back of my head
and held his own eyelids open with his fingers, grinning at
me, telling me to stay awake.

By sunset I was extremely tired, but my stances did not
sag. Each position was read into the muscles and joints
themselves, as the pieces of a truss bridge know its shape
and support it. I no longer had to create tension or energy
to hold a stance. My legs were the stance. My head, my
shoulders, and my unused arms were lolling with fatigue,
but my hips and legs were working like machines.

I looked up at Shizuka and grinned.

"It would be appropriate to give him a present." The
voice came from the ground, below the stage. It was the
Master. "In return for his gift of teaching you."

"But . . . I have nothing to give."

"Ahhh. It is known to me that the roof of his house is
aging and lets in the rain. He would fix it but must also
work to support his family. You are skilled at patching
roofs. You may take tomorrow and the next day off to do
his."

"Thank you, Sensei."

I stayed in the clearing at Hakusan nine months. Every
day we were immersed in karate training, or in the simple
actions and transactions of keeping our bodies alive. In
that time, I wrote nothing, spent nothing, touched no
machine more complicated than a hoe or a knife. I could
talk in complete English sentences only with the Master,
and he had little time to spend with me.

He taught me almost nothing, the other students barely
more. Yet I learned a great deal in those months. Karate is
like that: it is the process of teaching yourself how to move
in your own body, how to walk the earth on you own feet,
how to dodge or defeat the blows life sends you. For every
minute you spend learning a technique or absorbing a

graceful movement from others, you spend an hour teaching it to yourself. What comes out of the mountains is not a deadly fighter, neither a great warrior nor a magician—just a man complete in the knowledge of himself.

And that is the source of all skill and magic.

I never sparred with the Master, although he sometimes watched me spar with other students.

"Not so hard!" he called out one time. "You do *kumite* like a man who fights enemies."

"Isn't that what karate is for?" I asked after the match was over. I was lying on my back and breathing hard, having been tripped, thrown, and brushed with five feather-touch punches. Meaning that I had lost.

"Karate is for itself," Matsu said.

"Yes, of course. But what if you were attacked? Wouldn't you use it to defend yourself?"

"I would run away if I could."

"Suppose you couldn't?"

"Then I would not put myself in a place where I could be attacked and have no room to run."

"Well, what if you had to protect someone." I was thinking of that night on Cannery Row with Alice Wycliffe and the boy I had killed, Emilio Lopez. Sensei Kan had been mad as hell and demoted me because of that fight. Would the Master give a different answer?

He just shook his head. "You may think of a thousand reasons to fight. None of them is enough. I teach you to fight so that you may never have to.

"A man so formidable that he cannot be beaten has no one to contend with," Matsu went on, in a rare mood. "Such a man has no enemies. He has nothing to defend. He is like light and air: When others punch at him, there is nothing to hit. To make war against him is useless. When they see that, they stop trying to fight, which is the beginning of peace."

I thought about Sybil Zahedi and her scar-faced lieutenant in the helicopter. They would have been amused by the "light and air" analogy. To them, I had just been a side of meat to barter for their cause. Arguments wouldn't have stopped them, only bullets and finally the executioner's sword.

"And if they don't stop?" I asked. "Don't you finally have to kill them?"

He just shook his head. "Disable, if you must and have no other choices, no other skills. But to disable is not to destroy.

"You think only in terms of winning and losing. You say, 'My win is your loss.' I would rather have you seek a third way, that both can win. Or else both lose something."

"Perhaps," I said, "you've been too long on this mountain. The world out there is full of people who don't give up until either they're dead or you are."

Matsu's face never lost its smile.

"Do you think the world was any different before I came up here? If the people around you cannot learn, if they understand the *Tao* so poorly that they break their heads against it, then you must teach them, if only to save your own life. There is always a way. Even the rocks learn from the water."

"If the water has enough time."

"Time is an illusion of the body, as the *katas* have taught you. There is always a way around time."

"But . . ." I was running out of arguments. I was a rock standing dumb against the flow of his simple optimism.

"To be human is to be apart from the natural world," he said. "The rock wears away in the water or tumbles along the streambed because it can do nothing else. The vine reaches toward the sunlight and withers in the frost because it can do nothing else. The owl pounces and the mouse squeals because they can do nothing else. But the human has a mind that can see alternatives, a will that can choose something else. There is always a way. You only have to find it."

He paused. Time stopped. His eyes were looking right at me for once, not past me. But he gave the impression of seeing not me but someone else, far away, in memory.

"And if there is not a way," he said slowly, as if reciting a lesson he'd learned fifty years ago. "If you lack the skill to find alternatives, or your—opponent—cares so much about killing you that none will satisfy him, then you can submit to the natural world and die. As the mouse to the owl. The world will not end. The *Tao* continues."

My head went down in submission. "Thank you, Sensei. I understand that now."

Right then, I was lying, a little. I still thought, deep down, that you had to fight enemies and find justice, that winning was better than either losing or patching up a compromise. Since then, his words have proven to be wiser than I could have guessed. And I'm not talking about just a fistfight. . . .

The cycle of days at Hakusan went around, more months of training and learning and living. Then one morning after the class had formed up on *Hajime*, the Master called out, in English: "Student Corbin!"

I knew what to expect, as he had done this several times since I had come to Hakusan. Still, it was a shock that it was happening to me. I walked forward and faced him at attention, biting my lower lip.

"You have learned as much as you can hold at this time," he said. "I advance you one degree in rank and send you back to the world." Sensei Matsu gave me a quick grin and then turned a sober face to the class.

It took ten minutes for me to gather my few possessions from the cottage I had rebuilt and start walking down the trail. The cadence call of the morning class was soon lost on the wind breathing through the pines behind me. By noon I was back in civilization.

And did I ever learn the thirteenth *kata*—which was the whole reason I came to Japan? Yes, a student named Kudasaru taught it to me one afternoon. It has only eight moves, and in half an hour I could perform them perfectly.

Chapter 9

Billy Birdsong: Easy Money

Stuffing a cork up the backside of the Feds had always seemed like a good idea to me. I mean, who had been my biggest source of aggravation right from the start? The Feds.

The Bureau of Indian Affairs had put my people on a piece of land even the coyotes avoided. The Drug Enforcement Agency had tried to queer the pitch on selling that twelve pounds of coke I had lucked into. The Internal Revenue Service was always hassling about my profits from running the kiddie tricks. The Department of Defense had sent me to Nicco—and jammed my system full of poison when they dusted Managua. The Central Intelligence Agency had probably been behind the kidnapping in Arabia. If anybody was going to clap and cheer when those debt and tax laws finally passed, it was me.

For a time it looked like the worst depression anybody would ever see. All the money dried up one morning. The stock market and real estate went bad overnight. Everybody I knew lost his job.

But the funny thing was, some things did not change. In San Francisco, anyway, the Safeway stores still had food on the shelves, more of it than before, I think. Pacific Gas & Electric still gave you light when you flipped the switch. Hetch-Hetchy water was still coming out of the tap. The cable cars still rolled; the streets got cleaned. And the main cop was still around the corner in his squad car, dammit.

For a while Bank of America was issuing paper scrip backed by its own assets, whatever they were—mostly loans the bank would never collect. On the street, we said "backed by its ass." But people took it.

After about six months, MasterCard and Visa got together and fixed a rate of exchange, the New Dollar, at about thirteen cents on the old on. Everyone grumbled, and a few of the larger cities tried to issue their own bills. Except they turned into colored paper when you got past the city limits—no good for a national economy. So, in a few weeks, American Express, Diners Club and most of the banks went along with the McVisa Plan, and the currency stabilized as much as it ever does.

And about that time I got steady work in the pollution control field.

Happened this way. The Twenty-ninth Amendment had turned the Environmental Protection Agency into a kind of advisory council to big business. A million pages of regulation got squeezed down into The Little Green Book, which everybody thought the big boys would ignore while they stuffed asbestos and other crud into their landfills, poured raw sewage into the Bay, and blew smoke where they felt like it. Except the people still wanted these messes cleaned up. So the EPA hired guys like me.

I bought a bond for a million new dollars and filed it with the Agency. They in turn gave me half of Santa Clara County, the heart of Silicon Valley, for inspection and enforcement. Which means that I looked into all the citizens' complaints; sampled air, water, and garbage trucks; and "counseled with" the businesses and private individuals who broke the Green Standards in my jurisdiction. Otherwise I lost my bond and went on my ear.

Who watched the watchdog—that is, me? Everybody. Neighborhood associations, consumer groups, county health agents, Naderites, you name it, they all had their sampling gear plugged in right alongside mine. Three unresolved complaints in a quarter and I would be out—with the bonding agency looking for a piece of my skin.

Right away things got very hostile.

I had a fistful of complaints about an etching lab called P&L Partners that was shown to be dumping one-tenth-molar solutions of hydrofluoric acid into the sewer system. That is the kind of acid that scratches glass, really bad stuff. So I went and "counseled with" them.

The guard at the gate paused over his racing form to send me to Reception. The dish at that desk stopped chewing her gum long enough to sign me in and point me toward the office of the Environmental Director. The secretary there put down her coffee, the phone, and a paperback novel and pushed open his inner door. And from inside came a yell: "You got a warrant?"

"No, sir. But we have had several complaints about—"

"I don't do business with you jokers unless you get a Federal warrant. And that's with the whole specification: the dates, the times, the names, and the complete chemical analysis for each alleged infraction. You got me, Chief?"

"Maybe we can short-cut some of that paperwork with a simple—"

"No way, Chief. You just go the whole nine yards with me and then we'll be in a position to talk."

"But you see—"

"Am-scray, Redskin. You got no business here."

What could I do but leave? I put my head down, apologized for bothering him, and walked out.

And came back that night—you have to work fast to make an impression on these people—with a crew from the midnight paving company. We opened the sewer line two feet south of the P&L fence and pumped in nine cubic yards of fast-setting concrete.

They must have had concrete slopping out of the toilet bowls. It closed them down for a week while they laid a new sewer line. This one went the other way, across the parking lot, back under the building, and into the creek under a culvert right on the edge of their property.

Inside of another week P&L was pumping acid again. So we went back one foggy dawn, down into the creek, and pumped that line, too.

This time the Environmental Director came to me, at my

hole-in-the-wall office in back of a petshop on First Street
in San Jose. He threatened me with a suit for breaking and
entering, trespass, and vandalism. I introduced him to
Elmo Garcia, who dealt Doberman pups and, in turn,
introduced him to his breeding stock.

After two more of these counseling sessions and about
six weeks' worth of downtime, the director's boss got the
message that it was cheaper to put in concentrators and
filters than to rebuild the sewer system twice a month.

The P&L people were tough but they never heard
about suffering in silence. They complained plenty and to
anybody who would listen, especially to their trade association, the Chamber of Commerce, the Better Business
Bureau, and the Rotarians over lunch. Word, as they say,
got around and soon I had the cleanest jurisdiction in
Northern California.

Now you are probably wondering how I made money on
a deal like that. After all, I had to put up the bond, appear
before the Environmental Protection Agency to answer
complaints, pay for the sampling and testing, and arrange
for enforcement. So who was paying me?

When I applied to the Agency for relief, the few remaining bureaucrats in the local office, the lucky survivors
of waves of fiscal decimation, grinned at me without any
sympathy at all. They surely had no money to pay for
enforcement; that was why they had been taken out of the
business in the first place, to be replaced by rude amateurs like Billy Birdsong. Let it go to hell, they said
behind their smiles. Then the people will wake up to what
they have lost. Amendments can be repealed. The budgets will come back. Washington will rise again. As for my
problem, the bureaucrats trusted to my "ingenuity and
spirit of enterprise."

They were disappointment number one for me.

Well, when I had first gone into the pollution business,
it seemed that the State, county, or municipal governments—
any one or all in a row—would gladly pay for a cleaner
environment. Now I discovered they had no budget for it.
And so long as my bond was on the line with the Agency,
why should they? The local administrations were growing

fat and strong by choosing carefully among the pieces of the Federal mantle they would or would not pick up after the Twenty-ninth Amendment.

Disappointment number two.

Up until the P&L affair, I had half-thought that the polluters themselves would pay for my "consulting." But a few subtle approaches—and the unsubtle responses—convinced me they would only cough up to be left alone. Not to have their sewers broken in the name of clean water.

Disappointment number three.

Cash flow—the incoming side—was becoming my biggest problem. I was seriously thinking about abandoning that million-new-dollar bond and going back into the kiddie trade when Jay Corbin came back out of the mountains.

He telexed me from Japan, using the old address and blindly trusting that someone would forward the message. He also expected me to meet him at the airport. Probably carry his bags, too. After brooding about it, I decided to meet him anyway. What else did I have going that day?

Corbin was the same man but different. I could see that even as he walked up the jetway. Browner, quieter, with eyes that were older and saw more. He was more like an Indian, a tribal elder perhaps, than the brash kid who had shot up a pink helicopter in the desert. Corbin looked like a wise old man—until he smiled and showed teeth. Then he looked like a hungry jaguar.

And he carried his own bag.

"What have you been doing with yourself, Billy?" he asked as we settled into my car.

"This and that. Losing money, mostly."

"What, at the beginning of a great flood tide like this?" He was smiling, teasing me. "I thought there'd be opportunities coming out of this fiscal thing that 'any sucker could fall into.' "

Suddenly I remembered that line of bullshit I had once handed him when he was down on his luck. Yeah, me.

"Sucker is right," I said and proceeded to tell him all about the pollution control business.

Corbin heard me through. He was staring out the wind-

shield, down the road, with his lips all puckered up.
When I ran out of words, he did not leap right in with a
lot of great ideas and free advice. Just held his stare.

After a while he said, "Seems like there should be
money somewhere in that mix . . . somewhere . . . Have
to think about it."

Then we talked about Japanese culture, the U.S. economy, or what was left of it, and things generally. That
night he stayed in my apartment, which was on the edges
of the San Jose barrio, and slept on the couch.

Corbin was stone broke and alone. Which took me some
getting used to, because he still spoke and acted like a
Harvard Law grad and senior partner in an East Coast firm.
He could never wash cars or cadge drinks with a manner
like that; so the world had to find him something decent to
do and ripe to live on. It found him me.

Jay spent five days lying on the couch, mooching in the
refrigerator, drinking with my friends, and listening to their
songs. I still called him "Jay," but among my friends he
introduced himself as "Gran," or "Granny." That was short
for his first name, Granville, which I had never known.

Sometimes he did karate exercises in my living room.
The quick jabs he would make with his hands at the door
frames, and those fantastic spinning kicks with bare feet
that ended up half an inch from the chandelier, looked like
they would turn the place into kindling and broken glass.
But he never touched a thing.

Most of the time, however, Corbin sat and stared out
the window. Or went down to the library and took out
books that he just flipped through and put aside. I thought
he was in some kind of a funk. I should have known he
was thinking hard.

Finally, on the fifth day, as we sat down to my special
California ranch breakfast with chili-salsa eggs, he quietly
observed, "You know, garbage is a really undervalued
resource."

"Hunh?" I put down my fork. "Something wrong with
my food—?"

"No, no. I mean *garbage*, trash, wastes, what comes out
of the dumpsters, pollution, your current problem."

"What about—garbage?"

"Looked at the right way, it's valuable. I mean, our thinking is shaped by our definitions, right?"

"Ahhh-ummm." That was Corbin's way: leap out onto the loose, leafy end of the limb and work his way back to what he was really talking about.

"Right, definitions," he plowed on. "And we have always defined garbage as something to be thrown away. Prehistoric peoples had their middens and shell mounds; we have the town dump. Everyone knows that colorful characters can find useful and interesting things in the dump, at the wrecker's yard, in garbage. But there's a stink such things have that goes beyond the nose. It says, somebody didn't want this, it has no value."

"So, perfesser?"

"So, if you redefine garbage, it works out to be the most valuable product in the natural world."

"What product?"

"Mineral ore! You look at the big open-pit copper mines that people were digging in Utah, Montana, and Arizona early in the nineteen-oughts, teens, and twenties. Were they pulling nuggets of solid metal out of the ground? They were not. The ore at Ajo, Arizona, was something like one-half percent copper. They'd raise a ton of dirt to get maybe ten pounds of metal—and that was after a lot of chemical processing. And how much copper is there in your average pile of city garbage?"

"How should I know?"

"Two to four percent. Forty to eighty pounds per ton."

"Of pure copper?"

"Well, some of it, the wire in motor windings and electrical parts. More of it's in alloys like brass and bronze. And that's just one metal. There's steel and tin, about eight to twelve percent, mostly from thrown-away food cans. Aluminum, twelve to fifteen percent, from beer cans, pie plates, and packaging. There's glass from bottles and jars. All of these products are in an already energized state—"

"What does that mean?"

"These things are refined from their basic ingredients

with energy. Huge amounts of electrical energy to smelt aluminum, which is why so many Third World countries that build hydroelectric projects put in an aluminum smelter, even if they have no bauxite. Aluminum is exportable electricity. Look at how many smelters grew up around the Bonneville projects in the Pacific Northwest.

"Steel and glass are also made with energy—that is, heat. The cost of the iron ore or silica is incidental to the energy inputs to the process.

"And all these products are just lying there in your garbage, waiting for someone to pull them out, process and sell them."

"*My* garbage?"

"You've got the territory and—oh, boy! In Silicon Valley you're getting gold salts, specialized acids, rare earths, and other unique chemicals, probably in attractively large concentrations. Billy, you're a rich man."

"Okay, garbage has percentages of metal in it. And glass. But most of it is still trash." I was grumpy because my specialty eggs were getting cold on his plate.

"Definitions again, Billy. Most of it is still paper and plastics, vegetable fiber and animal fats. Garbage to you, but wood pulp, oil products, and organic chemical feedstocks to an industrialist, or anyone who has studied our scarce natural resources.

"At the very least you can pelletize this stuff after you take the metal and glass out. The cellulose and fibers, helped along by the fats and plastics, burn with about the same Btu rating as bituminous coal. And just about as cleanly—which is to say, not all that clean, but scrubbers and filters will take care of the smoke.

"Of course, pellets are just the quick buck. Long term, you will want to fractionate that material into wood and oil precursors, backtracking your enterprise into their natural resource markets."

Corbin loved words like "fractionate." I would have to spend an evening with the dictionary just to understand half of what he had been saying. But I could see a problem right away.

"If garbage is such a God-damned delight, why has nobody ever gotten rich off it before?"

Corbin puckered up his mouth and thought about that one for ten seconds, max.

"Because," he said, "no one has taken in the scope of it. Like a kid going to the town dump, every one has looked for a particular prize. Aluminum, they say, we could take that out! Except the market isn't high right now. Or the cost of separation is too great. So the project isn't feasible.

"Or take the old recycling programs. They'd go after a wider range of products, sure, but only if the people throwing them away—the recyclers' suppliers—would spend the time to separate the green bottles from the brown, the aluminum cans from the steel, then haul it all in their cars to a collection point. It was too much trouble for most people, so the volume was never big enough to compete, economically, with scraping away whole forests and raping the Earth.

"But when you go after the whole enchilada, 'every part of the pig but the squeal,' as the old-time packers used to say, then your separation costs are lumped together. They become a smaller part of the overall cash flow. And by dipping your hand in half a dozen different markets at once, you can weather the periodic slumps. When aluminum's down, wood pulp may be up, or chemical feedstocks, or gold."

"How do we get this garbage?" I asked.

"You already own it, under the same legal fiction by which the EPA made it your responsibility for cleaning the garbage up. City scavengers will already truck the solid wastes thirty miles to an approved landfill—so let them send it to your reclaiming station. The sewer system runs twenty miles to a wastewater treatment plant—so build a fractionating plant next door."

"Who is going to put up the money for all these plants?"

"Anybody who wants to get rich. There's a venture capitalist born every minute, Billy. All you have to do is dazzle them out of the trees."

Corbin picked up his fork and began eating the eggs, cold salsa and all.

Dazzle the investors we did, with colored brochures showing artist's renderings of processing plants. We gave them reams of computer analysis showing discounted cash flow and return-on-investment projections. We even had tiny lucite capsules made up with samples of real garbage sealed inside.

Corbin and I raised such a big chunk of working capital that we seriously debated, for half an hour, putting it in a satchel and flying to Mazatlan. Finally, Jay—or Granny—pointed out that three times that amount was available in credit lines and bond underwritings, but we could only get our hands on it by going ahead with the project instead of running.

I had to take that on faith, but we went ahead.

We started with a demonstration plant in Alviso on the edges of the Bay's marshlands. It was sized to take in 50 tons of municipal solid waste a day. The machinery that worked with the garbage was really simple: It ground up whatever came in, metal and all; cooked it till the fibers and plastics were softened; mulched it to digest the organic matter; and ran the whole mess through a set of centrifugal separators. We could then reprocess the almost-pure fractions of metals, glass, organics, and oils: melting the first two, pelletizing the third, refining the fourth.

The only thing our first plant could not do was separate the green glass from the brown. For a while we let them mix and added a heavy shot of deep-purple dye to the molten glass. That turned it all into black glass, which has an industrial and artistic market. But we soon found a high-temperature process to settle out the green and brown dyes and make clear glass, which is more widely saleable.

The Alviso plant cost us about N$2.5 million to build. It returned more than N$1.5 million a year at the market rate for refined products, not even counting what we charged the local businesses and municipalities for taking their "wastes." Oh, we did give them a nice walnut plaque, laser-engraved with the signature of their local Environmental Protection Agency representative—me—affirming that they had complied with all regulations for safe disposal of solid refuse blah-de-blah-de-blah.

When we branched out with city scavengers, our cash flow started seesawing. It took five months for Corbin to figure out that the secret to the residential market was seasonality.

"Bid up the price of metal in December and January," he advised. "There's more aluminum foil then: Christmas tree tinsel and wrappings for gifts, leftovers, and the neckwrappers from champagne bottles. There's more other metal, too, when people are throwing away last year's bicycles, ski poles, and video recorders.

"Bid up cellulose in April and May, when everyone is tossing scratch paper away while they figure taxes and throwing a year's worth of old magazines out during spring cleaning.

"In summer," he said, "the profit comes from plastics. Everything from suntan oil to franks is packaged in plastic bottles and film. And we'll eat it all."

So I would reset the separator equipment in the plant to track these greater seasonal volumes, and we made an even higher margin. Yes, I was the manager, the chief operating officer, and the practical hand. Corbin, with his polished manner and his feeling for the money end, became our chief executive and front man.

What did we call the company?

The paperwork said "Alviso Associates, Inc." Which was smart, you see. To our suppliers of municipal solid waste, we were just garbagemen. To our buyers of refined products, we were metals servicemen, glass wholesalers, paper makers, oil retailers. And when we branched out into sewage sludge—selling end products like methane, garden fertilizer, and animal feeds—well, the separation of our image became even more important.

At the end of our first full year, we toasted in 2001 and the new millennium with a magnum of champagne that we drained then dropped in the grinder. Within five years, Corbin and I had ten plants going all over Northern California and were well on our way to owning half of the markets we sold to. Who could compete with us, when we got paid to take our raw materials and produced just as much as each market needed?

I was content with getting good at this business, making my fortune from it, and being comfortable, but not Granny Corbin. He was too restless.

As soon as he had a few hundred thousand out of the garbage business, Corbin backed a turn at the Montana State Lottery. All he had to do was put up a share of the prize money and pay off the administrative costs for a week. Then he could take fifteen percent of the receipts, off the top and no taxes to pay. The balance went into the State fund. Corbin was guaranteed a two hundred percent return, minimum. He made six hundred percent that first week.

The only hitch to this little moneymaker was that the backer could not return to the well whenever he wanted. No, he had to sign up for a slot five weeks in advance. And until then he had to put a percentage of the stake on deposit with the State Gaming Commission, which of course got beneficial use of the money in the meantime. However, the only risk was that, while he was waiting, the people of Montana might lose their taste for Lotto-Jotto. You should sooner bet against sunrise.

In nine months, Granny was making as much money on the games as we had made in two years with the garbage. And still he was restless.

So he bought a seat in the Southwest Electric Energy Pool. The usual asking price was five million, but he knew a broker who was in distress through a series of dumb deals that went sour. He would sell out for three.

Corbin bought the seat but did not occupy it himself. Instead he staffed it with professional representatives from Barton & Badger, the biggest pooling house in the nation. Corbin himself could sit back and watch the really big money roll in.

How did S.W.E.E.P. and the other regional markets get so big and—um—powerful? It was another fallout from the Money Warp that the economy went through.

After the power crunch of the Nineties—which some people say was caused by deregulation of the national electricity grid, and others believe just happened at the same time—local utilities were hurting for available sources of energy. Of course, they had all long ago negotiated complex interconnection agreements, through their regional power pools. But in the palmy days of easy energy, these agreements were for mutual, short-term coverage. In formal language, the utilities told each other, "You help me meet a peak load this afternoon and I will pay you back with power tomorrow morning." Their contracts merely specified a set of exchange rates, which were based only on the amount of power and when it was taken.

These mutual pooling agreements did not, could not foresee a time when local regulators, on the State or county level, would turn the simple decision to build a power plant into a twelve-year session of People's Court. When the cost of capital would push the price of a kilowatt of installed capacity to as much as N$170,000. Or when, as a result, a couple of loose megawatts kicking around in a utility's resource plan would draw a dozen bids from other utilities, industrial parks, shopping malls, housing developments, and growers associations strung out over wires a thousand miles in any direction.

Anytime resources are scarce and demand is high, you create a market. And for electricity, the market centered around those early power pools. Except that instead of remaining helpful industrial associations, they became cockfighting pits where brokers wheeled and dealed energy from supplier to distributor to end-user. All it took was money and a telephone—and a seat in the pool.

Through enterprises like our joint garbage processing, Lotto-Jotto and S.W.E.E.P., and a dozen real estate deals and side investments, Granville Corbin was worth about N$150 million by 2005.

He quickly discovered, or maybe he knew all along, that this kind of money had *velocity*. He had no Federal taxes, not on income, capital gains, excises, nothing. Most of the State taxes he might have owed could be ducked by operating interstate and moving assets around at opportune times. The States had not learned yet to cooperate by sharing data bases and holding joint audits. The net result was, his fortune was growing at about sixty percent a year, minimum. Which meant that in four years he was worth almost a billion new dollars; in six years, two and a half billion; in seven years, over four billion. And that was just figuring on the bad years.

Corbin did have some braking mechanisms. He gave money to charities. He built a new wing on the law library at Harvard. He funded a home for orphaned Hispanic children in Monterey. He even set up a foundation with an educational bent, which he once told me had access to ten percent of his assets. These were all good works, from the heart. They had to be: After all, he got no tax deductions from them. Of course, he was making a name for himself. On the two coasts he was known variously as a smart financier and a great philanthropist.

I just looked up that word and it means he loved people. Women especially.

But Corbin was cleaning up his act. Putting a polish on it. Where once, when he and Anne were living in San Francisco, he would chase anything that had two good legs and an itch between them, now he was only seen publicly with respectable young women of the marrying kind. And, at the end of an evening, he was only seen to kiss them chastely in the elevator lobby and saunter off to the Rolls. In five years Granny had earned a reputation on both coasts as a gentlemanly heartbreaker. Until he met Tracy Starrett—she was the pretty one.

Corbin and I had grown apart during those years. I was still managing grubby little garbage operations that now were not worth more than five percent of his time. It was a full-time job for me just becoming the municipal solid waste and sludge king of the West Coast, while Granny was always in motion, making money and a name for himself. He flew in just once a month for Alviso Associates' board meetings.

So by the time he turned up with Tracy Starrett on his arm, and she had a rock ring on her finger, it was too late to give him any fatherly advice.

You see, I had seen the face and remembered the name. Tracy was from one of those families that are richer than the Rolling Stones and all of them orbiting farther out than the asteroid belt. Her father was some kind of money connection to the Overthrust Formation gas fields out of Denver. Her brother wholesaled crack, cobra, and a collection of designer drugs along a 2,000-yard strip of the beach

at Venice, California. One sister became a big mama in
the kiddie porn around Portland, Oregon—which is how I
knew the family—and was giving her younger sister lessons. Tracy had done some fly-weight modeling while still
in high school, then had a couple of walk-ons in those
low-budget formula flicks where the superhuman ghoul
cuts up lots of nearly undressed teenage girls and also, by
the way, boys.

Denver in the Oughts was one huge house party for
white-anglo girls like Tracy. Corvettes, cocaine, and cock
till it was coming out of their ears. The local police did not
even try to stop it, just keep them from using their Porsches
to score points on little old ladies crossing the street.

Tracy, however, had been busted on a morals charge
when an almost-hit-and-run was followed up to a motel in
Arvada where she and seven other mixed sexes were surprised in various states of undress and also penetration.
That was no problem, except Daddy's VCR was rolling and
the movie lights were disturbing the neighbors. Ditto the
heavy-metal beat. You see, the action was poolside. The
oldest one there was Tracy, who at nineteen was considered an adult and a bad influence. The judge gave her a
stiff lecture and probation, which still constitute a record
in the State of Colorado.

Since that time, Tracy had evidently been polishing her
act, too.

I did not know all this when she first turned up on
Granny's arm; I just remembered Tracy's name and face
and a faintly bad aroma. It took me a week to track down
the references. By that time they were back in New York
and all over the society pages. Wedding bells were in the
air, as they say, and who was I to call long distance and
spoil the fun?

Maybe they deserved each other.

Chapter 10

Granville James Corbin: 100 Lost Days

I personally witnessed the start of the Hundred Lost Days.

Well, I wasn't actually in Washington to *see* it, because then I would have been dead, right? Or my eyes would have burned black and my head been torn off. But I was nearby, in Laurel, Maryland, which is on the Patuxent River, halfway to Baltimore.

It was during a research trip, a tour of Old Line State Scavengers' new solid waste plant. They were trying out a new dry process, first shredding the material with diagonal cutters and then spewing it into an air column for gravity separation, like wheat and chaff. All the heavy stuff fell to the bottom of the column, where they took out the ferrous with magnets.

The process had a couple of disadvantages. For one, their handling of nonferrous metals was clumsy. They just tumbled all the aluminum, copper, and fragments—plus any steel the magnets didn't pick up—in a big drum that settled it out in layers of, they hoped, similar material. However, the process was more suited to separation by size or weight than by specific gravity, which is what they were groping toward.

But frankly, our own wet process wasn't doing such a hot job with nonferrous either. We were selling some pretty strange alloys and couldn't promise more than about fifty-five percent purity.

For another thing, Old Line was losing all the oils. That didn't matter to them too much, because they were pelletizing all their paper and fibers for furnace feed; so the embedded organics and plastics just made a hotter fire. But they knew what they were missing and had called me in to consult.

It was a clear December day, bright cold, about four in the afternoon. Our tour of the plant had just arrived at the maw, where the trucks from Baltimore dumped their loads. This was a concrete funnel, twenty feet wide and fifteen deep, with a shiny screw conveyor thirteen inches in diameter running along a trench at the bottom. We were on the southwest side of the building, and the low sun was casting long shadows.

I noticed quite a pileup of loose paper and aluminum cans along the concrete wall on the southwest side of the truck turn-around. That told me they were using open trucks and the light stuff was fluffing off the top as they positioned for the dump. What would they be losing in that?

While Walt Doury, the plant manager, talked on about hauls per day and tons per haul, I bent down to study the sludge of stuff by the wall. Under a loose top layer, most of it was wet, slushy pulp with the cans flattened by truck tires, so their losses were worse than I thought. I turned my head, still bent over, about to call their attention to my findings, when the group's shadow suddenly leapt into focus. The metal siding of the building behind them brightened until its tan paint shone almost white, with the outline of their heads and shoulders in deep black.

Some instinct held my body, kept me from straightening.

"Jesus Christ! What was—" Doury broke off. His face in the white glare was slack with surprise.

"God, look at—" One of the others began.

"Don't look!"

And, after a few seconds, from a third man: "I can see—see something like a—a white blob. But I can't see you, John, and I'm looking right at you!"

"Was that Washington?"

I counted ten under my breath, raised my forearm—ready to shield my eyes—and stood up. Real slowly.

There to the southwest was the setting sun. And beside it, brighter, redder, rose a ball of fire that was mottled and veined like the head of God's penis. It was connected to the treetops by a glowing rope of smoke.

I knew by my guts that it *was* Washington. And I knew by the map it was about fifteen miles away.

What could we expect at this distance? Radiation poisoning? Probably. How much we picked up would depend on the megatonnage of the blast, with the radiation's intensity dissipating under the inverse square law, of course. That scurf of paper alongside a concrete wall may just have saved my life, but the Old Line men with me could all be dead and not know it yet. Nothing we could do about it now: We took our dose twenty seconds ago.

What else? If there was going to be a firestorm, we'd have felt it already. A flash burn from the ultraviolet? Possible but, like the radiation, nothing to be done about it.

Then there was the overpressure, shock waves in the air and maybe the ground, too. How big they might be was also defined by megatonnage and inverse squares. They were coming at the speed of sound, 750 or so miles an hour. That made them due here in about seventy seconds, and I'd already wasted, say, half a minute screwing around and watching the fireworks.

Forty seconds to do something.

All around me the Old Line people were staggering in circles or standing still, mostly blinded and unable to help themselves. I grabbed the elbows of two wandering off toward the parking lot and into the direction of the blast. They promptly sat down on the curbing around the garbage maw.

We had to get under cover. I looked up at the corrugated siding of the plant and debated taking everyone inside. When the shock came, it might punch all that metal right through the steel frame and wrap it around the machinery inside. I had seen the moving pictures from

White Sands and Yucca Flats—frame houses exploding
into kindling wood while the ground rolled under them.

Thirty seconds now.

About fifteen men were working in the plant, I knew.
Some of them were coming out the side doors.

"Get back," I shouted to them. "Go through to the
east side and *get down!*"

The foreman, identifiable by his red hardhat, took one
look toward that still-hanging fireball, waved at me, and
shoved his crew back inside.

It would take too long to gather up the blinded managers out here and herd them around the building. I tried. I
pulled them to their feet, pushed them in the right direction, explained that a big wall of sound was coming this
way.

They just whimpered, said their eyes hurt, wanted to sit
down and worry about the radiation, began walking off
again in different directions. They were all going to die,
flying away on the wind like dead leaves, unless I found
some close place of shelter.

Behind the wall that had sheltered me? The ground
wave would bounce us up and the air wave serve us
against the building like tennis balls.

Of course, we could hide down in the concrete garbage
maw. I looked into it. Walls sloping at forty degrees and
slimy with pieces of garbage. This was going to ruin a few
three-piece suits.

Fifteen seconds.

I started pushing them into it, and they resisted. They
could smell the rot down there, probably remembered the
sharp edges of the screw conveyor, too. All I could do was
agree with everything they said and just keep grabbing
and pushing.

Ten seconds.

Doury fought me and I lifted him bodily over the curb,
let him slide on his ass in the slime. Maybe a second too
late I told him to try braking with his heels, to bend his
knees, to get his feet *between* the blades on the conveyor.
One or two were more aware and began climbing in
themselves.

Five seconds.

As I put my own leg over the curb, the air all around suddenly thinned out, as if God was taking a deep breath. The papers and cans on the sill opposite pulled free and flurried past me toward the storm. I jumped.

Underpressure preceded overpressure by half a second. The wavefront came with a skull-knocking *boom* riding on the echoes of the loudest sounds you've ever heard: train wrecks, stamping plants, dentist's drills, air horns, fire sirens. That wave of sound pounded six-inch-deep dimples in the metal siding over our heads. Dust, grit, paper, and leaves swirled down on us.

I landed in a heap at the bottom of the maw. The curve of the screw blade cut a finger-wide gash in my shin. That was our only visible injury so far, but we would be seeing a *lot* more.

If this was Armageddon, then Washington would catch three of four MIRVs just for luck. Baltimore, not fifteen miles east and north of us, would have its own bombs. The whole BosWash Corridor, in fact, would be getting slagged. Somewhere—perhaps sitting in a shelter far below that red cloud, or interrupted at a political rally in Minneapolis, or flying in *Air Force One* high over the Rockies—the President would be trying to contact his scattered or now-dead advisors. Somewhere in the Iowa corn, perhaps, flights of missiles might even now be launching on computer control. The incineration of the world was seconds away.

Poking my head up over the concrete lip, I could only stare at the fading glow, the already wind-smeared cloud, and wait for the inevitable second, third, fourth . . . nth blasts. At the back of my mind, like a clown knocking on my coffin lid, was the thought that I was spending the most important—and final—minute in American history inside a garbage maw.

What no one could know at that instant, neither I nor anyone else in the country, was that this one was the single bomb to go off that day. But only hours of waiting, watching, and praying, hours of tense quiet, would tell that. And in the meantime the whereabouts of the President, Vice President, members of the Cabinet, and leaders in Congress had to be confirmed. And first, of course, somebody had to locate the officials, the senior staffers, undersecretaries, newsmen and anchors, who would do the confirming. Washington was buzzing like a beehive that had been smoked, pounded, and burned—and no one could find the queen.

President Geddes was dead. He had been holding a meeting of his full Cabinet, including Vice President Stokes, in the White House not more than a mile from ground zero. But all the staff members who might know this detail of the President's daily schedule were also in the White House and also dead. So it took a while for the nation to piece together who was alive and who not.

A collateral but more strategically critical question for the nation to answer was: Who had launched, or placed and detonated, the bomb?

We will never know.

It is certain—almost certain—that no incoming missile had been detected by the Eastern Seaboard's radar net.

Like the rest of the Federal government, the Pentagon and the Department of Defense had been strangled by the Twenty-ninth Amendment. Their functions had been either eliminated or distributed piecemeal to any State or private enterprise that could fund or afford them. The nation's standing army had stood down; its bases and materiel were auctioned to local National Guard units. The Ballistic Missile Early Warning System had been subjoined to the Air Traffic Control network, which itself operated on a State-by-State basis only loosely coordinated into regions. The Eastern Seaboard net insists that they saw nothing, and if there was anything to see, it was on the other guy's screens.

The U.S. nuclear arsenal had actually been left intact after the Twenty-ninth Amendment. It was operated by the new International Strategy Subcommittee of the House of Representatives, paid for out of the Congress's tiny General Fund. Rumor had it that fees paid by citizens under the Firearms Registration and Testing Act of 1999 actually went to keep the missiles in fuel and oxidizer. The fact that some bright-eyed lieutenant sitting in a silo under Missouri did not launch against the Soviets or someone else handy is either a tribute to the intelligence of the 2,000-odd officers who remained in the U.S. Air Force, or the fault of inadequate funding. Certainly no one was left alive in Washington to either call for or call off a retaliatory strike.

If the radar saw nothing, then the bomb may have come from a low-flying, Cruise-type penetrator. Or it might have been locked in the trunk of a car parked by terrorists, the infamous "Islamabomb." The country waited days and weeks for someone to claim it, or take secondary action, or at least make good on the U.S.'s time of confusion. But nobody did.

What was the megatonnage? My uneducated guess, based on the force of the shockwave by the time it reached me, was thirty-something. Experts later published a figure of fifty megatons. It was a dirty blast at ground level, they said, evidence of a terrorist's implant instead of an incoming missile strike. The mushroom cloud sucked up a lot of dust and dumped hot fallout over the Atlantic and into the Gulf Stream. Fish died on the Grand Banks and in the Irish Sea for months afterward. The Europeans were understandably upset.

To this day, analysts have picked over the world situation in the weeks and months preceding 4:09 p.m. EST, December 19, 2002, looking for some clue, some precursor to the bombing. Nothing very convincing suggests itself.

"Nonsense, my boy. We know exactly who did it," my Uncle Aaron boomed when I tried to argue this lack of causes with him.

I had run into Aaron Scoffield, my mother's younger brother, walking down Charles Street in Baltimore at about eight o'clock on the evening of The Day. Finding him was a relief because he was a congressman from Oklahoma now serving as House minority whip. If anyone was going to be in Washington the day before the Christmas recess, twisting arms to get those last-minute votes, it would be Uncle Aaron. What was he doing in Baltimore? I could guess by the loose knot in his tie and the smudge of dusky powder on his collar tab that he had been enjoying a midafternoon quickie at an uptown hotel somewhere near the Washington Monument. Far uptown.

"Well then, who?" I asked.

We were still together after midnight, sitting by a hastily strung telephone in the Postal Express office on the first floor of the Federal Courthouse, off Fayette Street. Grim-faced young men and women walked past, and every few minutes the phone buzzed with another congressman returning Scoffield's calls to private numbers. So far he'd gotten eighteen Republicans and a dozen of his fellow Democrats. Out of 433.

"The Russians, of course."

"But that's crazy! What provocation did we give them?"

"What do they need, boy? Just another turn in this Fifty Year's War we've gotten ourselves into. We appear to be weak right now. That damn-foolish Tax Repeal amendment gives them ideas. Maybe they can win on a sneak attack. Provocation enough. It's worth one bomb as a probe, isn't it?"

"Unless we retaliate. Anyway, their reconnaissance satellites can just about look down our silos and see we still have—"

The phone cut me off. Aaron's face went from weary contempt to soft apology two seconds after he put the handset to his ear. I could guess that, instead of reaching a living member of Congress, he'd called a widow or an orphan. He talked a few minutes in consoling tones, then put the phone down.

"—missiles active," I pushed on. "Same as we can see theirs."

"But do we have the will to use them? Are we still a nation, or a raggle-taggle of States who will debate foreign policy for six weeks before returning a shot? Oh, I tell you, the States'-Rights men are in hog heaven on the Hill. Any Russian worth his vodka would try just one bomb to see how that gaggle react."

"Yeah, but not *Washington*. You launch a probe against the periphery, something your opponent does not absolutely have to fight for. Like the Japanese did at Pearl Harbor."

"I thought we all agreed the Japs did something stupid there," Aaron countered. "Provoking Roosevelt without finishing off the American will to resist."

"Well, yes, but they could hardly have delivered a knockout punch. . . ."

"Right, they didn't possess nuclear technology. Whosoever did this probably thinks they *have* knocked us out."

"But not the *Soviets*, Uncle Aaron."

We would have gone around and 'round on this argument, except the phone was heating up and my leg was beginning to throb again.

I had spent half the evening trying to find someone who would stitch up my wound. It seemed that every doctor, nurse, mobile unit, and medical tech within 300 miles had moved in toward the blast perimeter to help the survivors. I had gritted my teeth and swabbed the gash with rubbing alcohol, tied a handkerchief around my shin and, when that bled through, reinforced it with a napkin snaffled from the dinner tray they had brought over from the Lord Baltimore Hotel.

The point I was trying to make with Uncle Aaron was that, while States' Rights may have risen triumphant from the ashes of the Twenty-ninth Amendment, the Federal government was hardly weak or confused. The pay-as-you-go society was paying off. Its system of licenses and fees was operating in an economy that had mushroomed after the terrible tax and interest burdens of the national debt were lifted. The Federal government was becoming rich beyond dreams. And, once it had discarded the involuted snail shell of the Federal bureaucracy, the men still in power could make hard decisions faster than ever before. Congress still proposed and passed laws for the common good and defense, and sent them to the President for approval or veto. The only difference was, they delegated the tasks of monitoring and enforcement to the individual States, instead of to a ziggurat of fiddling bureaucrats.

But now that system had been smashed, not by law or amendment but by a thermonuclear device. Over the next hundred days I would see the reins of government flopping while men scrambled to recover them.

At about 5:30 in the morning, with a cold, gray dawn still almost two hours away, Speaker of the House McCanlis called to order the last session of the 107th Congress, sitting jointly in the Fourth Circuit Court of Appeals on the top floor of the Federal Courthouse. He had appropriated Chief Judge Mabel Benwick's personal gavel for the occasion.

George McCanlis was a man fully in command. His huge lion head had the right bend of gravity and sorrow as he spoke both to those present in the room and to the videocams recording for posterity. He declared that, with only fifty-four representatives and thirteen senators, they lacked a quorum in either house. "However, the tragic circumstances being what they are, I am convinced we have a quorum of those members still among the living.

"Before us, ladies and gentlemen, we have four orders of business. In the interests of expediency, and lacking full representation from any of our committees, I hope you'll permit me to outline our immediate agenda.

"First, we must regain that duly elected representation as soon as may be practicable. Toward that end, I have authorized telegrams to be sent to the governors of those States which have lost sitting members of this body, so that they may hold special elections on or about the first Tuesday in April. That date will allow sufficient time for candidates to announce themselves and become known to their electorates."

It would also, as we were to discover, allow McCanlis and his coterie sufficient time to weld together the sort of government *they* desired.

"Second," he continued, "we must consider our colleagues in the Senate. We are reasonably assured of the death of Vice President Richard Stokes, who was duly sworn as president of that body. Now, lacking a bare seventh of their members, those senators here present may feel some embarrassment about naming a president *pro tem.* Therefore I propose that, until such an election in April shall bring up their numbers, the Senate continue to sit in joint session with this house."

What McCanlis was omitting, of course, although he knew it perfectly well, was that a certain number of freshman senators, as well as newly elected representatives, were waiting in their home States to be sworn in as the 108th Congress on January third. That omission—purposeful or not—would confound the legitimacy of the incoming Congress for many months.

"Third," he said, "we must appoint a special committee to propose, in accordance with the Constitution of these United States, the names of candidates to fill out the vacated term of President Martin Geddes, who has likewise been declared officially dead."

Uncle Aaron, three rows back in the spectator seats, was shaking his head slowly side to side.

I wondered briefly about his reaction, until I'd worked it out for myself: McCanlis could more easily have proposed himself as acting chief executive and taken office this same day. He had the votes right here, and Aaron knew it. Most of the surviving congressmen seemed to be from the Rust Bowl Conservatives, of the same stripe as McCanlis. (Had there been a secret caucus, held outside Washington, last evening?) Anyway, that the Speaker should name a committee to propose candidates could only mean he had some deeper game to play. And that might mean more trouble for everyone than an outright grab.

"Fourth and last," McCanlis said, "we must prepare for a full investigation of yesterday's tragic events. As this body, in my own opinion, lacks sufficient members to fill a second extraordinary committee, I propose that we request a commission be appointed by the governors of the adjoining States of Delaware, Maryland, Pennsylvania, and Virginia to sift the ashes, as it were."

Evidently McCanlis was not quite as concerned as either Uncle Aaron or I was about who had launched or placed the bomb that destroyed Washington. A governor's commission would take months simply to convene—not an effective forum for either strategy or diplomacy. I hoped the boys under Kansas were still watching their screens.

Then a chilling thought occurred: Would a . . . could a
. . . nascent dictator arrange to bomb his own capital?
With a nuclear device? To take power in the confusion?
And cover the traces—those not already fused to glass in
the rubble—with a ponderous official committee?

No, even McCanlis would not. Could not.

"Now, I know all of this proposing is quite a mouthful. I
hope our secretary *pro tem* can formulate these sentiments
into an orderly set of motions that you, my colleagues, can
second, discuss, and then vote in favor of." The wink and
nod McCanlis gave the front row was only partly humorous.

The measures were seconded and approved in half an
hour. Discussion took only ten minutes of that, and Aaron
Scoffield was ruled out of order six times in three of those
minutes. I marveled that the 107th Congress was certainly
an orderly place to work in.

Uncle Aaron had no staff—all dead in Washington—so I
agreed to stay on in Baltimore and help him during the
transition. He began that very day, saving three hours for
sleep in the morning, to pull together a coalition that
might beat McCanlis. He had eighteen Democrats and a
handful of leaning Republicans to work with.

On the other side, McCanlis's party was not made up
entirely of fools. They would back him on a tariff bill or
States' Rights, but in deciding the presidency they just
might think for themselves.

As the history books tell it, thirty-four potential candidates were named between then and March 29. The lob-
bying went on night and day, over meals, side by side in
the men's room, in the hallways outside of the courtroom—
which remained their meeting place all that time. Bearing
Uncle Aaron's card, I made concessions to Helpfuls, cor-
nered Hesitants, and confronted Hostiles. I made more
promises than I can remember, and some of them my
uncle never knew about.

However intent I may have been on staying for the
fighting, my leg ruled otherwise. Within days it began
oozing pus, probably from germs in the garbage smeared
on that cutter blade, and I kept doping it with alcohol and
off-the-shelf disinfectants. Finally the leg turned septic

and puffed up like a blind white grub with an angry red mouth. The doctors were back in town, but the hospitals were full of burn and radiation cases. So I flew back to California to lie down and try to avoid an amputation. To this day I still have a shiny purple scar across my shin.

During those hundred days, the nation saw everyone from rogues to saviors to sycophants proposed to fill the highest office in the land. At one point even Uncle Aaron was just three votes shy of a majority. But it always came up short. I followed the action from California by television and later got the complete story from Aaron. He was sure, from the fabric of the deals that were being made around him, that McCanlis was rolling logs *against* his own candidates. It was as if he wanted the confusion to go on and on.

Finally, toward the end of March 2003, the Joint Congress passed a resolution declaring themselves unable to name a President and requesting Speaker McCanlis to serve out the remainder of Martin Geddes's term. It was known as the Emergency Powers Act.

I never understood the part called Title VI. Aaron had fought it like a devil and all the Democrats snarled when they talked about it. Yet to me it seemed like a technicality: Every two years, at the opening of a new Congress, the members were to assemble in caucus and name the Speaker of the House who would serve two years into the future.

According to the Constitution, the House had the power to choose its Speaker and apparently the freedom to do the choosing how it liked. A powerful man with a strong party behind him could serve again and again, for years. Look at Rayburn or O'Neill. Title VI would seem to break up this pattern, letting the new blood choose for the future.

When I tried this opinion on my uncle, long after the fact, Uncle Aaron only said, "You young fool." But he said it kindly. There were new lines in his face and tears showing in his eyes. He seemed to be exhausted by the struggle of those hundred days. A fast cancer took him just nine months later.

As a supplement to the Emergency Powers Act, almost an afterthought, Congress approved and sent to the people the Thirtieth Amendment, which eventually became known as the Speaker's Amendment. It provided for the Speaker of the House to assume the duties of the executive branch if both the President and the Vice President should resign or die.

The rest you know. This new but already worn-out Congress neglected to call a special presidential election, as provided for in that amendment. The regular election in 2004 was spirited, with the young turks pushing through John Ramos and Stephen McKenzie at the Republican Convention in Kansas City. They won a landslide vote and were assassinated before the inauguration, while they were technically still private citizens.

Both murders were well timed, well executed, and well covered. Three bullets each, all head shots, fired at medium range by a medium-size, medium-weight, medium-complexion man, or possibly a mannish woman dressed as a man, who left the scene in a late-model, medium-size car of no remarkable color. One witness thought it was yellow, but he was later proven to be standing at another corner, looking the other way.

George McCanlis called for a congressional commission to investigate the assassinations and thereby put off any special elections. Its members met for sixteen months and returned nothing but an array of rumors that the FBI had presented, with embarrassed smiles, early in the testimony.

For the country as a whole, the deaths were some kind of psychological straw. One aging anchorman in a jacket-and-sweater combination opined sententiously that "The People can take no more." As if these crises—the bombing, the assassinations, the political confusion—were acts of a stupid volition which, if somebody only wanted to, could be stopped or somehow made right. The pundits and the politicos generally felt that an immediate special election to fill the still-vacant presidency, another hotly contested national campaign within a few months of the last election, would somehow be "too disruptive" or "too costly" or just too much.

On that note, "The People can take no more," McCanlis was quickly confirmed as chief executive under the Thirtieth Amendment.

In the next presidential election year, 2008, the major parties rallied and chose their candidates. The pundits observed that they seemed to be second-stringers. Not one sitting member of Congress had consented to run. None of them was visibly involved with the conventions. None endorsed the candidates. And a month before the election the three presidential candidates and two of their vice presidential hopefuls—I don't remember their names, nobody does now—were assassinated. They were fragged by a wire-guide rocket, shot by a "jealous husband," crushed by a falling stage flat, snuffed by cyanide, burned in a head-on collision. All of these were creative ways to die. And, if some or all were actually murders, they involved enough *modi operandi* to give the FBI an excellent excuse not to link them to each other or to the assassinations of 2004.

Once again McCanlis assumed, or rather retained, the duties of chief executive.

By the time the presidential election of 2012 came around, power was firmly centered with Congress and not with the vacated Office of the President. So, although the columnists and anchors posed rhetorical questions about the possibilities of an election, it never attained the necessary political velocity to get off the ground.

Five times McCanlis was chosen in caucas as Speaker for a "trailing" (as it came to be called) two-year term. His future was secured.

Chapter 11

Granville James Corbin: High Times And Misdemeanors

I met my second wife, Tracy, at a ball.

No, I take that back. It was at the Norwegian Embassy, which was in a converted mansion along Fifth Avenue in the low Eighties. And the ballroom was where they held their receptions. This one was for the King's birthday, or maybe the Crown Prince's. Neither was there for the occasion.

Why was the embassy in New York and not the capital? After the bombing of Washington, you see, the Federal government may have been content to relocate in Baltimore; the diplomatic community, however, would have none of that. I think they were nervous about living so close to that wide, black-glass crater. And it didn't help that the local Baltimore vids were reporting the milly-milly each morning—that is, so many thousandths of a millirem riding on the wind from the southwest. Too much like the reports following Chernobyl. So when the new ambassadors and their staffs arrived, replacements for those who died in the bombing, they migrated to New York, where their U.N. consulates were settled in and would remain for a few years more.

Tracy Starrett was at the birthday reception, being squired by a flaxen-haired giant who was either some kind of unlanded baron or a renowned socialist. Perhaps both at once. Call him Peer Gynt. He introduced himself and

146

tried to get me into a confab about municipal sewer sludge and the problems they had with the wastewater treatment plant at Trollhaven. Or wherever.

In the meantime this woman, beautiful by any standard, and tanned, and blonde, and wearing a strapless sheath of blue-gray silk that was being held up by static electricity, was still on his arm but looking around the room like a pilot fish about to jump ship. And she still had not been introduced to me by Gynt.

At first I thought she was Scandinavian, his wife, and just restless. After the third time she made some extravagant flip-flap gesture with her left hand, I caught her third-finger code and tumbled that she was unattached and signalling frantically to be rescued from the ice giant.

I deftly inserted some wisdom into his talk about sewers and permafrost, sought her agreement, then excused myself for not being introduced. Even Peer Gynt got the message.

"Ah, may I present Granville Corbin, who is one of your countrymen, Tracy."

"Charmed," she said with relief.

"Mr. Corbin is an expert on—"

"I know that he's an expert, Karl." Her eyes never left my face. "He's an expert on money, experienced with women, and I hope he knows something about food and can offer me better than that mess of pickled fish and head cheese you call smorgasbord."

"What's your pleasure, Tracy?" I asked smoothly.

"Proscuitto. Pasta. Picatta. None of this piscati profanatti, hey?" Her accent was pizza-Italian, hinting at origins in the Midwest.

"Do you have a wrap?"

"Right here." Like a stage magician she pulled four square yards of silk out of her clutch purse. It was iridescent blue-gray on the outside to match her dress but silver-sheened on the inside. When I raised an eyebrow and mentioned the temperature outdoors was ten above, she made a small laugh. "Space blanket," she said. "Keeps two bodies warm for, oh, hours."

We walked away from Gynt without ever looking back.

Tracy and I did not make love the first night. Instead I left her in the hotel lobby with just a pressing of hands. But we had made arrangements. She was flying back to Denver and her family in the morning; I was going to be in Pueblo toward the end of the week to inspect a site. We would meet at the Brown Palace at six Friday, by the bar, white carnation in my lapel, purple gardenia in her hair. Use code. Wink. Nod. Goodnight.

Her family turned out to be rich. Chris Starrett, her father, was an investment banker connected with drilling for natural gas and petroleum. He may have known my father, although I never got a chance to ask.

Starrett handled hundreds of millions and, apparently, kept a few of them for himself. The family had a ranch, with horses, west of Golden, fifteen acres of lawn and fifteen hundred of scrub with a wedding cake house of white stucco and glass in the middle of it all. In a much grander way, it reminded me of our home in Asilomar.

Tracy had rooms there, when she wanted, and also kept an apartment up in Boulder. She had a part-time job keeping a computer warm doing the accounts in a doctor's office while completing her university degree. Busy girl. But she found time to work me in.

We made love on the fourth date, which in those times was a standard of propriety that the Pope would applaud. After that, she was about the only woman who registered on my retinas. Tracy was frank, witty, knowing, expensive, stunningly beautiful, and sensuous as a cat. With me. Before me, she claimed a state of near-virginity: She had known just one boy on her prom night—"and didn't everybody?"—and had experienced one long-term love affair with an older man—"which was almost like a marriage, it got so twisted"—during the start of her acting career. I was the first man she could relate to "at anything like her own level, thank God!"

We got married at the end of the summer on the Starrett ranch. As a social event in the Oil Patch, it was almost like a marriage of aristocracy. However, after the shocks in the energy market, this was a dowager aristocracy living on coupons and the tired cachet of the Nineties, while a new and more vulgar life surged around it.

The reception at Golden got a little fragmented. At one point the pills were running three-to-two against the champagne, and toward sunset a wing of the Arvada version of Satan's Slaves roared in on their spidery Harleys. Leather, lungs, and lusts. But a couple of the houseboys hustled them out quickly, without even wrinkling their own white uniforms, and after that I focused on the bulges in those boys' biceps. All in all, the party stayed remarkably decorous.

That night Tracy and I left for Bear Lake and two weeks at a cabin she had wangled from a friend for our honeymoon. When we got back I put her in a penthouse along San Francisco's new Embarcadero. I worked harder than ever to make her happy and keep her in the style she demanded.

Hard work doesn't mean drudgery. I learned that early enough. The garbage mining business was exciting. We were solving tough problems, beating out the competitors and the imitators, discovering new byproducts and new sources of supply. Birdsong and I founded an organics research center that was supposed to discover new ways to crack hazardous wastes, which are mostly human-made, very complex molecules. We were even thinking of branching out into radioactive wastes and reprocessing spent fuel from all those Federal reactors.

Yes, the business was exciting right up until it was making really big money; then it became predictable. And any business, once you're on top of it and the problems are knocked, becomes a bore. If you're selling high fashion, after a while the daring cuts, the textures and materials, and pouting models, all begin to blur and it's as much bean counting and nickel busting as running the bargain basement at Macy's.

Garbage got to be like that: all a blur.

You might think backing the lottery in Montana—and later in New Mexico—would be exciting, but only if you are a gambler and don't understand the business. For me, they were a cold-blooded investment with a guaranteed payoff. About as much fun as buying double-A-plus bonds.

For a while I dabbled in the developing futures markets for municipal solid wastes and sewer sludges. Of course, Birdsong and I had created that market, but what the hell, owners could be players, too. Except that I knew it so well. There's no fun when the pace is seasonal, the wrong moves are obvious to anybody, and the suckers are just handing you their money. Another guaranteed payoff.

Then I discovered S.W.E.E.P. Electric futures is the fastest-moving commodity market in the world. It was so exciting and unpredictable that I loved it even when I lost money. I just had to buy myself a seat on it—but why do they call it a "seat" when you never have a minute to sit down?

The actual trading floor—called just "the Pool"—is located in Las Vegas, of all places. Maybe because it's close to Hoover Dam, the first big regional energy project. Maybe because it's about the most central place in the southwestern U.S. that's not Los Angeles. Maybe just because of the action and the type of people it draws.

The timing for electric futures was on a dozen different interlocking cycles.

Longest cycle of them all was the rate at which the old privately or publicly owned utilities and the new Third Party Producers could build power plants. That cycle was in fives and tens of years. But news of a proposed big project could rattle contracts and coalitions just months out.

In a slightly shorter range, years and months, were the boom and bust of economics. Mostly boom in the Twenty-oughts. You bet against what the Imperial Valley's growers, the peach canners, and the electric-arc steel people would demand from the grid.

The seasonal cycles were fairly predictable. When would the fall rains come? What would the winter peak for heating in the mountains be? How about the summer peak for cooling in the deserts and California's Central Valley? Those were events you could bank on—just about. Climate.

Weather, however, was the biggest thing in the daily cycle: You had to study the forecasts and look out for heat waves. In the Southwest that meant air conditioners humming on every rooftop, drawing megawatts of power like a kid sucking soda through a straw.

And the joker, the wild card, was downtime. Who, among all the suppliers of capacity, would suddenly get a hot turbine bearing, discover a leaky steam generator, lose a cooling tower, or drop a control rod and have to trip off line? Then the scramble for surplus power was on and we brokers earned our commissions.

Well, we earned it secondhand. Our Poolmen did all the actual buying and selling. As brokers, we merely supplied the cash cushion and the tolerance for risk.

What's a Poolman? To work down on the floor of the Southwest Electric Energy Pool required someone who could speak a totally new language, a verbal shorthand made up of "gigs" and "megs," of delivery times counted in "moes," "dass" or "hows" from that morning's opening, of electricity as either "cap" (for dispatchable capacity) or just "ergs" (for available energy only).

That last may need explaining. You see, a wind turbine will give you electricity, but you can't switch it on and off; it only runs when the wind blows. The windmill is just ergs and so less valuable to the user system than a fossil or nuclear power plant which is switchable—you can run it anytime you want—and so "dispatchable" by the system operators.

And there are a dozen other, similar details to running the grid. Most of them are communicated with hand signs and body language down in the Pool. The pace is that fast.

Deals are made and kept on the word and memory of the Poolmen, backed by their brokers. The grid's computer system lags about twenty seconds behind deal and delivery for the real-time and daily transactions, and about ten *minutes* behind for the month-by-month futures trading. So the action is all in the head.

If I had tried to work the floor myself, the other Poolmen would have cleaned me out in fifteen seconds. They would have clustered about me shouting offers and orders at my head, making a deal on every flinch and twitch, just like an auctioneer running up the bids on a half-asleep buyer who's nodding in the back row. Breaking in a new Poolman costs a brokerage about N$300,000 until he—very rarely a she—learns the lingo and the body language. A seasoned Poolman has a useful life of about five years. Then he either gets out and starts his own brokerage with subcommissions he's earned, or collapses in a heap from the scoriations on his cardiovascular system. The pace is that fast.

My most exciting day in the Pool, even secondhand, was August 19, 2008. It was the third day of a heat wave that was held over our heads by a massive high-pressure system in the California Central Valley. No relief in sight for a week, at least. The heat in Vegas was so thick that the sweat popped out in just the five steps between your air-conditioned limo and the lobby of your air-conditioned casino. Oh, the hum of that lovely power.

I'd flown down from San Francisco to watch the action from the vantage point of the Pool's gallery and its on-line monitors. Even before I focused on the screens' numbers, I could sense the tension in the air. Electric! A glance at the joggling columns of figures told me that the market was, um, under-supported. Through his ear-plug I told my Poolman, Joe Dark, to buy everything he could for a week out, with delivery in hour lots.

Other sharks were moving in ahead of me. Joe actually took the time to turn and find my face along the gallery windows. He scowled and made a choke sign in my direction.

"Get in there!" I growled and made a strangler's grip that he could see.

Joe shrugged and waded in.

Inside of nine seconds, he had bought twenty-seven percent of Palo Verde, ninety percent of all five units at San Onofre, and eighty-two percent of Diablo Canyon—for a total of 9,300 megawatts in nuclear power.

"Good show!" murmured the broker to my left and signaled his own Poolman to sell.

Then Joe bought all of Hoover Dam, big chunks of Bonneville, Grand Coulee, and the Sierra hydro systems—another 2,000 or 3,000 megawatts at least.

"Daring, that," someone said behind me in the gallery.

I barely turned my head. Other Poolmen were now gathering around Dark. He was picking up antique fossil plants, all of The Geysers and the new projects with geothermal brines, half a dozen solar towers, and even the first-generation wind farms. All of this was on three- to seven-day delivery, counted in hours. For some reason, the sharks were dumping on him. Fast.

"You're going long," one of their handlers crooned past my ear.

As Joe finally went after any of the out-of-region power contracts that might be lying around, my insides suddenly sagged. Was something about to happen, I wondered, that everyone could see but me? An imminent change in the weather? Maybe a black cloud or storm front coming in? Were the other brokers planning to run me up and then gut me for a novice? It had happened before. And I was catching dirty looks from Joe over his shoulder as he went on buy, buy, buying contracts.

Then my spine stiffened.

"Keep going, man," I whispered into the mike. "Take it all."

Within two hours I owned 24.7 gigawatts of dispatchable capacity and another 13.6 in simple energy, all for delivery sometime in the next week. All bought at top dollar, or so near the top—an average of about thirty-two cents per kilowatthour—that the only way for that electricity to cost more would be to pay the secretary of the Exchange to rub two sticks together.

I *owned* the southwestern energy market for the next week. Since there wasn't but a handful of resources left to buy in that timeframe, the Pool's action immediately moved on to long-term futures.

The other brokers lining the gallery windows all looked at me with grim chuckles. One even patted my shoulder, telling me exactly what to expect. A shift in that high-pressure zone or five minute's worth of cold rain that week could break me. I mean, the payments would go on for *years!*

When I went out to lunch, I turned a hard stare up at

the sky. That same silver glare shone down, only turning a softer, smoggy yellow just above the peaks that surrounded the city. The Exchange building's air conditioner roared above me. A bead of sweat rolled down the inside of my leg.

"Maintain, baby, maintain," I said to myself.

By four in the afternoon I was sitting in my Vegas condo with the air conditioner turned all the way off and still shivering in reaction. Visions of a cold snap, sleet, a hailstorm . . . flash floods were passing through my brain, washing acres of greenbacks down the scraggly valleys. I stayed in that night, praying for the wind to die.

Then the following morning, Wednesday, San Onofre's Unit 4 developed a steam leak and had to trip. The operators ended up paying *me*—and triple for breach of contract.

Thursday a minor *temblor* in the Mono Lake area weakened the dam impounding Lake Wishon, at the top of the Kings River hydro system. The State inspectors ruled there was no alternative but to spill the water all down that stairway of reservoirs and powerhouses. The operators had to do it by day *and* by night—when their energy wasn't under contract. Another triple indemnity for me and a further squeeze on the region's electric resources.

God heard my prayers and raised the temperature three more degrees, average, all across the Southwest. And the wind died in the mountain passes, stilling those second-generation wind farms that Joe Dark had missed out on buying for me.

We ended up unloading that power at about a six-cent profit on every kilowatthour, of which there are a million in a gigawatthour. Paid in every hour. For a week. My take was N$390 million, just on two hours' trading one sticky morning in August. The pace was that fast.

As I say, it was my best day ever. But the action was all secondhand. More to Joe Dark's credit than to mine. And after a few years of it, even trading on the S.W.E.E.P. seemed to go pretty stale.

However, at the end of that week I went back to San Francisco feeling pretty good about myself. Then I walked into a fine old Italian tragedy.

The cab from the airport dropped me off at midafternoon along the seawall of the Embarcadero and I crossed to our apartment building in the South of Market. It was one of the new buildings, with three levels of fancy townhouses on the roof, seventeen stories up. The elevator opened on a series of hidden gardens. Around them were balconies, window walls, rounded arches on private pathways, grilled gates, fountains doing double duty as cooling sprays for the building's air conditioning, and ground lights tucked into the ivy. I had to walk through this twisting jungle to get to our door.

The first thing I heard was the music. Loud music. Our music. *Modo reggae.*

The first thing I saw was the door to our apartment. It was open six inches. Waves of that heavy *modo* beat were almost visible coming out of it.

At first I thought Tracy was throwing a party. I pushed on the door with my face working up a big smile for our old friends and the new ones Tracy was sure to have found.

The foyer was empty, neat as always except for the scatter of handbag, keys, and scarf Tracy usually dumped on the table there. Just the music coming through that space.

I climbed the six steps to the living room. It was empty, too, except for a weasel-faced man who was wearing one of my checkered silk robes, tied loosely, with his hairy chest sticking out one end and his hairy legs sticking out the other. He was sitting on the couch, grooving on the music, and drinking my scotch. Haig & Haig Twenty. From the bottle.

"Who are—?" I started to shout over the music. Then from the upper balcony leading to the bedroom I heard: "Gran! Help!"

Weasel Face did a double take and started to get up.

I nailed him.

Ten years of soft living and making money hadn't rotted my body. I ran through the *kata*s every other day, working out in a clear space at the resident's gym. My edge had lost nothing.

I nailed him. From a standing start at the top of the stairs I was across the living room in three giant steps and a quarter turn that brought my heel—six layers of Italian leather and one of hardened callous—straight onto the point of his chin. He did a backflip over the couch and balled up in the corner by the window. It probably broke his neck, although I didn't hear the telltale *crick*.

There had to be more of them. Right? They had to be upstairs. Right? So I took the risers three at a time, shrugging out of my suit jacket and clawing at my tie.

Number Two, a scrufbum with half a week's growth of beard, naked as a hairy ape, stood in the bedroom doorway. I put three stiff fingers six inches deep in his solar plexus. But I didn't finish him off. Somebody had to be around for the S.F.P.D. to book.

On the bed were Tracy and Number Three, who was looking over his shoulder with slack-jawed surprise. He seemed about as clean as his partners. Tracy and he were both naked. That is, from what I could see: They were *under* the satin sheets. On the top of the sheets was a smattering of fresh blood. Coming from Tracy's nose.

I was ready to leap on the bed and stomp him. But that might have hurt Tracy more: He was kind of on top of her.

Instead I grabbed his foot and pulled—except in the tangle of satin I got her ankle and she yelped. On my second try the foot was his. Sensei Kan always said, "Strike clean, never grapple. That's judo, and I don't teach it." But there I was, pulling 190 pounds of wife-molester down-bed, against the tuck of the sheets, going slower and slower all the time.

What else could I do? It was a big bed, and I wanted to get at him to pound him.

Tracy was screaming, the *modo* was still thumping, and the guy was saying things like "Hey! Wait a minute! I can explain!" Just what you'd expect, and I had no reason to listen.

But finally I had to listen. The disc player ran out of music, Tracy ran out of screams, and the friction—even with satin sheets—finally caught up with my tugging. I let go and he sat up in a pile of shiny white cloth.

Tracy used a corner of it to wipe her still-dribbling nose. She was giving bruised looks alternately to the guy and to me.

"That's better," he said. "My leg was comin' off."

"Better?" I felt my face go stiff again. "I come home, find three guys raping my wife, and you're worried about your leg? You should see your friends."

"Hey! What rape?" he protested. "She invited us in. I'm the engineer for this building. They're the gardeners. We got contracts to be here."

"Contracts? To rape my—?"

"Oh, brother! What you don't know. You think that little bit of blood makes it rape? She popped herself on the schnoz two seconds after we heard the door slammin' open. This is purely a setup. And if you've hurt those gardeners you'll have assault and battery charges comin' out of your ears. Not to mention a union grievance."

Tracy was strangely quiet. I looked at her. She was making no move to cover herself, even though my hauling had pulled the sheet down to her knees. Instead, she was working her face up to the right state of outrage.

"It was too rape!" she screamed after a second. "You guys forced your way in here. Knocked me around. You put on the disc player to cover the yells. Then you stripped me and carried me, biting and scratching, up here!"

"Oh come on, bitch!" he said tiredly. "Where are the bites? Where are the scratches?" He showed me his arms, mugged his face left and right. "And, about the music, she said she liked to fuck to that *reggae* beat. Mister, we've both been had!"

It was Tracy's word against his. And against the fact that, for a scene where three guys had set on her, the apartment was strangely neat. The men's denims were folded or hung over chairs. Her clothes seemed to have been put away.

Tracy's words and the blood on her nose were giving me a convenient reason to side with her. I could press charges against these guys and not a judge in the city would fail to arraign them. Except for the fact that it would be a huge scandal, smeared all over the media: the Case of the Penthouse Pests. I could read those headlines on the front screen of my mind. And except that Tracy might pull the same stunt the next time I went away on business. I understood all this just standing there.

"Get out," I told him quietly.

"Granny!" Tracy half-screamed, half-pleaded.

"Take your friends," I said, still talking to him. "If I hear one word about lawsuit or grievance, you're going to see some disappearing acts you wouldn't believe."

"Hey, I got rights," he whined.

"Not in my house. Get out."

So he went, taking the other two, Bruised Belly and the Undead One from the living room. On the way he gathered their clothes; they also got away with my robe and my scotch. I never heard a peep from them afterward, and maintenance on the grounds didn't seem to suffer—for the little bit of time we continued to live there.

"Well, you certainly embarrassed me, Gran."

Tracy slowly pulled the blood-spattered satin up around her breasts.

"Three at a party, Tracy? With the *gardeners*?"

"I guess you don't believe me. It was rape. They forced me."

"Damned considerate, putting your clothes away like that."

"They wanted to make it *look* like something else."

"Clever fellas."

"They *were*!"

"Pardon me if I don't believe you. It's really nothing personal. Just—this puts me in a very bad situation. A man in my position, who does the deals I must, has to give his word sixteen times a day. People rely on what, I guess, you could call my honor. So I really can't be vulnerable to blackmail. Or even to the snickerings of people who think they know what's going on behind my back. Not even discreetly."

"You cold-blooded bastard!"

"No, Tracy. It's simply that my wife—"

"You prancing freak!"

"—has to be above suspicion."

"Do you think I don't know about your *boys*?"

Poor Tracy thought she had a stopper there. Fact was, she didn't know anything and was only wild-guessing. And if I were doing anything, I'd be one hell of a lot more discreet than she had been. Christ, leaving the door hanging open! And her guesses were truly irrelevant, because the issue in question was not what I might have done, but what I found her doing. However, like a wise old woods wolf, I knew that the best policy with a discovered trap is to spring it, harmlessly, from the outside.

"Doing *what* with boys, dear wife?" I countered.

"You'll swing with anything, Gran, provided it hasn't been dead three days. And I'll bet you've tried that, too."

"Homosexuality, pedophilia, necrophilia—that's quite a catalog of fantasies. Do you want to add bestiality, or just leave it to be presumed? You have quite a few unfounded allegations, but not one of them backed by evidence or even hearsay."

"Don't wrap me up in lawyer's words, Gran."

"I'll wrap you in a bill of divorce, you hussy. I caught you *in flagrante delicto*."

"What does that mean?"

"Getting reamed and liking it."

She smiled at that, the slow, lazy smile of a satisfied woman. "Go ahead and sue. Do it now, and you can make the *Examiner*'s evening edition. We can be on the *Ten O'Clock News*. 'Prominent Dog-Faced Boy and Socialite Wife Wrangle Over Billion-Dollar Estate.' I *like* it."

Actually, the money was now more than two billion, with the latest S.W.E.E.P. transactions, but I wasn't going to tell Tracy that. Let her attorney dig through layer on layer of holding companies, joint ventures, stock options, and poison pills. Like Schliemann digging at Troy, he was never going to find the real treasure. But this matter wasn't going to get that far.

"Ride's over, Trace. I want you out of here in twenty-four hours. You can take what you like. Hint, hint: There's probably three hundred thou in Bophuthatswana's new gold rands hidden behind the bookcases. Keep whatever you can find. I'm turning my back now. If you disappear without a scene, I will make out a cashier's check for fifteen million for you. If you try to make a fuss, you will disappear without a sign."

"That's a threat! My lawyer will hear about it. It's mental cruelty!"

"Your lawyer will take half of that fifteen mill if you're not careful. See? I'm looking the other way. Take what you can and get out. Now!"

I really did turn my back on her.

From the rustling and the banging—of bedsheets, bare feet, clothes, and finally the closet door—she cleared out in nineteen seconds. I vacated the apartment for a few days, and when I came back it had been stripped. Empty. Everything gone including the runner in the hallway and the light fixtures in the bathroom.

Let her have it. I never heard another word from Tracy Starrett Corbin, her lawyer, or her kin. The check I had left in her name at the bank was picked up inside of thirty-six hours. This time around it was I who filed divorce papers *in absentia*. And like Anne Caheris, I did it from Mexico, too, but I didn't go there just for a legal dodge.

I went to war.

You see, ever since I was a kid Mexico had been a country on the edge of disaster, in terrible economic shape, dying, dying, and not dead yet. Transfusions of cash and technology from the United States had done nothing to revive the comatose economy. Oil and mineral wealth beyond the dreams of sheikh or shah had done nothing to improve the life of the people. But that year, in 2009, it finally happened. The *bandidos*, the petty revolutionaries, and the peasants finally got together and kicked the Institutional Revolutionary Party, the PRI, out of power. Like a dried skeleton in a sandy crypt, the country just fell apart.

Within weeks, Yucatan was trying to be an independent communist state and laid claim to the oil fields in the Gulf of Campeche. The west coast and Baja set themselves up as a free state, with tourism and drugs the mainstay of their economy. The rest of the country was balkanized in similar fashion, with a dozen family parties and warring factions scrambling for the few pesos left in the cashbox. The process was fearful and wonderful and wholly predictable.

The confusion raised anxieties in the United States, of course. The border States of Texas, New Mexico, Arizona, and California, which had grown into a loose confederation known as the TENMAC, were the most concerned. For decades they had absorbed—and, frankly, capitalized on—a trickle of hungry brown people seeping across the border, a few hundred each day at each crossing point. Now that trickle had turned into a torrent; thousands of human locusts were streaming north. Everywhere. Every hour. Many of them were armed, and most of them understood democracy and a free market economy not at all. It was the Southwest's worst nightmare come awake.

The TENMAC petitioned Congress for intervention. The States took their authority from the Mexican government's last series of requests for U.S. aid. They took their cause from the plight of the Walt Whitman School, an American institution in Monterrey which the local People's Revolutionary Socialist Council, or CSPR, had taken under its "protection." Rumor had it they were holding the teachers, mostly U.S. citizens who had come down to work and play in the sun, hostage to extract concessions from the local industrial managers, also American-based.

The image of helpless white females being held in ruthless brown hands played well in Baltimore. The House Subcommittee on International Strategy granted the TENMAC's request to form nearly independent militia units, formally known as the Gentlemen Volunteers, to intervene in Monterrey. In a further move, also inspired by the TENMAC, Congress put forward a resolution annexing the entire country. That passed by a four-vote majority. The date was February 8, 2010.

Technically, a state of war existed. Moscow protested and the U.S. government, in the person of Speaker McCanlis, cited the now-defunct Monroe Doctrine, bared its collective teeth, and fingered The Button. Moscow backed off.

Why did I get involved? Couple of reasons . . .

The first was boredom. I was tired of paper risks, with all the adrenaline flowing in somebody else's blood. I could buy a colonel's rank—maybe even a general's—in the G.V.'s and campaign with my own troops. It would be the ultimate game, the real "sport of kings." I might even get killed.

The second reason was part of the first. I was tired of being a victim of circumstances. My life to that point had been pushed right and left. By the rise and fall of the economy and the financial markets. By one wife's demands and another's appetites. By terrorists in Arabia and America. By the lusts and laws that my own childhood had imposed. By the stuttering thing in my head that I never talked about.

It was time I went out and made some circumstances of my own. And Mexico was the place to do it.

Chapter 12

Billy Birdsong: War Among The Ruins

God-damned white man!

I had almost gotten my life together, making something to be proud of with the sludgeworks and socking away big money, too. Sludge is almost soothing: a complex of fertile, life-supporting liquids that gurgle gently inside white piping and cook in gleaming steel vats. The farmers, the pharmaceutical makers, and the metal and water traders all depended on my products. It was a gentlemanly business, like aging wine and cheese.

Then Corbin decided he would go to Mexico and wanted me to take him in. More deserts and jungles. More killing. More sand. I did not want that, and I told him so.

"Aw, Billy! You've got this business knocked!" Granny's eyes were shining like a kid's. "What's left to do but just sit and watch the greenbacks grow?"

"An occupation I could like real well."

"You'd grow old. And fat. And respectable. You'd end up with a house in Woodside. A nagging wife and a pack of kids. Probably have a couple of horses, too. Do you know how much stable rents cost? And you'd have social obligations—have to learn to play golf. Do you know what greens fees are at the clubs there? Sky high!"

"Keep talking. I could die young in Mexico, too. Hip deep in sticky green vines, centipedes, and other poisonous crawlies. Let it alone, Gran. Enjoy life, now that we got it made."

"Mexico needs us. It's almost our duty to go down there and bring those poverty-stricken peasants into the twenty-first century. Teach them technology and a free market. Make them good U.S. citizens. And protect our backside, too."

"I did my duty in Nicco. Thought we learned our lesson there. And in Vietnam. And in Beirut. Our backside is better off when we just sit on it."

"It's the course of history, Billy."

"History is not my business. Sludge is."

"It'll be fun!"

"God damn it, it will be a tangle of hard work like you would never believe. To build up from scratch—what? A battalion? A division? With a table of organization to set up. Vehicles, arms, and equipment to buy. Officer and enlisted ranks, not to mention specialists, to recruit. And test. And train into a unit, so they shoot at something besides each other the first time you take them into combat. Do you have a base for that? What about logistics and support? And transport? And signals? And air cover? And—and—"

"You see?" he almost gloated. "You already understand the problems involved. That's why I need you to organize this, Billy. More than I need you to run a series of processing plants that are all under computer control anyway." There was a dealer's edge to his voice. I was hearing the whip in Corbin's other hand.

"What about money?" I asked. "A venture like this will cost two or three billion-with-a-B dollars just to put together. Running it will gobble down another billion a year. Maybe more. Can you cover that?"

"It can be arranged." Corbin smiled more to himself than for me.

"And the cash flow is one hundred percent outgoing: soldiers' pay and benefits, fees and bribes, food and fuel, equipment losses, indemnities to the next of kin. And what comes in? Nothing."

"Duty. Country. Glory. Adventure."

"Bullshit. Will you get use of the territory and markets you conquer? Will the people who surrender to you become your chattels?"

"Possibly."

"Bullshit. Becoming a general with your own half-assed army is a sinkhole you could throw money into for years."

"What rank do you want, Billy?"

"Colonel, at least."

"Don't you want to fly choppers?"

"Not going to be that kind of war. I hope."

"Then let's get on with it." Corbin reached over and squeezed my hand. It passed for a handshake. "I'll begin the negotiations and paperwork in Baltimore. And in Sacra-mento, if we're going to acquire a base . . . Oh! And I'll write you a letter of credit to cover the costs of starting up."

"I hope you know where it will end."

"In a free Mexico, Billy." He smiled like a girl going to a wedding, sure of everything. "And in glory."

Now, as Corbin said, I had a practical knowledge of military organization—from the inside out, as it were. I knew the table of organization for a standing army: corps, division, brigade, regiment, battalion, company, platoon, squad. Most of the units that fit in there were self-contained for moving and fighting—a squad with its riflemen, machine gunner, thumper man, radio man, medic, and team leader. The platoon combined several squads, just as a hand combined several fingers—for a practical purpose. And so the T.O. was built up.

Some of the units were highly specialized for staff and support—medevac, airmobile, quartermaster, press office, et cetera. Each of these fit in at the level—company, say, or battalion—that represented the right span of control or service. But how many new specialties had been thought up in the last twenty years since my war, I was not sure. Did the army of today need a company of computer programmers? How about economic theorists in each squad? An organ bank at the battalion level? Financial counselors? Insurance adjusters?

A corollary question: How would isolated militia units

like the Gentlemen Volunteers be different from a standing army? To start with, Gran was talking a division. We would operate without a corps level to call our own, a theater command we could depend on, a Pentagon, or a whole string of U.S. bases to stage from—or draw replacements from. It followed that many of our staff functions would logically be filled in at lower levels in the T.O., probably. The whole army would have to be more mobile, probably. And set-piece battles with high casualty rates would cripple us or wipe us out, probably.

Also, if Granville J. Corbin was planning to be *the* general, we could not afford to be top-heavy with high officer ranks. No room for promotion. So the lower ranks would have to take on wider responsibilities and have more authority. But be willing to march in place, as it were. That meant we would be paying more for experienced men. Running a GV unit was going to be complicated and expensive. Probably.

Sergeant Billy had a lot of boning up to do.

One thing Granny made clear from the start: He wanted his own press corps. I was to be sure we had writers, video producers, tape editors, lighting techs, makeup specialists, media reps. And all the equipment and blank tape they needed.

"Are we starting a war or making a movie, Gran?"

"We're making sure no one forgets this war."

Granny wanted to be a second MacArthur.

I had to strategize our recruiting. With other GV units already forming up, it could easily become a seller's market for bodies. Not that I minded taking a certain number of green kids with big dreams; after all, somebody had to hold a rifle and walk into the bush. But I needed that high proportion of seasoned men, and they would keep the kids walking forward when the shooting started. I also needed all those flinking experts.

My advertising plan covered *Fortune* as well as *Soldier of Fortune*, plus a healthy sprinkling of special-interest magazines like *Black Belt*, *Cycle Dad*, *Trucker*, *Chrome*, and *Playperson*.

Gran and I debated whether we should be an equal-opportunity employer and take on women recruits in all specs. He was for it, but I could see immediate problems of morale on both sides. The question was finally answered for us when the State of California passed a resolution grandfathering the GV units. A rider to the bill required EEO documentation. So we signed up anyone who could run two miles, bench press fifty pounds, and had a clean medical record. The rest we could teach—and motivate them to learn.

That State resolution also simplified a lot of the legal questions. Being a legitimate militia, we could get end-user certificates for all our arms and ammunition. We could legally buy heavy equipment like tanks and jet fighters, if we wanted them. And we could make war outside the country. No need to train in secret and push off across the Rio Grande in civilian clothes on a moonless night.

However, this last provision turned out to be not all that important. While we were still in training, Congress passed the Henderson Act, naming Old Mexico's thirty-one *estados* and the *Distrito Federal* as the fifty-second to eighty-third States. All we GV's had to do was go out and get them.

The news certainly made recruiting easy.

In three months we recruited 9,000 men and women. And we must have talked to 20,000 more to find them. Even putting the early officer-types to work right away as recruiters, I personally had to see, question, and grab or make walk six people each hour, ten hours a day, with only Sundays off.

"What name, Sarge?"

"Rusas, sir."

"Where you fight?"

"Nicaragua, Guatemala . . . Got my start in Lebanon."

"What are you, Shi'ite?"

"No sir! I fought in the Zone with Colonel Haddad."

"What specialty?"

"This and that. Communications, mortar man, computers, cook, point man. Whatever you need."

"Scrounger?"

"That too. Just tell me what you want—and what's off limits. The rest just happens."

"Terms are six months till shakedown, then we are all month to month, or duration of hostilities. Rank assigned at end of training. Pay is—" Flip, flip, flip. "—twenty forty-one a month, on the first. Report to the bus station in Escondido the first week in June. Need anything to keep you fed till then?"

"No, sir. I got my stash."

"Good man." Check the application "[ ] Approved" and initial it. "Next! . . . Okay, Sis, what name?"

"Beth Longacre and I ain't your sister."

"Listen, Beth. These collar tabs tell you I am a full colonel. 'Sir' to you. Now we can start over. Name?"

"Beth Longacre—sir."

"Experience?"

"Well, uh, I was in on the Madera Run last year, riding with the Road Fems."

"Baggage? Or do you sit your own bike?"

"I ride my own—sir. I'm hell with a knife."

"Put your down as a silent killer. Ever fire a gun?"

"I can learn—sir."

"You will. Any other specialties?"

"I graduated from high school—"

"Hmmm. 'Claims can read and write own name.' Anything else?"

"Two years of business college—"

"No typing pool in this army."

"I can do FASB accounting, program in Ada VI, field strip a Kodak 2880, and maintain a LAN—sir."

"Okay . . . okay. Quartermaster is light. You can start there. Terms are six months till shakedown, then we are all month to month, or duration of hostilities. Rank assigned at end of training. Pay is—" Flip, flip. "—eighteen twenty-two a month, on the first. Report to the bus station in Escondido the first week in June. Need anything to keep you fed till then?"

"I'm square."

"Great, Sis. Next! . . . What name?"

"Julio Garcia, sir."

"Experience?"

"Nicco, sir. For as long as *that* lasted."

"My first war too, Julio . . ."

They became a blur of white and brown and red faces, squinty eyes, twitchy hands, bitten lips, smiles and sneers, and sometimes cold, dead voices trying to out-John Wayne the Duke himself.

I saw kids who had learned it all on television and kids who claimed to have taken out entire villages with tactical nukes. I saw ex-cons and future-cons and men on the run. I saw women who thought Yucatan was going to be Cozumel and were already working on their bikini lines. And I saw women who wanted to kill something, anything, quick. I saw career soldiers from the Old Army who thought war was polishing buttons, filling out triplicate forms, and eating three flavors of ice cream in the chow hall. I also saw pros from the O.A. who would be the backbone and bootsoles of our unit. I saw everything that walked, talked, and wanted to go to Mexico.

And once I got the bodies squared away, and the Early Birds down in the desert building our base at Poway, I went on a shopping trip.

Uniforms, cots, blankets, and bullets we could buy from the wholesale catalogs. Jeeps, stoves, and radio transmitters I had somebody else look over. My concern was air power.

Although I told Gran it was not going to be that kind of war, a light and mobile attack unit had to be ready to jump long distances, land dry, and be firing as they unloaded. That meant helicopters or something better.

"Something better" was Stompers.

The Bell HU-1 Iroquois had been the main ass-hauler and gunship for Vietnam, the Apache and its brethren in Nicaragua. As I said earlier, Charlie and later the Chorotegas could hear those aircraft coming before they could see them. And it did not take too many attack approaches for those little brown people to figure that heavy thwock-thwock-thwock meant they were right on the flight path. Being no dummies, they prepared accordingly.

Well, at ground-level basic our soldiers and defense suppliers were not stupid either. In the decade and a half between Vietnam and Nicaragua, one of the airplane companies brought out a tilt-wing, short takeoff and landing, or STOL, airplane for ground support. It was light and fast, but not as maneuverable as a chopper. The Pentagon kept it from limited duty and went to updated helicopters for Nicco.

After those Constitutional amendments whirled the Pentagon's bright boys into oblivion, the country's defense contractors were scrambling to make the States' National Guard units and the international buyers happy. The big firms like Boeing and McDonnell-Republic finally did something about the status of airmobility. By the time we were heading for Mexico, the Western Alliance's infantry units were flying recon, ground support, and infiltration with the Boeing STM-4 Skyjay, the Stomper.

I took Granny to the airfield in Hayward, California, to try out the skinned, or troop carrier, model.

"Looks like a crop duster," Corbin said, squinting across the concrete at the stubby little plane.

"Flies like one," grinned the tech sergeant, Gonzales, who was going to show us. "Only better," he said after a beat. "She'll do vertical takeoffs and landings carrying twelve soldiers or 3,700 pounds of cargo. Range is about 800 miles, fully loaded. In the air, she'll cruise at 280 miles an hour or attack at 350—usually straight down. This baby *can't* stall and she'll only spin if you tell her to."

Gran went immediately to the Stomper's engines, which were mounted in swivel-and-tilt nacelles at the end of the short, broad wings. From the swept area of their fans, I could see they would give the pilot almost as much control and hover ability as a helicopter.

"The turbines are high-revving jetprops," Gonzales went on. "From the ground they're almost silent, until the plane's about a hundred yards out. And then your bush people hear just a bee-swarm whine that seems to be coming from everywhere."

The underside of the Stomper's fuselage was fitted with ceramic-sponge panels.

"Those'll deflect or absorb the energy of anything up to .50 caliber. They learned how to fit them from the heat tiles of the old Space Shuttle. Engine nacelles and fuel pods're protected with a titanium laminate armor. Supposed to turn back an armor-piercing grenade, but I've never tested that."

When we climbed in and I took the righthand seat, I could immediately see the weak link in the whole Stomper system: the controls. Every function was monitored or commanded by computer and routed to the pilot through the central display unit, or CDU, and the variac, or joystick. That stick and the "Engines start" button were the only two controls. Just like a kid's video game. No, I was not worrying about electrical glitcharillos: Backup circuits and tandem chips were probably stuffed into the console. But let something crack the gas plasma plate of the CDU, or a wire pull loose inside the joystick, and you plowed it.

Even the canopy jettison was set up from the variac.

It was a design vulnerability that, in combat action, everyone would chalk up to computer dependency, system efficiency, or low-bidder mentality. Everyone except those who crashed and burned.

Gonzales pushed the button and, before anything else, the CDU flickered on. Then the engines, right and left in order, kicked to vertical, coughed one puff of black smoke, and began to whine high and nasal like Gina Fong.

Sitting on the ground, Gonzales did a test orbit with the stick. I could see the nacelles rotate and tilt in unison. Through the airframe we felt them tug right-forward-left-backward. That plane wanted to *go*.

He twisted something on the variac and the Stomper leapt straight up into the air at 1,200 feet per minute. The CDU said so. In about ten seconds we were looking a long way down at the field and surrounding rooftops.

"Do you have to clear with the tower or anything?" I asked casually.

"We did," the pilot grinned. "All done by computer call sign and automatic delay. We went when the system told us. I don't have to use the radio unless I really want to chat."

"Oh."

Gonzales pushed forward on the stick, the nacelles,

pitched forward, and that 350 feet per second was translated into about 250 miles per hour, fast. My stomach—*mine*, and I was used to Fraggy Dan getaways in an Apache—was left somewhere over Hayward.

"With only three guys she's a little more responsive than usual," the pilot admitted. "A full load will slow her down. Some."

He headed for the rolling hills opposite the Bay. "I'm going to take you to a patch of live oak we use for assault practice. Show you how easy she is on the in-and-out."

For the next hour, he hopped that plane into little patches of ground among the scrubby trees. Most times, our chin bubble was practically resting in one set of branches, while the tail surfaces fought their way into another. Gonzales would touch wheels, pop the door, then pull her out like a champagne cork. When we parked back at Hayward, Granny flipped open his checkbook and was all ready to write.

I signed up for flying lessons the next week.

We also personally tested tanks and half-tracks. But aside from trucks for transport, I was dubious about taking in any heavy ground vehicles. I was even less enthusiastic about armor. In the desert, on hard gravel with not a lot of cover—maybe. But in among the vines and lowlands sinks and other shit, about the only tracked vehicle I wanted was a bulldozer with a big plow. Our main strike force was going to be the Stompers, supported with bladder trucks and rolling machine shops.

Corbin agreed, so that is what we sent down to Poway.

It sounded crazy to me, setting up a near-desert base to train our unit for a jungle war. Then I got out the topo maps and the atlas and looked over our theater of war: The northern end of the Yucatan Peninsula, where we would at least start out, is hardly jungle at all. Except for mangrove swamps along the coast, the land is a semi-arid plain vegetated with low scrub or *chaparral*. The most remarkable feature is the natural cavities known as *cenotes*, or water holes.

Not until you go south, across the central zone, do you find tropical vegetation—tall cedars, kapok, and mahogany trees, lianas, and all the rest. The only microclimate in California that approximates these rain forests is the redwood groves. And flipping around *there*, firing live grenades, and bivouacking a couple of thousand troops is—umm—contra environmental. We did try for a permit from Fish and Game, but they turned us flat down.

Poway was not bad. And our aim was not to climatize the men and women, anyway. It was to toughen them and make a team out of them. We could have done that in Antarctica or the Bronx.

I thought Granny was going to run the unit Hollywood style: show up when he felt like it, give a few orders, drink a few beers with the troops to be sociable, then fly home until next weekend. No way. He took basic right alongside the greenest of them. He let the temporary sarges chew on his butt. He went on the twenty-mile forced marches and ended up on one of them doing the fireman's carry, in relays, on a drill instructor who got snakebit. He even ate our food, which was intentionally subpar to weed out the grousers and the Cozumel-holiday-charter people. And, of course, he took the language classes with us. After all, they were his idea.

Teaching everyone a common, nonstandard language was a good idea for a lot of reasons. It was another way for us to blow away the chaff. It gave the unit, especially the fire teams, a common bond. And it gave us guarded communications at a subcode level. For silent work we all learned American sign language—at least a pidgin-patois of it that we had adapted to military situations. For radio and open communications, we considered a made-up language like Esperanto, but too many Old Army units had been using that for enemy-speak in their war games. We wanted something already spoken but really out of the way—from a country we were unlikely ever to fight in. I was hoping Gran would pick Navaho and make my life easier, but he settled on Malay. Think he chose it from a hat.

Malay is a knobby, many-syllabled language a whole world away from anything European. The only word I could recognize was *soldadu* for soldier. But then, I am really *hebat* [terrible] at languages.

We trained for six months, taking our initial 9,000 down to about 5,600. Which was my target all along. Then we held Career Day—kind of a graduation, mixed with rank assignments and some choice of duty. It was the first time many of the recruits discovered who the Granny Corbin among them really was. The General. Most had thought that, because I wore the oak leaves and gave the orders in public, I was top dog.

The paperwork finally caught up with us. By a special resolution in Congress, our unit became the California 64th Air Cavalry Volunteers. There were a whole bunch of authorizations: to make war in the public interest; to seize and hold territory in the name of the Congress of the United States; to commandeer vehicles, fuel, and food supplies; to issue script with a redemption period not to exceed two years; to execute military prisoners. We had quasi-judicial powers. We could set up a military state and run it while the bullets lasted.

Congress also set some restrictions: We were nominally under command of the House Subcommittee on International Strategy, known among us as HSIS or "Ha-Sis." We were required to coordinate our efforts with other GV units operating within our theater of operations—which was really meaningless, because what does "coordinate" mean? Finally, we were forbidden to conduct maneuvers in the original fifty-one United States as defined prior to the Henderson Act. Not even for further training and drills, Corbin explained. Once we crossed the border going south, we could not return to the country except as unarmed civilians, or in boxes.

That was clear enough, you would think.

Every division has two names, its official designation, like "64th Air Cavalry Volunteers," and some warlike *nom de guerre* like "Tropic Lightning," or "The Big Red One." I thought it would be Corbin's privilege, as sponsor and top dog, to pick a name he liked. But Granny was smarter than that.

In those final days of training, he let it be announced that we were taking nominations for a unit name. We would vote until a majority found what they wanted.

"After all," he told me privately, "if they're going to fight and die for the group, they might as well like how it sounds."

We heard everything: California Cobras, the Condors, the Seals, the Giants, and the Giant Killers, the Dodgers (which sounded pretty smart—for rifle teams—until baseball fever finally ran out), the Fighting 64th, Birdsong's Bastards (when they thought I ran the unit, the little ass-kissers), Snake Eyes, Silent Death, Sweet Dreams, Screamers, Day Trippers, Dandy Dogs (huh?), Legion of the Damned, Foreign Legion, Foreign Order, the *Valorous* 64th (for God's sake). The names went around and around, turning up nothing that more than six people at one time could like.

Finally, with the whole unit on parade at Career Day, a newly starred General Corbin performed the swearing in and read the congressional resolution making us an official unit of the U.S. government. They listened quietly. However, when he got to the part about not returning to the United States, someone from the rear ranks shouted out of turn: "Homeless Bastards!" Corbin picked it up immediately, used it in his remarks, and by chow time that evening the phrase was humming from one end of the division to the other. We were the Homeless Bastards, so rough and tough and dangerous that our own country would not let us back inside. It fit.

Staging for Yucatan was from Corpus Christi, Texas. We went south in seven coastal steamers modified as troop carriers. Clearly, we could never fly all our staff, stores, trucks, and heavy equipment out in the Stompers. And we could not march or roll from Chula-Vista, down the length of Mexico, to Merida, which was the capital of Yucatan and would be our new base of operations. The country was so broken up that a march like that would have meant fighting for every mile. Ten percent of us might have gotten through.

As it was, we hardly expected to make port, unload, and walk into town. Although technically the territory belonged to us by annexation, we still had to invade. The plan was to land on the offshore island strip along the peninsula's north side, at Progreso, form up, and dash forty miles south for the capital. If we moved quickly, preceded by the Stompers, we might just take the *Comunistas* by surprise.

The preparations for launching an invasion—anywhere, by any means—is an absolute *mind maze*. Every piece fits together and interlocks like a wooden puzzle: loading up your assault troops, setting up fuel points, scouting the disembarkation zone, making the first attack, establishing diversions, bringing up fresh support units, establishing a perimeter, contacting any local friendlies, tightening the perimeter, de blip, de blop, de bloop, right up until the point that your soldiers are drinking beer around a fountain in the plaza while you unload the presses for printing your new currency.

Every piece of the puzzle has its limitations: the operating range of your vehicles, the sleep-wake cycle of your troops, the firepower-to-weight ratio of the weapons they carry, the distances they have to move to engage enemy hard points. And every movement has its optimum timing, its window of opportunity, and a lockout dead zone where moving at all, let alone successfully, is impossible. They tell me bringing a first-run play to Broadway is a complicated span of action, with a lot to be done in a short time on interlocking schedules. Well, tell me if the price of failure for the theater producer is a few thousand men and women shot up on the beach.

Our limitations were distance and heavy stuff.

For Corpus Christi to Progreso is about 650 miles. Technically within the range of the Stompers, until you account for a full load, possible headwinds en route, and circling and maneuvering during the assault. You fail if you arrive with tanks sucking vapor.

I wanted a carrier, even a small one. But the U.S. Navy's heavy ships had been scrapped ten years earlier. Obsolete and unfunded. What we had was the loan of two Coast Guard cutters—at a per-diem fee that actually brought tears to Granny's eyes. The cutters had chopper pads on their bridge decks, and we persuaded them to each tow a fuel barge loaded with JP-5 and equipped with high-speed pumps. We were going to touch down, refuel, and fly off 150 of our first-wave Stompers in pairs. Loading ten soldiers per plane, that would bring in 1,500 troops in the first wave. Adequate.

We practiced at an airfield outside Corpus Christi until the pilots could average just three minutes on deck. At that rate, we were still looking at a dwell time over the cutters of *three hours and fifteen minutes!*

The Stompers could not possibly arrive as a single strike force. Given the fuel that first-comers would burn while orbiting the cutters and waiting for last-comers to touch and fuel, our immediate strike force, the first of the first wave, would be about 30 planes. Or 300 troops on the ground and firing.

I wanted a flotilla of amphibious assault craft, little tracked boats that could wade ashore and roll right over the enemy. But when you are running a war on a shoe-string, you do not have the bucks for expensive toys you will use once and abandon. I tried to rent them but no one had really done a beachhead landing in the sixty years since Normandy.

Why not just hold the attack in downtown Merida? Land, shoot them up, take over? Well, as I said, we had no plans to bring in the whole division in our Stompers, which basically were for light attack and recon. We had trucks to unload, along with the equipment, supplies, and materiel they would carry. We needed the freighters to move that heavy stuff. Which meant we needed a port to unload them. Which meant we had to take Progreso and march inland.

Finally, it all worked out.

Granny took me over the plan again and again: timing, load weights, distance, firepower, fuel burn, the enemy's strength and positions. We were mumbling the numbers in our sleep. We bought LANDSAT photos of the beach area, blew them up to twenty by twenty feet, and hung them on the wall of a warehouse on the Corpus Christi waterfront. Then we took the pilots and the first-wave troops over the assault again and again. Until *they* were mumbling the numbers in their sleep. But, in theory, they were ready.

In practice, it was a fuckup.

We were on the freighters, in sight of the coast off Progreso, with 150 Stompers in the air and some of them even circling our ships, when the beach opened up with rockets. Old Exocets. Hot shit.

"*Star. Captain.* Billy, how many do you count?" That was Corbin. He was radioing from the bridge of the M.V. *Inland Captain*, which was our flagship. For safety we had split the command, with me in the second boat, M.V. *Gulf Star*.

"Three launch sites, at least. Gran, if they hit one of these buckets, you can write it off."

"We can't shoot them down. Can we maneuver?"

"I suppose we could widen the range," I replied. "Let any natural error in their flight path take its course . . ."

The *Gulf Star*'s captain, for whom this whole adventure was just another charter-for-profit, overheard that last comment. He quickly put about and headed out to sea.

Still holding the radiophone, and squinting toward the beach, I pulled my 9mm automatic and stuck it in his ear.

"Not yet, Barney."

Our wake fell back into formation.

"Billy, can the Stompers take out the launch sites?"

"Worth a try, but the delay will blow our timetable."

"Turning back blows it worse."

"We could divert," I offered. "Say, to Puerto Juarez?"

"As bad as turning back. Two hundred odd sea miles . . . about fifteen hours . . . and who knows what the reception will be like there? No, whistle in the Stompers."

"All right, General."

"And Billy . . . Have the command ship pick you up. I think you better take the lead on this."

"Unnhgh . . . Yes, sir."

I was not happy about that. Not that I was scared—just concerned more about the main movement than cowboying around with the first wave. But Gran's intuitions were right: He had a major problem with the rockets and he wanted his most experienced man on it. Me.

The command Stomper was a special ship. I had directed her outfitting—radio gear, guns, map cases, computer, crew of three to tie Bird Leader into the network, plot the ground action, and keep score. When I was aboard, however, the lefthand seat was mine. So flying the first wave had its compensations.

Pete Beckwith, the alternate pilot, brought her right down on the *Gulf Star*'s fantail, where I was waiting in my flight gear with a fresh copy of the battle map, marked with all the launch points we had spotted, in my thigh pocket.

"Welcome aboard, Colonel," Pete said, scrambling over to the right seat. The copilot hopped out that side, and I slid in around the variac stick. During the transfer, the fans were under full control from three sets of hands, overlapping for about three seconds. Teamwork.

I twisted the stick, the nacelles countered, reversing thrust direction on our port side, and the Stomper spun away from the ship on a rising curve.

"Got a problem, Johnny," I said, handing the map back to our computer jock. "Exocets, we think."

"I saw them. This map is out of date, Colonel. We've laid in a couple more sites you didn't see."

"Great . . . The formation is set up for ground assault, not a raid. We got four, count them, gunships."

"This ship has rockets and quad-fifties," Pete said. "We could take a crack at the sites, too."

"War hero," I said cheerfully. I had figured the attack to go that way. We were already vectored in on the center launch site.

A corner of the CDU was showing me a silhouette line of mangrove swamp with a hard point shadowed in. Johnny was a fast programmer. I armed the rocket pods and tipped the fans far forward. We ate up the surf.

When were were 300 meters out, the operators in the trees panicked and tried to take *us* out with an Exocet. Dumb. Better they had frozen like a fawn in the woods. I sideslipped with a twitch of my wrist and used my thumb to send a Beeswarm down its backtrail. There was a blue-violet flash followed by a sincere *thud*. When we swept over, an acre of swamp had flattened out to black mud and sucking tidewater.

"Bingo," Johnny shouted behind me.

The war was on.

We cleared out two more launch crews the same way. The third fought back with something that, finally, could kill us: a ten-kilogram SAM-9. It was a ducted, air-breathing wasp-thing under control from the ground. Coming up beneath our chin bubble, it looked like some kind of model airplane. It was too small and maneuverable for me to dodge, and it was carrying too much C-4 explosive for me to ignore. The only solution was to outfly it. I cracked on the power and surged straight up. The SAM came right up with us, which surprised me badly. The sweat broke out under my collar. Next I tried rolling forward and shooting off at 300-plus toward the mainland. That worked; I could see the SAM tumbling in our fanwash. So I flipped over, loosed a burp of .50 caliber in its general direction, then homed a rocket on the launch site picked out by the CDU. Flash, thud, flatten.

The beach was pretty well worked over in twenty minutes. I had Pete get on the radio and call in a vee of five skinned Stompers—again, planes carrying assault troops, not aerial guns—to secure the area, while I flew on to Progreso proper to see what else the *Comunistas* had waiting.

From the main plaza and the waterfront we only drew flashes of small arms fire, plus a half dozen or so of those SAM-9s. Hardly a room-temperature reception. We took a high hover for air control and sent in the other twenty skins of the first wave. They settled like a flock of pigeons and our boys and girls tumbled out shooting.

That morning I spent twelve hours in the lefthand seat of my command craft. As soon as Progreso was halfway pacified and the freighters were heading into the harbor, I took a flyby south down the highway toward Merida to scout resistance. Nothing, nothing, and then a circle of trucks at Dzibilchaltun. Or however you say it.

It was a clearing in the coastal undergrowth, covered with a million square, white stones. Atop a mound near the center of the area was an old stone blockhouse, looking like a military hard point, except for some kind of friezework around the roof. The trucks were parked south of it. I gave the blockhouse my last Beeswarm rocket. Flash, thud—but all it did was knock some stucco loose from the frieze and blacken the west wall. Killed anybody inside, though, I bet.

We flew back to Progreso, set down near the fuel bladders—which by Gran's orders had been unloaded first—ran another 700 gallons of JP-5 into my ship and rearmed her. Then we took off to give some more grief to that concentration at Dzibilwhatever.

I gathered the other four gunships and a dozen skins that were just coming in from the cutters at sea.

"Column headed this way," I told them over the radio. "Near Zibblechaltun on your maps."

"That's an historic ruin, Colonel," one of the pilots protested. "It's preclassical Mayan architecture."

"Right! Also, a bunch of stones with guys behind them trying to kill us. Now, fly!"

We engaged that column of trucks north of the ruins and moving toward Progreso. About fifty in all this time. If you figured twenty men to a truck, plus heavier armaments than we could airlift, then they had our first wave outnumbered with a force of a thousand, or by about three to one.

As gunship leader, we burned the first two trucks in one pass. The rest of them circled and scattered in among the trees and stone temples.

"Skin leader, take them down." I was committing a large fraction of our available forces to a pitched ground battle against terrible odds. Well, the alternative was to let the *Comunistas* dig in and bottle us up in Progreso. We would have to stay in those mangrove swamps for ten years.

The Stompers dropped straight down and unloaded battle-ready troops right into the enemy's cluster points, while the other gunships zipped around and blew up anything that was not occupied with our boys and girls. Meantime, I got high and diverted every Stomper we had coming in from the cutters. I wanted to put the best part of 1,500 men into Zibble-*gesundheit* as fast as possible. The war was going to end right there, as far as I was concerned.

The first of the reinforcements were coming south, high over the trees, like a flotilla of Canada geese, when I got a radio call from Gran in Progreso.

"Colonel, proceed with a raiding force southwest toward Celestun. Intercept a force en route for one of the oil derricks, *Zanja del Norte* No. 32 at map coordinates YJ-0016/ZJ-0028. Intercept and interdict. Over."

What was this shit about an *oil derrick?*

"But, Gran!" I turned a fast circle in the sky over the ground battle while trying to figure out my response. I had my adrenaline up, telling me to fight, fly, fuck, or die, and Granny wanted me to go off chasing rabbits somewhere to the west.

"We are right in the middle of clearing the road—" I started to say.

"I don't care how important you think your action is, Billy," Corbin cut across me. "Those rigs are three-quarters of the reason we're down here. Now crack on the power and check it out. . . . Clear."

"Yes sir." I said into a frequency that had already gone dead.

Not a lot of choice about what happened next. I handed control of the battle over to the number two gunship and tipped our Stomper to the southwest. I took one other guns along as escort.

The eastern end of the Bay of Campeche, the body of water between the Yucatan Peninsula and the Mexican mainland, was a new oil field. It was richer even than the western end, around Tampico. Some of the rigs were too new to be on my maps. But I found *Zanja* 32 all right. Three hundred miles offshore, or about ninety minutes by air. It was going to be close on fuel. I hoped they had a stock of JP-5, or even -4 for their service choppers. In a pinch I could burn kerosene, but that was about the limit of my fuel specs.

We flew northwest to cut across the direct sea line from Progreso, then swung southwest and followed the route of this supposed insurgent force all the way to the map coordinates Gran had given. We found the rig but no boats on the way, not even fishing boats.

Zanja 32 was a big one, with dual chopper pads and three drill towers. It was no shallow-water walking rig but a permanent tip-and-flood installation. In a hundred years it would be the center of a coral-reef *cayo*.

"Rig *Zanja* three-two," I radioed. "California six-four bravo-hotel. Request permission to land."

"*Si,*" came a quiet Spanish voice on that frequency. "*Con permiso.*"

Which should have been my first tip-off. The language of air traffic is always English, even on a Mexican rig in Mexican waters. But I was too worried about fuel, cross winds, and the size of the landing pad to link up little facts like that with the overall situation.

I had the wheels down and was feeling for the center of the pad when it blew. A wall of lacy orange flame, roiled with black smoke, rose up around the cockpit bubble. The ship jarred and sagged badly to port as one of my engines took in a piece of shrapnel and exploded in a shower of fan blades. Pete and Johnny worked quickly to shut down systems, while I fought to keep the ship upright and disarm the rockets at the same time. For a few seconds the external air filters fought against the heat and smoke, but soon a gray, sour version of the hot death outside seeped into the cabin. Then the bubble itself was melting in dime-sized holes, letting in gouts of flame. Our fingers were still punching off systems when the smoke knocked us out.

Chapter 13

Granville James Corbin: A Clean, Well-Lighted War

The momentum of that first attack took us as far as Merida, the provincial capital, which was our primary objective. Colonel Birdsong was wise to force the enemy's stand at Dzibilchaltun; we were able to roll them right back to the city so fast they had no time to prepare its defenses. That was vital, because we didn't have an armored column, and a single artillery battery inside the city could have stopped us cold. The extent of my generalship in taking the city was to lay out a simple encircling movement, bringing our ground troops in from the east and west simultaneously, in trucks.

As it was, we had to subdue Merida on a house-to-house basis, clearing and securing each district. Our singular advantage against the enemy was more modern weapons with a higher firing rate than the Communists, with their Soviet castoffs, could achieve. In two days of hard fighting we cleaned them out and drove them south into the bush. The first part of our war was over in 72 hours. It was almost too easy.

I only regret that the fine ruins of Dzibilchaltun had to suffer. They are—or were—an excellent example of early Mayan architecture and culture. I was deeply disappointed that the enemy forced us to destroy part of the people's heritage in our advance.

As we brought the trucks and headquarters vans through

this area, I asked the tapemen to stop shooting. Because they had been rolling continuously since we had docked at Progreso, this request raised some comment.

"It would be much better," I told them, "if we show some of our men at work putting the stones back and washing down the burn marks. We are going to be builders in this land, not destroyers."

"Good line, Gran. We'll use it in the biography. But while we're here, how about just one clip of you examining the damage and, maybe, shaking your head sadly."

"Later, boys. We have work to do."

I did let them shoot as we formally entered the city, after its submission. It would have been more dramatic if I had been standing in a tank's open hatchway. Again, if we'd brought any tanks. Instead, I made my driver slow the jeep down while I stood on the front seat, holding onto the windshield with one hand and waving with the other. We located some sympathetic residents to pose by the roadside, smiling and waving back at me.

Once we were based in Merida I found time to make inquiries about Birdsong. The crew of the second ship that had flown out with him to Rig 32 was fully debriefed on what they'd seen.

"Some sort of boobytrap, sir," the pilot affirmed. "The colonel touched down on the landing pad and it went up right away."

"What do you mean, 'went up'?"

"It looked like a carpet of shaped charges. Or maybe a dozen or twenty grenades wired up under the decking. We saw a ball of fire rise around the plane."

"And he couldn't have flown off?" I pressed. "Maybe on the other side, where you wouldn't have—"

"No sir," the pilot and copilot said at once.

"We stayed until the fire burned out," the pilot, a major named LaCroix, continued. "Took only about twenty seconds, sir. So I don't think his tanks ruptured. When it cleared, I could see the outline of the Colonel's ship sunk in among the tangle of support struts, on the derrick's main deck."

"Any signs of movement? Could they be . . . ?"

"We really couldn't see, General," the copilot put in.

"Excuse me, sir," LaCroix said, hesitating. "But what is this all about? I mean, why were we diverted to that drilling rig? What did you think we could accomplish?"

In any regular army those questions would have been a breach of discipline, and LaCroix knew it. Volunteer units, however, have different standards. Because my soldiers were half-mercenary, I had to lead them with a combination of trust and discipline. If I were to give orders they didn't understand or agree with, on the strength of my authority as their general and my experience as a soldier—and that last was admittedly pretty slender—then they might respond with either massive desertions or a mutiny. And in neither case would that congressional resolution with my name on it mean damn all. LaCroix deserved an answer.

"We had prisoners, taken in Progreso," I said, "who indicated that an expedition had sailed a few hours earlier to capture the oil fields. I wanted Colonel Birdsong to check it out, so that we could prepare a plan to stop them."

"You'll pardon me, sir," LaCroix said after absorbing this, "but it looks as if you fell for a trap. Those prisoners must have been lying. The people on that rig were definitely settled in, and they were a lot farther from Progreso, by sea, than a few hours."

"You may be right. We're lucky I didn't split the force further. As it is, we've lost both the oil fields and my second in command."

LaCroix only nodded. I dismissed them both.

I was set up in the former *alcalde*'s office. He had a corner suite in the admin buildings that overlooked the main plaza and was air conditioned like a meat locker. The windows were sealed shut with neoprene strips and actually sweated on the outside.

The square below me was quiet. Two of our three-ton trucks were parked along the south side. We had set up a sandbagged nest for two machine guns on the northeast corner, with a field of fire that covered four of the five streets entering the area. An ancient Mercedes 190D, painted a depressing aqua color, paraded up and down as Merida's only taxi. It was missing its back window.

The Communists would certainly try to come back from the bush. In an hour . . . a day . . . a week. We could only dig in so far, and then we had to be ready to fight for the capital all over again, from the inside.

How much the local people—the European-descended growers, their modern Mayan and Olmec peons, the Chinese traders, the state oil men—how much these various groups had supported the new Communist regime, or merely tolerated it, I did not know. How tightly organized it was, what kind of party discipline it maintained, I did not know. What kind of cracks might exist among its various bureaus and cadres, and between it and the tribal chiefs and village elders in the area—cracks into which I could insert my weedy toes and begin prying the whole fabric apart . . . Again I did not know.

The California 64th was a fighting unit. In the local people's lives, we were still the *gringo* from the north, the "them." We had only limited liaison with the village structure, just a few ears out along the main roads.

I called in my intelligence officer, Major Michael Alcott. He claimed to be a great-nephew at several removes from the American author Louisa May Alcott, and I had no reason to doubt it. He was a cheerful young man, with a plumpness that two months at Poway had not melted but only hardened.

"Yes, sir?" Alcott raised an eyebrow at me, which pulled the whole side of his face up in a smile. I wondered if he practiced that in front of a mirror.

"We need an approximation of the local situation. Not only where the insurgents are, but when they'll move, who their friends are, what their resources are."

"Already working on that now, General. They burned all their paper files and did a bulk erase on everything in their stationary cybers. Not unexpected. But what they forgot was, the BLX switches in the phone system keep internal billing records. We've got every call they made, who to and how long, for the past two months. We're dumping it all through a pattern-sampler program now. By this evening we should know who the friends are. That will begin to give you an idea of where the enemy has gone and what they have to work with."

"Excellent, Major. What have you got in the field?"

"I've sent our best Spanish-speakers out with good-will baskets. Hand tools, mostly, a few biolumes, how-to books, some familiar foods, and a few pickled delicacies for the village elders. Peace Corps stuff that's all appropriate to a rural setting with rudimentary power and data resources. Nothing political or cross cultural."

"What's their mission? Diplomatic?"

"Mostly. Show the local authority structure that we'll support them. That they can work with us. It's the standard beads-and-blanket number Columbus used."

"But no fast results."

"Afraid not, sir. If you want a semipermanent base here, the relationships will take time. Villagers' time. It would be different if we were just passing through."

"Of course." I kept him standing for a minute more. And after a pause: "Tell me, Major. What are your contacts like in the southwest, down near Campeche?"

Alcott's brows came together. "There's no GV unit assigned down there yet. Not that we've heard. Technically, you have a temporary charter that carries all the way to the Rio Candelaria."

"I know that. But what about an American Express office or a bank branch? And is anybody, um, 'passing through'?"

"I'll get you a name, sir. But it might help if I knew why."

"Somebody's pulling some cute tricks with the eastern oil fields—"

"I heard about Colonel Birdsong, sir. Very sad."

"Yes, well, I want confirmation. This end was clearly a setup, some kind of false trail. My guess is that anyone who knows anything hard is going to be in the south."

"Excuse me, sir, but what does 'confirmation' mean? Do you want the bodies back?"

"I want to know what happened, why, and who did it. You get me those answers, and we'll know more about what kind of war we're fighting. And yes, I want the bodies back."

"I'll get right on it, sir."

Alcott left, and within three hours he had a contact name and probable location: Tom Pollock, a major, heading up an intelligence battalion that had splintered off the 29th New York Volunteers, the Irish Rogues, working out of the State of Tabasco. Pollock was now based somewhere along the coast between Champoton and Campeche.

Pollock? Well, well . . . Probably just coincidence.

In a few days, when the situation seemed to be running itself, I mounted a small expedition to go find this Mr. Pollock. We had two Stompers loaded with assault troops as an escort, while Alcott and I rode in a command gunship. We flew south from Campeche, moving in interlocking squares that quartered the forest, searching for some kind of settlement or camp. It took us two days to cover the thirty miles between the two cities this way. At the end of the time, far in the south, we caught a flash of light, a reflection off metal, deep among the trees. There was barely room to set the planes down.

"Guns ready but safeties on," I gave the order. "These are friends."

We walked forward through the undergrowth, coming to a circle of barracks tents. A circle, not a double line or square, which was the military way we'd learned to pitch tents. It looked more like a native camp than a soldier's bivouac.

No one in sight. No guards. No cooks or orderlies. I was about to suggest we'd found an abandoned site, except Alcott was on one knee by a trash heap. He had his nose into a green-foil ration pack.

"Hard to say, with the preservatives," he said, "but I'd guess this was just opened. An hour—maybe two—old. They were still here this morning."

"Any idea who 'they' are?" I asked. "Is all this stuff American? Or do we see any—"

"Nothing Russian." Alcott's eyes were moving, always moving. "No baskets or blankets that look like the locals . . . Hello? What's this?"

He stood up and went to the corner ribbing on one of the tents. Tied there was something furry and black, like a big, short caterpillar or some kind of uncamouflaged jungle animal. A panther's black fur? He touched it, smoothed it, blew on the hair to test its depth and texture.

"It's a scalp."

Alcott was fascinated: He did not draw back his hand. One of the men turned away, making gurgling sounds. I could feel my jaw tighten of its own accord.

"General?"

It was the trooper who had been sick. We turned and found two dozen men standing beyond him, in the gap between two of the tents. They wore green fatigues, jungle boots, belts with pouches and knives. They looked like American soldiers, except for a week's beard growth. And there was something else, in the look of their eyes. A look that mixed deep fear and—and sexual excitement.

"Who are you?" That came from one slightly apart, a pace in front of the others. Their leader. His blouse had no insignia. He was tall, with curly brown hair and gleaming hazel eyes, but they had the same hooded look as his men's. That broad forehead, wide mouth—the family resemblance was ringing alarm bells inside my head. This could only be a brother of Gordon Pollock.

"We are the California Sixty-fourth Air Cavalry," I answered. "I'm Corbin, commanding."

That seemed to relax them—by about two percent.

"The Irish Rogues, New York. Major Pollock of the intelligence unit," the leader said. "What can we do for you boys?" He tried to make it sound both hearty and casual, but his mouth worked as if he was gagging on a fine hair.

"We need some information, Major, if you can give it."

He nodded. And his men began to spread out around the camp. However, they kept themselves between my men and the tents, effectively encircling us.

"I need to know," I went on, "what kind of activity you've got in the eastern end of the Bay of Campeche, in the oil fields. We're new in our sector and getting conflicting reports of infiltration."

"You could find that out in Campeche town, better than here. Pemex stages its operations from there, you know."

"We don't necessarily trust the Pemex organization, do we?"

"Oh, we trust them," he was nodding, slowly and judiciously. Then fast and eager. "On the oil business we trust them completely. Don't we, Lieutenant?" He turned to one of his men on the fringes, who was barely paying attention to our exchange.

"Sure, sir," he drawled. Flash of teeth. "Trust 'em with our peckers. For sure."

"See?" Pollock said. "You go to Pemex. They'll tell you all about the rigs."

When we landed, the wind had been from the west. I remembered that because we'd had to swing the Stompers into it for the landing. Then, while this strange verbal ballet was going on, the breeze had stopped. Now it picked up from the east, the direction Pollock and company had come from.

"Gah!" Alcott, beside me, suddenly choked. "What's that smell?"

It was sweeter than jungle rot, deeper than the dark earth. Every human nose can identify it, instinctively. This was the stench of a battlefield at every stage of its lingering life, from the first moment of quiet after the firing stops, to the long weeks of silence after the flies, the crows, and the buzzards have done their work. It was the ancient stench of the slaughterhouse, with old blood worked deep into the grout between the tiles and rotten there.

Pollock's men froze at Alcott's exclamation.

My men sniffed and then they froze, too. But their rifle barrels came up by millimeters, and I could hear the safeties go off, like crickets all over the camp.

"The smell?" Pollock asked, as if he had just noticed. "Oh, that! We were just down in the ravine. Butchering a cow. Messy business. But we like to live off the land. Real soldiering. Have to eat, you know."

I looked down at the empty ration pak near his boot. The rifle barrels came a tad higher.

"That's no fresh kill, Major," Alcott said.

"Well, we've had to kill two—no, three—cows since we came here. Been here a while."

Half of me wanted to take Pollock and his men at their word, smile and wave, and fly out of there. The other half wanted to know what the hell was going on. That half won.

"Let's take a look in your ravine, Mr. Pollock."

"You really don't have any authority here, General."

"Oh, but I do. All the way to the Candelaria River . . . Let's go."

I didn't have to tell my troops to follow. Instead, I had to signal three of them to stay behind and guard the camp. However, all of Pollock's men hung back.

The ground underfoot to the east was soft and the slope was gentle. The trees seemed to grow taller to compensate for the falling off of the land. The trunks became more widely spaced, the foliage higher and thinner. From the air we had noticed none of this. The ravine opened up like a great, columned hall. The misty light under the trees brightened. The smell got stronger.

We had passed the first tree that was not a tree before I recognized it for what it was. A smooth pole had been raised in the dirt. Hanging at about eye level was a dead leaf, or it was a piece of dried leather, or it was a mummified human foot. I looked up.

The top of the pole went straight up through the corpse's withered buttocks; its sharpened point emerged from the ribcage. The limbs hung slack and smooth from this center. The skull tipped far back; the neck's cords and vertebrae were so rotted that the head was about to drop like a ripe fruit.

In one breath, the ravine came into focus for me: ten, twenty, fifty, more of these horrible trees leapt out among the natural foliage. The early dead were on this side. Across the way the bodies became fresher and the smell even stronger.

"What the fuck is going on?" I said back in my throat.

"Prisoners, General. We had to—interrogate—prisoners. These natives are very stubborn. Indians, you know. Have some kind of code of silence. Or just too dumb to know when to talk. You have to do this to a few of them just to get the rest to look at you. It's really not a lot different from what—"

"Shut up, Major." I said that as gently as I could.

"Yes." He sounded relieved.

"Alcott."

"Sir?" His face was white, but his voice was steady.

"Special duty for you. Go to the other side and see if any of those poor people are still alive. If so—"

"We'll take them down, sir." He waved a squad of our men to follow him and trotted down through Pollock's awful forest.

I looked over at Pollock, who was leaning against one of the poles, as if it were a normal tree. As if he were an innocent bystander in the whole affair.

"This was pure sadism, not interrogation," I said.

"Oh, it was the only way."

"Nonsense, Major. Torture—pain—only work when you can offer the prisoner some hope that it will stop. There has to be some reason to talk. What could you offer these men?"

"A bullet."

I held his eyes for a long minute. "They will try you for this," I said finally. "And I hope they hang you."

"Who, General? Some court in New York? In California? Did you plan to take this up with some judiciary committee in Congress? Or do you think you could find a 'jury of my peers' in Mexico? No, that may not be so hard: Everyone in this country is a butcher. But just who has jurisdiction here, do you think? And who the hell cares?!"

"I do." And as I said it, I knew it was the truth.

Tom Pollock believed this rain forest existed in some other moral dimension, separated by the gap of a million miles from the society and values in the States. That the old rules did not apply here. And that, coming here, he had stripped off his human feeling, as well as his soldier's honor, as easily as kicking off his city shoes. A plastic man. The chameleon.

He would get away with it, too. Unless this crime was made a public example, which meant a media scandal, he would put on his shoes and walk out of here clean. Probably even a hero. Creating a venue for that scandal, and then selling it, was almost hopeless. All the Stateside politicians were orating their heads off about a morally just war to save our economically depressed brown brothers and sisters to the south. They were jingling on the theme of our brave, cleancut boys—of whom, with a shave and a haircut and a new pair of shoes, Tom Pollock was one. The effort to smear him would absorb time, money, ingenuity, gallons of newspaper ink, miles of videotape, and luck; it would return only a tiny burp of indifference.

There was a logistical problem as well. I had twenty troopers and two airplanes to take in Pollock and his squad, who outnumbered us, knew the countryside, and were clearly feeling ugly. If I yelled "Hands up!" he would whistle up his friends and, after a pitched battle, mount my survivors by their assholes on ten-foot poles alongside his Indian prisoners. Would Pollock's men follow him? Well, he didn't plant this forest with his own delicate hands, did he?

All these thoughts went through my mind while I stared into his half-crazy, white-showing eyes. And a final thought came to me, as if I could read it off his retinas: Were some of his men even now quietly gathering up their weapons and moving to disable my Stompers?

"Major Alcott!" I called.

"Sir?" came back across the ravine.

"Leave that crap and get your ass back here!"

Through the light of leaves, I could see him and his men turn and begin trotting back.

"Don't move, General." The point of Pollock's knife made itself felt in my ribs, three inches above my holstered side arm. He had about five pounds' pressure on it, enough to prick my skin through the military blouse. It hurt.

What happened then was instinct. My body turned to the right, toward the blade, narrowing the field of entry for a thrust. My move precipitated his, and he pushed hard up and in. I could feel the tip snag, cut my skin and the upper layer of fat, then break out. Pollock stumbled forward with the give, and there he was—off balance, with his blade caught up under my arm in the heavy cloth of my blouse. I brought my right forearm under, across, and up; that effectively pinned his knife hand against my biceps. Then I pivoted left, swinging my arm right at the same time and putting intense pressure against his elbow and shoulder joints. They gave with a hollow grating sound, preceded by Pollock's scream of pain. I ended that by pivoting right again, bringing my left fist up from the hip and into the side of his throat. He sagged. I unlocked his arm. He stumbled back and sat down. Then he fell over on his back, gasping and coughing blood.

Pollock's men stared in shock. One of them started to move toward me and I nailed him in the solar plexus with the heel of my boot. He doubled over and the second snap of that kick cracked the top of his skull. The rest of them backed off, hands wide at their sides to show they had no weapons.

"Trouble, sir?" Alcott asked, arriving with his squad on our side of the ravine.

"Put these men under guard. Then get on the radio and bring a force of at least company strength down from Merida. But tell Barrows to send no fewer than six officers of battalion rank or higher. Got that?"

"Yes sir!" Alcott saluted, then paused. "Why so topheavy with officers, sir?"

I pointed at Pollock. "We're going to try that son of a bitch and execute him right here."

Alcott nodded grimly and ran off.

Within ninety minutes, men and women of the 64th AirCav were mobbing the place. I wanted to retire to one of the tents to have the gash in my side dressed, but the smell in there drove me out. So I ordered a sergeant to unpack and set up a clean one.

Alcott at one point was conducting tours of the ravine. I think he enjoyed the green faces and sometimes unexpected "upheavals" the sight was causing among our delicate lads and lasses. By the time he was through, not one of them was able to see Pollock and his men as quite human. I had to make it an order before one of my officers, a Lieutenant Longacre, would volunteer to defend them at the court-martial.

"I can't do this, General," Longacre said when she took me aside. "All I want is to shoot these creeps. There's nothing anyone can say to defend them. This was just inhuman butchery."

"True. The last man to plant a forest like that was Vlad Tsepes, the Impaler, who was the historical antecedent for Count Dracula. Still, these men are U.S. soldiers. Someone has to at least say words over them—before we execute them. Just try to explain what happened."

"I'll do my best, sir."

"Sure you will."

We tried Tom Pollock and his men as a group, not singling him out as their leader or making a special case against him. Five of my majors and lieutenant-colonels sat as the court, along a log we had pulled up to the head of the ravine and cleaned off. The defendants squatted on the ground, their hands tied behind their backs, facing their judges. Between the squatters and the log, opposing counsels stood. Around this space the rest of my soldiers watched and waited.

Major Alcott spoke for the prosecution. He worked strictly from the evidence, his own personal survey of the dead in the ravine. He had counted the bodies, noted their condition in life and in death, and drawn the necessary conclusions.

"Four months," he told the court. "That's how long our medevac corpsman, Gregson, believes the oldest body has been hanging there. There can be no plea of temporary insanity here, because what act of desperation or rage goes on for four months? No, these soldiers systematically hunted, caught, and killed, in most barbarous fashion, every Mexican national and Indian who came near their camp.

"There can be no justification of war here, that they were, as claimed, carrying out some kind of interrogation of prisoners. What military secrets does a five-year-old baby girl hold? Who would mistake a man well into his seventies for a combatant?

"This was simple brutality. Done by men who have put themselves beyond the bounds of justice. For which you can never find . . ."

Et cetera. Et cetera. Alcott spoke for almost an hour, working himself up into a fine lather. I believe in civilian life he had studied for and practiced corporate law; he should have gone into criminal practice.

Longacre, as I expected, took the more emotional approach. She tried to describe the psychological state Pollock's men could have entered, stationed week after week in this gloomy coastal forest, surrounded by enemies speaking a strange language, losing touch with the realities of home and loved ones.

"I think the least this court could do," she said softly, without much conviction, "is send these men back to the States for psychiatric evaluation. Then, if they are fit to stand trial, they can be dealt with as humanely as possible."

Finally, Pollock was invited to speak for himself and his men. Kneeling on the ground, hands still tied, he rambled for twenty minutes trying to justify the torture of old women and babies to obtain military information. He dug his grave with his mouth.

The court voted unanimously for the death penalty. Then they stood up and stepped back over the log. A team that I had personally counted off moved in among the prisoners. Their rifles were switched to manual, for single-shot firing. They gave each of the men a bullet in the head. Some of the prisoners tried to scramble out of the circle on their knees, but the rest of my soldiers kicked them back. Tom Pollock was the third to die, and he never took his eyes off me—until the high-velocity bullet pushed them sideways out of his head.

A group of volunteers cut the corpses down from their poles. One hundred and six bodies were laid in a new mass grave, alongside the fresh kill of Pollock and his men. I wrote a short description of what had happened, signed it as military governor of the area, and sealed it in a plastic pouch that had once held fruit cocktail. That we put under the stones of a three-foot-high cairn to mark the spot. The impaling poles we left where my men had cut them down.

I tired to make contact in Champoton with whatever remnants Pollock had left of the civilian authorities. We had set up my headquarters in a tiny whitewashed hotel on the edge of the town square.

On the evening of the third day, an ancient panel truck drove into the square, drew up before the hotel veranda, and parked. It was painted dull gray, splashed with mud, and stained with the green juices of jungle travel. Clots of mud and dust obscured the windshield. In two seconds my men on guard duty surrounded it with their rifles leveled.

The driver's door opened and an Indian climbed down with his hands locked over his head. He was shaking it side to side, as if denying a string of terrible accusations. Slowly he moved through the soldiers and, when he reached a clear space, ran for the side streets.

Longacre, who was on duty that night, later said they opened the van cautiously. They half-expected a delayed mine to blow them all up. Inside, on simple canvas stretchers, they found three men in torn uniforms and white bandages. The unconscious bodies were hung with intravenous drips and webbed with restraining straps. It was Billy Birdsong and the two crewmen who had crashed with him on Rig 32.

There was no note, and never a communication since, to say why they had been returned. My guess is that there were hidden witnesses to that court-martial in the jungle. Somewhere deep in the collective native mind, some tide of opinion may have turned. But that's just a guess.

I had Billy and the other two flown out of the country, to a clinic in San Diego. They had bad burns and scars on their lungs. Recovery would take some months.

However, before Colonel Birdsong was fit to continue service with the unit, I had left Mexico myself. The Homeless Bastards of the California 64th AirCav stayed in Yucatan, under the active command of Michael Alcott, who had recently been promoted to lieutenant-colonel. Nominally, I was still in charge as general.

"Remember," I told him the night before I flew out of Merida in a transport, "you want to work among the village structure. Support the traditional headman or *jefe* whenever possible. Keep sowing doubts about the aims of the Communists, of course, but don't try to ram a free-market economy, two-party system, and all that *norteamericano* crap we brought with us down their throats."

"No, sir," Alcott said with a smile.

"If these people are going to take up American systems, they'll do it in their own time. In their own way. Your job is to keep them from flopping down toward the East, not make them over into good little Iowa corn farmers overnight."

"Yes, sir."

"Infiltrate the Communist cells where you can. In the deeper war, don't try to destroy them, but guide them. The opposition clearly serves some need among the people. Don't deny it, but use it where you can to shape your own ends."

"I think I told *you* that once, sir."

"What? Well, possibly. At least you understand what we're trying to do here."

"Building, sir."

"Exactly. Take local volunteers into the unit if you can. Make them auxiliaries, specialists. Train them. Don't just use them for runners, spies, and gun fodder. And pay them parity wages, minus our out-of-country stipends, of course."

"What about the local economy, sir?"

"I'll give you a blank check up to three hundred million. Put it where it will do the most good. Hospitals, schools, real Peace Corps stuff. But remember, too, that a starving sheep dog is a species of wolf. Keep the local *funcionarios* just a little fat for now."

He grinned at me.

"Oh, and I'll be sending a team of archeologists down."

"Archeologists? What for?"

"To see if they can put back together the ruins at Dzibilchaltun. There must be photographs and drawings in the States they can work from. I'll see what we can turn up."

"Good idea, sir."

Alcott and Birdsong ran the war in Yucatan—although we preferred to call it a pacification—for two years more.

They fought pitched battles at Tikax and Ticul. They helped another GV unit repel a Soviet-funded armada that sailed up the Caribbean side of the Peninsula from Livingston in Guatemala heading for Puerto Juarez in Quintana Roo. The rebels were fools to hug the coastline. Our people sank the lead vessels in the strait between Belize City and Turneffe Island with rockets, then picked off the stragglers with coordinated air and water attacks.

The most powerful sign was the large numbers of Mexicans, of both European and Indian background, who joined that fight. They said they didn't want to be ruled by the Guatemalans, anymore—they said under their breath—than by the *norteamericanos*.

At the end of those two years, our small corner of Mexico could feed itself. It was raising a crop of children who could read, write, and fight for themselves. And it was ready to hold civilian elections under a three-party system—the *Democratos*, *Republicanos*, and *Independientes*. By that time, the 64th Volunteers was half-Mexican and doing double duty as the *guardia civil*.

So, eventually, we had won the war. But the Mexicans, as we were to find, would do more to change the United States of America than we could do to change Mexico.

It's a push-me-pull-you universe.

Chapter 14

Granville James Corbin: Deaf Smith District

Carlotta Hurstford was not my ideal woman. However, after falling in love with the sweetly practical Anne and the practically insatiable Tracy—and divorcing them both—I was ready for a marriage on some other basis.

Carlotta's face and body were adequately attractive, I suppose. Today I can hardly recall what she looked like. She had gray eyes, I think, and dark-brown hair in great falls, with a streak of silver that she may have put in with chemicals. All irrelevant. It was her brain that interested me: She was wired like a computer.

Name a district or a State, and Carlotta could break down the voting pattern for almost any candidate or issue. Show her a loaded banquet hall, and she could count the contributions with a sweep of her eyes. Set her in the middle of scandal or crisis—with offers, deals, and dodges coming down on all sides—and she could thread a path of promises and quid-pros that would leave everyone owing us, and us with no commitments to speak of. Outline a piece of legislation to her over *daiquiris des modes*, and between sips she could reel out fiscal impacts, likely amendments, the final vote on it, and the ultimate date of enactment plus or minus five working days. Then she would go on to predict Supreme Court challenges and their outcome.

Carlotta cared very little about the issues. They were grist in her mill, not the mill itself. Like a good general, she viewed all personal or political stands purely on their tactical merits. She thought of them as stepping stones, stations from which she could advance or retreat. She was completely nonfanatical and almost nonpartisan.

Carlotta cared almost nothing about money. Her brain converted it automatically into media coverage and, from that, into votes.

And she cared absolutely nothing about security. It was static, boring, dead. Carlotta lived like Eliza, scrambling, tipping, sliding from ice floe to ice floe. But I never discovered whom she was running from—or where to.

We first met when I returned to the States and settled briefly in Vegas. There is something about that shallow, dusty valley between the black mountains, possessing no green grove, river, or other natural feature to focus it, with a city laid out like a bedouin camp and lit by a million light bulbs. Vegas was a human dynamo, running on dreams. A rich scent hung in the air, like yeast or human sweat. I planned to live there a while, tend my S.W.E.E.P. brokerage, and possibly run for the Nevada State Senate.

Why think about going into politics? I was forty-three years old and had tried everything else worth a man's time: making love, making money, and making war. I had become reasonably skilled at each of them. And now the wielding of power, by making law, seemed to be the next step. Besides, the mind scars from that disastrous San Francisco municipal campaign had just about faded.

"Get a campaign manager," one of my business friends said. "Running for dog catcher, let alone senator, will run you ragged. You'll spend so much time and energy projecting that boyish charm of yours and scoring points that you'll have nothing left over for plotting strategy and wheeling deals. Let alone details like meeting times, contributions and campaign accounting, plane tickets, meals and rooms, et cetera."

"Okay, how do I find a manager? You volunteering?"

He pulled his chin. "Somebody said Carlotta Hurstford is in town. Claim is, she's never lost an election. But even you probably couldn't afford her."

"Did this somebody say where she was staying?"

"Try the Crown."

It helped to be discreet in Vegas. I had my secretary make polite inquiries. The Crown's concierge agreed that a Miss Hurstford was in residence and had not discouraged the use of her name. We set up an appointment.

"Granny Corbin?" she said with that cool, imperious voice when I was invited up to her suite. The accent was stage English with a slight nasal twang. Maybe something western Canadian? "*Granny?* How did you get a handle like that?"

"It's Granville, actually."

"Distinguished. But useless. *Granny!* Do you have any other names?"

"James."

"James. James Corbin." I could see her tongue rolling it around. "Not Jim? Westerners can live with a Jim."

"Jim if you want. And I was Jay as a kid."

"Jim Corbin. Jay Corbin . . . We can work on it."

"Excuse me, but what's this—"

"Politics, am I right? You come to Carlotta for politics. And I have to presume that a man with your money, your background, Mr. Corbin, has ambitions. Not for a friend but for himself. Am I right?"

"You're right," I admitted.

"Carlotta is the best political talent you'll find in this country, sir," she said with a toothy grin. "And I don't work cheap."

"I'm sure we can negotiate—"

"Oh, we will. But there's just one non-negotiable condition."

"Which is?" I said drily.

"I'll stay with you as long as you win. You go rabbit on me, or get a case of scruples, and I split. Deal?"

"Whatever you said. Deal."

It turned out Carlotta was to stay with me a long time—as she counted time.

"What are you running for?" She settled on the couch, arranged her full skirt, and patted the cushion beside her for me.

"State Senate."

Carlotta made a face. "In this State?"

"Something wrong with Nevada?"

She looked around the room. I guessed she was spotting
likely places to hide bugs—which was futile, unless her
handbag carried a labful of electronics equipment. Later,
when we really began working together, it did. She
shrugged.

"No, of course not. It's beautifully managed. You talk to
the Gaming Commission, put in your name and resume,
and in about five years—if you measure up—you go on the
ticket. You get to stay in office as long as you like, until
you get tired of voting the line. . . . Simple and clean.
Like everything here. Including the rattlesnakes."

"What do you recommend, instead?"

"Go to Congress. It's smaller scope than in the old days,
when they were making gigabuck appropriations and setting social policy through taxes and entitlements. But the
fun is faster now. And you'd still be writing the law of the
land."

"Kind of a big first step, isn't it?"

"Well, you've already got something of a national
reputation, after executing Congressman Pollock's little
brother."

"That was a mistake, I guess."

"Oh, no!"

She jumped up and turned to face me.

"Your man Alcott got it all on tape—the corpses, the
shock on your troops' faces, then Pollock the Younger's
rambling, psychotic monologue. It caused a flap in Baltimore that's just now cooling down. Gordon Pollock had to
say publicly that his brother had gone crazy and probably
did deserve the death penalty. He just wishes you'd brought
the boy back to this country for trial."

"It was a proper military tribunal," I said stiffly. "And,
according to law, it was carried out in the State of Yucatan."

"Of course, and it left no loose ends, no jury to muck up
the law, no court of appeals, no clemency or paroles. It
was a solution every American could feel in his guts.
You're the biggest thing since Wyatt Earp."

"So, I should run for Congress from Nevada?"

"No. Only two House seats here and they're both taken."

"Why not run for the Senate?"

"It's a backwater. Old men's club. The action is in the House. Play it right and you might-could lunge for the big enchilada."

"Which is—?"

"The Speaker's gavel," she tossed casually. "Where else are you known? What's your power base?"

"I'm a native of California . . ."

"So is half of the West. The field's a little crowded."

"Then—"

"There *is* a back door. Known in the business, but not much outside. However, I'm not sure—" Carlotta narrowed her eyes at me, clearly making a decision. "What the hell," she said, "if you're not the one, you probably can't use it anyway."

"I don't understand."

"The districts in West Texas and the Panhandle have seen their populations decline steadily for almost twenty years—since the cotton crop died for lack of water and the rumors said it was atomic dusting. Now they're almost deserted, but they have never been reapportioned. In some circles, they're called the Armadillo vote. You can buy in fairly cheaply, and *no one* is looking over your shoulder."

"How do I—um—apply?"

"In Austin, with the electoral commission. Let's see, '13 is an off year, so you could try to run for a vacancy, if any. But it'll be November before you get squared away—a little late for anything to turn up this year. Or you could position yourself to run next year. The campaign season is abnormally short in Armadillo Land, so you'd have plenty of time to make your other contacts."

"Which are those?"

"Get you tied into the Baltimore circuit. Scout the committees you'll want to serve on. Get your hand into the lobbyists' pockets. That sort of thing."

"Then you'll manage me?" I finally asked.

"Are you kidding? I've been billing you for the last half hour. You're a natural, sweetheart."

So I went to Austin, got on the ticket—Democratic, for

old times' and Uncle Aaron's sake—and thirteen months later took my seat in the House of Representatives. It wasn't too different from booking an airline seat, with Carlotta as my travel agent.

By that time it was clear to her that she could go farther as Mrs. The Honorable James Corbin than as a behind-the-scenes field marshall in what was becoming, in a small way, the Corbin political machine. We were married in a simple ceremony at Annapolis. The honeymoon was a working session, I'm afraid, a fast tour of Yucatan to see how Alcott, Birdsong, and my Homeless Bastards were faring. Carlotta found Chichen-Itza by moonlight a place of sovereign romance. The north coast and Progreso she compared favorably to Cozumel. She was really trying hard.

While we were gone that summer of 2014, the first riffles of hot wind were blowing through the Old U.S. In Miami, a six-day running riot broke out. The videocasters dismissed it as another effect of the now-institutionalized drug trade: a spasm of indigestion when the local economy tried to swallow the gross domestic product of a small country. Yes, the Colombians and the Cuban exiles were involved. But no, trade rights weren't the issue.

The next cork to pop was Taos, New Mexico. Wealthy, artistic, settled Taos. It started with a car bombing—which was read as a terror technique instead of any attempt at assassination. Somebody was sending a hate message to Taos, and the city responded with vigilantes and guns. The countering move was with pipe bombs, grenades, and molotovs. And the party was on.

That same week Pasadena erupted. Not Watts or Venice, but *Pasadena*? Then Marina Del Mar.

Reading the papers—actual newsprint, in Spanish, with stories off the wire service in Merida—I kept looking for a linking cause, but nothing suggested itself. Carlotta, whose Spanish hadn't developed yet, got a trailing synopsis from me at breakfast. Her brow furrowed.

"Who are the leaders? Who's claiming responsibility for these disturbances? What are they demanding?"

"Nothing yet."

"That's really weird. You don't hold a riot until you know what you want."

"Maybe it's a natural phenomenon. The heat. The burden of poverty. Or the collective sense of injust—"

She was shaking her head at me.

"Hot, tired, poor people don't shoot up their own homes unless somebody is offering them something better. There has to be a payoff. Video coverage is the lever."

"Then it will all come clear in a couple of days, huh?"

"Ought to," Carlotta said.

We went back to our rolls and chocolate.

On our return to the Old States, it seemed as if we had brought half of Mexico with us. When we flew up to Baltimore that January, the town was overrun with Spanish-speaking brown people. Most were newly elected congressmen from Mexican States that, for the duration of the war, they dared not return to. And they had come north with their staffs, families, lobbyists, political backers, bank-rollers, chauffeurs, sideboys, and bodyguards.

Everywhere about town you could see signs of a language warp. Notices in Spanish pasted up alongside the English on billboards, city directories, storefronts, and buses. Inked translations on menus. Posted exchange rates for pesos. (Although the peso was now legal tender in the Old U.S. and accepted in most places, the rate fluctuated somewhere around 279,000 to the dollar. My wrist calc ran out of decimal places when I tried to convert the price of lunch.)

But physically it was still the old Baltimore: Fort McHenry on the Patapsco River; the National Aquarium and the frigate USS *Constellation* in the Inner Harbor; the music, shows, and games of the Power Plant; the broad streets around Federal Hill with their narrow brick townhouses—and their white marble steps, of course; the Florentine clock tower with "Bromo Seltzer" inscribed around its face; the restaurants of Little Italy and the sailors' bars of Fells Point; the mystery writer Edgar Allan Poe's house and the humorist H. L. Mencken's; the McCormick Tea House, with its spice scents still lingering.

You might think the Spanish-speaking newcomers would

have the courtesy to be amazed and abashed by all this history and heritage, or at least act like it. No, they and their ladies ran around the city speaking English or Spanish, whatever came to their tongues, sometimes a mixture of both. They paid the tab and made change in mixed dollars and pesos, which really confused the issue. If the locals didn't like it—and most didn't—then the Mexicans took their business elsewhere. Baltimore was being Miamized. There would be some scarring.

My first night in town, the Speaker's office sent a courtesy bouquet and orientation data pak up to my suite at The New Omni. It must have been confusion about my name and my district, which was so close to the border: the text of the greeting and the pak were in Spanish. I gave a laugh and read them anyway.

The laughing stopped when I realized what was going on. For any freshman congressman who had just arrived from what was essentially a foreign country, this message from the Speaker of the House would be the gospel on democratic institutions in America. After all, McCanlis was the Old Man of the U.S. Congress, father of the New Republicans, and de facto chief executive of the richest nation of the West.

His orientation pak, at least the Spanish version, read like something out of Banana Land. It was the monotheistic vision, with McCanlis as chief deity, pope, and political oracle. Separation of powers and the U.S. Constitution were lost in the murk of words. What came through very clearly was the NR—or *Nuevos Republicanos*—party line: support the Speaker in this time of crisis, protect the Federal cash flow, preserve peace and order. For statesmen who went to school under the *Partido Revolucionario Institucional*, the message would be both powerful and reassuring. It told them this foreign place was a lot like Old Mexico.

I grated my teeth, but what could I do? With his own brand of audacity McCanlis had once more outflanked everyone.

The first session of the 114th Congress in January 2015 was the now-traditional joint session with the Senate. Which meant the New House chamber was crowded asses to elbows, waiting for McCanlis to arrive. And with the heavy infusion of congressmen from Old Mexico, it had the flavor of a border-town rodeo.

The mixture of gringo and Spanish was jarring. Among the sober sharkskin and occasional polysatin suits of the congressmen from the East and the Midwest, the older Mexican politicians stood out in their immaculate white linen or their too-conservative charcoals, like pieces of sea shell and chunks of burned wood in the sand. They had the obdurate manners of Old Empire, smoking thin black *cigarillos* and, among the low murmur of voices, carrying on distracted monologues in Spanish with whomever was in earshot. It was the younger members, however, with a reputation for guerrilla politics to preserve, who added the real noise. They wore green fatigues, pistol belts (with the weapons removed at the door by the sergeant-at-arms), and boots that they hiked up on the desk, railing, chair back, or whatever was in front of them. If they disagreed with what they heard, they drowned it out by clapping their hands on their knees—in less decorous circumstances they probably rapped the table with a pistol butt—until the House chamber echoed like a football stadium. It was a circus.

And then there were the Mexican politicians who dressed like *norteamericanos*, spoke like *norteamericanos*, and thought like *norteamericanos*. They were the smooth ones, the ones we would have to watch out for.

At this opening session, however, I was wedged in between white linen and green duck, trying hard not to inhale the evil cigar smoke. Then I caught sight of a familiar face across the room.

The tall forehead was higher than I remembered, helped by a receding hairline. The pale hazel eyes shone like headlamps, and I fancied their beams would sweep up and lock on me like a truck zeroing in on a rabbit. The body seemed athletic as ever, although the waist had thickened.

He was in deep conversation with two senators, their little group ringed by aides and, even in this powerhouse, awed followers. While one of the senators with his back to me was be speaking, Gordon Pollock raised his eyes, looking right at me. There was no dividing instant between casual glance and recognition. He looked up as if he had been keeping an eye on me for hours. Those arched eyebrows raised a fraction. His head nodded minutely. Then the eyes returned to the senator.

I felt like a distant satellite receiving a high-speed, blip-squealed message from Earth. With a look and a nod, Pollock had said: "Hello, hello. It's been a long time. You're looking about as old as I expected. Do you still have your wagging tongue? Are you fit for a fight, boy? We are finally matched in an arena worthy of both of us. You killed my brother. I don't have but a second to spare for you now. I will destroy you later, at my leisure."

End of message and close the circuit.

I'm not telepathic, but this one time I could hear every word in that casual-cool voice. His hatred was beautifully masked, but it gleamed there like something rotten and phosphorous under his smile.

From the congressional directory, I knew Pollock was a ranker in the majority Republican party. He represented the New York district that included Nyack and most of Rockland County, the rich semifarming communities west of Tappan Zee on the Hudson. His unofficial position was third-assistant whip and shepherd to the new Mexican congressmen who had landed on his side of the aisle. As always, Pollock was a comer.

In the opening address, Speaker McCanlis tallied the problems facing the nation and the legislation that Congress would, in response, be proposing during this session.

First among the problems was the condition he quaintly called "unrest." Rioting had continued in the cities. It had gradually shifted and focused, ending up in the poorest pockets of the East and South as a free-floating phenomenon. Any big city, however, was likely to catch fire; Denver, Los Angeles, and Oakland in the West had all erupted in their turn. Military jurisdictions in Mexico had not stabilized either—although there the guerrillas vanished into the mountains and jungles, instead of across the tenement rooftops. Everyone still used automatic weapons and captured grenades.

McCanlis conjured words like "breakdown of civil and moral authority" and "unresolved racial tensions." But they were just smoke. Every skin color was represented in the vandal bands that washed through these cities. And the police forces and National Guard units—if they represented any kind of "moral authority"—were hardly broken down. They were better organized and equipped, with more firepower, than ever before.

No, the problem, as framed in the garbled *communiques* that had been issued by the loose-knit guerrilla associations, was a breakdown in popular expectations. The pay-as-you-go society was leaving larger and larger segments of its people behind. Not everyone is a capitalist entrepreneur. Not everyone wants more opportunities than assurances in his or her life. A lot of people can't even see straight enough to tie their shoelaces before 10 A.M.; so they resent the burdens placed on them by true economic freedom.

This long-simmering brew of want and envy had boiled over when the Mexican war began siphoning loose cash out of the economy. I knew well the extent of that drain, having personally funneled a billion or two off to support the Homeless Bastards in Yucatan and to build a few schools and hospitals along the way.

Compared to the free-for-all running fire fight in the cities, the nation's second, third, and fourth runner-up crises were minor league. Violence in the expanding drug trade. Collapse in key financial sectors as the government fine-tuned the prime interest rate. Soviet violations of air space, coastal oil fields, and fisheries. Et cetera. Mostly economic problems.

McCanlis spoke like a stage magician who has a single card up his sleeve and wants you to believe it's a flock of live doves. I could see that the man had outrun the limits of his power and imagination. The floor was hardly listening to him.

On coming to Baltimore, I had picked my committee assignments carefully. I tried to get on the International

Strategy Subcommittee. There, if anywhere, a successful general in the Gentlemen Volunteers could make use of his experiences and expertise. The old-line career politicians, however, had that bench all filled up. The Insurance Subcommittee of the House Banking and Finance Committee had been my second choice. I thought it would be fertile ground, representing an industry on the edge of ruin, and it was. Almost as an afterthought, I took the junior seat on the Urban Affairs Committee. And that, of course, was going to land me right in the middle of the cities' running fire fight during the next couple of months.

Early in my first term the Larkin-Redgren bill came up. It was approved out of International Strategy unanimously and went to the floor with a strong recommendation to pass from the majority Republican side. It was a measure to revoke the commissions of the Gentlemen Volunteers and withdraw all troops from Mexico, returning those States to independence as a nation. Larkin-Redgren was clearly an attempt to reverse the collapse of our cities, as the preamble admitted in stumbling prose.

Whoever cooked this one up must have parked his brains in the side lot: The text of the bill was issued in both English and Spanish, to accommodate all of our new members. The majority whip and all his elves, including Gordon Pollock, chased all over the floor, praising Larkin-Redgren to the skies, in both languages. The honorable members from Mexico nodded and puffed their cheroots. The bill crashed and burned on the first vote.

Urban Affairs had a selection of instruments for dealing with the national unrest, but our new members from south of the South had some very direct ideas. The abortive Mendez bill called for martial law, a 7 P.M. curfew, water cannon, and suspension of *habeas corpus*. There was one piece of legislation—a perennial, I was told—that proposed a separate Black Nation to be formed in, variously, Montana, Arizona (if the Indians didn't mind), and Rhode Island (if the Old Money didn't mind). It had to be a joke, right? Except that the authors, an estranged coalition of the Black Caucus and old States Rightists, were deadly serious. Nothing even resembling legislation that could pass constitutional scrutiny was sent out of our committee in my first term.

The rioting went on, picking up the pace of violence as the summer of 2015 heated up. The Old Man of the House, McCanlis, showed his age as he called on us repeatedly for some kind of action. With each speech his lion's mane was a shade whiter; the hand that gestured with the gavel shook more; the heavy baritone reached for a higher note and cracked on the vowels. The country was killing him before our eyes.

Finally, during an August heat wave that baked the pavements and muffled Baltimore and the East like a pillow, Speaker McCanlis resigned. But I wasn't in the House to hear his farewell speech. On a Thursday evening, after a late session of the Urban Affairs Committee, I was introduced to an urban affair of my own.

It was while driving back to Baltimore from the new Capitol Complex, which was northeast of the city proper and across the Patapsco Inlet from Fort McHenry. To live in, Carlotta and I had bought the old Commerce Exchange, on Commerce and Water Streets. Its simple brickwork, round-topped windows, and extra-high ceilings had appealed to me. The south-facing windows on the top floor looked down two blocks past the World Trade Center to a slice of the Inner Harbor. And the building could be made defensible. So we lived there and I commuted to the complex.

"Driving back to Baltimore" sounds like I was honking along at sixty, arm out the window with the top down, doesn't it? No, I was in the back seat of a plain blue GEM sedan, with my driver and burly boy in front. The car was special and didn't look it: armor plate under the plastic skin, bulletproof glass all around, tires filled with high-temp, ripstop jelly.

Out ahead somewhere, weaving through the traffic and watching for us, was a Harley motorcycle with a leather freak astride it. Leather freak had a radio in his ear and a mike on his larynx, talking to burly boy. He also carried a silenced 9mm and a handful of penades.

Somewhere behind us was a white van, Parker House

Rolls, with four more burlies, a .50 caliber recoilless on swivel jacks, and a collection of shoulder-mount rocket and grenade launchers, plus the heat they were carrying concealed. Slam on the brakes, and in three seconds they would be outside and making little ones out of big ones over a 200-yard radius.

They were all trusted men, special picks from the Homeless Bastards, trained in the desert and sharpened in Yucatan.

My own armaments? Well, the honorable representative from Deaf Smith District carried a pocket knife with a scissors and nail file on it. And my own hardened hands and feet.

This rig was our normal commuting convoy. The colors of the vehicles changed. Sometimes there were two motorcycles. For state occasions we laid on a helicopter with "TV-52 Sky Eye" markings. But reinforcement in depth was our formula.

Somebody had figured it out . . . or sold our secrets.

That Thursday evening the first hint of trouble we had was when Chickie, the cyclist, went off the air. Burly Amos in the front seat was still tapping his ear and whispering deep in his throat when we spotted Chickie. He was in the middle lane of the turnpike, under the rear wheels of a city bus that was flashing "Not in Service" on its route sign.

Both Amos and I swiveled to look out the rear window for Parker House. John, the driver, kept his eyes ahead and picked up speed by a fraction.

Parker House was closing the gap when a truckload of kraft paper, a flatbed trailer piled high with brown rolls four feet long and a hundred-odd pounds apiece, swerved. The strapping on those rolls came loose and the van disappeared under a pounding avalanche. I saw one side of it collapse before our guys slid over into the guardrail.

"What should I do, General?" John asked.

"Keep driving," Amos answered for me in a harsh, strained voice.

"Right," I affirmed.

Suddenly the highway was empty—of course, with all

that wreckage behind us, and our not slowing down to rubberneck. The driving was smooth and eerily quiet. Up ahead the sun was going down in our eyes.

"It could all be coincidence," John began. "I mean, the bus . . . Chickie always did take chances on that hog . . . and then the truck. They never check those—"

"Shut up, John," Amos grated.

"Don't think," I said soothingly, as Sensei Kan would have done. "Spread your senses. Look with your ears and listen with your eyes. Trust your guts. Be ready."

John drove on like an oiled machine. But I could see Amos' head going side to side like a frightened horse.

We didn't have to look far. Four cars, heavy-sprung oldstyles, closed in on us from the front, back, and sides, like white blood cells mobbing a germ.

They had bronzed privy-glass in the windows, which had been fashionable a few years earlier. So we couldn't look in, except through the windshield of the vehicle behind us. All we could tell was the faces were dark, maybe masked.

Our revised motorcade was slowing down. John tried once to ram the car in front, but hemmed in as we were, there was no room to fall back and get up decent speed. Next John nosed into its rear bumper and floored the accelerator. But the other car just snugged in and let us burn rubber. After a few seconds, John took his foot off it and let the inevitable happen.

Amos rolled down the window on his side and started to take aim at the driver in the car on our right. They rolled down both back and front windows and bracketed Amos's head with about six assorted rifle and pistol barrels. He put down his weapon and closed the window.

"Anything else we can try?" I asked.

John shrugged in answer.

Amos slumped.

"Then we sit back and see where we're going. If they wanted us dead, they would have rolled a grenade under the car two minutes ago."

"If they wanted *you* dead, you mean," Amos said quietly.

With that thought spoken, we stopped being a team and became three men in a sedan.

Where we were going was the waterfront district, east of Fells Point. Our car cluster took the offramp three abreast, which raised a lot of dust from the shoulder, and one of the outriders peeled off a NO LITTERING sign with its bumper. That didn't slow them.

When we got to the narrower surface streets, the formation slid into two ahead and two behind. John was ready to dodge down any likely side street, except our escort kept us moving so fast we probably would have flipped out and rolled. I ordered him to stay in line until they dropped the speed.

They never did.

The first *zing* of sniper fire peeled a strip of plastic off our hood. The second pocked the fender on the vehicle ahead of us. From a side street came a burst of automatic fire that must have chewed up number one's tires, possibly also its riders. The car swerved out of line and crashed into a mailbox, carrying it on into the closed grille of a storefront.

Evidently our escort was crossing enemy territory to get to wherever they were taking us.

Still moving at seventy miles an hour, we roared down a cul de sac and into the open drop-door of an abandoned warehouse. Loose planking thundered under our wheels, so I guessed we were on a wharf or pier over the river. That's when the car ahead hit the brakes. We all slid around in circles on the oil-soaked, dusty wood, smashing up fenders and doors pretty badly. A couple of tires blew before we ended up near the far wall, all upright, and pointing every which way.

Our escort recovered quickly. They were out of their cars with a dozen weapons leveled before we could get our restraint belts off and the sedan's doors open.

Even in the dim light, reddish with the setting sun, we could see the deception. They were supposed to look like black men, but it was makeup. I noted the pale flesh of their eyelids, the light color of their lips. They would only be taken for urban guerrillas from a distance.

"Drop weapons! Hands on heads!" one of them shouted.

Amos and John made a great show of letting the hardware slip from their fingers and clatter on the planking. We all cupped our skulls.

Poking with shotguns and pistols, the captors separated us. My bodyguard and driver were taken toward the still-open door and into the early evening. To be killed? To be paid off? I don't know. After the affair was over, we tried to trace them and got no leads at all. That works out either way, doesn't it?

But, as Amos said, it was me they wanted. The warehouse had an inside structure built along the river wall. It looked like an old wooden meat locker with four doors into it. Half a dozen men with weapons dead-centered on my stomach—they must have appreciated my skill at hand-to-hand combat—walked me over, through the one door that was standing open, and slammed it on me with a *thunk*.

It was absolutely black in there. The first impression that came to me was the faintly sweet smell of old, dried blood. Like a butcher shop on a Sunday.

As my eyes adjusted, I could see faint differences in the blackness. Gaps in the wood were letting in the evening glow and new fresh scents: water, sewage, tar, spices, and strangely enough—popcorn. Sooner or later the smell of my own sweat, urine, and shit would join them, then overpower them. If I was kept here in hard accommodations. Or if I stayed long enough.

As my senses adjusted, I began exploring with my fingertips. The door was faced with sheet metal. It had been scratched and gouged. Somewhere there would be, as required by law, a plunger to release the latches from inside. Were they that careless . . . ? No, here was a stump of iron rodding, sawed off recently by the feel and taste of it.

Door hinges were on the outside.

The interior of the locker seemed to be paneled in matchboard. I measured distances with my hand, then gave it a hard back blow with my elbow. Nothing gave. I explored the point of impact and could feel neither dent nor splinters. Nothing.

So it was oak or some other hardwood, backed by a solid subsurface. I had been hoping for pine backed by studs.

And where was the light coming from?

Ah, the ceiling of this locker had been ripped out. Above it, beyond the top of the locker structure, was a dead space between the inner and outer walls of the warehouse. Vents high in the outer wall were letting in enough of the evening light for my adjusted eyes and enough air that I wouldn't suffocate.

Jump, heave, and leg up. I could move around in the dead space, but I found there was nothing loose up there. The refrigeration machinery had long ago been stripped down to bulky bare frames and motor parts. There was no way into the other lockers.

I dropped down, deciding to take it slowly. I might be here a long time.

Chapter 15

Billy Birdsong: First Foray

I had taken three platoons east to clean up a guerrilla nest near Chichen-Itza. During a break in the fighting, my wing of Stompers had settled on the parklike grass that stretched between the crooked columns of the Temple of the Warriors and the stepped pyramid known as the Castle. With the green grass, the white stones, and a hot sun in the blue sky, it was a beautiful place—except for the random crack of sniper fire.

I was standing outside my command ship, jawing with a recon group, when the signals section from Merida broke in with a priority transmission. They said it was a call from the States, relayed through our satellite downlink, which over the months had grown pretty wobbly. So the voice quality was shot to begin with; it did not help that Carlotta sounded on the edge of tears, too. Incredible as that was to anybody who knew her.

"Colonel, can you hear me? Colonel? . . . Colonel?"

After ten seconds or so, I thumbed the mike and told her: "We are on open air here, Carlotta. It is polite for you to say 'over' so I can switch to transmit and answer."

That was a fuzzy old bit of radio protocol, as out of date as Samuel F. B. Morse himself, but with Carlotta Corbin I played by the numbers. Never cared much for her. Probably because she did not like soldiers, or Indians, or me,

219

and she showed it. I return the love they give me—my choice, right?

"Thank you, Colonel. Can you hear me now, over?"

"Five by. What can I do for you? Over."

"They've taken Gran."

Two, three, four . . . "Who has? And where have they taken him?"

"I don't know. Nobody will say. He just disappeared one night in Baltimore. And then we got a ransom note—with an ear in it."

That last part was broken up with what might be either her sobs or dropouts in the downlink. I would bet on the link. Carlotta felt about Gran the same way the owner of a winning horse feels. If she was sorry about the ear, it was because without it he was no good on video.

"Are you sure it was Gran's ear?"

"Well of course it was—! What do you mean?"

"Just that, a couple of hours after being cut off, you might not be able to tell your own ear from a dead baboon's. It could be anybody's ear. So stop having hysterics. . . . Over."

"I wasn't having hysterics."

Three, four . . . "How much was the ransom for?"

"Five—five hundred million."

"Can you raise it?"

"I don't think so. To get that kind of money out, Gran would have to sign a lot of paperwork. I don't have the power."

Good! Smart man, our Granny. Keep her hands off the big chunks. But to her I said: "All right. A demand that high—they are not going to deal anyway. Just stalling. We have to find out why. Over."

"What should I do?"

"Wait for me. I will come north with some tough friends. Where are you, Baltimore?"

"No, home in Vegas. Come quickly. I don't want to get another ear, or worse."

"On my way. Good-bye and clear."

"Good-bye."

Three, four . . . "Say 'clear,' Carlotta."

"Yes, that's—clear."

Close enough.

I left a captain in charge at Chichen-Itza and flew back to our base. First thing, I looked up Mike Alcott. He had just returned with a mixed company on a training exercise. His face and uniform were colored with sweat and red dust. I pulled him right out of the debriefing anyway, ducked us into an empty office, and explained Carlotta's call to him.

Mike whistled.

"You're actually thinking of taking half a battalion back to the States?"

"No, two platoons, and without air support." That was about seventy troops.

"Do you want to slow down and give that some thought?"

"What do you mean?"

"Title Twelve, for starters," he said, referring to a section of the Gentlemen Volunteers enabling legislation. "You can be court-martialed—not some pantomime in the bush by Gran, but the real thing, ordered by Congress—for 'maintaining an armed presence' north of the Rio Grande. We can travel to the States—the Old Fifty—as civilians. We can ship weapons, munitions, and supplies there under bond. But you go back with the ordnance in your hands, and they'll swing you. Those are standing orders, Billy. Gran's, too."

"I think we can get in and out unseen. Go the cocaine route through the bayous. Dressed in civvies and with the ordnance in crates. Once on dry land, we can buy a bus and head north. Or something."

"What about police involvement, during and after the action?"

"Then we just have to keep an 'armed distance' from everyone until Gran is safe."

"Planning to take passports, idents, anything?"

"I will think about that," I said. "Not having them kind of burns the bridges for everyone. . . . We end up as foreign terrorists, that way."

"Wouldn't it be simpler just to pay the ransom?"

"If that would get him back, yes. Personally, I think the ransom is just a stall. They want Corbin for another reason. Maybe to kill him. Or to brainwash him. No way to know until we get in there."

"What do you want me to do?"

"First, keep up the same level of activity here. Maybe increase it. So any audit team coming through has no reason to suspect part of the division is out of country.

"Second, loan me your best intelligence operative. Preferably one with a police detective or investigative background. It would help, also, if he knew the Baltimore area."

"I'll give you Randell," Alcott said. "Born there and spent three years on the police force—but uniform, not plainclothes. Does that count?"

"He any good?"

"She. Robbi Randell. Yeah, good as I've got."

"Then brief her while I pick the action teams and find some crates big enough for our 110-millimeter rockets."

"Anyone catch you with those, you're cooked for sure. What do you want 'em for?"

"We may have to blow a few doors."

The team prepared in secret and left Mexico by charter plane two days later. Taking a fishing boat across the Gulf and in through the bayou country would have been too slow. Instead we flew hard-ass in the world's oldest DC-10, which had been converted to long-distance freight hauling around the Caribbean sometime before the Nicaraguan War. The inside looked like a beer can that had been housing chickens. One engine would not stay in synch but warbled all over the scale like a drunken Paiute. Our pilot-owner, Poco Pete, insisted, "She fly good, no problem."

For the sake of Tampa Air Traffic Control, we were shown as miscellaneous cargo and machine parts out of Merida. For the sake of U.S. Customs, we developed "engine trouble" somewhere over South Carolina and made an "emergency landing" at the Calhoun County Airport. Four trailer trucks were waiting there, by prearrangement with Carlotta, to make a transfer—loading on real "general cargo," including maching parts, in exchange for men and materiel—before a flying squad from Customs could arrive and seal the plane.

We changed the trucks' markings and plates before crossing the county line.

Carlotta was waiting for us at a farmhouse she and Gran kept outside Loch Raven, Maryland. I bedded down our troops in the barn and then took Randell and my second in command in to see the lady.

Jumpy as a cat, Carlotta leaped off the sofa and came over to us. She was decked out in some kind of satin afternoon dress, like this was going to be a tea party. It occurs to me now: She must have been watching from the window as the men and weapons unloaded, gone to sit down—elegantly—for our entrance, and then been unable to hold the pose. She really was nervous.

"Have you found Gran yet?"

"Slow down, Carlotta. We just got here."

"But you brought soldiers."

"We need them no matter what we find," I said reasonably. "This is my second, Lieutenant Larry Stalk, who I think you met in Merida. And our intelligence expert, Corporal Randell."

"Charmed," Carlotta said at ten below.

Robbi Randell was petite, black, and tough as tarpaper. She was dressed for hard travel, in high-top motorcycle boots, pink denims with a grease smear across the seat, and a pearl-gray pullover sweater. Even wearing civvies, she walked like a soldier—or a cop. She took the three-fingered handshake Carlotta offered her and acted polite over it.

"Do you have the ransom note here?" Robbi asked. "And the ear?"

Carlotta looked startled for a second, then went to her desk. She took a folded and refolded piece of paper out of her handbag. From a bottom drawer she took a sealed plastic bag with a blackened scrap in it.

Randell accepted them both. She stared for two seconds

at the ear, set it aside, and focused her attention on the letter. She was quiet for several minutes.

"It would have been better," Randell said at last, "if you had kept the letter in the baggie and the ear in the open air. The paper's been so handled we'll never get finger-prints, and I can't even find a watermark or tell much about the fiber structure. It's definitely cellulose, not rag. And I'd guess it's sulfate process, but that's about all.

"Using word fragments out of newspapers is a corny old trick—easier to pull off when there were more papers and less screentext. The idea was to hide the sender's identity. But scraps like these give us a lot more clues to go on than just using a new impact printer would. If we had a dozen tireless clerks—or two months with just me—we could scan and trace the fragments through media from all over to find out when this was put together and where. I'll short-cut all that by guessing the *when* was after they took the general, the *where* is somewhere around Baltimore. Half this stuff looks like the *Sun's* print edition and adwork. But that doesn't necessarily mean they're holding him here. Be a lot better if we could lift prints from this."

"But where would we go to match them?" I asked. "We are not officially in this country. And we would have no legal standing if we were. . . . What about the ear?"

"It's definitely starting to rot," Randell said, "which makes identification harder."

She picked up the bag again and stared into it, kneading the scrap gently with her fingers.

"No doubt that it's a real ear, and not a piece of leather or some other skin. I can feel the cartilage. It's probably human—they're easier to find around here than, say, chimpanzees or baboons. If I had a gas chromatograph with me, I'd run some of this residual liquid through. Bet we'd find traces of embalming fluid."

"This is a dead person's ear?" I asked.

"Easiest kind to get. It's hard to find volunteers in your own cadre who'll give up an ear for authenticity. And if you go around maiming innocent bystanders, it gets into the media and spoils your story."

"But this ear is definitely *not* the General's?"

"No. His lobes are longer."

Carlotta let out a sigh. "Thank God for that!"

"So what do we know?" I asked the corporal.

"That General Corbin is probably not hurt," Randell said. "Though he may be dead. And they could be holding him anywhere in the country."

"Is that what you would do—take him out of the area?" I asked her. "Be difficult to buy a pair of plane tickets and march him down the jetway at gunpoint."

"Of course you could. Masquerade as a State's marshal with a prisoner. Or a doctor with a comatose patient. But look, speculating like this is useless. You want answers, you got to ask questions."

"Where do we start?"

Randell looked over at Carlotta, who seemed to be listening to other music. "When was the last time he was seen?"

"Thursday night. Leaving the New Rotunda. By car."

"Going where?"

"Our house, the Exchange, near the Inner Harbor."

"His aides agree with that?"

"Yes, of course."

"He have any favorite routes?"

Carlotta shook her head. "There aren't many ways to go, but Gran and his people used them all, in random rotation. They had a convoy system that's pretty complex because, riding with him, I've never spotted all the other vehicles."

"We can check out the accident reports for that night. Should give us a lead to the route. And we can see how they took out his escort."

"Check the reports where?" I asked. "With the police?"

"Look, Colonel." Randell rolled her eyes up and counted ten mentally. "These're public records. We go in under cover and make like civilians who have insurance claims on a fender bender."

"You might be recognized by old friends."

"So we send Stalk here. So relax, Colonel. . . . Now,

once we've idee'd the route, which is still going to be in the east end, we get down on the street and start talking to people. I know some of the juvie gangs in the area. They talk tough, but they think a bicycle chain is a deadly weapon. When we go in, they'll be sincerely impressed."

"And what will they tell us?"

"What they saw."

"Then what?"

"Then we take the next logical step. Detective work is a process of building knowledge, Colonel, not wild-ass theories. It takes time."

"According to that note we have three days, until Wednesday morning, to deliver half a gigabuck or they send us another piece of the General."

"Or a piece of somebody else. Don't worry. We'll go pretty far in that time."

Randell was right about almost everything. The accident reports showed a motorcycle and a bread truck in two closely timed incidents on the turnpike. Corbin's Stateside security man was able to confirm both vehicles. That gave us the route. One witness described to the police a tight huddle of cars banging fenders as they left the turnpike. That gave us the deviation from the route. Somebody else, from an apartment window, had heard the squeal of tires and seen the same five cars go by, down near the water. That gave us the probable location where the kidnappers went to ground. In the Vice Lords' territory.

She was wrong about the gangs, though.

"I don't recognize any of this," Randell whispered to me as we crept down an alley early on Tuesday evening. We had less than twelve hours until the kidnappers' next deadline.

It was just the two of us, Randell and me: a recon and negotiating team. But Stalk was flanking us with a squad of riflemen on either side, over the roofs, just in case.

In the shimmering heat, and with what little of the evening sun could penetrate the screen of storefronts and warehouses, we were reading the spray-painted walls beside us:

"Whisper Fish." Whatever that meant. It was in blue.

"Honkey Meat, US Govament Grade AA Choyce."

"Otha Govament."

"Outa Mexico, Outa Baltimo, Outa my Head."

"Slim 'n' Lady Dee make it Right Here."

A sting of jagged stars, exclamation points, and lighting bolts—like cartoon swearing. This was either a code or spray-paint doodling.

"PanTango Rules." That one was heavily crossed out in several colors.

"Put yo guns down!" This was sprayed in yellow with a silver border.

"The sign mean it, Fish," said a voice from a recessed doorway. This was followed by the muzzle of an old M-150, whose pronged flash suppressor looked like a spearpoint in the gloom.

Other gun barrels poked out of windows and doors, and around the corners ahead of us. I looked up at the roofline and saw three more pointing down at us from either side. There was not a bicycle chain in sight.

Randell and I laid our carbines on the cobblestones and I added my sidearm. Then we stood with hands loose at our sides.

The alley filled with young black men and women, all silent and staring. Their clothes were a patchwork of jeans and rainbow tee-shirts, but each had at least one piece of military apparel—fatigue blouse, web belt, beret, or jump boots. Like they were saving up for a complete set of uniforms and sharing the wealth until then.

Quickly they bound our hands and blindfolded us. Then they led us on a tour of the neighborhood, spinning us around corners, ducking us under real or imaginary doorways, slapping our shins to make us step over unfelt door sills. Twice they jammed us up against the wall, as if waiting for a patrol car to pass, then jerked us along. There were no police patrols in that area—Randell had checked.

Finally they led us into a large, echoing space and sat us down on crates. The air was hot as an oven, and I could feel my sweat sprouting immediately. The blindfolds came off with a snap and we were looking into a bank of klieg lights.

On the floor in front of us, bound hand and foot and gagged, lay Stalk and his riflemen. For a "juvie gang," these kids had made a clean sweep of my jungle veterans.

"What are you honku-racist-fascist-'cudas doing in *my* territory?" The voice was deep and mature. It came from behind the lights.

I gathered my spirt, my *chi* as Corbin had taught me, and set my voice deep to match this man's. "We are looking for a friend of ours, Congressman Corbin, who disappeared in this area."

"And you blame us?" Quick and sharp and proud.

"No. We *blame* no one. We only want to find him and take him home."

Ten seconds of silence, then: "The black woman beside you, is she your prisoner? Bait for us?"

"Corporal Randell is a soldier." I was about to add that she had fought for Corbin in Mexico, then I remembered the spray-painted slogans.

"A soldier! Another bottom fish of the white cesspool, hey lady?"

Randell curled up her face to say something, but I cut across her.

"We are hired mercenaries. We did not come for a fight, just to do our jobs and find the congressman."

"Do you think we'll help you?"

Ahh! "We have some operational funds . . ."

"So you can buy off the Revolution?"

"I hope we can buy information. If you are not holding the man for some political reason, perhaps you saw, or know of, others who are. It would be fair for us to pay for such knowledge."

Ten more seconds of silence.

"What good is money to us? We can get all we need."

"I can also negotiate for a certain amount of Congressman Corbin's good will and—um—support."

"Now what can a white blowfish politician do for me?"

"Well then . . ." I could feel the sweat coming down

beside my ears and along my upper lip. "We could leave you our weapons."

"Already got 'em, Red."

"These are just carbines. We have heavier stuff, grenade launchers and rockets, such things you cannot buy in a sporting goods store. We could forget them in a convenient place—when we have retaken the congressman."

Two seconds. "We could trade your living-and-breathing selves for those things."

"Trade with who? And what says they want *us* back?"

"Too true. All right, your weapons—them and a free pardon, signed in the guy's name, for any of the Vice Lords who might be caught in, like, an unjust 'cuda-police raid. Or something."

"I have Corbin's power of attorney," I agreed. "I can sign a blanket release right now." For what *that* might be worth, I added mentally.

"Then my chief scribe will just write it up." He laughed.

I did not see anyone move to start writing, but the lights were too bright to see much of anything.

"And about the gen—er—congressman?"

"Five cars went roaring through the projects about a week ago," he said simply.

"Last Thursday. We know that. What else."

"Nothing else. We shot at them. Hit the center car straight on. Bullet bounced."

"Where did they go?"

"West. To the river."

"And then?"

"Disappeared."

"What, with a flash of light and a puff of smoke?"

"Went into a warehouse."

"Any name on it?"

"You are a pushy bastard, ain't ya?"

"Part of my job. What name on the warehouse?"

"LaTiffe Fine Meats, used to be."

"He still there?"

"Ah now, Red! That's what you *don't* know, is it?"

"Did I tell you, the rockets we will be carrying are

110s? Blow the door right off a warehouse like that . . . Blow out a D-block wall . . . Put an armored car over on its side and across the street . . ."

Another deep, lively laugh came from behind the lights. "Yeah, I'm just a pantin' and a droolin', huh? Don't worry, Red, we'll get everything you got. So you might as well know. The crew that took him were white, but done up blackface, and for *that* shit we'll make an example of those fish ourselves. Want to play at Black politics and give us a bad name, they get the death sentence. We put the eye on that building. We see men, white men, come and go. But always in singles, always alone and looking around. . . . So you work it out for yourself."

"The congressman is still inside."

"Hey! You ain't half dumb."

"That's what we came to find out," I said, relaxing finally. "So, what happens now? I sign your release paper, you cut the lights, blindfold us, and take us out the way we came, right?"

"Yeah, sure, Red. All of you, except the girl. When we get the hard goods—and that pardon, signed on nice legal pa'chment by the man himself—we'll let her go."

I glanced at Randell. Her face was pinched, but she had the courage to nod at me.

"Deal," I said.

"Ain't no *deal*, Red. That's the way it *is*."

Twenty minutes later we were out on the street—with our carbines but minus our intelligence operative. It was full dark, sometime after nine o'clock, or 2100 hours.

I sent one of our comm men back to the vehicles to get a dozen sets of talkies and all the IR gear we were carrying. I also told him to patch us into the nearest voice-and-data lines, making a relay that would connect us with the rest of the force back at the farm. Then Stalk and I dug out our city maps and traced the nearest route to the waterfront and the LaTiffe warehouse.

It was difficult to get near the building. The neighborhood was so densely overbuilt that sidewalls leaned against each other, with not even slither space between. A network of alleys wound their way to almost anonymous panel doors.

We finally took up position in a recessed doorway, wide enough for a truck, a block and a half down the alley from the front of the warehouse.

Stalk wanted to go over the nearby roofs on a recon, and I approved it. He and a squad, all wearing running shoes instead of boots, put on the IR goggles, tachpads, and harness, and went up the walls across the alley.

The rest of the troop and I kept watch on the only entrance we had found to the LaTiffe building. The door next to us was a roll-up, and every couple of minutes one of my men would lean on it or bang it with an elbow. The boom and rattle this caused was making us all jumpy.

Twenty-two thirty hours.

"Talk to me, Larry," I whispered into the comm set.

A mouse-sized voice came through my earplug: "Getting the slope of the roofs now. Looks like our building goes right out over the river. It's wedged in on either side. So unless a door goes through into an adjoining warehouse, no exits there. Over the river is a half-dock and a cargo hatch. No boats tied up there. Anyone goes out that way, he's gonna swim."

"What about the roof line?"

"Row of cupola ventilators and some flat boxes that might be skylights. Do you want me to cross over and check them out?"

"No, keep off the LaTiffe roof for now. Tell your men to hold position and scan for movement."

"Copy that."

I went through the relay to talk to Jeanne Powers, my other lieutenant at the farm. I gave her directions to the warehouse, places to park our light trucks, and two assembly points for men and equipment.

"I want you rolling by 2330, Jeanne."

"We're going in tonight?" She seemed surprised.

"Half an hour before dawn. Unless we spot some major activity. Now, what are we missing?"

"Medevac?"

"We got three corpsmen. Have to do with them."

"If we rush that building," she said, "they may shoot the General before they start sending it our way." Powers was a smart soldier, thinking ahead.

"Suggestions?"

"We have some canisters of Null-B."

"Bring them. I know just where to use it."

"Anything else?"

"Put Carlotta to bed with a stick in her milk, and get down here by 0300 latest."

"I copy."

The rest of the troop who were with me, I sent back to the vehicles to sack out—and so they would stop thumping on that door. Meanwhile, a runner and I settled in to watch the LaTiffe main entrance.

Half an hour before dawn, everyone was in place except the rocket man who was going to blow the warehouse door.

I was getting really worried. We were supposed to be dealing with fairly professional outlaws. Slick enough to time a four-vehicle accident and snatch a U.S. congressman. Now they were supposed to be holed up in a perfectly blank building. My men had been clumping over nearby roofs and rattling roll-up doors all night, and still they had not yet run into a peeper, a sleeper, or a perimeter walker. I had a deep-gut feeling that, no matter what the senior Vice Lord believed, we were going to blow the front off a long-empty building.

At 0550 hours I signaled the rocket man to start setting up for a straight shoot down the alley. Then for Stalk to walk barefoot over the LaTiffe roof and start pumping Null-B down the ventilators.

That gas was the best thing that ever happened to crowd control. The old tear gas and mace were hysterical stuff: One whiff and everyone around you is choking, crying, screaming, vomiting. It stung. But if you did not get enough to knock you over, you had a powerful urge to *kill* the sonofabitch who was shooting it at you. Smart rioters learned to hold their breath, grab the gas grenade, and lob it back to the police.

Null-B was different: colorless, odorless, and strong

enough to work by skin contact alone. It went straight to the brain and scrambled the signals. Under its influence, most people simply went to sleep. The most violent cases became twitching paralytics, dizzy and disoriented. The effect lasted about twenty minutes, and I never heard of a healthy person either dying or suffering relapses from Null-B. Best of all, there was an antidote, administered by slapshot, which completely countered the effect. I made sure all of our people had taken it.

In other words, in five minutes we were going to blow the door just to see the fireworks. Behind it there would be no one to shoot at us.

"What do you hear, Larry?" I knew Stalk would have his ear to the ventilator.

"Nothing," he whispered over the comm set.

"Any light inside?"

"Yes, not much. Wait. Sounded like something—maybe metal—dropped on a plank floor. A couple of words. Half a shout. They're in there. Blow it in two minutes, Colonel."

"Okay. Make sure you got a squad covering the river door."

"Already have."

The LaTiffe door was another roll-up: horizontally hinged panels, two inches wide, and made out of forty-gauge steel. You could probably cut a man-sized hole in it with a torch in ten minutes.

Our rocket flew forty-five meters and went off with a great yellow flash. Like kicking in a venetian blind. Twisted pieces of metal came whickering back down the alley like Aussie boomerangs.

I suddenly got a sick feeling the same twisties were cutting up whoever was inside. Including, possibly, the General. Too late. We were already running toward that gaping archway.

Someone on the other side of that door still had enough coordination to begin firing an automatic rifle. Half a clip. At least three slugs caught Powers, beside me, and tossed her back on her ass.

I was number two through the door, saw the man—half

on his knees—swing the muzzle toward me, and put a bullet into his brain.

Everyone else in there was either down and twitching or down and dead from flying metal. I signaled the dozen or so of my people to begin tagging and bagging. Sent somebody back to help Powers, if they could. Then looked around for the General.

It was a desperately empty place. Bare wood floor with grease and other stains. Red brick walls going up to the rafters. A few buckets and some scrap lumber. A table stood small to one side with a cluster of chairs, probably where the guards ate and played cards.

No place to hide a man. Except, along the back wall, a row of heavy, old-style meat lockers. Four of them: three with simple safety latches and one with a padlock and chain.

"Bolt cutters!" I called. I gave up shooting at locks the first time I saw what a lead-splattered mess it made—and still had to cut the lock off with a torch.

Stalk was down from the roof and handling the cutters for me. "Powers is dead, sir," he said under his breath.

"Aw, shit! She was a good woman . . . A good soldier," I said. All the epitaph she would need from me. "Work the jaws more to the left. Take one side of a link at a time."

Cut through, the chain slithered to the plank flooring. I got three fingers behind the door latch and pulled hard.

Velvet blackness inside. Our flashlights drew zig-zags across the floor until we found a foot, a pantleg, and finally the General. He was lying on his side, twitching with the effects of the Null-B. But his eyes were aware.

I gave him a shot of the antidote. As fast as it got into his blood, his palsy stopped. He knew enough not to try sitting up right away.

Only then did I cautiously, half-fearfully shine the light on either side of his head. He still had both of his ears. Randell's analysis was the right one.

"Colonel Birdsong," Stalk said, one hand to his earplug still taking messages. "Perimeter reports hearing sirens. That rocket blast must have caught somebody's attention. We ought to dust off this place."

"Right. Are the prisoners loaded—dead ones, too?"

"Yes, sir."

"Then withdraw the perimeter. Crank up and move out by the numbers."

Stalk touched his throat and began giving orders.

"Gran, can you move your legs?" I asked.

"Sure . . . Have to."

With a surprising surge of energy he rolled to his knees, then rose straight up. I put an arm under his ribs and we stumbled out through the empty warehouse.

Our last three-ton truck had been brought down to the ruined door. Stalk climbed in back. I pushed Gran across the cab seat and climbed in after him. We were moving before my door slammed.

At the far end of the alley, ahead of us, a patrol car swung into view, its gumballs flashing. It was cruising down toward us.

Our driver licked the sweat off his lips. "What do I do, sir?"

"Keep moving."

He gunned the big diesel engine and the truck picked up speed. The police car did the same. The two cops inside it hunched forward and glared at us through the windshield. Neither vehicle was going to stop, and there was no room to turn aside.

Beside me, I felt Corbin start shivering. I looked over and saw his eyes, fixed on the squad car's revolving lights. A dribble of saliva was starting down from his mouth.

"Sir!" our driver called. "We're gonna—"

I threw an arm across Granny's chest and braced myself against the dashboard.

Our front bumper hit the forward front edge of the patrol car's hood and rolled it right back into the windshield. The glass crazed and sagged, hiding the cops' surprised faces. Our crankcase caught somewhere on their engine block, and our momentum pushed them, wheels spinning and screaming, back out onto the main street.

The police car was still pushing into us on little slicks of burning rubber when our driver switched gears, hauled the steering wheel around to the right, backed off a yard, switched again and drove to the left. Our big tires thumped the car's fender, and the vehicle spun around and drove itself into a brick wall. We tore off down the street.

I looked over at Gran. By this time his eyes had rolled back and the tendons were standing out around his jaw. He was halfway into a *grand mal*. I ripped off my shirt cuff, rolled it into a tight plug, and jammed it between his teeth. All I could do then was keep him from flopping around too much.

"Gee, what's wrong with the General?" the driver asked.

"Bad reaction to the Null-B, I guess."

"Never saw it do that before," he said doubtfully.

"Just drive, soldier."

Chapter 16

Granville James Corbin: S.X.

One of the advantages of paying for a good staff is they know which stories to tell under which circumstances. After my security team had verified me as missing that Thursday night, the Baltimore office told all callers that I was at the district office in West Texas. Our part-time secretary there told them I had been called away to an emergency in Vegas. And the home phone in Vegas said I was unavailable for comment, hinting at a bereavement.

Only Carlotta and my security chief knew about the kidnapping. If others on the payroll guessed, there was an incentive bonus for keeping their mouths closed.

After the dawn raid the following Wednesday, Colonel Birdsong and his troops drove back to the farm at Loch Raven by three different routes. They put the three live prisoners, thoroughly drugged by our unit corpsman, in the woodshed. When we wanted to talk with them, we could wake them up fast.

I told Birdsong to see that the two dead kidnappers were buried at least twenty miles away from the farm in opposite directions. Lieutenant Powers we put deep under the vegetable patch at noon with full military honors— against Billy's strong advice.

"What if they are watching the farm?"

"Who's watching?"

"Anybody could be—the Baltimore PD, the group that snatched you in the first place . . ."

"This property is not in the public knowledge," I said. "We've never entertained here, or even declared it in holdings. It's deeded to a third party."

"What if we were tailed? What if—two days, two months, two years from now—the Baltimore police come with a search warrant? How will you explain a woman with three machine-gun bullets in her?"

"I will take responsibility for the lieutenant."

"We could return her to Mexico with us."

"Not on the route you'll be taking, Billy. . . . Powers will have to rest here."

Birdsong flapped his arms in disgust, but he gave in.

Right after the funeral, Lieutenant Stalk took a farm truck loaded with the remaining weapons back into the city. In his pocket he had a blanket pardon, drafted in the most legal language I could summon, for "any and all members of the unchartered association operating generally under the name of The Vice Lords." There were fourteen whereases and six therefores. It was signed by a congressman with two USGV officers as witnesses. It might even stand up in court. The lieutenant was going to make the trade for Corporal Randell, who as our intelligence operative would lead in processing the prisoners.

That same day Carlotta went west to Vegas. There, she said, she would lie in the desert sun and try to recover from the shock. She no longer felt safe in the city, I knew, and what my soldiers planned to do at the farm disturbed her.

I returned to my seat in the House. To protect against a further attempt at kidnapping, we integrated about half of Birdsong's clandestine troop with my in-country—and quite legal—security force. Now, even as I walked across the marble floor of the New Rotunda, we had plainclothes watchers in the gallery. The weapons they carried were made of glass and plastic and nonaromatic chemicals that would pass the metal detectors and gas sniffers that guarded every entrance.

What a difference a week's absence made! It was clear

to anyone with a fresh set of eyes that the country was falling apart. Uncontrolled urban rioting, committees of vigilance roving in the countryside, roadblocks and militia units at the State borders—all added to the atmosphere of rising general panic.

During that week, Speaker McCanlis had resigned. The trailing candidate, Vorhees, a man handpicked by McCanlis and voted by the House to succeed him eighteen months ago, had now attempted to take the gavel and been shouted down—literally—from the floor. The business of the House hung suspended. Not only were the wild horses of civil disorder carrying the country away from them, the members could not agree on a strategy for dealing with the breakdown—nor even on a successor who might lead them to a strategy. The government was paralyzed by lack of options, and the howling depths of Hell followed on the unchosen alternatives.

In spite of all my staff's routine denials—and perhaps fed by them—the rumor on the House floor had linked my disappearance to the rioting. So, when I entered the chamber a week later, the 692 other representatives rose in a body to applaud me. It was spontaneous, I believe, and even heartfelt—but who could say?

The membership then returned to what the minority leader had termed "debate by the numbers." The roll was called and each member was allotted one hour to express his or her views on the succession. It had been going on for four days. Yankel of Delaware was just finishing up, having claimed an extra three minutes for the interruption occasioned by my entrance, and a linguistic and alphabetical squabble broke out over whether the District of Columbia or the *Distrito Federal* should speak next.

That took up most of the morning and allowed time for the real political business to take place—that is, hammering out the shape of the coalition that would finally rule the House and so the country.

Being the junior member from the tumbleweed constituency, I could only watch the huddles from the other side of the chamber. Someone sitting closer might have heard

my name mentioned more than once, for reasons I will
explain shortly.

While these overt and covert debates went forward in
the House, my intelligence team at the farm worked on
the prisoners we'd taken in the raid. If Randell and company had been given unlimited time and a hospital-sized
facilty—with a complete psychiatric panel, a well-stocked
pharmacopoeia, and full-sensory digital and tape imaging
equipment—they could have regressed and drained the
prisoners completely and painlessly. Unfortunately, they
were working under field conditions. Three days of non-
stop processing had uncovered only tantalizing fragments
and dream sketches. It also killed one of the prisoners and
destroyed the minds of the other two.

On the evening of the fourth day, the team reported to
me at our safe house, an antique brick townhouse on
Warren Avenue behind Federal Hill.

"The men were hired," Randell said. "From what I
could get, they were brought together for the snatch.
Never seen each other before."

"Backgrounds?" I prompted.

"New York area . . . It's a big place." She shrugged.

"Is that it? Any connections? Associations? Are they
from the drug circuit? The rebel groups? The old mobs?"

"Yeah, all of that, a real grab bag. One was a small-time
hood, did a little arson and insurance fraud. Another was a
freelance chemist in the methadyne trade. He couldn't
have been very good, though, to have taken a job like this.
The third one—he was strange."

"Half his stuff was in Russian," Birdsong said. The
colonel was standing outside our circle, at the window,
looking toward the lights of the distant Capitol Complex.

"What was he?" I asked. "An emigré?"

"We think he was MIS. He actually used the phrase
Ministerstvo Inostrannych Svedeniy—Ministry of Foreign
Information—or pieces of it, at least once. The rest is
babbles."

"Well, there must be something that ties them all together," I said. "Who hired them?"

"One name came up in each, um, interview," Birdsong said. "Pollock."

"Not Gordon!"

"No first name, but you guess."

"If it's him," from Randell, "he's got Soviet friends in low places."

"I have trouble believing that," I said. "Gordon may be a creep, but he's not a foreign agent."

"Here are the alternatives," Birdson said, turning from the window. "First, the Soviets are playing their own terror game inside the U.S. They probably are hip deep in the social reaction to what our armies are doing in Mexico. That makes you a target, primarily as a GV officer and secondarily as a Federal lawmaker. And the name Pollock is either a red herring—"

"You're excused for the pun," I said.

"—or a freak coincidence," Birdsong plowed on. "Second, the majority Republican party wants you out of the way and sent their third-choice errand boy, Pollock, to arrange it. Again you are a target because you are a power in Mexico, an important man in the U.S. Southwest, and, with your connection to Aaron Scoffield, a possible rallying point for the Democrats in Congress. That makes the Russian bully boy a coincidence.

"In either scenario, they—whoever—wanted you out of the action, and ultimately disposable, at a time of their choosing. Setting the ransom astronomically high was just a way of saying they had no plans for giving you back anytime soon."

"There's a third possibility," I said. "That Pollock was acting on his own against me. For spite. For vengeance. For his brother."

After a pause, Robbi Randell looked up. "Does it really matter who did what and why?"

"Well, of course . . ." from me.

"But you have to . . ." from Birdsong.

Then we went quiet and let her point sink in.

"Knowing all that doesn't help us decide what to do next," she continued. "If you could know for sure who was behind the attack, would you retaliate? Probably not. Would you trust anyone less—or more—than you do now? Again, no.

"General, you have a lot of enemies, always had them, and you know it. Up until two weeks ago, your security was equal to whatever they could throw. Now we've learned someone out there has thought of a new, more violent approach to taking you off the street. So we've changed the procedures and doubled the bodyguard. Tactically speaking, that's all you can do."

I looked from her to Birdsong. "Comments, Colonel?"

"Randell is probably right, sir . . . Gran. Still, I would watch my back around Gordon Pollock."

"I always do."

"What do you want us to do with the prisoners—whatever is left of them?"

"Make them disappear."

"And us—the rest of the troops?"

"Split up and make your way by different routes to Brownsville, in Texas," I said. "Cross the Border Strip by night into Matamoros. Tamaulipas is under protection of the 94th Nebraska, General Barton. I'll give you letters for Bart. He'll move you down to Tampico and get you a plane for the crossing to Merida. . . . Unless he decides that you've all volunteered to join up with him. In which case, *vaya con Dios, muchachos.*"

"Won't you come get us, sir?" Randell asked seriously.

"Be simpler if you just stole a transport, wouldn't it?"

She grinned at that. Birdsong laughed outright—for the first time in days. Then they said their goodnights and left. I would not see either of them again for three years.

The wrangling in Congress went on. At the center of it was the Speaker's gavel and rule of the nation. Which, to those most personally concerned, only coincidentally implied the responsibility for solving the rat's nest of civil, military, and social problems afflicting the nation.

The fight would have ended sooner if the party bosses who lusted after that gavel had not hated and feared each other more than any one of them wanted it for him- or herself. For every member of the House who had the political connections, the years in Baltimore, the favors

owed, and the secrets buried to qualify him or her for the
Speaker's chair, there was someone with equal weight to
block the nomination. It was a shoving match, with everyone intent on keeping the other guy out.

In this arena, those of us whose only attributes were
skill and knowledge, personal fortune, the backing of constituency, and standing in our home States—we counted
for nothing. This was an infight among the in-crowd.
Freshman congressman, cloakroom conspirators, and up-
and-comers like Gordon Pollock, me, and six hundred
others could only wait and watch, speculate, and resign
ourselves to the inevitable.

Finally the party bosses and old-line committee chairman reached a kind of truce. The shape of it was an
understanding that none of them would let any other of
them have the chair and the gavel. Instead, they might
agree to a timeout, a freeze frame while they discussed the
deeper game.

Let a dummy take the seat for the time being, they
decided, someone we can control impartially and remove without prejudice when our differences are finally
settled. . . . Someone? No, even a dummy might get ideas
and begin to exercise the shadow of power he thinks he
holds. Instead let us, they agreed, empower a committee
of dummies. Yes, and choose them carefully—for their
differences. Let them splash around in the shallow pool
and make a public mess, while we, their elders, work on a
more permanent solution.

So, behind closed doors and with the microphones turned
off, working only by verbal contract, they created the
Special Executive. I can trace the time to within days: It
must have been just before veiled references to "S.X."
began appearing in open conversation among the grownups and cognoscenti—to the confusion of the other six
hundred. A month after my return to the House, as the
gentle rains of September took on the first cold tang of
autumn, it was all hammered out.

All they had to do was pick the dummies.

They wanted a committee that would represent, oh so
democratically, all those qualities they cared nothing about:

geography, constituency, skill, knowledge, and personal reputation beyond the grounds of the Capitol.

Let there be one dummy from the East, they decided. Someone who could speak for the Rust Bowl, the Silicon Beltway, the Glass Hats of Hartford, and the Money Moguls of New York.

Take another dummy from the Sun Belt, the Energy Empire of the New West, the Fantoccini of Hollywood, the TENMAC States that were falling into the sticky goo that the cognos were beginning to dismiss as "the Mexican Adventure."

And add a third—three is a good number, isn't it? —from the Midwest, from the Oil Patch, Hogland, and the Granary which, in bad years, they deplored as the Dust Bowl.

By a series of cocktail interviews, feelings out, mysterious assurances, and pats on the back, the grownups began weaving their picked candidates, the three shiny new members of the Special Executive, into the fringes of the in-crowd.

Without warning, I suddenly found myself bumping into Gordon Pollock at committee room huddles, in the side aisles of the library, going into staff lunches, in the foyers. Each time, there would be an instant of recognition between us, a narrowing of eyes and lips, and then an instinctive drawing back. Like bringing two north magnetic poles together.

The other person who was suddenly at hand and under foot all around the Capitol was an elderly senator from Minnesota named Martin Luther Cawley. Twenty years he had served on the other side of the Rotunda and there was nothing to show for it—not a decent committee chairmanship, not a position in the party, not even a personal fortune. Cawley had the face of an old, saddle-broken camel, a voice like plain yogurt with a raspberry at the bottom of it, the deferential manners of a myopic old butler who cuts into the sherry twice in a morning.

A dummy.

I could recognize him for what he was. I just didn't recognize the similarity—which was clear in the eyes of the grownups—to Pollock and myself. We were too busy hating each other for past mistakes.

Finally a bipartisan press conference, hosted by the House leaders and the loyalists, announced the Special Executive as a "creative compromise in this historic moment of decision." The three dummies—Pollock, Cawley, and Corbin—were taken out of their boxes and propped up with references to virtues we never suspected we possessed.

Now why, you may ask, would the House, which had dominated the Federal government for a dozen years, include a senator in the new ruling body? Vulnerability. The vacuum that McCanls had left behind him was drawing attention and a few awkward questions from the other side of the building. Putting Cawley in the lineup was a subterfuge to muffle the gabby voices and tie back the grabby hands before they could latch onto any power—or any that was of real value.

About four o'clock on the day of that press conference, after the media crews had raced back to their studios to cut tape and write copy, after the new outsiders in the Congress and their staffers had gone off to soak each other in gin and speculation, there was a knock on the inner door of my office in the New Dirksen. Normally one of my clerks would receive and announce a visitor, but all of them had taken the afternoon off to celebrate. The office was empty. Even my security team was in the garage, four levels removed.

"Come in!"

Gordon Pollock moved in like a cat. His feet touched the carpet pile without thumping or scuffing. His clothes made no chafing or whisper around his limbs as he walked. He swung the walnut-paneled door shut like a bank vault's on jeweled bearings.

When he turned toward me, after latching the door silently, I could see the black stitch of concern on his face, drawing his eyebrows together and sewing up his mouth into a thin, sour line. The Apollonian young man, with his easy smile and his superior eyes, had been temporarily put away.

It struck me that this was the first time Pollock and I had met privately, not surrounded by other faces, the murmur of other voices, in all our long association.

"Well," I began, brightly, "one third of the nation's new power base has come to pay a call."

He stood over my desk, and I saw a panorama of expressions cross his face: contempt, betrayal, fear, anger, and finally contempt again.

"You are many things I despise," he said slowly, "but I try hard not to think of you as a fool."

"Should I be flattered?"

"Can we talk honestly?"

"Probably not . . ."

"You don't really believe we have been given the gavel, do you? Absolute executive authority—to us?"

"That's how it will look on the tapes. That's what they will believe on Main Street tonight."

"But really—in the reality that you and I know—?"

I knew what he was driving at. It *was* time for honesty. "Depends on what strings they have on you," I said.

"And on you," he shot back.

"No strings. No promises. No secret understandings. I was completely surprised by what happened today."

"Completely?"

"Well . . . After six weeks of whispers and closed-door sessions and rustlings in the bushes, then everything went quiet. Even the janitors knew *something* was about to happen."

"Yes, but you didn't know—?"

"Before this morning—?"

"That you would be—?"

"Jointly with *you*—?"

"Named to this Special Executive?" he finished the question.

"No."

"Neither did I."

"What do you know about this Cawley?"

"He's a zero. Not even a member of the chorus."

"What does that make us?"

A look of pain crossed Pollock's face. He was truly

offended—not by my question, but by its implications. "They don't think enough of us even to buy us off first."

"And how long does that give us?"

"But I was a whip!" he said, cutting right across my question. "I was part of their organization."

"Evidently not a very important part."

"That's easy for you to say, Corbin. You hadn't even *begun* paying your dues."

"Can you hear us? This is exactly what they want. We're cutting each other to pieces before the sun is even down."

"What do you mean?"

"We are just a holding pattern for them. Not meant to hold together very long, either. We're supposed to spend our time figuring ways to fuck each other over in public while they, in private, work out who's going to grab the power McCanlis let drop. I repeat my question: How long do we have?"

In Pollock's face I could see the awareness focusing in and shifting to a higher plane.

"How secure is this room?"

I laughed. "I've got four white-noise generators and an radio interfrequency scrambler running right now. The window surfaces are vibration-damped to mask any modulation from our voices, and distorted to discourage telescope-toting lip readers. The subframes in these walls are fitted with random vibrators, also to mask voice modulation. Once a week my people—the ones I trust completely—burn every exposed surface here with hard gamma. I have taps and warblers, activated on a voltage drop, on every wire and pipe going into this wing of the building. If anyone knows what we're saying, they're using Tarot cards."

Pollock almost looked impressed.

"We can have all the time we want," he said, "if we act right away."

"If we tried anything serious, they would block us in committee, wouldn't they?"

"Pick the two top contenders," he said.

"Akers of Georgia and Walton of California."

"Good choices." He did look impressed. "We'll have them killed."

"How do you plan to arrange that? I mean, cleanly?"

"Those people you trust . . ."

"They're just security forces, soldiers, not Mafia bullies—"
I waited a two-count then added, "—or MIS assassins."

"Then we do it politically," he sailed on, missing my
jibe.

"How?"

And he told me.

Two days later, standing together at the Speaker's Rostrum, Pollock and I heard Triss of Arizona, a very junior
congresswoman and another certified dummy, prefer charges
of espionage and treason against Akers and Walton. The
substance of the charges was that as chairman and ranking
minority member, respectively, of the International Strategy Subcommittee, they had sold maps linking the locations of ballistic missile silos with radio abort codes. The
deal was supposedly made with the Soviets through contacts in Baja. Ms. Triss produced consular documents forwarding the papers and naming their sources.

Were the documents genuine? Certainly the letterhead
and language were. So, incidentally, were the abort
codes—as of about nine months previously. Did it matter?

The affair might have ended right there, with the disgrace, if not the actual impeachment, of Messrs. Akers and
Walton. The score would then have been Dummies two,
Elders nothing. But we wanted more.

The specifications that Triss filed also contained twenty-five John Does and twenty-five Jane Does, listed variously
as accomplices and informants. We didn't have to advertise them, just let the fact be known—and hint that the
Does were all congressmen and -women—as the House
assembled an investigative committee. We made sure that
panel was packed with our fellow Dummies. Meanwhile,
other Dummies led the speculation on who might fill
those fifty pairs of shoes we'd put on display.

You've seen those action-adventure movies where the
hero is suspended over the side of a boat, or maybe over a
swimming pool, with a dozen triangular fins circling and
criss-crossing beneath his toes. To get out of the jam, he
pricks his finger and lets two drops of blood fall. That

excites the sharks into a feeding frenzy. The water boils, the foam turns pink, and soon there are no more sharks.

The sharks were thick where we were swimming. All we had to do was nick the two of them, Akers and Walton. Because Ms. Triss was recognized by all players as a Dummy, the other contenders took her charges as the signal for the grand melee to begin. Assertions and defamations flew around our heads, with the occasional crash and clatter of an actual resignation or recall vote. And, because we were supposed to be Dummies, too, Pollock and I were never touched. Within two months, all of the Elders were bloodied beyond redemption. There was a new order in the House, and the Special Executive's *prima facie* standing was accepted as real.

Finally, because the House investigating committee never actually called for an impeachment, the original evidence of espionage was never examined in any rigorous way. It disappeared soon after.

Pollock had arranged the whole charade. Now *I* was impressed.

It was about this time, and no doubt related to my sudden prominence, that my sister sent her son to me. Clary and I had drifted apart over the years. She had married badly—a burned-out computer software wizard named Ossing—but divorced well; before it was over, she had produced this one boy. I think the responsibility frightened her. Keeping a pile of cash intact through the Money Warp of the '90s was an impossible task. Raising a child in any American village big enough to support a closet-sized pot farm and a pusher was another impossible task. Clary understood that, if she stayed, she was going to lose one or the other. So she went.

She used her settlement to buy 900 acres of dairy farm along the Salmon River outside Truro in Nova Scotia. If she wouldn't lose the boy to corruption, she would lose him to yokeldom. I think he knew no books or music but what she had brought with her, and Clary had a rampaging taste for detective mysteries of all vintages and the *Jefferson Starship* as the rhythmic emblem of a childhood she never had in the 1980s. Gabriel Ossing grew up knowing other children by rumor only, and from a few withering mentions out of Dashiell Hammett. I'm told he had many fights when he finally was sent to the county school at Bible Hill. The boy was quiet and strange.

After he finished high school, and before starting a college course in law or medicine, Clary wanted him to see something of the world. Becoming a congressional page would broaden him, she thought, and with my new position of power I could arrange it immediately.

So now Gabriel stood before me in Baltimore, having been brought up to our top-floor living quarters in the Commerce Exchange by the doorman, who was also on my security payroll and claimed he saw a resemblance right away. The boy was tall and big in the shoulders, pushing out of the sleeves of his wool-tweed jacket and the cuffs of his gabardine pants. Both had frayed spots with the ticks of darning across them. His shoes were heavy and square, like something out of *Ulysses* or the Irish bogs.

His face was unmoving as an old dog's, but his eyes followed me quickly enough across the room, as I hunted in my Empire desk and various cupboards for the letters he had said his mother had sent. The eyes followed me— that is, when they weren't tracking Carlotta, who was deep in an electric book and not really aware of us.

"Are you sure she sent them here?" I finally asked. "Clary hasn't been heard from for ten or a dozen years. And you don't have any paper from her, do you?"

"No. She said you would know me . . . Uncle Jim." He said *that* as if trying it out for size. I was "Jay" to Clary then and "Gran" to my intimates now; where or whom would he have gotten *Jim* from?

"Well, no matter. The letter's gone—if it ever was." I dimly remembered letters about him, from sometime in the recent past. And the rural delivery services occasionally lost personal correspondence, especially from a backwater like the Maritimes.

"Do you *want* to be a page?"

"If that's what Mother wants," he said this in a neutral voice.

"It's a tough school, I'm told. Not the loving family you're used to, nor the polite society you might imagine Baltimore to be. The page system has other knives than steel ones to torture you with, if you're slow-witted there, and I won't be able to defend you. That's the first thing they will look for and the last they'll get."

"I understand." Spoken like a soldier about to go on a suicide mission.

"Then I'll see what I can do. Do you have a place to stay?"

"No, I just came from the shuttle depot."

Carlotta, who had heard more than I thought, looked up and said, "Front room, Gran."

"Of course," I answered quickly, "you can stay with us until you get on your feet and move in with new friends of your own."

He nodded once and flapped his arms in a kind of vestigial bow. Then Carlotta took him off to find someone from the upstairs staff who could make up the bed for him. All things considered, she was smooth at acting motherly.

I suppose at one time the congressional pages existed to do actual work for the representatives and senators, like little butlers or clerks, before electronics and automata took over those duties. And at one period the page system was a breeding ground for democratic idealists: Children with good marks in school, vaguely political ambitions, and good political connections could see the workings of government in action. But by 2015 that was pretty much a dream of the past.

Pages were the substructure of our political system. Like Fagin, each congressman sent his little spies to listen and learn and report back all they heard. In the hallways, public lavatories, and cloakrooms, these children—some of them arrested teenagers in their thirties—operated an intelligence market where rumors and facts were sold like hog futures. Some truths had the ring of pure gold, others the clank of brass. A quick-witted child would try out a piece of intelligence, testing the waters for his or her master, before the item would be spoken aloud by the grownups in their offices.

To give you just one example, the page circuit had been a-twitter with the rumor of a proposal for the Special Executive—and my name, among others, had floated on it—at least ten days before the act that made Pollock and Cawley and I.

Few congressmen loved, and not every one even tolerated, the pages. "Poison-toads" was the name that stuck with them for as long as I was in government. The new representatives from Mexico picked up the flavor of that and called them *los escorpiónes*.

It was a hard mother who would willingly send her son into that life. But Clary was a realist. If Gabe could survive there, he would prosper anywhere. However, I doubted this boy with the cow dung still showing in the cracks of his shoes would survive.

Admittedly, the idea of having a blood relation on the circuit intrigued me. For one thing, he'd be a perfect tool for disinformation. For another, I could pick over his brain to learn both what he was sure to hear and what he was sure *not* to but which could be read from the stub ends of other conversations.

Oh yes, I've sent spies into dangerous territory before. And lost a few, too.

Chapter 17

Granville James Corbin: Impeachment in the House

Pollock, Cawley, and I managed to hold the Special Executive together for almost three years. How we did it would make a study in social dynamics: We feared and distrusted the rest of Congress and all of the country more than we feared and distrusted each other. Like the forces working on the nucleus of an atom or at the core of a sun, the energies pushing the center inward balanced those trying to pull it apart.

But don't think the process was stable or static. If we were an atom, it was more fragile than uranium. If we were a sun, it was a wildly pulsing variable star.

"If that ninny proposes his inventory of aquifers one more time, I will strangle him with his own lolling tongue."

Pollock said this calmly, even judiciously. But I could tell he was furious: We were at lunch and he was buttering a piece of bread as he spoke, working the grease well into the knuckle of his thumb. The ninny, of course, was Senator Cawley, our third—and most often absent— member.

Pollock was kidding about the strangling. Sudden and unexplained disappearances were rumored to be his specialty.

"Well . . ." Here I was, taking Cawley's side just to keep us in balance. "He does have a lot of support from the Farm Belt, and they're drawing brine as far north as

253

254 *Thomas T. Thomas*

254 *Thomas T. Thomas*

Missouri, you know. The latest report on Lake Superior shows the pH drifting below 5.5. If water isn't a problem this year, it will be in another ten."

"Then it will be someone else's problem—certainly not Cawley's, because he will be long dead by then."

I raised my hands, let them settle to the tablecloth. "Hear him out, for a change. What can one study cost?"

"It's not the study, it's the conclusions he's pushing for. You know the horse he's riding—a freshwater economy to replace the energy matrix we've built. Cawley wants a string of solar generators driving water crackers and pumping plants that will feed a nationwide network of pipelines. 'Fuel free and fresh,' he chants. Yes, and at a cost of something over two terabucks. I say, let the farmers bid for wastewater as they always have. It's a natural check on the grain market."

I kept quiet at that point and concentrated on picking the chickpeas out of my salad.

The Federal government could certainly afford Cawley's water scheme, especially if it were amortized over twenty or thirty years. Hallowed Hell, the take on Mississippi tariffs alone was at least a quarter of a trillion dollars a year. But Pollock's last argument was the real one with him: A nationwide water system would upset other markets and ripple through the whole economy. It worried Pollock—me too, to tell the truth—not knowing who would profit and who would lose in the shakeout. And government is the art of deciding whose pocket gets picked, whose gets fluffed.

As the Special Executive found its equilibrium in those first months, this became our *modus vivendi*: One to make a proposal and the other two to stamp on it—a natural system of checks and balances. The only area that united us early in our career of government was the general rebellion.

Up until now, policies for dealing with the problem had been decided on a local level. Police forces had tried to contain the insurrection in the cities with the techniques of crowd control. They were opposing automatic weapons and mortars with rubber bullets and fire hoses. That's because the nation's political philosophy, patched together during half a century of civil rights marches and usually nonviolent protest, dictated that the police protect the civil rights of armed guerrillas as much as those of bystanders. By now the police were losing badly.

We took the text of our own response from a series of isolated incidents occurring in the late '80s of the last century.

In one case, a group of political activists—evidently sympathizers with the struggles of an African country named Simbio—had been tracked by the FBI to a small house in the Los Angeles suburbs. The group was "armed and dangerous": Over the preceding two years they had kidnapped a newspaper heiress and involved her in several bank robberies. In the final action, Federal agents and local police blockaded the house and provoked a shootout, during the course of which the building caught fire. They made no attempt to put the fire out because, the police said, the outlaws inside the burning house were still shooting at them.

A later incident, in Philadelphia, expanded on this example. The police were trying to evict a radical political group, which formed some kind of guerrilla community, or an extended family complete with small children, from the tenement they were occupying. When a police helicopter dropped a dynamite bomb on the roof to discourage a sniper's nest there, the roof started burning. The fire department claimed it could not fight the blaze properly because of shooting from that same rooftop. A whole neighborhood was burned out.

Clearly, those in authority were free to use massive force so long as the people on the receiving end could be shown as the vicious and stubborn sort who preferred burning to death instead of surrendering. Of course, nothing was mentioned—in the police reports we could find, anyway—about the conditions into which the outlaws might have surrendered. One can realistically assume the choices were burn or get shot in the crossfire.

The point remains: So long as we maintained the appearance of options, and publicly regretted the consequences, we could eradicate the insurrection with a minimum of political fallout. The American public does not really love a martyr.

Pollock and Cawley were all for issuing tactical nukes and a fill-in-the-blanks news release to the local PD. Then they would stand back and wring their hands.

I argued for a measure of subtlety. We should pick our targets for maximum lesson value, I said. Give the greater number of guerrillas a chance to lay aside their weapons and fade away. The words "surgical strike" even found their way into my argument.

Cawley pursed his lips like he'd bitten into a lemon.

"You think we're going to make *con*verts, Granny?"

"Ah, no . . . But what you and Gordon are heading for is a slaughter. That's a strategy for cattle. We're dealing with people—supposedly the same ones this country is governed of, by, and for. If we can set an example with the hardest cases, the fellow travelers won't stay to test it."

"But you're missing the whole point," Pollock said impatiently. "Our aim has to be elimination. Total suppression. We're removing garbage—a business I think you have some familiarity with? You don't clean up a city by letting the little scraps go with a stiff lesson, do you? We will, of course, *seem* to be offering them surrender and amnesty, but we cannot have anyone 'running away to fight again another day.' We don't want to stop the riots; we want to win the country back."

"Too right!" Cawley crowed.

So, in the end, I was overruled. Checks and balances, again.

By emergency order, Congress created auxiliary units of the Gentlemen Volunteers with a charter for operations *inside* the country. It was a total break with precedent. Further, these units had no State affiliation or support; they were called simply "Federals." It had an unpleasant ring to modern ears.

Praising my exploits in Mexico, Pollock and Cawley offered me command of them. I declined, explaining that it was illegal for a general in the GVs to accept a commission with more than one division at a time. This actually was the law, although most patron-generals were ignoring it by now.

However, Pollock and Cawley accepted this argument and gave the appointment to a Pentagon planner named Willoughby. He was a programmer by training and a poodle by disposition. You have to work with what you've got.

The new units were techincally airmobile infantry, but for urban operations they would go in by troop transport. The combatants carried the new 440T nuclear grenades, which gave each man roughly the firepower of a main turret off the USS *Missouri*.

Soldier's joke of the time: What's the only problem with a nuke grenade? Answer: Throwing it far enough!

The launcher, which even the manuals called a powzooka, was ballistic. That is, instead of holding it level like a carbine, the GV had to fire it up at an angle, like a thumper or a mortar. The only danger was in getting the angle too steep and having the shell come back down on top of him. An alarm system on the barrel was supposed to warn against this. But when the bullets are snap-cracking all around, who's listening for that little E-flat buzzer?

If you think I hated these things, you're right.

The new GV units went into their first action on the Loop in Chicago. The tactics were simple: feint and fall back, and when the rioters come out to play, plaster them. Not as elegant as the "Oops, look at the building burn" that was our model, but then, times change. For one thing, most of our buildings were fireproof.

For another, these were not the baby political fronts which had sprung up in the last century, long on Marxist theory and short on firepower. These were nine-tenths street gangs who had been knocking over sporting goods stores for decades.

And if you haven't been in a gun exchange or sports shop lately, they're worth a look. The hardware they sell is a lot closer to the jungles of Nicco than the deer country of Appalachia. It's amazing how much camouflage clothing and high-velocity, speed-loading, anti-tumble ammo a hunter needs for shooting woodchucks. A semi-automatic rifle with a filed-off cam seems to be *de rigueur* for deer, because they're quick and you might miss 'em with the first shot. And cleaning game evidently requires a nine-inch sawback knife, balanced for throwing, with spikes on the guard. Just in case the carcass wakes up and decides to charge, I guess.

Willoughby and his boys were up against a force that was better armed than any of the peasant brigades we fought in Mexico. And, like a nest of wasps on a hot summer morning, the Black Widows, Los Cuervos del Oro, and other gangs in the area were just waiting for an eager pushbutton soldier like him to come poking his finger into the inner city.

Oh, they knew he was coming, all right.

These wasps were also better coordinated than the *campesinistas*. Willoughby thought he was going to shoot down a blind charge by a bunch of screaming teenagers with zipguns. Instead, they were tracking him before he even got the ground carriers stopped along the lakefront. They let him unload his men and advance across the perimeter of burned-out and bulldozed buildings that defined their territory. Worse, they let him walk the streets unopposed and poke his guns into empty doorways. And the more inside he got, the more outside—and above—they got. Until these children had ten Federal companies, almost 1,400 soldiers with a collective firepower of almost 600 kilotons, right under their sights.

Willoughby had penetrated too far, letting the street fighters close the gap silently behind him. But that wasn't his first mistake. He should have worked his way into the downtown from the west. Our tactical consultants, who went over the ground eighteen months later to analyze the action, all agreed on that. The element of surprise he hoped to gain by approaching from the lakeshore was a very small potato. It was far overshadowed by the limitations of the ground: You can't "feint and fall back" when you're standing on the edge of the water. You don't have the lob-range to use your 440Ts effectively.

If Willoughby had gone in from the west or south, he

would have spent a week negotiating the passage of every two or three blocks with rival gangs that hated him and the Widows about equally. He would have had to pay them indemnities as well. But those gangs on the perimeter would have kept his secrets. It's a good bet, too—maybe sixty/forty?—that they would have let his units withdraw without swamping him. And they would certainly have stopped the *centrociudados* when they counterattacked. The gangs stay bought, especially when their territorial instincts are on the side of the agreement. Willoughby never paid off Lake Michigan.

It really didn't matter.

When the trap was tight around Willoughby and his 1,400 Federal troops, and the first burst of autofire came down from the rooftops and upper windows, his men forgot all about tactics. With the tracer streams coming down and the ground pocking all around them, they did the natural thing and fired back. With the 440Ts. Maybe only one or two hundred soldiers made that mistake, but they were in a panic and they all made it at the same time.

Our consultants estimated the combined force of the primary blast at about 85,000 tons of TNT. They arrived at that number by sifting the area, studing how the walls went down, working backwards from structural analysis, and so on. The force of that explosion would have been enough, they said, to ignite the grenades still in their launchers. It was the secondary blast that made the crater.

"We ought to give Willoughby a commendation," Pollock cracked, "for innovative thinking and initiative under fire."

"Give it posthumously?" Cawley cackled.

They could afford to laugh. Willoughby had destroyed the insurrection for them—in Chicago, anyway. We could even gloss over the political situation: We claimed to know nothing of the blast and opined that "terrorist and insurgent groups" may have built or stolen a nuclear device and tried to use it. That raised a useful specter on our side. And anyone who claimed to have seen a convoy of troop carriers with Federal markings driving up the lakeshore that day we dismissed as a crank or a co-conspirator.

But as a military operation it stank. The cost in lives and usable real estate, not to mention the blind stupidity, sickened a soldier like me. I was almost ready to do something rash, like offer to take the field myself, when Pollock and Cawley agreed not to undertake another military action like that. They argued, sensibly, that the States would probably object to any Federal force that successfully beat up on one of their cities.

So, instead, we authorized all sorts of new police weapons. We put a bounty on the head of every radical leader we could identify. And, as an emergency measure, we proposed suspending about half the Bill of Rights for a period not to exceed one year. Congress voted enthusiastically for all this. Our rumor that the street gangs were toting atomic bombs cleared away a lot of the political deadwood.

Within that year, December 2015 to November 2016, we broke the quasi-military power of the gangs in the cities. We couldn't eliminate them. The kids still owned the streets, moved their drugs, and ripped off whatever caught their eye. But they no longer invaded the police precinct houses, erected barricades, issued deeds to property, or bankrolled their own wholesale credit operations.

Enclaves like Denver Free State, Taos Colony, the Memphis Xone, Empire of East Oakland, the Century City Badlands, and Inner Houston were dissolved. But in Miami—there was nothing we could do with Miami, not for the past forty years and not today.

Our overall success against the insurrection cemented the Special Executive's position in Congress. Everyone had been sure we would fail—that had been the point of setting us up in the first place. But we had not failed, and it was too late to cancel the arrangement now.

The elections of 2016 completed our control in the House, as each of us brought in a few more supporters. I called Mike Alcott north to run for a seat from his home district in the Commonwealth of Massachusetts. With the right backing, he won easily. I took one or two others from the 64th's officer pool, knowing that Colonel Birdsong could always train up replacements.

At about this time the pecking order in the S.X. seemed to settle into a regular groove:

Step one, Cawley would do something stupid on his own, or refuse to do something intelligent that we wanted—it always came out the same in the end.

Step two, Pollock would complain about it to me, not because I was a sympathetic ear but because Cawley's slow smile and thick head were complaint- and idea-proof and Pollock knew it.

Step three, I would try to keep the peace between them by suggesting a middle course or occasionally by divining Cawley's point of view. (I never managed to step off this path and avoid the trap.)

Step four, Pollock would privately take offense at my support for our camel-faced friend.

Step five, like the workings of some Goldberg contraption of gears and levers, about 2.5 days later Pollock would find a petty and spiteful way to cross me up.

We were like three sides of an old marriage, knowing where to gnaw at the open places until the blood flowed again.

Over those months, I was satisfied with the decision to take my nephew, Gabriel Ossing, into the page system. The Special Executive formed the most closed society within Congress, and a friendly ear down in the cellars was serving me well. Time and again he brought me news of a plot or a coalition that might have upset our triangle, usually by cutting into my side of it. With enough warning, I could always wiggle out of the knife's way.

All of this is not to say that the S.X. never accomplished anything, or that the only thing we did achieve was the half-megaton destruction of the Chicago Loop. Our years were not all war and deception. Pollock endowed a magnificent theater in Baltimore, the New American. We underwrote the production of new plays and symphonies in many cities. We built new road systems and finally began work on an orbiting anti-ballistic-missile defense, based on plans and broken technological leads that were left over from the last century. We finished construction of the first commercial Troikamak mirror-loop fusion reactor at Syracuse. We even, in a small way, began a commercial program for distilling fresh water from brine domes in Louisiana.

But still that pattern of squeaks and chafing spots persisted. In 2017 we went to a new plane of animosity and angst. Cawley and Pollock were then engaged in a subtle war of political blockade. One would propose a bill, say to raise the tariff on coffee beans, and the other would launch an opposing measure to lower that particular tariff, or all the tariffs with that particular trade group. It was done with a lot of courtesy and secret smiles, but Gabriel told me that anyone in or near the Congress could sense the lines of force building up between them, like a static charge growing between two electrodes.

That, I think, is when I blundered. I began to care about the job of governing and, in one single area, really tried to do something right for the country and the people. In a politician, this is deadly folly.

It had its root in the insurrection.

A lot of urban property—homes, small businesses, office complexes, streets, and utilities—had been destroyed in the rioting and our suppression of it. The owners naturally had turned to their insurance carriers for compensation; after a single incident two or three thousand claims might be filed in a week. And the insurance boards rejected every claim out of hand. They pointed to the fine print about "exclusions in time of war," sat back and folded their hands. Let those who insisted take their case to the courts. The claimants did, and the dockets filled up so that the average person would not see judge or jury before 2035.

This was a tricky legal area.

While Pollock, Cawley, and I might have privately talked about the urban rioting as "insurrection" and our reaction as "going to war," we never said those words in public. The strongest terms we used were "disturbance" and "civil unrest." Only the mediacasters called it a war, and their pronouncements had no force of law. So the insurance boards didn't really have a clearcut objection. But then, a couple of trillion in hard cash was at stake.

And when was the wording of any insurance policy so clear that you didn't need six lawyers to define a sneeze?

What made the situation more onerous was that, for twenty years, the insurance boards had virtually managed every business in the country and prescribed the home life of every household. They were involved in every decision. For a small business: where to build, what to sell, how to arrange the stock, what to print or say in advertising it, how to do the bookkeeping. For a homeowner: what terms for a mortgage and collateral were acceptable, how often to clean the front steps, what kind of bleach to keep in the laundry room, how to discipline and counsel the children.

To get life insurance, a person was summarily enrolled in a health maintenance organization and an exercise program. Usually he or she was also given a list of proscribed activities, foods, and drugs; there would also be a list of countries and cities the person was forbidden to visit.

The objective of every decision, of course, was to find the path of least risk and greatest safety. The right of the insurance company or broker to hold surprise inspections was written into every policy. So the insurance boards had contractual powers that overturned the Fourth Amendment.

Of course, the boards charged high fees for this counsel and advice. Then they turned around and charged higher premiums because of all the potential risks their mandatory investigations had uncovered. This was just a huge, well-oiled money machine.

(And Gordon Pollock was the chief mechanic; of that I had proof. His vote on the Finance and Banking Subcommittee had many times protected the boards and their rogue power. No doubt he profited handsomely from the business. More than that, he had a personal hand in several sectors—real estate, banking, entertainment—that ran most profitably when their economic environment was risk-free.)

Now, when the greatest number of the country's small policyholders had lost almost everything, the boards and their client insurance carriers disappeared through a loophole. It wasn't right. It wasn't fair. And, if I had anything to do about it, it wasn't going to happen.

For six months my legislative staff and I drafted and redrafted a package of reforms. On paper, the legislation bore the title "Insurance Industry Fair Claims Act," but it went a lot farther than that.

It redefined the relationship between the insurance carriers and the boards that had been set up to regulate them. It specified the findings of fact and conclusions of law any court would have to make before denying a claim under an existing policy. Further, we streamlined the entire litigation process. We created new standards for risk and compensation that fairly apportioned the burden of a loss between the individual and society. We redefined the Banking and Credit Act so that terms for "adequate indemnity against all losses," as written into most loan agreements, were not a license for the insurance companies to shear the sheep and take the skin, too. And, to boot, we imposed new antitrust restrictions on the largest insurance carriers.

Oh, we brought in a broom and meant to sweep hard.

And while we polished the wording on our draft legislation—using computer systems that were isolated from the national network and locking everything under my private codes—I had my spies out tasting the winds for me. Gabe turned up a surprising talent for a farmboy: He was a first-class data dabbler. For three months he had been nibbling around the edges of private storage blocks in the net, especially Pollock's. Finally, around the middle of December 2017, he claimed to have found an entry point there.

"He's on to you, Uncle Jim." A grim smile bent the boy's horsey face.

"How much does he know?"

"Congress is really ready to support legislation about the insurance mess, and Pollock's staff are passing memos about it."

"General memos? Just tone of the times stuff? Then he doesn't have . . ."

"Your name or initials come up as a cross reference sixteen times out of twenty possibles. When you pop that bill, he's going to be looking in the right direction."

"We'll have the votes to beat him."

"If you get a chance to."

"He wouldn't—"

At this precise instant, the door to my private office banged open and my personal secretary, Janna, backed into the room, propelled by Pollock himself. If I'd ever seen a man with a black cloud over his head and little lightning bolts shooting off, it was him. With a hook of his thumb he sent Janna out of the room. Then he turned his mammoth attention on Gabe.

"Get out of here, Puppy." Pollock said with a glare that should have cleared up the boy's acne for good.

"But I am Mr. Corbin's—"

"I know who you are, Snot. Go."

Gabe glanced at me, and I nodded him to go. He did, with his head down.

Then the searchlight of Pollock's gaze came around and settled on me. He advanced on the desk and leaned over it, supporting himself on his knuckles.

I stood up to meet him, instinctively going on the ready. My karate reflexes were humming.

"There are ground rules, Corbin . . . I didn't think we'd have to teach you about them."

"Yes? What rules are those?"

His fury relaxed marginally and he went smooth before me.

"Let's—ah—see if I can find a metaphor that you can comprehend. If you were a farmer, like your clod-footed nephew there, I would tell you not to plow across another man's field. If you were a merchant, I'd tell you to keep out of my markets and off my sales floor. If you were a real politician, I'd tell you not to canvass among my constituency. . . ." Then the words choked up in his throat once more and his face went pale where before it had merely been red-brown like a brick.

"You're angry about something, Gordon. I can tell."

"Of course I'm angry! Each of us has certain spheres of responsibility and influence within the government. You are about to poach on mine."

"Do you want to tell me what it is you're talking about? Or would you rather remain mysterious?"

With a visible effort, he took control of his face and emotions again.

"You are about to launch major legislation—"

"That's an interesting idea. How do you know?"

"Oh, come on! You reserve twenty-minute blocks of video time and schedule half a dozen enabling votes, we all can guess it's not to propose a national ice-cream flavor. There is only one subject that could interest you and your pack of Dem-Nat Coalition populists."

"You mean the insurance scam—um—scandal?"

His face went dead sober, even reasonable. "We've built an orderly system of indemnity and risk coverage in this country. We've created safety in an uncertain world. Brought order out of economic chaos. You're an outsider to that system, Corbin. You can't expect to understand the intricacies—"

"I understand grand larceny when it splashes my shoes."

"I'm telling you: Don't interfere."

"I'll have to think about it."

"Don't think too long."

"Or you'll *what*?"

Pollock's eyes locked with mine. He said nothing. He just smiled. But as clearly as if he had spoken aloud, I heard him tell me how I would be killed. By torture. With wires and springs and tiny, tiny knives. After I was made to disappear.

Then, without another word, he turned his on his heel and stalked out.

I wasn't afraid, but after he was gone I blinked back cold tears of rage. Who was this character to try and intimidate me? *He* was mortal, too; *he* was fallible, and—I suddenly realized—he was *scared*. He knew what would happen if I went ahead with my legislation. The economic matrix would shift. He would lose a measure of control. The ripples would unsettle too many of our small boats. And no one could say where the new powers would rise.

Pollock's display of anger had given *me* power over him.

The urge to use it immediately, to push ahead just because it would surprise and hurt him, was irresistible.

That night, I told Carlotta about our encounter. Her reaction was swift.

"You must stop work on that bill immediately," she said, with real fear in her eyes. "Dump the program and destroy your files. Who's your chief aide on that—Ronson? Send her to the Deaf Smith office tomorrow. Or fire her. I only hope it's not too late."

"Why? We've got Pollock on the run. This can hurt him."

"Yes? Ah, Granny, you don't put a man like Pollock 'on the run.' He's like a great hunting cat: His brain is wired for the kill. He can't think about meeting an enemy and turning away. He *can't* run. Now, you must go to him as soon as you decently can and tell him you've seen it his way. Apologize and hope with all your heart that he believes you."

"Oh, not now! No, Carlotta," I said. She was telling me to do something *my* brain wasn't wired for.

She gave me a level stare. "I told you once, I would back you as long as you won and kept on winning. Crossing up Gordon Pollock on his home turf is not a winning strategy."

With a slow shake of her head, Carlotta left the room and went to bed. Since the first day of our marriage, she had been drawing lines. Somewhere in the course of this conversation, I had crossed an important one. And that still wasn't going to stop me.

I had thirty-six hours left.

The next day, Gabriel Ossing disappeared. He was late for our routine morning meeting. After half an hour, I had Janna call down to his cubicle in the Page Room. The voice message he'd left there was at least a day old. When it finally rolled over on the sixth ring, Janna discovered that no live human had seen him that morning.

She called his apartment in the city, and the answer machine there told her to call a woman named Jenny Tancredi in Cleveland, Ohio. Being the thorough type, Janna followed up that lead. She got a sleepy voice that

sounded, she told me, a lot like Gabe's saying his aunt was
out of the house and could she call back. Janna wisely
excused herself, said she had a wrong number—which was
almost impossible with the new BioComm liquid switches—
and hung up.

Janna was mystified, but the tangle jelled a suspicion for
me.

"Call my sister in Nova Scotia. Tell her to send her son
to my place in Las Vegas. She should buy three different
plane tickets in his name and hers out of Halifax, then put
him on a boat for the mainland. He's to go by bus to—
umm—Augusta, and *then* fly. Use the scrambler on this as
far as you can, at least on the beampath out of Baltimore.
And have someone from the security team get up to Augusta's
airport or bus station, whatever, and snatch him."

"How will they know him?"

"He'll probably look a lot like the young man we've
been calling Gabriel Ossing."

"You mean our Gabe was a plant?"

"Don't unhinge your jaw, Janna. His information was a
little too good, especially toward the end. And Clary never
called me 'Jim' in her life; so why should he? Now move
on this, the real Gabe's life might be in danger."

"Yes, sir!"

The business with "our" Gabriel was all smoked herring, meant to distract me. And to deprive me of a set of
ears.

The following day, when I was tied into the House's
electronic agenda, working up the timing for our legislative package, an action flash came across the net. I keyed
to check it out and found my own name on a bill of
impeachment. The detail was sketchy, but it had something to do with my "aiding and abetting insurrectionist
elements." The bill called for my trial in the Judiciary
Committee and, if I was found culpable, my removal from
Congress, a separate trial in the criminal courts, and revo-
cation of the charter for my GV division in Mexico. This
action was signed with the personal codes of Harry Colpat,
the chairman of Judiciary, and Winifred Ponce, a nobody

but also on the committee. Both were New Republican cronies of Gordon Pollock.

While I watched the screen, the preliminary enabling vote was scheduled. A counter bill to examine the evidence was introduced almost instantly. And, bless him, Mike Alcott's code was on it. He was the junior-most representative on Judiciary.

The data came across in a dump that tied up the network for almost two minutes. There were names, more than 2,000 of them, streaming down the screen: Kareem Ahmed, Kenny Avery, Mohammad Azrael . . . Burton Calhoun, Abu Conan, Mohammad Crockett . . . Abraham Davis, Myra Davis . . . John Doe 121, John Doe 122, John Doe 123 . . . none of them was familiar to me. At the tail end was the explanation.

These were members of a revolutionary supergang, the Vice Lords, which had been operating in a dozen eastern cities. Each of these people had been apprehended in a felony or a criminal misdemeanor, and each had carried a plastic laminated card that reproduced in miniature a blanket pardon to all Vice Lords, signed by Granville James Corbin. A member of the House of Representatives and of the Special Executive had authorized purse snatchings, felony homicides, breaking and entering, and a catalog of crimes almost as long as the list of apprehended suspects.

I knew immediately what had happened. The Baltimore Vice Lords must have used that piece of paper Birdsong arranged to spread their name, if not their influence, to hundreds of gangs up and down the East Coast.

It might, in other circumstances, have been passed off as a joke. After all, Colpat and Ponce could have no proof that my signature on the card was genuine. And the idea that I would grant immunity for urban mayhem to a bunch of kids was absurd on the face of it. But those with a will to see me in the wrong would believe. Pollock and his henchpeople would have a lot of will in that direction.

Again as I watched, Alcott introduced another counter bill challenging the evidence and calling for a nonbinding tally. This was crucial: If less than 30 percent of the congressmen and -women currently logged onto the agenda network accepted the bill of impeachment, it would die. If more than 30 percent, Judiciary would try it.

I stabbed my thumb down on "N" and prayed that a majority of the members would have the charity, or the sense of humor, to see the absurdity of the charges.

The numbers flickered on the screen: 18 . . . 23 . . . 24 . . . 28 . . . 29 . . . 29 . . . 30 . . . 31 . . . 33 . . . 37 . . . 37 . . . 37. And there they settled. Pollock had more friends than I'd thought.

I picked up the phone and tried to call Carlotta. The message she had left with the front desk at the Commerce Exchange said she was going to San Francisco for a few days. Shopping trip, she said.

I tried to call Mike Alcott's office, over in the freshman wing. His incoming lines were all tied up. And while I waited, another bill of impeachment went across the network—one with Alcott's name on it. This one was a war-crimes charge, for some fictitious bit of torture-interrogation he was supposed to have committed in Yucatan. A fine touch of revenge for Tom Pollock there.

Gordon was going to sweep us all into a bag in one morning. By the end of the week we could be on the street—or in jail.

And my options were crumbling about me.

Chapter 18

Billy Birdsong: Rio Grande Rubicon

"Evacuate! The whole division? Impossible, Gran!"

We were talking on an open satellite link, speaking in Malay. I was pretty rusty because, fighting in Yucatan, just speaking English was enough to confuse any comm-circuit eavesdroppers.

"What's impossible?" he said. "I thought the military situation there was fairly stable. Besides, even if it's not, I need you back in the States."

Now that was crazy: He needed the division in the *States?* I had understood what he said clear enough, so Granny had to be using the wrong words in Malay.

"Gran . . . No way I can bring the division back," I told him. "It would be illegal, bang, dead. You *know* that."

"Yes, illegal. I'll take responsibility. But can you do it? Physically, that is?"

"What? Uproot 6,000 troops, their bases, vehicles, and hardware? Take them across 600 miles of the Gulf? Then what? Just where do you want the division?"

"Go through to Southern California. Regroup at our old desert base, Poway."

"Okay. So we march through six GV military jurisdictions in Mexico . . . or, alternatively, through the TENMAC States. I guess we can do that. Do we have to fight our way through?"

"I don't know yet. I'd try diplomacy first. General Barton in Tamaulipas will probably help you; he did before. So will Poniatowski in Nuevo Leon and Coahuila. If they won't, hold up the specter of the GVs being eaten up piecemeal—"

"Christ! Is *that* happening?"

"Not yet . . . Let's see, Jenkins in Chihuahua can be bought; I'll arrange that. Wackley in Sonora is touchy; promise him whatever he wants. But he'll balk anyway. Dodge around his positions if you can; beat the shit out of him if you can't. Then, in Baja, you'll be crossing such a narrow strip that Clarkson, who's based down in La Paz, probably won't notice you. After that—"

"Gran . . . all this omits a minor geological quirk—two bitch mountain ranges called the Sierra Madre, Oriental and Occidental. *Nobody* takes a ground army across Mexico east to west, not since Cortes, and *not* in the north."

"Oh."

"And after all that, what do you want us in Poway for? Are we being disbanded?"

"No!" Gran barked. "Not while I can help it."

"Then this is a—" Strategic? Check out my Malay dictionary. "—*menurut siasat* situation?"

"Yes. I am to be impeached on trumped-up charges in the House, followed by a criminal trial, probably for treason. Pollock is finally going to do away with me. He thinks."

"Well then, falling back to Southern California does nothing. Will you wait for them to come and get you? Lick your wounds? You can do that here in Yucatan. No, instead, we ought to go on the attack. Straight across the Gulf and capture New Orleans or Houston. It would be less work, for one thing."

"Whom do I trust in New Orleans? Or Houston?"

"Well," I answered, "who can you trust anywhere? Certainly no one at Poway anymore."

"The real objective, of course, is Baltimore . . ."

"That is a long way, by sea. And we have no Navy . . ."

"Can you go east? Land in the Florida Panhandle, then right up the coastal lowlands—Georgia, the Carolinas, Virginia—"

"Skirting the black-glass crater that used to be Washington?"

"Yes, and then—"

"They—the Congress, Pollock, the States themselves—would be organized to fight us before we even pulled out of the swamps. We are talking civil war here, Gran."

"Yes."

"We are going to invade the continental United States, without securing a strategic nuclear capability or even heavy air support? That could be suicide, you know."

"Yes . . . But then, the country has no opposition in the field, and no standing army since '98. We can walk ashore, I think."

"So." I thought for a minute. "Who is on your side?"

"I can probably swing the GV patron-generals—thank God, all the professional military men are there in Mexico. And the Southwest, TENMAC for a start, will trust me more than they trust Pollock—at least, he's no soldier. The rest of the country, that we'll have to fight for."

"Then we go for your strength. Land at Corpus Christi or Houston and appeal to Texas history. If the State rallies to you, we have a chance. If not, get out of the country entirely. But Gran, *you* have to land in Texas. Personally. They will not accept me, or any other surrogate."

"All right. Prepare the division for the crossing, then. I will come down." And he hung up without even saying good-bye and good luck.

The job Corbin was leaving me could be compared to moving the circus out of town without letting the town know.

An infantry division is that big. Officially we were listed as 5,600 combatant and support personnel. Plus ground vehicles, Stompers, auxiliary aircraft, and boats. Plus cyber and communications gear. Plus armories, supply dumps, maintenance shops, mess halls, dormitories. Plus a few thousand inventories, from bonding lists to bedding to burial records. Add to that the community of families, merchants, mendicants, scroungers, and paid spies that any occupying force gathers to itself during seven years in one location.

All of it had to be either moved or left behind. And moved or dumped secretly, because the bastards in Baltimore would have spies following Gran, and more spies watching Gran's personal army in Mexico. If he made a beeline for Yucatan, and then that army pulled stakes and started north, the Federals could choose our landing site with a coin toss. They would meet us with overwhelming force.

I began pulling the plugs very quietly, making it look—wherever possible—like we were demobilizing. We paid out the spies, sold the bedding, and burned the burial lists. We sent the families into exile in British Honduras. We took the unit colors down from our headquarters building in Merida. All very public and sad.

Then secretly I began buying steamers, the old kind with cargo cranes on their decks, not container hoists or air slides. I also did a quiet deal with the Israelis for a hundred of the new Jonah landing craft, to be shipped air freight to our port at Progreso. These vehicles were personnel-carrying hovercraft with armor mesh knitted into their skirting. The airfloods were all collapsible titanium ducting; so the whole boat folded flat. We could pile a dozen of them on deck in a stack fifteen feet high. The propulsion systems were Netanya Industries KK-4 jet turbines. These were stored separately from the boats, would be fitted at sea and fired up just before launching.

Clips on the front of the air boats would take our .50 calibers and a rack of the powzookas that Gran hated so. We were ready to go up Galveston Bay into Houston spitting like a fire serpent. Just in case.

As these preparations moved forward, Corbin worked his way across the country. He went first to Vegas, making it look like he was going to ground, just to throw off Pollock's watchers. But he kept in touch with me—always in Malay and usually by electronic maildrop.

January 19 was the day we picked to move out. That was a Friday and, allowing travel time and make-ready, put us in a perfect position to land in Houston at dawn on Sunday, the 21st.

I had big surveyors' maps of the city and began training

our officers in their attack roles and contingency moves. We met in the warehouse on the edge of Merida, plugging numbers into our battle cybers while the rains came down on the leaky tin roof. We drilled each other on landmarks, rally points, and acceptable kill rates.

What we were going to do after we took the city, I did not know. Cross one mountain at a time. If our charade went as planned and we achieved surprise at Houston, then we might be able to move west, rally the TENMAC, and fortify it before the Federals could build up a standing army and get moving our way—if the State militias would come out on our side. If not . . . maybe better we lose a glorious battle on the Houston waterfront.

I never liked loser's odds. We needed an edge for our one slender division. Faith and friendship would only take us so far: we needed to give the opposition a reason to fear us. I had a few ideas along that line. Knowing Granny would not approve, I went about researching them quietly. I even went so far as briefing an action team that would . . . but later. I will tell the story in order.

Granny turned up in Merida during these preparations. He rode in on one of our gasoline trucks coming from Celestún. The rain was rolling off his Baltimore topcoat and the mud of the roads was squishing in his Baltimore shoes, but he was grinning, looking fit and ready for anything.

Like some Roman general, Corbin insisted on an eve-of-battle speech the day before we loaded up the steamers in Progreso. Any other modern GV officer would just post general orders, usually as a data dump of time ticks and map coordinates to all unit cybers. What does a soldier need to know besides when and where to fight? But Granny wanted them to know why, and he wanted to tell them in person, all at once.

There was no amphitheather in Merida big enough to hold all 5,600 troops in the division, plus casuals and native reinforcements. Or, there had been no amphitheater since we bombed the *fubol* stadium in our first fight for the city, seven years ago. So we made a special day of his speech and assembled the entire division at Uxmal, on the green grass surrounded by the dead white stones.

Luckily, the rains held off.

Granny stood high above our heads—a couple of hundred steps up the eastern side of the Pyramid of the Sorcerer, with enough sound equipment that his voice could be heard back in Merida. He began bravely enough:

"Women and men of the California 64th. By now some of you probably have heard or guessed why I'm down here with you, and not up in Baltimore doing my job. It's difficult to keep anything from people as sharp as you—though your officers try pretty hard. . . ."

That brought a laugh, especially from the officers themselves, arranged near the foot of the steps.

"Anyway, it's all over the satelcast by now, what a bastard I am. . . ."

More laughs—and a few shouts of "No! No, Gran!"

"I'm supposed to be the man who sold out his country to the mobs. Taught innocent little children to go shoot their parents, loot their neighborhoods, rape their sisters. Then I'm supposed to have promised these brat psychopaths a free pardon, free ice cream, and a chance to do it all again. Oh, the stories you can hear in Baltimore! And in return . . . in return, I was supposed to get—what? You tell me! What?"

"Pussy!" some joker down in front shouted. I saw people on either side turn and punch him out.

"That would be a good reason!" Gran cracked back, and the crowd dissolved in laughter, even the women in our ranks.

"But it's more reason than the politicos give me! Anyway, it's all a fiction, lads and lasses. A lie, but with a core of truth.

"And truth is that we, Colonel Birdsong and I, *did* pardon a group of black youths who helped us when we were being persecuted—just as they had been. They helped us when no one, not in the Federal government, the Baltimore police, the FBI, no one could be trusted to help us. And in return for that favor, these young people have been themselves been hunted and persecuted. And now these children are being used against us.

"The truth is, lasses and lads, you cannot believe *anything* from the 'duly elected Congress' that leads our country. Take that from someone who tried to work inside it, tried to do something for the people, tried to follow the soldier's path of honor—and got kicked in the teeth.

"If I return to the States, I will be tried for treason and imprisoned. Then I would probably be shot. If *you* return to the States, you will be detained and jailed, then sent back here. . . . The Special Executive means to disband the California 64th and exile you—*here!*

"We are exiles together, lads and lasses, while the pigs of Congress sit up there in Baltimore and eat our country alive. Are you going to hold still for that?"

"No! No way, Gran! No way, man!"

"Of course you aren't!" he shouted back at them, his amplified voice dominating the field.

"There is only one course open to us. Only one way to follow that path of honor. . . . We must return to the States and challenge those bloated pigs. We must return to the States and claim our rights as citizens. We must return as a unit. We must return armed. To save our country—we must go to war!"

Six thousand breaths caught on the same inhale. Six thousand pairs of eyes focused on the tiny figure that was poised on the steps of an ancient Mayan ruin.

All night, I had argued with Gran about this. Take them to Texas, I said, but without fanfare. Move first and explain later; they will follow you and be returning fire—if they are fired upon—before they can think about it. But if you stand in front of them and tell them what will happen, they might have time to decide against you.

And all night, Gran shook his head and insisted it was immoral to trick a person into history. And these were not innocents. They had read and understood and fought under the charter of the Gentlemen Volunteers. They had minds. Long before we came in sight of the Texas shore, they would be worrying themselves with rumor and speculation. No, better that they heard it said straight out.

"That's right, ladies and gentlemen. We are going to a war. Just like the shopkeepers of Boston in 1775 who, for reasons they knew were good, picked up their flintlocks and ran for Lexington and Concord. Just like the farmboys of the Carolinas in 1861 who, for reasons they knew were good, manned the guns that fired on Fort Sumter and then marched up the road to Washington. So we are going to war in 2018, for reasons we know are good.

"I can't tell you what kind of opposition we'll find in Texas. If the State militia comes out against us, we'll have to fight our way up from Galveston Island. Pound for pound and round for round they can probably outgun and outmaneuver us." He looked from side to side at his volunteers—a gesture that must have been invisible to the back of the field. "But can they out*fight* us?"

"*No!*" they roared back at him.

"I didn't think so." He shook his head with a huge grimace that would carry, at least into the front ranks of the crowd, as a smile.

"You are all free men and women. It's your choice to follow me. Choice is something not many people have these days, in the machine society they've built for us in Baltimore. It wasn't meant to be that way, you know. But even the best designs can be brought to nothing by small men. Now, it's your choice to help me change history. Can you do that?"

"*Yes!*" they roared.

"Then, you Homeless Bastards . . . the adventure begins tomorrow!" He left a pause for them to cheer. They did.

"Your officers will have your wave assignments in the order of battle. Good luck. I know you won't let me down."

Corbin turned off the microphone then, intending to end it there, simply, with dignity. He began climbing down the pyramid's steps, a hundred of them and more. They were steep shelves of cut rock, which forced him to take long, careful, jackleg steps.

However, the troops would not let it end. They began to call his name: Gran, Granny. At first it was scattered, said barely above a normal voice. But they soon found a rhythm, with each step he took: Gran—ny, Gran—ny, *Gran*—ny, *GRAN*—ny.

In response, Corbin paced himself, step by step, letting it build, then raising his hands over his head. Their voices rolled up at him. They pressed forward to the base of the Pyramid of the Sorcerer, took him onto their shoulders when he reached the bottom. Still chanting his name, the soldiers carried him off the field. And into glory, they thought. . . .

We worked the crossing in reverse of our invasion of Yucatan. The ships left first, with the assault forces. When they were almost a hundred miles out from the target, one of the steamers that carried the third wave broke off and stationed itself to begin refueling the Stompers from a bladder on deck. The rest of the ships crept to within five miles of the gap between Galveston Island and the Bolivar Peninsula. We could only hope the harbor authorities' navigational radar would not ring any bells because five assorted cargo ships stopped to dump garbage or fuel oil or whatever this close to port.

There at 0620 hours on Sunday, with more than an hour to dawn, they began mounting the KK-4 turbines on the boat shells, firing them up, blowing up the skirts, and putting the craft over the side with cargo cranes. Then a hundred troops swarmed down nets and began mounting weapons and settling in, while other crews went to work on the remaining shells. The honk and whine of those jet engines starting up echoed mournfully across the black water.

Or so I am told—this time I was in the air, leading a wing of the Stompers. With no reconnaissance, no spies, not even a media scan at the target, we had no idea what the reception would be. I wanted to be high in the air and moving from the start for this one. Gran was going to be on one of the air boats, he said, somewhere in the first wave. We had shaken hands in Progreso on the nineteenth, before the ships moved out, and known that we might never see each other again. It was one of those dry-mouth moments. Not much to say.

Now I took the Stomper high, looking down on the sleepy, minimal glow of the city. Behind me was the great black of the Gulf, and ahead the raggedy, patchy glow of street lights and buildings on Sunday morning safety lighting. Houston is unlike any other American city. From the air, most of them look like concentric circles: a big, splashy center city, then congested inner 'burbs, spaced outer 'burbs, radiating interstates, and farmland satellite villages. The Houston downtown by comparison was a pimple—maybe a dozen tallish buildings huddled together, surrounded by greenery and subdivisions. The ship channel, the docks and refineries were far removed from the city itself. Beltways ringed Houston, connecting a dozen isolated office-hotel-shopping complexes which were an architect's dream: glass and steel shaped and set in their own spaces. Like a futuristic chessboard.

The city was shaped by its laws, as most were. Houston had no zoning ordinances, reflecting a Texas tradition of inde-goddamn-pendence. A man could build on his own property whatever the hell he wanted, pard! So an office building might go up right next to a residential complex, a gas station right beside a single-family mansion. Owners' property rights were supreme, restricted only by the covenants written into their title or lease documents.

I flew over this web of spider light, seeing mostly the red gems of aerial beacons on the tall, wide-spaced buildings. No other air traffic rose to meet me. Air Control queried me on the radio, and I made up some trash about being a private aircraft with a flight plan forty-eight hours old. That would keep them pawing through back paper. The rest of our air force was five miles out and low to the water—below the controllers' radar horizon, I hoped.

The city was asleep, or so it seemed from up here.

From the air boats, it was a different city. They moved up the ship channel, seeing the yellow-green sodium lights of the docks and cranes draw closer. Then a dozen, twenty, a hundred similar lights were between Granny's flotilla and the shore. They swarmed, crossed, raced around, forcing the air boats to dodge and cross their own wakes.

Then, from a clear black sky full of stars, it started to rain, great lashing gusts that almost swamped some of the boats.

Granny's talkers had a lot to say about all this, calling to each other, jamming up communications. He told me later that it was some minutes before the lead boats identified the source of the rain as a tugboat-looking thing, or possibly two of them, that bore down the channel toward the air boats.

As the sky grayed with dawn, Gran could see it was a pair of fireboats, waving their lacy veils of water back and forth. "As a weapon against our hovercraft, those pounding streams were almost ideal," he told me later.

But they were not a weapon. The fireboats and small pleasure craft—which is what all the little lights were—had come down the channel to greet Corbin and his forces in friendship. A large police launch carried the mayor of Houston and a joint delegation from the States of California and Nevada to welcome him to the city and offer him the support and protection of the TENMAC, or at least half of it.

"Did you arrange all that?" I asked him, after we had linked up at his temporary HQ.

"When would I have done that?" Corbin grinned at me.

"When you were in Vegas, say, on your devious way into Mexico?"

He made a swimming motion with his hand. "Let's say I dropped some hints. That, and my reputation as a member of the Special Executive, which preceded me. No one has forgotten what happened in Chicago."

With the mayor and the delegation was Mike Alcott. He had a bundle of messages for Gran, most of them secret agreements from members of Congress who were unhappy with the rule of Pollock and, fading into the shadows, Cawley. Alcott had stayed in Baltimore as long as he could. Then he had been impeached in an electronic vote that lasted fourteen minutes. A new record.

Now both Corbin and Alcott had prices on their heads. Literally. Pollock had convicted them *in absentia* of high treason and was offering a million new dollars, apiece, to anyone who returned either them or verifiable pieces of their bodies, no questions asked, to Federal authorities in Baltimore.

So the war was on in earnest.

Corbin moved his troops into Houston. He adopted the old Galleria center, in the city's Southwest Corridor, as his headquarters. We grounded the Stompers in the parking lots on one side of the shopping center, put a small ammo and weapons dump on the other, at some distance from the hotel and office towers. Granny commandeered the top floor for his immediate staff.

I did not see Carlotta anywhere around, and thought it was just my good luck. I wondered about her. Walking barefisted into Texas with a price on your head was definitely not Carlotta's style.

While Corbin was settling in and soldering up the political situation, I put into action the plan that had come to me in Merida, the one to get us some teeth.

One of our cyber sergeants, a woman named Alice Tanno, had once worked as a systems integrator in the maintenance section of the Federal Strategic Forces. This tiny cadre of pushbutton soldiers kept the missile silos, which were the country's loaded gun to the heads of the Russians, the Chinese, the Middle Arab Jamahiryat, and every other power bloc that might want to march into North America. Tanno had admitted to me that she knew the locations, entry points, and access codes for the Central Kansas Complex.

At 0300 hours I took off from Houston with a wing of twelve Stompers. We filed bogus flight plans for California with the Air Control radar scan, then flew north. Aboard each plane was a fire team of eight troopers and a two-man specialist team that Tanno had trained in Merida.

For a group working in complete secrecy, we had been amazingly thorough: Tanno had set up maps, models, and cyber mockups for these teams to work on. They cracked codes, popped circuits—even fired off a simulated multiple strike. The team had everything to play with except real live guards in FSF uniforms to garrote.

Our formation split up over Oklahoma and diverged for three separate points in Kansas. Dawn was still two and a half hours away on our right wings when we dove for the deck, flying radar-low and only rising over the field breaks of trees. My string of four flew east towards Wheaton in

Pottawatomie County, the others headed more west to Abilene and Concordia.

Three miles out from our target sites we split again, one plane to each of the fenced reservations in this strategic group. To confuse everybody later, we came up on them from opposite points of the compass, low and fast.

On the first pass over the ground, we knocked out satellite dishes, domes and antenna arrays, anything that looked like communications. We also hit the powerlines we could see, forcing the sites onto backup generators.

At the end of that run, we did a climbing turn, wing over, and went back for more. On the second pass, we released the heaviest nerve gas I had been able to buy on the arms market. I was not interested in secondary effects—whether it killed the victim, made him dizzy, knocked him cold, caused him to swallow his tongue and choke on his own vomit, or just mutated his kids in the nth generation—so long as it met two simple criteria. One, it had to incapacitate anyone who got even a trace on his pinky, put him out of action immediately and totally. Two, it had to be dense enough to settle quickly into ventilation ducts, stairwells, and elevator shafts. To protect against this poison, our fire teams, specialists, and pilots all wore fitted suits and gas masks that filtered incoming air through a neutralizer specific to this gas. I remember the product we used happened to be made in France.

After that pass, we were on the ground inside the fence and pouring out of the Stomper. No one was alive aboveground where my ship set down. It happened to be our luck that there was not much wind—let alone a blizzard—blowing that morning. The gas hung in yellow streamers in our flashlight beams.

Our educated specialists popped electronic locks and released hatches. The gas puffed and swirled downward. There were no alarms that I could hear, but that did not mean much. Then down we went, following a trail of sagging, twitching bodies into the earth.

Alice Tanno had been right about the controls: The team recognized the layout of the control pod and all the access panels. They immediately began throwing switches. Somewhere in the fabric of the underground complex I could hear heavy motors rumbling, the blast doors opening.

One of the site's duty technicians regained control of his muscles long enough to draw and aim his pistol. His first shot went wide of my neck by two feet. He never got another shot, because I took off the side of his head with the butt of my carbine.

As soon as the locks were all released and the circuits open, my team was out of the pod and into the silo. There they began working on the missile's side covers. The work was both electrical and mechanical, to isolate the warhead both physically and sensorially from the booster mount. They had taken the equivalent of a six-month tech course in two weeks with Tanno. Actually, they had only half the course—the disassembly part.

After twenty minutes' tickling and tweezing, they rolled over the silo's bridge crane and hoist, latched onto the freed nose cone, and lifted it off the rocket.

"Where do you want it, Colonel?"

"Topside," I answered.

He looked up. The crane and hoist had rolled out *under* the blast doors; no way it could lift the warhead *above* the doors. The man shrugged.

Just then one of my trucks arrived, right on schedule. Our second team had bought or stolen a fleet of auto wreckers in Houston, painted them with plausible colors and signs, changed the plates, and started north from Texas the day before. The wrecker driver lowered his wheel cradle, hand-cranked it down below the lip of the silo, and cupped the warhead hanging beneath the hoist. When he had raised it above the surface, his helper rolled the bomb—gently—into the truckbed, strapped it down, and flung a tarpaulin over it.

Then we pulled everyone out of the hole, climbed back into the Stomper, and got the truck out through the fence and onto the road. By radio I confirmed that the other eleven teams were just finishing up. We cranked up and roared off in two different directions.

For the trip back to Houston, all the teams spread out across Kansas, heading more or less south by twelve different roads and air routes. So far as I know, none of them even came close to being stopped.

It was a perfect GV commando operation.

Corbin was furious.

"I was hoping you might not hear about it," I admitted when he called me up to his office to chew on my butt.

"Oh? Right! And how did you figure that?" His face was twisted in that snotty-potty, upper-middle disdain he did so well. "When there's only one military force in the States right now that could have pulled off that raid *and* had a reason to. The newsats were linking my name with it before you were halfway across Oklahoma. If the FSF had its own air force, or maintained better liaison with the Kansas National Guard, you never would have reached Texas soil."

"You could claim it was one of the State militias that did it." I felt the heat rising to my face.

"I've already played that lie," he snapped. "For all the good it does . . . Hell's hinges! The State units have to *live* here. I'm—we're—just passing through. Don't you understand? We're *vulnerable*."

"Not any more, Granny. You got nuclear teeth now. Your enemies will have to think twice about mobbing you. Or betraying you."

"Oh, sure! We'll just do a little nuclear blackmail. . . . 'Mad Dog Corbin' they'll be calling me. Wonderful!" He ran his hands through his hair, what was left of it. "And just how did you plan to *use* those warheads, without launch vehicles?"

"Put them in stripped-out Stompers, wired for remote control. Fly in at hedge level like the old cruise missiles. They would be real hard to knock down."

Corbin stared at me, hollow eyed, for a whole minute. "Not bad," he said at last and grudgingly.

I was proud of this idea and could not help smiling.

"At least you haven't taken total leave of your senses. . . . How many megatons are they?"

"The casing codes say forty—"

"And you bounced them halfway cross the Southwest in the backs of tow trucks? You crazy Indian!"

"But—"

"Now listen carefully," he rode right across my objection. "If you ever pull a crazy stunt like that again, I will break you. Worse, I will have you shot and toss your worthless body out for the coyotes to gnaw on. *Entiende?*"

"Yes, sir."

"Very good. Dismissed."

I about-faced and marched out. As I went, a smile was growing on my face. I had accomplished my mission. Granny was not as angry as I expected him to be. And he did not order me to return the bombs.

We would soon need them.

Within a week of our landing in Houston, the country fell apart. I had expected the rest of the States to rally against us, sending armies in a wedge that would split Texas and California and drive us back into the deserts of Sonora. But not at all. Instead, it was like watching a beakerful of clear chemical solution suddenly turn cloudy and rain down crystals after you added a catalyst. The catalyst, of course, was Granny Corbin and his defiance of Congress.

The political outcry started with the formalists and legal purists, who objected in principle to our "invasion." But they were soon joined by every political and economic faction that hated the Mexican War and all it represented— the stain of military adventurism, the trend toward non-neo-isolationism, the Hispanicizing of America, the new marketplace of cheap labor and abundant energy.

Their objections were raised to boiling point—it took about three-fifths of a second—when they learned Corbin's private army now had nuclear capability.

Those bombs changed the situation for the TENMAC, too. Many local politicians had thought they were only protecting a native son who had got himself into a squeaky place in the corrupt East and so earned a price on his head. Now they saw clearly that he was forcing them into civil war.

When the secession pact was signed, I saw tears in the eyes of representatives from Arizona and New Mexico. These were States that had entered the Union just over

100 years ago. They were people whose parents had crossed the border on foot and fought hard for their citizenship.

War makes hard choices.

The initial split of the country was along the lines of Sunbelt versus the Rustbowl and Heartland. The West was progressive, independent, and inclined toward Corbin and self-determination. The East and Midwest were conservative, formalist, and sided with Pollock and the Congress, as representing the "legitimate" government.

However, the New England States came in on the side of the Sunbelt, largely because of their independent attitudes and their revitalized economies, a legacy of the Silicon Revolution.

New York City remained neutral and offered to bankroll any State, political coalition, army group, or corporation that looked like it could survive two consecutive quarters and pay out the going rate of twenty percent. Upstate New York, on the other hand, sided with the rest of the agrarian Heartland.

The Old South also came in with the Heartland, largely because of its prejudice against importing anything, even a new country.

"Ecotopia"—that is, Northern California, Oregon and Washington State—aligned themselves with the Sunbelt, largely because the people could not bear to be thought anti-progressive and anti-Hispanic. The Rockies sided with the Rustbowl because of their energy and water reserves—and they feared any pattern of forces that might try to realign the national wealth.

Louisiana declared itself a Free State and tried to become a duty-free port of entry serving both sides in the civil war.

Of course, any analysis of the Second Civil War would fail if it ignored underground economic interests. Each State had its own unofficial position—intolerant or tolerant—on the trafficking in pele, crack, and cochineal; on the trading in shady securities and unclean cash; on insider investing and corporate buccaneering; on moonshine liquor revenues and the trade in girlflesh. And that position helped decide whether it leant toward the Heartland-straight-Anglo side of the war, or toward the Sunbelt-hip-Hispanophile side.

The strength of the States was everything. Repudiation of the national debt in the 1990s and the Money Warp that followed had strengthened the positions of State and local governments: They still could levy taxes. Then, with the pay-as-you-go society, the Federal government got wealthy— but did not necessarily regain the dominant economic position it had held in the sixty years following the Great Depression. What the States won, they kept.

This centrifugal tendency was abetted by the Hundred Lost Days. The muddle at the top and the evolving power struggle with the Speaker created a vacuum in which each State of the Original Fifty developed its own power, special interests, and political alliances. Finally, Corbin's break with the Special Executive and his violation of the GV charter, bringing troops back into the country to defend himself, gave each State the option of siding with Congress to hold the Union together—or not.

At first, those other regions which chose against union did not so much secede as wander off. Corbin did not press them into confederation with him, he just offered to defend them. If and when.

On the other side, Pollock and Congress were desperate to attack Corbin in the TENMAC. But without a standing army, they had limited options. Pollock appealed to each loyal State to send its militia into the Southwest. But it was a long way to go. The threat to State interests was not clear. The lines of communication and supply were scrambled. And, as we knew, Pollock was no general.

The States on both sides of the secession expressed a towering apathy. So, right after the TENMAC split off in January 2018, the conflict entered a Phony War phase that lasted until August.

During this time, there *was* a group of top military men who were waiting to be asked to the dance: the GV generals and their private armies in Mexico. Granny and I had thought many would sympathize with our position as a former GV unit and come in on the side of secession. Of course, we were forgetting the cussedness of the entrepreneur. Some of the generals were sitting on the fence, trying to predict the winning side; most, however, were simply waiting for bids backed by cash.

Pollock had a lot of cash.

General Clayton Poniatowski, whose division controlled Neuvo Leon and Coahuila, entered secret negotiations with Congress in June. We never would have learned about them if Granny, before his flight from Baltimore, had not thought to bury a few tapeworms on time delay in the congressional net. These automated spies gave us just enough hints to look south across the Border Strip late in July.

The human observers we sent in mufti to Piedras Negras and Ciudad Acuña reported back that, yes, quartermasters from the 22nd Illinois, Poniatowski's group, were in the Strip buying passage rights from the local gang lords. An army of 9,000 airmobile infantry was poised less than an hour away at Allende, Morelos, and Zaragoza. If they crossed over, we could expect them to fly northeast and strike directly at our strength in Houston.

H-hour was maybe a day away.

"What are we going to do, Gran?" Mike Alcott asked. The three of us were closeted with the reports from our observers. We sat on the top floor of the Galleria, looking out over the dusty greens and browns of Houston baking in the summer heat. Not a breath of wind came up from the Gulf.

"They got us outnumbered," I said. "We can fly, fight, fuck, or die. And that is about all."

"Can we intercept and take them in the Strip?" Corbin asked.

"Our people are stood down all over Houston. If we had beeped for assembly and moved out twelve hours ago . . . But that would just be picking the spot we die in. We can not match 9,000 troopers with equal equipment, no matter what the ground."

"What about the Texas militia?" Alcott asked.

"If we are spread all over the city, they are all over the State. It would take a week to call them up, point them

south, and start them marching. By that time, Poniatowski
will be here."

Corbin's eyes took on a hooded look. "Colonel, do you
have three old STM-4s you can spare?"

I looked at my hands. "We have some hangar queens.
They fly, but two have glitchy armament circuits, one has
a busted fan—insufficient thrust to hover with a full rifle
squad aboard."

"They won't need to carry any troops. Or defend
themselves."

"Are you thinking of a one-way trip?"

"I am."

"I will give the orders, General."

"Do so."

Alcott was looking from me to Corbin with a puzzled
expression. He could not know that Granny was giving me
the go-ahead to incinerate three Mexican cities. As far as
Mike was concerned, our meeting broke up in mystery,
deciding nothing that needed a decision.

Was Corbin crazy, really the "Mad Dog"? That thought
did cross my consciousness as we walked out of the meeting. At first, when I had captured those nuclear weapons,
he did not want them, even for strategic purposes. Now he
was willing to use three warheads to stopgap what should
have been a purely tactical confrontation. Crazy? No . . .
But . . . "Erratic" is the word that came to mind. In the
overview, putting his actions in perspective, what we were
doing could be both a military necessity and political suicide.

Within two hours I had the drones in the air, flying with
one-quarter of our stolen nuclear warheads. I handled the
remote controls on the lead ship, the one for Allende,
myself. My two best pilots took the others.

We flew the Stompers low, as always, and fast. It was a
wild ride, streaking diagonally across the field rows, contouring the hills, dipping into ravines, blasting leaves off
the upper layers of bramble bushes.

These video images, compass readings, and flight data
were telemetered through a signal scrambler. Our enemies probably could not have done anything if they had

intercepted these signals and read them correctly—but why should we leave a probability wagging out there?

I was flying compass headings and contour maps. From the city library we had tried to get ground and air views of Zaragoza, Morelos, and Allende. We found some prints taken in an aerial survey of Allende forty years ago, when the population was a tenth of what it was in 2018. However, our maps told us the cities were laid out in a line ten miles long, northwest to southeast. So our strategy was to fly a spread until one of the planes crossed this pattern, then we would circle back and home on our selected targets.

Allende, coming up under my right wing, looked like a shanty city, a sprawl of tin shacks and adobe blocks. A million poor city people living on the edge, waiting for their chance to slip into the Strip and find their fortune. Somewhere in the center of this mass were a few thousand *norteamericanos* armed and aimed at us. For expediency's sake, we were going to take them out at a civilian kill rate of a thousand to one.

So be it.

Watching the video monitor with one eye and the horizon repeater with another, I pulled back on the joystick for a wingover and dove at the center of this huddled mass. With my left hand I typed in the code sequence that would detonate the forty-megaton warhead strapped into my cargo bay.

The screen flickered once and broke up in carrier snow.

I lifted my hands off the controls. Whatever was to happen now in America, we had sealed our back door behind us. With the outcry that would follow this bombing, there could be no retreat through Mexico. And no exile in South America. Whatever the war brought, we would live and die in the north.

Chapter 19

Granville James Corbin: Civil War

My decision to bomb those three cities in Coahuila raised a public outcry that gave Gordon Pollock the leverage he needed to raise his armies.

As I had feared, the politicians and the video people called me "madman," "public enemy," and a dozen other clichés of contempt. They demanded that Pollock personally unite the State militias and march into Texas and California to clean up "that scum." They screamed for "justice." They wept for the "poor peasants of Zaragoza." They honored Poniatowski as another Eisenhower, but one cut off in his prime. The hysterical bullcrap clogged the satellite channels for days.

Pollock could have cut through that—and saved himself four years of bloody war—if he had followed my example and called for a strategic strike on Houston. Just one bomb, a ten-thousandth part of the FSF arsenal, would have finished me right there. He might have gotten away with it, too.

But Gordon cared more for his image than for strategic necessities. And the direct approach was never his style, anyway.

Perhaps he was smarter than I give him credit. In the public reaction to my strike, there was a calculated measure of racial prejudice. To everyone with the entré or wit to pick up a microphone or stand in front of a camera, the civilians I had sacrificed were "and-of-course Mexicans." They were "innumerable peasants," uncounted because they weren't worth counting. They were just a bloody rag to wave at me.

I am indeed a bad man. I will probably go to Hell. But my errors do not make a saint out of anyone who mouths that brand of biased crap.

Pollock must have known this in his guts. If he were to use nuclear weapons on Texas, on "home soil," on—shall we say it?—*white* people, he would never recover. His closest allies in Congress would frog-march him to the nearest wall. His own Federal marshals would draw their own sidearms to shoot him.

So he had to whip me the old-fashioned way, the messy way, the way of Hannibal, Caesar, and von Clausewitz. He had to march down and get me. Which meant that he would make mistakes. And he could lose.

Pollock had no training for this. He had no Federal military men with active experience whose judgment he could trust. And he dared not turn the job over to any general in the State militias. Besides which, the best of them were running the GV forces in Mexico, and I had already shown how I could deal with *that* threat. The tenuous political hold Congress had on the country demanded that he, Gordon Pollock, Speaker of the House *pro tem*, personally whip the rebel babykiller Corbin.

So he did what every politician and modern manager does when sailing into unknown and possibly dangerous waters: He made a great show of his preparations. He sent the States' generals off to the hastily re-established War College outside Harrisburg, Pennsylvania, to learn "unified military tactics and communications." He called in consultants. He ordered a feasibility study. He ran the computers through every possibility and approach to the problem while he took various militia units on joint maneuvers through Lancaster and York counties. In a word, he delayed.

Maybe he hoped I would get bored and give myself up. Or die of some rare disease.

Well, I felt fine. I wasn't bored. My staff and I were

well along with integrating the militias of the TENMAC and the California 64th under my command. And I had no need of feasibility studies: When the alternatives are win or die, you don't waste time exploring the possibilities.

Which is not to say that I didn't plan and prepare.

When I was in Japan, studying karate with Takusan Matsu, I learned to play *go*, the game of black and white stones on a board of intersecting lines. It's the best way to learn strategy and tactics without taking whole armies on maneuvers, or getting people killed as an amateur general in a for-real war.

One of the principles of the game is that position is power. A blocking move is better than a pitched battle. A trap, laid out for all to see, both warns the enemy off your territory and saves stones—which is to say, lives. And a commander who wastes lives on either side has lost control.

With a neophyte like Pollock, the easiest trap would be to push him before he was ready. While he prepared his mind and his men for an assault on Houston, I could march out and force the issue on ground he had not chosen or studied for. Better, I could pick the ground myself. As our armies approached, I could speed up or slow down my airmobile units so that the clash came where *I* wanted it.

I chose Tennessee, the eastern end, around Knoxville. It was on a direct line of march. It was the psychological "danger distance" for a man who considered the East his home. And it was deep in Appalachian river valleys that ran northeast-southwest: They would funnel our armies together, forcing the battle in a way that might spook a new general like Pollock. I wanted him nervous.

Billy Birdsong and I went over the maps, and he had a few suggestions.

"Lot of lakes in those valleys, Gran. Wet ground. You might have to fly by Pollock's forces just to avoid a dunking."

"So much the better," I said.

"You might get a more decisive victory by holding back. Take him on in the north of Alabama, say."

"Yes, but then we'd have our whole left flank closed by Lakes Wheeler and Guntersville on the Tennessee River, our right barred by that dribble of lakes on the Coosa River."

"All right, maybe there is no dry ground. But in those valleys around Knoxville, your flanks will also be blocked."

"Our flanks, Billy. We're in this together, right?" Lately, since leaving Yucatan, the colonel had occasionally needed his spine stiffened.

"Yes, *ours*. Now, maybe *we* could find ground a little more open? Somewhere we can get a pincers or an encirclement going?"

"Look at the maps. Tell me where. We're in hill valleys or wet lowlands from Arkansas all the way to Baltimore. Unless you want to feint west into Iowa or Nebraska . . . ?"

"Nobody would follow us, of course."

"No. Then we'll fight where we fight. At Knoxville."

Birdsong made a shrug, his face closed off. "Your game, General."

At two minutes after sunrise on Sunday, August 7, 2018, we assembled the fire teams beside their Stompers, a field full of ships with their nacelles canted for takeoff, posed for the video crews. We had waited for a little light in the sky to accommodate the cameras. It was good planning to take off on Sunday, because news is usually slow on the weekends and we could be sure of the first pickup Monday morning.

I personally shook hands with the men and women on the five nearest flights, again for the video crews, before climbing into my own machine with immediate staff. Birdsong had arranged landing zones and refueling points for the 800-mile journey, especially the critical one, just before we were calculated to meet the Federal armies around Knoxville.

We had allowed two days for the advance. That was enough time for Pollock to learn of us, mobilize his forces in an indecent hurry, and get in the air and moving toward us. All worked out by computer.

A jumbo wing of 1,500 Stompers took off from Houston. A thousand of them were loaded with the full complement of troops; that is, a fire team of nine plus one noncom or officer. The other 500 ships carried either air-to-air or ground suppression weapons.

That gave us a strike force of 10,000 men and women. By modern standards it wasn't very large—well, even by antique standards. In Caesar's armies, we would have filled about two legions. In Genghis Khan's, we would have been a single horse column. But we were the biggest single armed force afield in our time in our country. That would be big enough. We hoped.

Leading reconnaissance for this army was a wing of the 83rd Texas Air. They were pushing fast jets, the new Seimens-Cessna F-33 Gyro Bat, out in front with two fighter groups.

Would it have been better if we'd had access to the satellite observer networks? Of course, but they were still under FSF control. And did it hurt us that Pollock thereby did have access? Not really, because we wanted him to watch our approach and be alarmed.

We might have sent up a high-altitude radar platform, something like the old AWACS—but why give the Federals something big and slow to shoot at? Besides, the Gyro Bats saw almost as much as the satellite net, and they were a lot closer and more maneuverable in case we wanted them to do anything about what they saw.

That turned out to be crucial in the Battle of Knoxville.

What everyone had missed—my computers, my strategists, me, and probably everyone on Pollock's side, too—is that it had been seventy-five years since two modern western armies had met in battle. In that time, while our theories of war had been sharpened for a presumed final conflict with ICBMs, TRIDENT submarines, XB-6 strategic bombers, and a tank invasion in Europe, our actual experiences had shaped our weapons and expectations toward a single, and much more limited, mode of warfare. Air mobility, tactical fighter-bombers, ground control techniques, communications, all had been developed to fight the kind of unequal little brushfire wars we had fought in Vietnam, Nicaragua, and Yucatan. That is, go in from the air, secure a landing zone, spread out, and capture or control a radius against native guerrilla forces which were using technologies anywhere from twenty to two thousand years out of date.

This was a mentality suited to old Rome: invade the barbarians' territory and suppress their disorganized hordes with superior weapons and tactics. Then hold your new borders against the next set of unwashed crazies over the ridgeline, while exacting tribute and exploiting tribal intrigues among the newly conquered peoples.

But now, two of these modern air cavalry charges were rushing toward each other. And what were we going to do? Land, deploy, and begin shooting up the citizens of Knoxville and surrounding suburbs?

Tumbling through the lower stratosphere in their erratic, radar-evading flight, our Gyro Bats made their first firm contact with Pollock's army in West Virginia. He was twenty miles and two hours ahead of schedule. They estimated his force at 2,400 planes, about a third larger than ours. His force wasn't all Stompers but mixed in a fair number of antique Apaches and A-10s. Not quite as versatile as out little STMs, but the Apache had a lot of bite for a helicopter, and the A-10 was still good in a roughhouse. He also had a supply of fighter jets, the F-25, a sissified version of the temperamental X-29. The fighter plane's everted wings were stiffer and the canard larger, which slowed its instability to the point that it might survive ESM scrambling of its fly-by-wire systems in combat.

With all this data in hand, I ordered our front to expand slightly and pick up the pace. We moved the refueling ahead by ninety minutes, which was a good thing, because it took longer than we had calculated. ETA was 8 P.M. Monday evening, twenty miles east of the city.

With the delay, we were just coming into visual contact with the enemy at 8:45, a good ten miles *west* of Knoxville. The Gyro Bats were mixing in at our altitude, about 9,000 feet, looping and diving through our front ranks like circus acrobats cartwheeling and handwalking through a marching band. Ahead, the Federal forces were spread across the width of two valleys, flying in three echelons vertically separated by a thousand feet. Behind them was the green-yellow sodium glow of the city.

I had hoped to have some sun still behind us. Instead we had dusk, only the sky's red and purple shadings. It was probably better than nothing.

The opposing lines speeded up, shedding altitude, both diving for the same patch of . . . water. It was the surface of Lake Fort Loudoun. We had almost meshed with their lead elements when the same thought must have occurred to both Pollock and me: Why fight on the ground when he, the other guy, the hovering, descending, spiraling mass of planes, is so vulnerable in the air?

"Red Guns Leader, take them in the air, in the air!" I interrupted on the tac freqs, speaking English because our combined troops weren't all drilled in Malay. Other orders went out as fast as I could push the radio's frequency buttons: reverse the descent, climb for advantage, assault ships hang back, air suppression ships move to the forward center, Gyro Bats lock on and fire at will. It took me a minute and forty seconds to get all that out. Those on the listening end relied mostly on the sound of my voice for the authority to change the battle plan. Bad military etiquette, but it saved us the minutes that hacking through channels and response codes would have cost.

Our alternative wing of Stompers, deformed with rocket pods and cannon snouts, cut across from the right flank, bending their head-on intercept course into a strafing run across the Federals' front line.

Maybe Pollock hadn't thought to change tactics. And maybe the Federals, working other frequencies, hadn't heard my orders in English and *en clair*. Their front line was still descending, into the darkening valley, with dark water below them. We could see by the wobble of their flight that the pilots were suddenly confused to be assaulting a pond. And that's when Red Guns hit them.

A dozen Federal Stompers took rocket bursts and fell out of the sky. Half a dozen more put their nacelles over and went into controlled dives, hoping to make the shoreline.

"Get over them! Alpha, Bravo, move in! Mob 'em! Keep 'em low!" I was shouting into the radio, hoping to reach as many of our pilots as possible on the common frequency.

Our own front line surged back, above the confusion near the lake's surface. On my order, our pilots who were mixed into the fray put on their running lights, hoping to separate friendlies from bandits in the deepening dusk. I also ordered our lowest echelon of Stompers to pop the side hatches and spray the planes below them with rifle fire, even with mortars and flares, anything to keep up the pressure and confusion.

The Federal's F-25s tried to rip up our formation, coming in from overhead. But they were too few, moving too fast in a straight line, with the wrong kind of munitions— laser-guided, not heat-seeking. They took out less than five percent of my top echelon.

Pollock's reserve gunships, mostly Apaches, were closing in, climbing to get altitude above us. They almost made it, too. But out of the sky, from a fast arc to 20,000 feet, the Gyro Bats came down like sharks feeding on a school of sea bass. God, those planes could roll, yaw, and fire while in a two-gee vertical drop.

That broke the Federals' formation. With full dark closing down, the lines of assault ships split and dove for the ridgelines where they could flee in the shadows. It looked as if the greatest mass went off to our left, toward the northwest.

"Guns to break and follow. See where they go. . . ."

I sent my gunships on a long tail chase. At best they could harry the fleeing pilots, push them far away, use up their fuel, and keep them from regrouping—after all, the enemy's planes still outnumbered us. The rest of our force I set down on the west side of Knoxville and ordered the troops to bivouac. My thought was that our unloaded Stompers, being lighter, could follow and fight this air war better than the Federals, who had flown off with their full complement of troops.

It turned out not to be necessary.

Pollock's planes never regrouped but instead split into five masses that fled west into the mountains. They did not slow down until they got into the Mississippi River bottom lands, somewhere in Missouri. By that time, near midnight, they were too scattered and exhausted. The

Federals kept moving west, across Missouri, trying to link up. Which they never did. Finally they settled down for the night, giving each colonel or general in command of his own piece of the army time to think. Apparently they were all thinking mostly about what a mess Pollock had made of his first battle and what their chances were for an honorable peace.

My own gunships put down at the Cape Girardeau County Airport about two o'clock in the morning to collect themselves. Then, an hour before dawn, they went into the air again and continued moving west. As they went they received radio signals and position coordinates from the Federal stragglers. The signals were almost all petitions for surrender. Pollock and his immediate staff, however, were not reported in. Neither were their bodies among the wreckage we took from the lakes.

The Battle of Knoxville had taken less than twenty minutes and ended in rout.

Two days later in Kansas City, the "City of Fountains," I accepted the surrender of the Federal officers and their company units. We mustered them in the city's broad avenues, marched them up to the plaza at the Crown Center, built with the glad money of greeting card sales.

These troops presenting us with a legal, or perhaps the word is "diplomatic," problem.

"I want to absorb them and their precious equipment into our army, Mike."

Alcott and I were closeted in a suite at the stately old Hyatt Regency, the morning of the surrender. From the windows we could see the Federal troops forming up. The streets around the hotel went dark with bodies.

"I want to win by winning," I said, almost petulantly.

"Not possible, Gran. They all have State loyalties, as well as their busted allegiance to Pollock. They can't legally come over to you, not while their home States still oppose you."

"Well then, the next best alternative is to execute them, the trained officers at least. That would remove them from the playing board."

"Yes, but—putting the morality and ethics aside—how

would you do it? Take them into a cornfield and shoot 'em
one at a time? One whiff of that and you'll cause a riot in
the streets out there. Plus, it would scotch any further
surrenders in this war."

"I know . . . just thinking aloud."

Finally, we made them they all sign a paper swearing
their peace with the forces of the TENMAC and pledging
not to take up arms against me in the future. And if they
did, *then* I would execute them. It was the best Alcott and
I could work out on the spur of the moment. After all, I
never expected to have 18,000 men and women at my
feet, baring their necks and asking what I would do with
them.

With the plaza fountains surging and splashing behind
us, Alcott and I took 1,500 signatures, with verbal promises, spoken in cadence, from the rest. The sun went high
and came down the other side of the sky while this ceremony went on. Name after scribbled name, verify the
signature against the enlistment papers, raise hands, swear,
salute, about face, next! The fountains were a white sea
noise I can still hear in my head today.

We did keep the Federals' weapons and planes. We also
offered generous contracts to their technical ranks: pilots,
cybers, comm tenders, armorers, and so on. About 2,000
volunteered to change allegiance.

It was ten days later that we learned Pollock had fled
north into Illinois and raised another army from the legislature in Springfield. I don't know what line he fed them,
but it must have been good. It worked for him again and
again in the years ahead.

The situation was really unfair. Pollock could keep on
raising armies, sending them against me, and losing them
until he ran out of glib words, the Rustbowl States ran out
of money, or the Heartland ran out of patience. And
supplies of all the above seemed inexhaustible. I, on the
other hand, had to lose just once. Then it would be a
solitary cell in Baltimore and bullet in my skull. My only
way to win was to see Gordon Pollock personally dead.

One thing at a time.

To oppose this new Illinois division I split our forces,

giving Alcott an aircav wing under independent command.
I also gave him a field promotion to general. General of
what, I didn't explain. My authority was shadowy at best,
but it was good policy to grab all I could and then give it
out with both hands. The historians would justify it all
later, or they would scorn me in Hell. No matter. Alcott
was to contain Pollock in the Midwest while I returned to
our main column and took up the march into the East,
toward Baltimore.

While I was in Missouri, the bivouac in Knoxville had
been attacked by a mixed division of the Kentucky Rifles
and the Nashville Guard. They were defending Old Southern turf more than allying themselves with Pollock and the
Union. Birdsong rolled them back into the hills. For thirty
days we owned the City of Knoxville, but we tried to make
peace with the mayor's office and keep off the flowerbeds
in the parks.

On arrival, I discovered that Carlotta had filed for divorce, Nevada style, with a fourteen-page telex sent through
a judicial cyber. The text of her filing itemized and claimed
for herself one-half of my financial holdings, which at the
time were something over forty billion new dollars. The
half, that is. Her grounds were noted simply as "incompat-
ibility."

Poor Carlotta. She was so smart about other people's
affairs and so dumb about her own. I don't know where
she got the idea to make a grab for a man's balls while he
was in the middle of a war to save his life and, by the way,
take control of the richest, most complex nation on Earth.
And to think she could do this by *legal* means! When you
boiled it down, my word was all the important law there
was between the Pacific Ocean and the Gulf, including
Nevada.

I sent off a one-page memorandum asking Governor
Wade Winston to put Carlotta under arrest. Treat her
gently, I wrote, but make sure she got on the first plane to
Salt Lake City or Denver, her choice, with only hand
luggage and *no* financial paper. She was to understand
that, if she returned to any State that I controlled, she
would be arrested as a spy, tried, and executed.

So much for the law in this matter.

One result of the exchange was that my nephew, the real Gabriel Ossing, left Vegas on his own and traveled through nominally hostile territory to join me at Knoxville.

This was my first look at Clary's boy since he was about four, and I liked what I saw. Not the hulking farmhand that our impostor was, he was slender and serious-faced, a young man just turned twenty. He had eyes that took you up—I remember them even as a baby. His glance would thoughtfully rub the weave of you this way and that, then set you back down without seeming to pass judgment. A quiet boy. He was fortunate to have missed my nose and chin, but he had the curly Corbin hair, though not quite in my shade.

"I can do recon work for you, Uncle Jay," he said after a thoughtful pause. "I was an Eagle Scout in the Truro troop. They gave me twelve merit badges and four electronics projects, before Mother sent me down into the States."

I tried not to smile. A Boy Scout in my front ranks!

But I was to learn that the new unisex Scouting organization in Canada had sharpened their training, making it almost a younger version of the British National Service. No more badges for tying knots and starting fires. One of Gabe's represented a black belt in judo, another a brown in aikido. His "electronics projects" were one senior dissertation in transcomputability and three summers of full-time work at a laser spectroscopy lab in Halifax, starting at the age of fifteen. Standing right before me, he could probably field strip a comm scrambler and reset the codes with his penknife.

I put him on my immediate staff, but I smiled and told him to keep out of trouble. I almost patted him on the head.

Colonel Birdsong and I regrouped our column, adding reserves from Texas and New Mexico, before continuing the advance on Baltimore. We had 22,000 combatants moving on the ground, with a rolling headquarters complex in eight armored vans.

The route grew complicated here. We wanted to avoid

the Washington Crater, which was on our direct line. And the governor of Virginia had sent us a stiff little note saying he would oppose us at the State line with every means in his power. Hubert Garrison was a one-man dynasty, twenty years in the making. He had gotten into the Norfolk Naval Base during the government auctions in '99 and started building the State National Guard into a personal army. In the events of the last few weeks, Garrison had backed Pollock with everything but troops. Those he reserved for a last, private effort against me, as now.

So our planned line of march took a wide swing, through Morgantown, West Virginia, and then east through southern Pennsylvania. The only way we could go.

While Colonel Birdsong took the Army of the TENMAC north on the ground, I went in search of a diversion.

My financial broker in New York City had arranged a meeting for me with Dr. Henry Lee Voles, the Supreme Vice Lord. It was to take place on his ten-acre estate at Sea Cliff, on Long Island. The negotiated arrangements specified one aide, no side arms; so I took Gabe along. It would be good for the boy to see real grass-roots power.

Voles, a PhD in nuclear physics and former member of the New York State Education Commission, was heir to the nominal organization that had grown up around the little plastic card with my signature on it. From street gangs and housing project hoodlums, Voles had built the Lords into a political party, a community voice, and a private army. He had at his command not only the muscles and minds of the East's young Blacks, but also the minds and money of a spectrum of Black professionals and political caucusers. A remarkable man.

He met our car in the driveway with an old pointer dog dancing paw to paw by his knees. Voles was dressed in rubber boots, a watch jacket, and a deerstalker on his head with the flaps pulled down. Picture Santa Claus, short and round, with twinkling eyes, a tight gray beard, and skin the color of antique mahogany.

"I was just going on my October ramble, to see how the fields are turning," he said with a smile, all bright cordiality, the professor turned landed squire. "Will you come with me? We have boots in the garden shed. . . ."

Gabe and I went around back with him and tried on musty rubber galoshes until we had our feet covered. Then the three of us and the dog, with no bodyguards or watchers in evidence, went out by the back gate into a screen of beeches or aspens or whatever whose leaves were just going yellow.

Voles set the pace with short, purposeful strides. The two of us hurried to keep up.

"Let me guess," Voles said drily, businesslike, when we were out of the line of sight from the house. "You want an army on the other side of Baltimore, a nutcracker around Mr. Pollock's power base. You want my boys, who are just now, for the first time, learning to walk tall without interference from white men anywhere in their lives. And you think you can call in a 'chit' to get them. What chit did you have in mind, hmm, General?"

I let us move forward eight or ten paces in silence.

Then: "Some people would say, you built your whole organization on a piece of paper I once signed."

Voles laughed quietly. "An accident of history," he said. "Most of the people who, ah, look up to me have never heard of you."

"Your accident of history eventually cost me a Federal impeachment."

"You would have found other reasons for breaking that stupid triumvirate, you know. The Vice Lords were merely convenient."

"We also have common interests," I pushed ahead.

"Really?" Voles turned with a face of comic surprise, his eyebrows arched high and his mouth forming an O of wonder. "A rebel's army out of Mexico by way of Texas, and an East Coast social organization for oppressed peoples? What common ground can you see there?"

"It would serve us both to see Gordon Pollock dead. If I remember correctly, he has in the past caused some interruption in your local activities."

"Would serve you. Not me. I'm very pleased to have him occupied with political intrigues in Baltimore, or haring off to points west chasing you—in either case proving just how useless a Federal government really is. Besides which, those untimely interruptions were initiated by the Special Executive. Your work too, General."

"But, among us, New York was Pollock's home turf, his personal preserve. And besides, I am no longer—"

"Ah! You are going to tell me that you had nothing to do with the urban riot controls? With abrogation of the Bill of Rights? That they were the reason, perhaps, that you left Baltimore? You are going to stand in my meadow and rewrite history with your tongue?"

"No . . ." I walked on in silence, finding myself forced to re-evaluate this jovial-seeming man. Gabriel had the good sense to hold his tongue perfectly still through all this.

"This issue still remains," I said at last. "Pollock is after total control. His intentions are easily read. Once he has mopped me up—if I can't stop him—he will come after the independent power bases. Like yours. Especially yours."

"And you offer your friendship, your support . . . perhaps another piece of paper?"

"Something like that."

"So that we can deal with Mr. Pollock now, rather than later?"

"When he will certainly be stronger."

"Unless you can weaken him badly in the exchange, before finding your inevitable end."

"Don't think you can skulk on the sidelines, then rush in to pick the bones of his carcass."

"We're not jackals, sir. All we want is to be left alone, to go our own way, to *grow* in our own ways."

"In Pollock's city? In Pollock's world? He will not tolerate that."

"Yes . . . of course. And if the Lords have sided with you and *lost*, what then? He is stronger than you or us, you know, with the resources he can command."

"Life is full of risks, Doctor."

"And some we can avoid. . . ." Now it was his choice to prolong the silence. Four paces, five, and turn toward me. "But not always and not forever. Would you be satisfied with this? My promise that, if Pollock brings troops into my area, say east of the Hudson River, I will not join with him or provide refuge. Nor will I fight against you. Not here. Not yet."

"I'd hoped for more. . . ."

"Do you want a piece of paper?" He laughed. "For now, you may have to be content with mutual nonaggression between us. And see what chits *you* can bring *me* in the spring."

"I may not need you in the spring," I said. "One way or the other."

Our path had unobtrusively looped around to the main access road, where our car was now waiting.

"Oh, you'll still be here, General. And so will I. This will be a long war."

Voles did not pause by the car but continued walking up the road, leaving us with no farewells, no handshakes. However, he did call over his shoulder, "Keep the boots. I have more."

And then he was gone around a curve, hidden by the red-yellow leaves of a stand of oaks. Gabriel and I got into the car and rode into New York City in silence.

Voles was almost wrong about that last. Not the boots, the war.

Birdsong had brought the column north, as we agreed, into Pennsylvania. He was moving our combined force on the ground, mostly in truck convoys, with only a fraction of the infantry in the air.

To shepherd the trucks he had a new kind of armored personnel carrier, or APC, that we called the Turtle. It was just now being turned out at our GM plants in Texas and California, and a dozen had been flown in by cargo plane to rendezvous with the column at Morgantown.

Unlike older, tracked vehicles, this was a low-slung, articulated shell with a twelve-liter, sixteen-cylinder diesel engine at either end. The wheel treads were spring-steel walking hoops equipped with hard-rubber cleats. By specification, the Turtle was all-terrain capable and could still reach 120 miles an hour on clear roads, although at that speed the rubber cleats flew off and the steel feet ripped up the road surface. It was no battle tank, being armed only with a cyber-track .90 caliber twin recoilless—a pop gun. Birdsong was taking the Turtles on this roll toward Baltimore as their shakedown. We'd know whether we wanted more when we saw how these worked in a real fight.

Birdsong's column wasn't just an assault team, meant to rush the Federals' main advance. We were planning to take Baltimore and hold her for the duration.

The Eastern Coalition must have figured that out—and decided against it. We knew that Pennsylvania's own militia might move to block our dash across the Commonwealth's southern skirts. We did not know they had allied with Garrison and the Virginia National Guard, who were moving north parallel to our line of advance, a few ridges east of us. Nor that the Ohio regiments had been called out and were moving to intercept somewhere south of Pittsburgh.

With Pollock occupied in Illinois, the Easterners had brought in their own general, a young instructor from the War College named Raynier. And he was good.

He waited until Gabe and I had rejoined the column—how he knew that, we never found out—and let us bunch up in the Monongahela Valley around Monessen, Pennsylvania. Then he hit us with air power, our old trick, plus two fast-moving ground armies totaling 40,000 combatants. They were coming at us from the northwest, the Ohio units, and from the south and east, those of Virginia and Pennsylvania.

The only thing that saved us from annihilation was the shape of the land. They had to bring their forces over the ridgelines. We could break and run up the valley. The Alleghenies aren't steep mountains, not carved ridges like the Swiss Alps. But they were hilly enough that not all of those 40,000 could move into battle at once. Our main body was saved by maybe twenty minutes' delay on their part.

We had no choice but to move north, fast.

It wasn't a complete rout, but we burned out a slew of transmissions in our hurry. And when a truck stalled we kicked it out of line. The troops aboard it we asked—not ordered—to hold our rear for an hour, then surrender quietly.

We raced through Pittsburgh, across the bridges and up the highways, and on the other side of town dove into the Allegheny River valley, still moving north, toward Butler. It was no way to go, because all that lay ahead of us was upstate New York, probably a fresh army, and the muddy waters of Lake Erie.

The best we could hope for was to wear out and scatter those 40,000 in the chase, regroup our own troops somewhere ahead, and get as many as we could out of the East. Somehow.

Gabe was with me on that wild ride, in the forward pod of a Turtle at the head of the second square. Bracing himself with a hand on the fire control panel, turning away from the driver and toward me, he asked in a low voice: "Why don't we call down one of your planes, get on it, and get out of here?"

I thought about it for two minutes, still staring ahead through the armor-glass slit at the curves of the road coming at us. A cold rain had started, and I could see water flying up in little goblin drops from the Turtle's blunt snout. We were sealed and heated against that miserable weather. The troops in our canvas-backed three-tons would be a lot less comfortable—although the cloud cover was keeping off the next air attack.

"Because these men and women are my responsibility. As long as I stay, they are an army, and I am their general. If I leave, we are all just criminals."

The boy absorbed this in his quiet way. When he understood, I imagined I saw the boyhood go out of him. Real actions have real results. One of them might be a copper-jacketed bullet spinning into your brain. And you take that bullet because somewhere, a thousand-thousand moves and words ago, you made a single decision and acquired this "responsibility." Some things you cannot deny.

For a hundred miles, as we dashed north, I was pulling the Turtles out of line and letting the unprotected trucks

move ahead. I set Gabe to counting them as they passed,
so we always knew our relative position. It was a dangerous ploy, bunching up the Turtles at the rear, because
what would we do if a force was gathering ahead to cut us
off? But the known danger was on our hindside, and I
wanted some armor plating back there.

As the miles ticked off in the rain, we took regular
reports from our own low-flying recon Stompers. When
they finally said the troop strength following us had at-
trited and was now about equal to our own, we made bets
on the pilots' eyesight.

"Your choice, Gran." That was Birdsong, by radio from
the first truck in the vanguard. "Turn and fight? Or—"

Or go on until we met another army, were up against
the lake, or crossed the International Bridge into Canada.
And what then?

We were almost at the New York Border, in deep pine
forests, with no place even to pull aside, about five miles
south of a dot on the map called Tidioute.

"Next valley we come to, Colonel. You break right and
left, circle back through the fields and close the road
behind our last truck."

"Yes, sir."

I changed frequencies. "High wing, give us a topo
reading—the next open space down the road."

"About twenty-five miles," my lead Stomper relayed
back. "There's a broad, shallow valley west of Youngsville.
But with dusk coming down—"

"So much the better." Change freqs again. "Hit them at
Youngsville. Lead with rockets, then walk up the road
with mortars. See if we can bottle them. . . . Okay, count
off by serials." That was to get a hard tally on the remaining trucks.

"One—AB66547."

"Check," came from our surviving quartermaster.

"Two—AB95203."

"Check."

It was a long twenty-five miles. The rain got worse, the
evening light got dimmer. I could feel my stomach tighten,
my guts suddenly heavy, my leg muscles singing to protest

three and a half hours bent into this seat cradle. It would be worse in the trucks, where the troops had been quietly peeing down their own legs because we could not stop for the ritual stretch break.

We reached the valley on the odometer and knew we were there because of the farmhouse lights on either side.

"Break and turn," I ordered.

One man in Birdsong's number two vehicle was assigned to count off truck headlights, aloud on the radio. He got to us, number 287, then a gap, then two stragglers; we knew he'd spotted the end of our line.

Our Turtle slewed around in the field mud and clattered to a stop with its pad anchors out. The driver dialed the cyber-track in on the road and popped the rear hatches for our troops to unload and set up their fields of fire.

After a ten-count we got another pair of lights. Let it pass down the road. Got three more. Then we opened up. Twenty or thirty rocket streaks, green flares of gas in the darkness, followed by cramped orange flashes when they hit. The thump of explosives and screech of metal came back to us, and over it all, like a drum beat, the sound of mortars. A steady death march. After the rockets our soldiers were running forward, firing automatic bursts that looked like little strobe flashes across the field.

That bloodied the Easterners' noses. It also blocked the road to the main force that was still coming up from the south.

We weren't there to take prisoners. After the ambush had done its job, I ordered the troops back into the trucks and onto the next wide road going west into Ohio. With any luck, we could outflank the body of Raynier's army, move off into the flat country, and link up with Alcott's forces.

Of the 22,000 troops that Birdsong had marched into Pennsylvania, I brought out 9,216. Pollock, the Federals, and even a contingent in the TENMAC called it a defeat. I called it victory, compared to what it might have been.

So the war continued. For four years, 2019 to 2022, we seesawed back and forth, Pollock and I. We raised armies from the States where we happened to be bivouacked, if they were friendly to our first cause. We each ran through a couple of hundred thousand men. But we lost most of them in maneuvered surrenders and demobilizations—like the 12,000 I'd lost along the road from Pittsburgh—rather than in killed and wounded. However, we broke up and burned out more light-armored vehicles than you can pile in a hundred wrecking yards.

Through it all, the country never got on a full war footing, not like during the First Civil War, both World Wars, or the Vietnam Cold War. Instead, the national economy dissolved into a patchwork of nation states, some in boom, some in bust, and some watching a parade of green trucks with haggard men and women driving through. The whine of Stomper turbines coming down at the county airport meant that a battle was about three hours away, pack your belongings and get out the claims forms. One side could usually be made to pay up.

My wallet was crammed with folding money in a dozen different colors. Each State or region was printing its own by 2021, although they all took New York credit on plastic.

The war seesawed because Pollock was a bad general. He never could quite put me in a box and kill me. He just never was fast enough. Nor smart enough.

The war seesawed because I would not walk him into a bloodbath. Like an experienced *go* player I wanted, first of all, to block and disadvantage my opponent. Better to intercept an attack than to rush two armies together. In the clash of battle, too much depended on luck and the weather. In the delicate thrust and parry of maneuvers, a general's brains and experience counted for more.

So we wrangled back and forth across the country for four years: St. Louis, Witchita, Denver, Omaha, Decatur, Fort Wayne. My army never again got as close to Baltimore as that drive up the Alleghany Valley. Pollock never even tried to attack me in the TENMAC. We were both too busy running, dodging, and standing to set up a proper diversionary front.

Yes, Henry Lee Voles finally brought the Vice Lords in on my side, fielding an army of 4,000 teenagers armed with light weapons, Czech machine guns from the last century, which my agents helped purchase. But they were a city corps, not air mobile. They hardly counted in the balance.

Pollock tried to buy Michael Alcott away from me. He had the right coin to do it, too: full command of the Federal armies, with Pollock's promise to retire to the sidelines.

"But how could I trust him?" Alcott told me later, after he had turned the offer down. "I'd be his lapdog for life. At best we could form another Special Executive. And look what happened to you."

Alcott stayed loyal because I made him no promises.

With all this confusion and mayhem going on, why didn't some third party, the Russians or the Chinese or the Canadians, walk in and take the country? I don't know. I suppose the Pax Atomica still held, despite a few moth holes gnawed in the concept by past detonations in Washington and Coahuila. The little fight between Pollock and me didn't really involve the boys hunching over their buttons in the silos or watching the screens under Cheyenne Mountain. And they were what really held off the international raiders.

I also have a creeping suspicion that—after the dislocations of the Repudiation and the Money Warp, after the inward-turning focus of the Hundred Lost Days, the McCanlis Revision, and the annexation of Mexico—the Old U.S. was not a superpower anymore. From an international standpoint, we were a second-class, isolationist, troubled country, no longer the World's Policeman, no longer the Prophet of the Capitalist Dream, no longer worth the effort of annihilation. But while the war Pollock and I were fighting might be for the revenant of a once-mighty country, it was *our* country and a deadly serious struggle all the same.

The turn came in '21. Arkansas sued for peace after the Battle of Little Rock and offered me command of their State militia. Oklahoma and Kansas joined in the terms of the peace, even though Wichita had been hotly fought eighteen months earlier. The two Dakotas claimed me for their own—that story of my being a "native son"—and subscribed to the peace. Indiana withdrew from further fighting because, they said with Hoosier wit, they were "tard of all the noise."

I was splitting the country.

When Colorado and Utah closed ranks with the TENMAC, Pollock was caught in the north. He had his eighth army—counting serially the ones he'd lost—outside Fort Laramie, Wyoming, in May of '22 when Nebraska began making fed-up noises. They sent him polite warnings that if he dragged another shooting war across their cattle ranges, they'd hang him for me. I obliged by sending an aircav unit west from Kansas City as fast as I could.

There was nothing Pollock could do but retreat further to the west, into Idaho. To have gone north into Montana, which was wavering, would have meant eventually ending up in Alberta or Saskatchewan. And to cross the international boundary now would lose him the war for sure. So he went into Idaho, with Oregon—my part of the country—facing him on the other side of the Snake River.

My army, with Alcott in tactical command, caught up with him at Shoshone and stripped away his ground forces in a dawn strike. The air component they chased another 120 miles and the rest of the day, finally bringing them to heel at Eagle, just west of Boise.

Because most people don't know where Eagle is, this clash went into the history tapes as the Battle of Boise River. However, given a map and three guesses, most people couldn't have found that either without a key.

Alcott had his orders: cut it short and clean it up. With the war going my way, at last I wanted either a high casualty count or humble prisoners to parade back to the East. No more daring escapes, no more lucky heroes.

So the Battle of Boise River had to be an air war of attrition. It's hard to surrender a Stomper or an F-25 convincingly. What do you do—promise over the radio to give up and then fly with your hands linked over your head? The only certain surrender had holes in it, with flames coming out. We littered a pretty little valley with burned-out birds.

Two days after the battle, I walked the ground with Alcott.

"So, Mike, where's Pollock?"

He was looking over the aluminum cradle and starred plexi of a Stomper cockpit, one of theirs. Apparently the plane had hit the riverbank in a flat spin and come apart like a toy, without much fire. The bodies inside had already been tagged and removed.

"We shot down everything that was flying that day," he said after a pause.

"And there's nothing here in the wreckage." I concluded the thought.

"No—no papers, no prints, no teeth."

"And your observers didn't track any low-flying bogies, no blips . . ."

"Not in this fight. But . . . right after we hit them at Shoshone, there was a lot of scrambling." He said this with a tight grin, embarrassed by the professional sloppiness. "Pollock could have snuck off then."

"Abandoning his army in the first twenty minutes." I made a face.

"He was already losing."

"And he'll never get another one. . . . Worse than a dead hero."

Alcott kicked a fragment of spar, spinning it away over the sand. "This area's clear, Gran, and no one's going to find his body. Does it matter?"

"Not anymore."

Chapter 20

Granville James Corbin: War Among the Lotus Eaters

Late in life, I found love.

Love. Not the brittle mutual-advantage syndrome that my other wives and I had practiced. I finally found a woman with a perfect sense of herself, who fitted perfectly inside her body and her chosen life. Who could share openness and candor with me, yet remain caring and committed. I finally found someone who was like me in her loving.

I found her in California, that great state of anarchy that had shaped so much of my early life. Actually, I went there looking for someone else.

Three weeks after the Battle of Boise River, a game warden patrolling the Malheur River basin in eastern Oregon found the wreck of a Command Stomper. This was a larger version of our aircav workhorses, fitted with extra comm and cyber gear for airtac, or airborne tactical control. It was the kind of plane a general would take into battle with twenty of his staff advisors. It had FSF markings on the fuselage and tail.

The crash site showed a short gouge in the rangeland grasses, ending in a bounce that broke the plane's spine. The pilot had flown to the limit of his, or her, fuel reserves, then come in at a shallow, controlled angle from about 50 feet with the landing gear up. Why she, or he, hadn't popped the gear and set down VTOL two or three miles back, in country no more rugged or closer to anywhere than this was, was a mystery. The game warden reported no bodies, no evidence of injuries, no telltale papers or personal effects, and the data banks were purged. Twenty anonymous men and women had crashed on a hillside and walked away.

Alcott sent a tech team to the site, and the mystery became clear. Two sets of truck tires had gone cross country, cutting into the ground a mile west of the plane and—judging from the vegetation's recovery—at about the same time as the crash. So the pilot had been stretching it for a rendezvous and run short of fuel. One answer.

Now, which way had they gone? North into Washington State and ultimately Canada? West to the coast, Coos Bay, and a boat? Or south into California? The tire tracks ceased to give evidence the minute they touched paved road, five miles from the site.

We settled it by process of elimination: North or west took them out of my jurisdiction; south was the place to look. But if they, he, Pollock had gone into California, we might never find them, him.

Over the years since the breakup of Federal power in the late '90s, California had become more and more isolated, especially in the north. The great eastern road, Interstate 80 from San Francisco to Reno and out across the deserts of Nevada and Utah to the rest of the country, had suffered when Federal money was no longer available to maintain it. The Californians paid to plow snow and repair potholes on the section through the Sierra to Reno, where the gaming action was. Then they figured it was cheaper to allow gambling in their own cities; Reno withered when there was no reason for people to go east.

I-80 was also the main truck route into and out of the region. When the road closed, the Sante Fe Southern system had regained its rail monopoly, which drove up the price of eastern freight, at least for bulk commodities and manufactured goods. In return, Northern California had turned its face more and more toward trade with the Pacific Rim for these things. Lately there had been rumors of exchange difficulties and embargoes with Asia, although this was all too far from my field of activity to bother sorting out.

In the south, connections through Vegas and Phoenix had remained more open, but mountains and deserts were still to be crossed. The water way, to Japan, China, and Southeast Asia, would eventually draw their eyes and their dollars, too.

Except for air travel to the eastern States, which only the rich could afford, the Pacific Coast became as isolated as it had been in Gold Rush days, when goods and news came around the Horn and were never less than three months out of date. The Californians, avant-avant and a little crazy by nature, developed a breed of anarchy that even I couldn't control. They were part of TENMAC by geography and personal choice, not because they submitted to anything like a regional government.

We would be following Pollock into the worst of it. The Redwood Empire stretched from Crescent City to San Francisco along the Coastal Range. And facing it across the strip of upper Sacramento Valley were the dark forest counties: Modoc, Lassen, Plumas, Sierra, Nevada, Placer, Eldorado, Amador, dense, green, secret, ingrown. The people of the valley towns like Red Bluff and Chico were sane, plain farmers compared to the ones who lived up in the forests.

The hill-country tradition had started fifty years ago, in the '70s, when independent marijuana growers had taken over the national forests and held them with automatic weapons against backpackers, game wardens, Federal narcs, and the National Guard. Commerce Department statistics for the period might have said Northern California's biggest crop was wine grapes. Pooh! The biggest *cash generator* in the State—bigger than financial paper, food processing, or petroleum—was maryjane. And all of that cash was going into private, very private hands.

The sherriff's deputies learned to unbuckle their holsters and leave them in the patrol car whenever they stopped to take a leak. County extension agents learned to draw their salaries from the comfort and safety of their offices and keep off the land, thank you. State officials learned to check with the growers before proposing any tiresome legislation that, ten to nought, would be righteously ignored wherever the roads left the flatlands. A situation like that, carrying on for fifty years, erodes the social contract. It draws lines around what people will and won't do. It leaves a lot of shadows where the mushrooms of not-sane behavior grow.

And we were going on a manhunt into this legal wilderness. I told Alcott I wanted at least five rifle companies at my back when we moved south from Oregon. But I left Mike in Oregon. Someone had to be outside, able to come pull me out if things got sticky, and Birdsong was rallying forces for the final push into the East.

I took a battalion of about 600 troops down I-5, which *had* been maintained, from Medford into Siskiyou and Shasta counties. We were mostly in Turtles, with a convoy of supply trucks behind and a short wing of Stompers overhead to provide high cover and spot ambushes. I'd ordered that everything be painted with TENMAC markings, the yellow sun-and-sea, at twice normal size. We didn't want to be mistaken for an invasion force, although that's what we felt like. I also ordered the pilots and Turtle gunners to keep their safeties selected. I'd preferred they took the first hit than spook the locals with nervous bursts at shadows. The shadows would probably fire back.

I-5 took us around the knees of Mount Shasta, across the spidery lake that was backed up by Shasta Dam, and down into the Central Valley. The highway purposefully bypassed the smallest cities and towns, which our recon flights said showed evidence of recent occupation but no people in sight. That didn't surprise me: The phones still worked, and you'd crawl into the storm cellar, too, if your neighbors up the road reported an army coming south.

The point was not to track Pollock, like a posse with dogs, nor locate him with detective work, asking questions door to door. No, we wanted to see the land, see what there was for him to encounter. And so far we had found a typical early-summer day in the Sacramento Valley. Which is to say, the sun was just baking the green out of the fields and turning the concrete highway ahead into a river of white lead. No wonder the people kept indoors.

We were following the interstate south, beyond Cottonwood, when it ended. Not a washout but a cut, as clean as if it was made with concrete saws, thirty feet wide. The roadbed layers of aggregate, rebar, and gravel had been carefully dug away to the underlying soil, and that removed in a ditch fifteen feet deep. If we had been moving at night, we would have lost the head of the column into this hole. As it was, we pulled up, popped hatches, and looked in while the Stompers circled and swooped overhead.

"Turn back. You are not welcome here."

The voice, electronically amplified, had come from a windbreak of trees a hundred yards away from the highway. There were trees on either side here, I noticed, dense ones. Backed up by knobs of hills that could have hidden a column of heavy tanks, although the Stompers reported nothing. They couldn't see into the trees, however.

I went to my Turtle and fished out the handmike for its bullhorn,

"Who asks us to turn back?" I blared.

"The Federated Growers of Tehama County."

"We have come in peace. We do not want to disturb your plantings."

"You won't, Bub."

"We are looking for a party of men and possibly women, who may have come through here less than a month ago. About twenty people with—"

"No one comes through here."

"But we have every reason to believe—"

"You have your feet planted on a piece of ground, Bub, that's zeroed in for a dozen wire-guide, armor-piercing rockets, which we're gonna let loose in about ten seconds if you're not packin' into your clamshells and gettin' out of here."

The morning sun was raising a dome of heat under my combat helmet. The sweat was leaking through my hair and running down my neck. I decided to try the obvious approach, an appeal to authority.

"I am General James Corbin, chief military officer of the States of the TENMAC, to which California is an original signatory. I respectfully request your civilian assistance in locating an enemy of the—"

" 'Corbin' did you say?"

"Yes. General Granville James—"

"Then you're the one."

I didn't know how to answer that. Shouting "One what?" seemed undignified, a slack-jawed dumb question for a commander to be asking in front of his own troops.

The silence grew.

Then, from the trees, a party of men, ten or so, came toward the road. They were dressed in patchwork cammies but were still civilians from their walk, the way they bunched and straggled in the face of an armored column. As they got closer, we could see that they were carrying machine pistols and carbines. Their rockets and their reserve troops, if any, were still in the trees. I noticed that the one in front was carrying a twenty-inch, tripod-mounted bullhorn, an awkward thing you *would* leave back there, if you had any sort of installation. One of his friends lugged along the twelve-volt car battery that powered it.

For the first time, I focused on a slat-sided green farm truck, parked innocuously on the other side of the ditch, about half a mile down the highway.

"I'm Jerry Dorner," the man with the horn said. I recognized his voice without the amplification. He held out his hand to me.

Caught off guard, I took it and shook with him.

"Your rockets are back on the latch?" I asked levelly.

"Oh, yeah." He smiled. Then he turned and pointed off to the right side of the road. "Look, the bank's not too steep over here. If your vehicles can negotiate a twenty-three percent grade—"

"They can."

"You can get them across to the other side."

"I suppose you'd like a lift down to your truck, too."

"In this sun, we'd surely appreciate it." He smiled again.

"And then—?"

"Then we take you to Mandy. Like she said."

The farm truck led us thirty miles down the highway,

past Red Bluff, and turned west into the mountains. The hills rise quickly here, about 1,500 feet in three miles, on switchback roads that had my drivers grinding gears and blowing blue smoke. No matter how friendly Dorner seemed, I kept the Stompers on high patrol, but they reported nothing.

This was sheep country, green meadows broken by white, cheese-textured rocks and cut by rambling stands of live oaks that ran through the country like dark veins in marble. They were goblin trees, bent and twisted, arthritic but incredibly tough. At the crest of these hills, the coastal fog blew enough moisture into the air to support streamers of Spanish moss on the trees. Gray-green lichens covered the exposed stones. It was land that felt old.

We took State routes, then county roads, then paths of oiled dirt. If Dorner was leading us into an ambush—which the Stompers denied, every time I asked them—then he was going to great lengths for it, in country he seemed to own. Somewhere in northern Mendocino County, by our maps, he took us into a small, level valley and pulled us over.

Dorner sauntered back toward my Turtle. We watched him through armored glass, waiting 'til he was right alongside before popping the hatch.

He was still smiling. "You can park most of these tanks and your men down here. No room for them up at the house, you see. Mandy wants you to come up, of course. And bring these fellas along." He waved at the inside of the Turtle. "Have everybody else make camp, why don't you. I saw you got all kind of supplies, but if there's anything you need, just whistle on Channel 33, and we'll try to provide."

He turned back toward the truck, paused, brought his grin around. "We don't get much call for diesel in here, not since the loggin' trucks left. But if that's all you burn, and you need some, we can bring in a tanker. Suits?"

"That's very kind of you."

"Mandy said to keep you happy." He grinned and walked off again.

We set off uphill, just the truck and my command vehicle, after I ordered the rest of the column to dig in, stay close to camp, and expect a call-in signal from me in four hours or come looking.

"Up at the house" was humble phrasing for what we found. Someone had taken over the top of one of these ancient hills, left the best parts of the rocks and trees, and rearranged the rest. The house was a fortress, set on ramparts of dressed stone which filled in the natural dips of the ridgeline and lifted their skirts across the stone outcrops. Above this foundation rose walls of white-washed adobe, ranked in three receding levels, like a Chinese pavilion. Each level was cut with a long Spanish arcade; the arches of the second level were half as wide as those below, the third's half as wide as the second's. Thousands of red-clay tiles topped it all; the roof was interrupted twice, however, by zags where the hill's gray-green oaks sprouted through. The house was as big as a small abbey, and no doubt there were outbuildings, garages, gardens, pools, and gracious living hidden in courtyards behind those Spanish arches.

As we caught glimpses of this gem, while switching back and forth on the road approaching it, I was trying to match lines and shapes with something in my mind. The form was too good, the modern interpretation of a classic theme too subtle. This had to be a Frank Lloyd Wright design, the plans bootlegged from the society that guarded his architectural estate, and unauthorized modifications made to fit a good design to a better setting. I thought it might have started out as the plan for the Marin Civic Center— except for the severe roof line broken up by the trees, and for the red tiles instead of the Center's delicate sea-blue. Also, there was no flat dome.

Looking closely at that roof, I detected a patina, a glint of green-and-silver on the red ceramic. I guessed that someone, finally, had perfected my solar tiles. If so, that house was pulling in about thirty kilowatts.

Coming to a gate that was crafted of oak six-by-threes and bound with steel, set in the eastern end of the foundation's stonework, Dorner's farm truck pulled aside and he waved our Turtle through. The paved road took us into a tunnel, up a ramp, and brought us to daylight in a cobbled court surrounded by more covered arcade, with planters hanging between the white arches. We shut down the engines and sensor systems, checked our weapons, and cracked the hatches. The scent of some heavy flower perfume came in to us. There was also moisture: A fountain sprayed and gurgled at the far end of this open space, cooling the hot afternoon air. Some kind of big pond lilies or other flowers danced and jiggled on the water's surface.

A brown hand, bigger than a triple-oh waldo, gripped the outer edge of the hatch near my head and lifted it to full open, pulling against the hydraulics. If they hadn't given, he might have bent the hatch. Behind the hand was a grinning face, dark-skinned, Dravidian, as broad as an iron frying pan, with moustache like ropes of tarred hemp. This genie wore cowboy boots, white jeans, a jerkin of red buckskin, and a tightly wrapped turban of pale-green linen. He put a hand under my armpits and half-helped, half-lifted me out of the vehicle.

"Very pleased to meet you, General Corbin. I am great admirer of your exploits."

"Why, thank you—umm?"

"My name is Ram Sen Devi, but Mandy prefers that you call me 'Punjab.' It is a small joke with her."

"Thank you, Ram. Are you going to take us to Mandy?"

He nodded his head deeply, almost a bow. "She wishes it."

"Do you need to take our weapons?"

Devi appeared to consider this. "You will want to keep your sidearm, General. Your men may feel—less encumbered—if they can leave their carbines and grenade launchers here. I assure you we offer no violence."

My driver whispered behind me, in my ear, "That wasn't their story back up on the highway."

"We sometimes have too many visitors," Devi said directly to him, "and not enough hospitality. You, however, are very welcome."

"Because Mandy wishes it?" I said with a smile.

"Of course, sir."

He led us in through one of the arches, through panels of sliding glass, and into a hallway floored with cut slate that had been waxed to a high gloss. Our boots clicked and scraped across it.

Beyond was a room, about twenty by forty, with a high ceiling. More slate on the floor, covered with Middle Eastern rugs in blues and greens. The windows along one side looked out through deep, second-level arches onto the valley. We could see the outline of our convoy, parked in serried ranks, in a field about three miles away. The room had the feeling of a working area: a few large tables, covered with maps; three computer terminals in a row; a small PBX switchboard; a rear-projection screen in the end wall. In front of the screen was a single chair, a folding director's chair with canvas seat and backstrap, set up like an impromptu throne. And on it was, presumably, Mandy.

She sat with one foot in front of the other, leaning slightly forward, her jaw and neckline perfect, like the white bust of Nefertiti. Her eyes were like the queen's, too—large, dark, and luminous, with a light that came from ages of experience and understanding. When she looked at me, I could see her seeing me see her. It was a dizzy feeling.

Everything about Mandy was long and smooth, supple, brown, and silky: her legs, her arms and hands, her neck, her hair. Without perfume or other devices, she sent her sense of self out on the air to strike at a man's most vulnerable parts. To know her was to want her immediately, to need to twist her graceful limbs around yourself and rut until your brains fell apart.

She was wearing a white dress, sheer linen worked with fine stitches of white thread at the neckline and sleeves. It flowed loose across her breasts, arms, and thighs, accentuating where it lay upon her, tantalizing where it fell away. On her slender feet were sand-colored leather pumps, flat heeled and practical for dancing.

How old was Mandy? My eyes and senses said nineteen or twenty. My memory says now, by her own admission, thirty-three. But around Mandy, time was a liar. . . . She told lies, too.

Devi brought us forward, toward the chair, and bowed himself aside. "General Corbin, memsahib."

"Welcome to our estate, sir," she said in a voice that was liquid gold, taught to sing contralto. "My name is Amanda Holton. I am the—ah—proprietor here."

Holton! Mandy *Holton?* It could not be a coincidence. But it also could not be the same woman. My Mandy Holton, who had taught Palestinian politics and household explosives at the Commune in Berkley, had been older than I. That would make her well over fifty now. Besides, my Mandy had been a good-looking girl, but she had not the visceral-sexual power of this woman before me. And yet, there were flashes, hints in the bone structure, glints in the skin. This was not a coincidence.

The quiet in the room stretched out. I suddenly realized she had stopped talking while I had gone on thinking. Everyone was watching me for a reply.

"You are not . . . possible," I stammered.

She smiled. "How not?"

"I knew you . . . a different you . . . years ago. A woman who had your name and some of your face. I loved her. Years ago."

"I know," she said, still smiling. "That was my mother, who named me after herself."

"Where is she?" I asked, too abruptly.

"She died, near here, two years ago. It was an ambush, a setup along the road, by competitors in the business. I hate to believe she finally got careless, but . . ." Mandy shrugged.

"And your father?"

"Mother was married to a man named Aguilar. He died. Also."

"And now you are the—proprietor?"

"Among those who will accept me."

"What *is* your business?"

The smile faltered on her lips. She rose from the chair; it took my breath to see the fabric of her dress slide over her body. "Enough, General. You did not come all this way to ask questions about me."

"No, I suppose not." It took a minute to remember why I *had* come.

"You came looking for someone," she prompted, not a question.

"Yes, we suspect that . . ."

"I know. We also believe General Pollock came south into California. That is why we cut the road, and why we watch there constantly. But my people do not know the man on sight. Perhaps you can help us identify him?"

She turned her head slightly, looking off to the right, raised her right hand, snapped her fingers once. From an inconspicuous side door Devi's broad buttocks—he must have slipped out silently while we were talking—bumped into the room. He was pulling something very heavy, or maybe just fragile, a rolling cart of some kind, that made a clinking sound as the front wheels went over the threshold.

It was a laboratory cart, loaded on both shelves with open glass beakers. Each had a capacity of about three or four gallons. They were filled with an amber fluid, which glistened darkly when the sunlight in the room touched it. Some of it spilled out as the rear wheels went through the door. The room was suddenly filled with the piercing odor of a good scotch whiskey.

"Oh my God." That was from our Turtle driver. His comment served for us all. One of the men behind me gagged. I heard him turn and stumble away toward the far end of the room.

There was nineteen beakers, and inside each one, veiled by the liquor and some darker tinge, was a human head, severed raggedly at the neck. Some were men, and a few were women, whose longer hair clouded their faces. Some had eyes open, and some closed. Some had their mouths peacefully shut, and some screamed. From the neck wounds, a few of the heads still bled a wisp of blood to stain the fluid more or less.

Amanda Holton walked toward this deathly exhibit. Then she turned toward me with a pale, sinister stare. "Can you tell me if General Pollock is here? I hope he is, because this has used up my last five cases of contraband Suntory. Don't tell me I've wasted good booze."

Pollock was there, all right. Second from the left on the top shelf. That high forehead was wrinkled for the last time in a look of disdain. The sleepy lids were half-closed over those smoky hazel eyes. The mouth was half-open, as if about to offer an objection. Athlete, aesthete, scholar, a natural attraction . . . politician, general, enemy . . . and finally, corpse—with the rest of his body left somewhere to rot. Good-bye Gordon Pollock.

"Why did you kill them?" I asked.

"They were trespassing," Mandy said simply. "And we knew what you wanted done with them, with him. General Pollock *is* among them, isn't he?"

"Yes." I pointed.

"Good," she said. Then, "Punjab!" and she made a flicking motion with her hand. Devi rolled the cart back through the door. The scent of scotch-and-something-else lingered.

Mandy turned back to me, the pale expression gone. Her chin came up to about my collarbone, I noticed. "Well, General. Will you stay and share our hospitality? At least for a little while?"

"What is your business?" I asked my question, at last.

"We are pele growers."

This was a virulent mutation of marijuana, first discovered in Hawaii. It had a euphoric rush and produced mild hallucinations, a sense of power, and at the same time, relaxation. The best of all possible drugs. It was fiercely addictive.

"You grow it in this valley?"

"No, sir, along the whole North Coast. It likes the natural shade of the redwoods."

"We can stay for a little while."

"Good. We need you."

My men were shown to rooms on the next level down and invited to rest. I and two of my lieutenants, Pet Gervaise and Barney Wong, were also told to dress for dinner. "Dress" meant casual civilian clothes, not evening wear. This was still California, after all.

The meal was held in another hall, this one with a more intimate view of the back of the hill and its live oaks, colored yellow-green by the westering sun. We were seven for dinner: Mandy, two of her "officers," the three in my party, and Mandy's brother. Ram Devi, whom even I was beginning to think of as "Punjab," stood in attendance at the main door and supervised the serving. The dinner was lamb and spring vegetables in a Middle Eastern preparation of strong herbs.

The brother, Eduardo Aguilar, was an insolent youth of seventeen. He was trying too hard in a party of adults, working his opinions on us as a stand-up comedian works his material. He must have been taking something; perhaps it was just contact with the pele plants, because he had worked a shift on patrol with the harvesters that afternoon. Anyway, two glasses of their excellent local cabernet went right through him. Or seemed to.

"You made a real ass-sh of yourself in Wichita," he said to me. He was referring to a battle of more than two years before. "If you hadn't been late at the river, you'da caught Pollock and saved us the trouble."

"Ed, please," Mandy urged him to quiet from the head of the table.

"General Pollock made a career of staying two steps ahead of me," I said lightly, to evade the insult.

"Yeah, he really led you a cherry mace—um—merry chase. He had to come to California to find real sol-jers. Not your buncha pretty boys and—" His eyes swiveled left to Barney Wong. "—slants."

Barney stiffened. He wasn't used to ethnic slurs—nobody in my army was. Suddenly I had to interpose myself to force the issue, before Barney took a table knife to the boy.

"Are you calling me out, sir?" I said.

Aguilar focused back on me, his eyes taking on a calculating look. Beneath the calculation was his certain belief that anyone over fifty, and showing as much gray as I had gathered, must hobble with a stick and pee with great pain. If his answer was at all affirmative, I would choose bare hands for weapons and give him at least a metacarpal fracture to remember his manners by.

"No, I—ah—"

"Eduardo is not used to wine," Mandy said smoothly. "Nor to polite company, it seems." That with a glare at her brother. "I want to apologize for us both."

"No offense taken."

"You are very gracious, General."

The dinner went on, but with strange tensions in the room that seemed to pull about Wong—from the way the others' eyes and conversation avoided him. The boys' insult had been more than a child speaking the worst he knew. I would have to discover more about this.

After dinner, Wong, Gervaise, and I went down the hill briefly to check on the camp and reassure our men. When we returned it was after midnight.

The room assigned to me was dark except for the frosty light of a gibbous moon coming through the draperies. I hesitated with my hand on the switch. Someone was there ahead of me. And I was making a perfect silhouette in the light from the hallway. I left the switch off and slid sideways out of the doorway, closing it with my foot.

"Don't be afraid, General." Mandy's voice. From the bed. Low and liquid.

"My lady, one reaches an age when there is nothing to fear but much to be cautious about."

"Oh. Not *that* old, certainly." As my eyes adjusted to the light, I could see that she was under the sheets, lifting them in invitation, and she was wholly nude.

I was halfway out of my clothes before I was halfway across the room.

Mandy tasted of cinnamon and anise. She twined like a vine. She rolled like the waves of the deep Pacific. I don't know if she used some drug on me, either put it in my food or smeared it on her own body, but I stayed erect and hard as a bar of iron, yet painlessly, for most of the night. We rode each other like wild horses.

In the morning, as the sun first came over the hills, I felt clean and washed, empty and light, strong, and very pleasantly tired. Mandy slept beside me like a beautiful child, with a smile on her face.

After four years and more of back-and-forth war, with all its intrigues, manipulations, and shifting alliances, I needed a woman of clear and simple lusts. I needed a place where the problems were all microscale. I needed a time that moved to the rhythms of growing things, not to the mechanisms of politics and technology. I needed to be here and now.

After four years and more of chasing Gordon Pollock across the country, always two steps behind, I was tired. Now, with my rival dead, I could relax for a while, enjoy this valley, this woman, this season of youth and simple colors. In that clarity that morning brings, I decided to award myself a furlough. Let Alcott and Birdsong handle the war for a month or two.

And, besides, I was already halfway in love with Mandy. Make that "completely."

If she had used a drug on me—and I did think the world had an aura, a brightness to its color and sounds, that morning—then it was one that imparted a feeling of power, optimism, freshness, strength. But I felt neither giddy nor silly, as sometime happens with lifters. And none of the mushmind that comes with tranks. Mandy's drug must have been the legendary chericoke, or a close derivative. And if she had used it without my knowledge, then so be it.

The staff knew to bring a double order of breakfast to this room. A soft tap on the door and, when I looked out, a tray with cereals and cakes, yogurt and fruits, and coffee. I poured some of the latter, and the smell of it appeared to wake Mandy. Her sleepy smile blossomed in a telltale instant as she focused on me.

We took the food out onto the small terrace, an open space under the house's arches, hanging over the valley. The sun warmed us and chased the haze of fog that drifted below us.

After the passion of the night, however, Mandy was very contained and quiet. She dipped her yogurt with the tip of a spoon and lapped it with her tongue like a cat.

With the light of day, I was careless of personal signals and decided to pursue a matter from the evening before.

"What was that comment at dinner about 'slants'? And Lieutenant Wong was treated coldly, I thought. Yet Asian prejudice has been a dead issue in California for decades."

"Don't ask," she said, lifting her head between laps of yogurt.

"But I do ask."

"Very well . . ." She sighed and pushed away her dish. "We're in the middle of a little war of our own here, General."

"The rest of the country calls us 'dream merchants.' By accidents of geography and climate, this region grows a most potent brand of pele, one that commands high prices. The weed grows in other places, of course, but our plantings are the largest and have the strongest alkaloid concentrations. This year, maybe this decade, our pele is the drug of choice in America. That gets us a bad rep with other retailers, particularly with the great pharmaceutical houses of Japan and Korea."

"What do they have to do with it?"

"Simple competition. People flashing out on pele aren't buying methaluude, diodreamin, cocolaide, or most of the other chemical dependencies. Our Asian friends are working through an American front company, Hajimeru Kara, Inc., to change that."

"What can they do?"

"Look out there." She pointed off the the east, between the fog and the sun. Her finger did not hold steady but wove a short line against the horizon.

"See them?" she asked.

I looked hard, and finally detected a pair of gnats, diving among the hilltops, two ridges away.

"Crop dusters?"

"Very good, sir!"

"Not yours."

"No. They come every morning when they can see through the fog to fly. They get a few patches where they think we aren't looking. They don't try to destroy the plants, just poison them. It's more fun if we put all the effort into cultivation and harvesting, then kill off a few customers. They think we don't know about it."

"Can you stop them?"

Mandy shrugged. "No air force. Just a few private jets, and they aren't armed."

"I have a wing of Stompers here. . . ."

"How many in 'a wing'?"

"A dozen planes."

"Would you fly them against civilians? That would hardly be honorable, would it?"

"I've done worse."

She stared at me with a hooded look.

I moved my eyes away—and noticed that those planes were growing larger, and they were no longer zipping around. Coming right at us.

"Do they often do that?" I pointed.

"No . . ." She hesitated.

The two dusters came in straight and level. If they opened up with cannons or machine guns, they could pick Mandy and me off this ledge. Their silhouettes grew against the sun, larger, wingtip to wingtip, separating, their engines a drone, a blast, a thunder. And then the planes pulled up in a hard climb.

Were they trying to frighten us?

Something tiny broke off from the belly of each. Without thinking, I dove across the table, tackled her in the chair, and crashed the both of us back behind the foot of the archway. Mandy banged her head, scraped an elbow, and cried out as I fell on top of her.

The bombs went off with a shallow concussion that had the undertones of a timpani section, with flutes and fifes singing over it. Sonic grenades. They were meant to cause neural damage, but you had to be line-of-sight to receive the full effect. Behind a parapet, with the blast below us, we were only shocked and deafened in the midrange. That effect would wear off.

I helped her to her feet.

"Next time," I said, my own voice sounding muffled in my head, "we'll come out and play."

"What?" Mandy shouted beside me.

Next time came the next morning. We went down to the valley before dawn, readied four of the Stompers, and waited under the fog. A fifth plane already in the air, high over the valley, pulling radar watch.

"Guns Leader from High One. Two bogeys on scan. Bearing east southeast at ten miles. Crank 'em and spank 'em."

Because the excursion involved little danger—unless there were more than two of the dusters, or one decided to ram us—I took Mandy along on the foray. We circled around the hills, contouring them with our ground radar, and came out of the mist behind the bogeys. We checked on visual to make sure we weren't dogging a pair of innocent Cessnas on private business. But as soon as we broke, the dusters went into wide evasive turns, one left, one right. We split, tracked them, and blew them away with rockets. The whole operation lasted five minutes.

Mandy's eyes fairly gleamed.

That evening, as we were getting ready for bed, an emergency signal came up from the valley. An intruder had been found near the Stomper pads, a man dressed as a *ninja* and carrying a string of clock-detonated bombs.

"Send him up to the house," I told Gervaise.

"Sorry, General," she said, "he didn't survive getting caught."

"See if you can get a live one next time."

Next time turned out to be that same night. Mandy and I were in bed, lying quietly after our lovemaking. We were in her corner suite, above the east gate, with one set of windows looking into the hill, the other across the valley's end.

I was almost dozing and Mandy's breathing had slowed to sleep, when a tiny *tink* came from the window. My eyes popped open. Turning my head, I caught a shadow against the drapes, on the outside. I slithered off the bed and rolled into the darkness beside the window's moon-lightened square.

Whoever it was had climbed two stories of stonework beside the gate and now hung or clung on the sheer stucco face of the building, without balcony or ledge. He was cutting a circle of glass above the lock. I let him in.

A hand came through the hole, pushing out the curtain, and worked the lock. The window swung out, pulling a bow of the material with it. Then a leg swung through and found the floor with the knee and ankle slightly bent to cushion and absorb sound. The weight followed, anchoring the figure on this side of the window. And I hit it.

A straight kick pushed the knee in directions it didn't want to go. The intruder cried out briefly, rolled into the room, and tried to bring up a weapon two-handed, aiming it at the bed, not at me.

A second kick hit clenched hands and hard metal. The weapon *phutted* once, well off target, as it went flying. The intruder was curling into a crouch to deal with me. One arm hung lower than the other and at an angle.

A third kick came up, heel and edge, under his chin. A hard crack echoed in the room. He somersaulted backward into a chair and lay still.

Mandy turned on the lights.

"Are you hurt, Gran?"

"No. You?"

"Nuh—he's moving! Behind you!"

I spun, stepped, and put a fourth kick into the black-clad, staggering body, right on the solar plexus and four inches in. It whistled and collapsed.

Crouching on guard above it, I did a quick pat search, pulling out weapons and tossing them onto the bed. Then I unwrapped the black cloths around the head, and discovered a girl. Her jaw was a shattered, blotchy mess where my third kick had taken her, but that had absorbed the shock and saved her a broken neck. I used strips of her clothing to bind whole arm against broken one, straight leg against bent.

"I have interrogators at the camp," I told Mandy. "We'll know soon enough what's going on."

"But her jaw—?"

"I saw a man speak clearly with half a tongue once. It all depends on having the right persuasions."

The *ninja* held her silence for eighteen hours, then broke. She told us a lot of babbled mush about secret rituals and codes and an interlinking trail of Japanese names that meant nothing to us, but hidden among all this was one solid fact. That she had known which room to attack because we had a traitor, not just in Mandy's organization, but in the house.

"Why is all this happening now?" Mandy asked me as we stood over the dying girl. "They've been spraying and harassing us for months. But trying to kill me, that's new."

"When I brought a couple of companies of heavily armed

soldiers into the valley, it might have looked like bringing in reinforcements. As if you were escalating."

"So we *are* escalating," she said. "What now?"

"You go for the win. There is no losing position, it would seem, that leaves you alive. And first we find the traitor."

The way to locate an informer is to color his data. We couldn't very well tell everyone in the house where we would be sleeping—and mention a different room each time. But we could pour subtle scrambles in the harvesting instructions for the next week. If the Hajimeru agents took any action, it would finger their insider.

It was fun, helping Mandy that summer. We went up almost every morning to chase the dusters, and after a few weeks of straight losses they stopped coming. We fought two pitched battles in the valley. After that, we went on the offensive. With my lady at my side, we went on a raid to the Oakland Inner Harbor to blow up a shipment of Japanese drugs. Two limpets placed at the waterline put the freighter on the bottom and blocked the channel. The cargo was in watertight containers, but we brought in the Stompers to strafe and bomb. Then we put a tap on the Hajimeru headquarters building in San Francisco and hit it a week later with another night raid.

Pet Gervaise and I were planned to go in with fake IDs making us for Midwestern clients. The cover story was that we wanted to wrap a deal with the Hajimeru right after the theater and before we went off for a late supper. Such a busy schedule . . .

We would indeed be dressed for the theater, but under the polysilks, strapped to our legs and torsos we'd be carrying a full kit of nonmetallic weapons and unsniffable explosives. The idea was to get in, go for position, and disrupt everything in sight. Wong would come by in fifteen minutes with a backup team and comb the building. There was just a chance we might not hold out that long, and that's what made the plan exciting.

Mandy nixed it.

"Why are you going with her?"

I was listening carefully for emphasis. Was it my taking

part in the plan that she objected to? Or Pet's? Couldn't tell, so I picked my own interpretation.

"Why, I have to go, Mandy. I'm about the only one here old enough to be a believable buyer. The white hair does it."

"No, you bear, I mean why *her*."

"Lieutenant Pet's a good soldier," I smiled.

"But *I* want to go with you."

"Nonsense, you'd be recognized."

"Not if I wore a wig . . ."

"With cheek pads and a funny nose?"

"You won't know me."

And I didn't. Mandy looked sassy and brassy when she modeled the disguise for me at H minus three. A silver-blonde acrylic wig, ironed straight and with bangs to her eyebrows, put her two cycles out of fashion. Subtle crow's feet painted next to her eyes and a little padding stuffed against her flat stomach added fifteen years to her age. She looked like a midtown jolly girl, nearing the end of her working life but just the thing for an old coot from the cornfields.

"You're hired," I told her. "Got your briefings?"

"Cab to the front door. Make the checkpoints on the strength of your appointment and a bunch of cards. Get to the elevators, and freestyle it from there. Where do we lodge, the executive suite?"

"Oh no! Going through with the appointment upstairs puts on their terms and under their guns. If we get as far as the elevator, we punch for the second basement and head for the computer center."

Mandy's mouth tightened, cracking a layer of lip gloss. "We're going below street level? Down in a hole. We could *die* there."

"Shall I call Pet?"

"No, just an observation."

No one tumbled to us at the first checkpoint, a magnetometer and sulfate sampler. At the second, a body patdown, the Japanese guard paused over the latex thigh pads that hid my spring gun. He probably thought I was in really good shape to have muscles like that.

At the third station our hosts, the Okane brothers, met us themselves. With just a short-form bow and smile, they led us across the building's green-marble lobby toward the elevator bank. Mandy, walking beside me, wobbled drunkenly on her high heels and put a hand to her new potbelly. She was unobtrusively working a penade up from the stuffing.

The brothers ushered us into the first open car, followed behind us, placed themselves against either sidewall, still smiling, and pressed "Door Closed." The car was a big one, about seven feet wide and six deep—an awkward space, with both their eyes on me, and their hands never far from the first button of their coats and the pistols that would be underneath.

Before the doors were fully closed and either of the men could punch for an upper floor, Mandy pressed her stomach again, moaned, and bent over. As the brothers moved forward, I swept up my hands in a crossed-uncrossed double strike that went to the limits of my extension and two millimeters more.

The first brother was caught square in the throat and put up his hands, after the fact, to do something with his larynx. The second brother took the edge of my hand just below the orbital ridge of his left eye. Whenever you double strike like that, you divide the force of your blow. I had enough behind that hand to split his eyebrow—the sort of wound that makes a lot of blood in the boxing ring but never stopped anyone.

He actually got his gun unseated before I could bring my other fist around and bury it in his solar plexus. His gun hit the floor in the same second my knee came up to flatten his descending nose.

The sight of the gun must have reminded the other brother, who left his throat alone and fumbled for his own weapon. He fumbled long enough for me to turn that rising knee into the cock for a back-kick that broke his wrist across his stomach. Then I half-turned and smashed his temple with a two-knuckle back-fist. The Okane brothers slumped across each another.

What was Mandy doing all this time? When she doubled over with her sick act, she let it carry her under my first strike and up against the doors. There she slid around like a snake to keep out of my way and pushed the B2 button. Before I had finished them off—it took all of nine seconds—the doors were opening in the basement. Mandy launched herself out into the white-tiled corridor in a drunken stagger.

A security guard, of a different flavor from the ones running the entry stations upstairs, came out of his glass booth to help her. He found himself looking down the barrel of a plastic squirt gun. It took him two seconds to figure it out; it took Mandy one second to fill his snoot with double-strength Mickeyfinn. He dropped like a sack of gypsum.

Meanwhile I was taking the brothers' guns and tidying their sleeping posture in the open car. I was just about to send it up to "Penthouse" with their special keys, when Mandy stopped me with a hand. She bent over one, set a penade in his ear canal, set the timer for thirty seconds' delay, and rammed it home with the sole of her shoe. She repeated the action with the other brother, setting his timer for fifteen seconds. Then she pushed the floor button and stepped out. We didn't hear the charges go off but inferred it from the way the telltale lights froze up around the twenty-first floor.

We turned to the double doors of the computer center. Time was six minutes into the operation.

Two batches of operators, about a dozen people all told, let themselves be herded into the corner of the room. Mandy held them there with the guns while I set penades and plastique in among the reader spindles and under the cabinet holding the core memories. I strung garlands of touch paper in the tape vault and fused it with my last penade. Then we took the operators out into the corridor and prepared our stand with a hostage shield while waiting for, first, the center to go up and, second, Barney Wong to get in with his infiltrators.

Things happened in that order, and we had a hairy minute watching the flames come out of the double doors and block our retreat to the stairs. The room itself may have been fire retardant, but I tell you nine tons of polymer substrate and ferrous carbon burn like merry Hell. There was a lot of stinky smoke in the corridor . . . only later did I think what the intense heat might be doing to the gallium arsenide on the semiconductor chips.

We held our ground for the full fifteen minutes, enough time to make sure of destroying the Hajimeru records, accounts, and data bases. They sent three waves of guards against us, but they were too concerned with trying to dislodge us and fight the fire at the same time, thereby making a botch of both tasks. Wong came through from the lobby and took them in the rear. Hajimeru's business limped so badly after our raid that I can only assume they didn't have their data properly backed up. Pity.

Mandy and I returned to the house in the late hours of the night, washed the last bits of makeup and sticky soot off each other with wash cloths, then made love to the singing of birds just before sunrise.

The traitor? We found him that first week: Eduardo, the brother. His dependency was something other than pele and red wine. Mandy should have spotted it months ago.

That summer was just what I needed: a break, a respite from the national scene. A time to fill my lungs with the quiet, moist air of the redwood groves. A time to deal with problems on a personal scale, a "pocket war" if you will.

In August, Mandy told me with shining eyes that she was pregnant and happy about it. She was the first of my wives—and no wife, really—to have a child. It filled me with strange emotions. She began talking about all the things we would do with the pele business: new land to cultivate, new strains to experiment with, new markets to trade in. She wove her plans for us, our new life together, and I listened.

A certainty was growing within me, however, that this hilltop existence might be fine for a vacation but it was no life. I had other business to continue, national business. Playtime was just about over. Soon now. Any time.

But it was soothing to listen to her song.

Chapter 21

Billy Birdsong: Speaker For Life

I had to go into California and get Corbin myself.

He left me with a mixed army of half a million men and women, keeping watch on the west bank of the Mississippi River and up the Ohio as far as Cincinnati. They were an uncongenial collection of State militias, my own TENMAC troops, volunteers, vigilantes, survivalists, reservists, freebooters, and carpetbaggers. A carnival show.

For every two of them who held a gun, a third was carrying papers and electronic ID that identified him or her as, variously, chairman of the fictitious board of Maybe Never Investments, Inc.; the newly elected governor of Erectorset County, looking for just the right kind of men to form a cabinet; the sole commercial representative for Nutra-Vita-Vim-Gro-Gen-Stuff, who just happens to have samples in the other pocket; a patent attorney with venture capital to offer the right young inventor who has just a tenner, or make it a hundred, to set the wheels in motion; the special agent-in-charge for the Canadian Bureau of Investigation, down here on official business seeking the beneficiaries of the Saska-Baska-Berta-Berry Case and a mere twenty will seal your claim; or just plain the heir to the throne of Roumania. These pitchmen were turning over a small geyser of currency every day on the flimsiest pretexts.

Why? Because we were an army with nothing to fight.

The station we were keeping, the line we were holding, was nominally against advances from the Old South and the East. But most of those States, while they had not yet declared for Corbin, had stopped fighting for Pollock when he disappeared after Boise River. They were content to growl at us across the frontier, occasionally, but they hoped to be left alone. After twenty-plus years of a Federal government that had served in, at best, an advisory capacity, they were quite happy to find their own level of provincialism, print their own paper money, and trade cows, corn, and not-too-bad moonshine whiskey with their neighbors.

The country was becoming balkanized. Most of the States kept their elected form of government, although I heard that Montana had promoted themselves a king. Most of them kept good relations within their region, although Florida was getting a bad name in the Old South by opening diplomatic ties with Cuba and Jamaica. There was a rumor that Soviet troops were practicing wet landings in the Everglades, but rumor was all it amounted to. People were seeing Russian spies, Japanese trading cartels, and Ayatollian terrorists on every street corner. That kind of fear contributed to people closing the borders, cranking up the vigilance committees, piling up inventories, and stockpiling canned goods and dry wood on the storm porch.

The carny folks in my army prospered, also, because the air on our side of the river was glittery with prospects. "After this war is over" they told each other—and went on to spin a dream. They would aspire to public office. They would set up a business. They would get married. They would travel, and see this beautiful land from some perspective besides the backside of a gun. They would get pregnant. They would carve a frontier out of the semi-urban wilderness of any State that would not submit to General Corbin. They would be on the winning side, you see, with a chance to become powerful and wealthy and famous and happy . . . "after this war is over."

I was nominal commander of a nominal army that was halfway demobilizing itself on the spot—and which had never been more than halfway mobilized to begin with—in the middle of a civil war that we were nominally winning but nobody knew. And Corbin was gone.

He had taken half a regiment down the road from Oregon and then disappeared. Yes, they had carried a satellite downlink with them. Yes, they had set it up and called in regularly. But they would not say where, exactly, they were bivouacked or what they were doing. There was a giggly note in the transmissions I was receiving. The lieutenant on the California end was smilingly evasive, yes-sir and no-sir, but he would *not* tell me where the General was. "He's out on hmm-ha"—secret smile—"on *maneuvers*, Colonel, um-ha-ha." Usually his link would drift off channel before I could get anything more out of him.

Sometimes, rarely, I even saw Gran on the link. "You just hold the fort there, Billy," he would tell me, with that same God-damned smile. "We're doing important military work here. Good liaison stuff."

Now that was more than just erratic. More like crazy. With the country about to fall apart like an ice-cream pie in the hot sun, what was Corbin doing "liaisoning" with the California natives? They were already on our side, supposedly—if they were really on anyone's side in this war.

Still, Corbin did look five years younger. The lines in his face had smoothed out, and it was no trick of the transmission. The squint was gone out of his eyes. The impatient little grind had disappeared from his voice. And that scared me: If Corbin was softening, ready to kick back and give up the war, where did that leave me and this vaudeville army along the Mississippi?

After five weeks of such nonproductive bullshit, I figured the only thing to do was go in and get him. But I would not take the Oregon road, not if it had been a trap for Gran. Instead I put a rifle company on a jet for SFO and arranged transportation north from there. How did I know to go north? My electron pushers had interrogated the satellite and gotten enough of a back-angle on Gran's signal to figure the bird's own azimuth and declination as seen from his transmission point. That put him somewhere within a forty-mile radius of Ukiah, California. Once on the ground, we could find his camp by triangulation.

We went straight in, there being zero percentage in screwing around. I put my company, about 150 troops, in chartered buses, except for the team with the tactical nukes. They rode in an open rental truck. It started out green; we gave it a quick coat of yellow paint and, where the owner's logo had been, painted in the three upside-down triangles that meant radiation danger. That truck led the column. There was no percentage in subtlety, either.

Going up Sonoma County on Highway 101, someone took a few pops at us. We countered with a thumper round fused to airburst over them, from the lead truck. It was a heavier than usual charge of gelignite, with a big fraction of magnesium shavings to make it flare. Whoever owned those hills cut out that shit right away.

North of Ukiah, the highway angled west toward Willits. We took the first road to the northeast, following our radio signal. We found Gran's five companies near Potter Valley. They were pulled up, parked, and dug in pretty hard in the valley of the Eel River. Petula Gervaise was in charge, kind of.

"Colonel Birdsong! No one—that is, I didn't—uh . . ." She took her size tens down off an ammo case and struggled up out of the camp chair where she had been dozing.

"At ease, Lieutenant." Although she *was* pretty much at ease. "Where is General Corbin?"

"Out on maneuvers, sir."

"Exactly where, 'out on maneuvers'?"

"He doesn't tell us, sir."

"How long has he been gone?"

"Couple of days."

"Did he take any men with him?"

"Yeah, some of ours and some of *hers.*"

"Do they have a radio with them?"

"Yes, sir, but it's set to *her* frequencies."

"Who is 'her,' Lieutenant?"

"Mandy, sir."

"Who is this Mandy?"

Gervaise shrugged. "She owns this place."

"Where is this Mandy?"

"With the General, sir."

"On maneuvers?"

"Yes, sir."

Tired of talking in circles, I looked at the hills around us. Just brown grass and scrub oak, an isolated farm site except for a California rancho, a house as big as a hotel, on top of one of the ridges.

"Does Mandy normally live up there?" I guessed, pointing.

"Yes, sir."

"And General Corbin stays up there, too? Sometimes?"

"Yeah, all the time, now." She grinned.

"We will go visit."

"They aren't up there now."

"Right. They are 'out on maneuvers.' "

I climbed into the yellow truck and waved the column forward.

At the last curve before the house, we pulled the buses over, parked them, chocked the wheels, and deployed my troops. They had orders to surround the house and make sure no one got out.

"Oh, and Sanders," I said to my major in charge, "pass the word not to eat, drink, or smoke anything they did not bring with them. Not until we find out what is going down."

He saluted and moved his first squad west around the house.

We drove the truck up to the gates and tooted the horn.

They opened and out stepped a cartoon character, all whites and pastels, dressed with a turban like a swami Indian's. He bowed low before our front bumper.

"Welcome to the house of—"

We put the truck in gear and drove right ahead, forcing him to dodge aside. We went through the gates and up the ramp. In the wing mirror I could see Swami whirl around, straighten his turban, and puff one of his mustaches off his lip. He was pushed aside again as half of my men came out of the bushes and advanced, weapons at the ready, behind the truck.

Taking this little hilltop fortress was that easy. Everyone

inside was armed with kitchen spoons and garden rakes, and they put those down fast enough.

After a sweep through the main corridors and rooms, I parked the truck in the middle of the fountained courtyard, put the men at ease in the shade, still with the order to ingest nothing, and waited. The turbaned houseboy tried to get a word in, but I ignored him.

At 1800 hours, with the sun still high, the men got orders they could squat by threes and break out their energy bars and cigarettes. Dinner, on maneuvers. They were told to answer the call of nature in the storm drains, not in the fountain.

"Please, sir!" Swami entreated. "There is no need for all this crudeness. There is comfort here for all."

I just looked at him.

"We truly intend no violence."

I did not ask him where the General and this Mandy woman were, nor when he expected them to return. The first rule of intimidation is self-containment. Plus, I did not want to get into any more circular conversations, which seemed to be popular around here.

After a while, Swami gave up and went inside.

When the sun went down behind the western roof, we slept—again by threes, in place.

With the dawn we made coffee, heating canteen water in a helmet shell on the truck's engine block. Swami was appalled.

At 1000, Sanders reported by talkie from the perimeter that a pair of Stompers—ours—had landed in the valley. And at 1027, that a car was coming up the road. I told him to pass it.

At 1042, the car rolled into the courtyard and jerked to a stop behind the nuke truck. Corbin got out of the back on one side; a woman, thin and dark and in her thirties, got out on the other. The driver stayed in the car.

"Why, hello Billy . . ." He looked younger than he had in the sateltrans.

"Been having fun, Gran?"

"Yeah, lots of fun."

"Doing what?"

"Fighting."

"Who?"

"The Asian drug lords, mostly. They were giving Mandy a hard time, trying to ruin her pele crop. I've been using our hardware and some of the boys to even the sides a little."

For the first time, I took a close look at this little Mandy. She had a good face and a competent body, and she used them like Jankowski uses a violin—for maximum effect. She was a stunning woman, actually. Then I saw in her face a nose, the shadow of a nose, that I had known for thirty years. And her jawline, her chin, her overall bone structure, hints and shadows. If Granny Corbin had ever sired a daughter—and I knew he had not—then this Mandy might have been her. But her manner and movements were her own. Most effectively.

"—about under control?" Gran finished with a question, whatever he was saying, and I had missed most of it.

"What? Oh yes. Of course," I covered.

"So why are you here?"

"To get you."

"And bring me back?"

"The situation is getting pretty ripe, out there, in the rest of the country, Gran. Falling apart, in fact. Small enclaves, regional nationhoods just forming up. If you want to—"

"Why are we standing here talking beside this—this truck?" Mandy broke in with a hard smile. "Why don't we go inside? And get this—truck—out of my courtyard!" The atom symbol was really spooking her.

Gran nodded and smiled, put an arm around her, squeezed her once for comfort and again because she was squeezable, and they led me under one of the cloistered arches. Before I left the area, I signaled my troops to stay put.

Inside, in a room you could play a fast game of touch football in, we settled into chairs of soft leather and took drinks that Swami brought us. I just sniffed mine and put it aside.

"The country's falling apart, did you say?" Gran began.

"First of all," I countered, "what happened to Gordon Pollock? Did you find him? Or still looking?"

"He's dead."

"Good."

"Mandy's people captured him and his party. One of her lieutenants executed them for trespassing. It was kind of an accident."

"Does it matter?" I asked.

"I don't want it said that I put him to death without legal process. Pollock wasn't a criminal. In fact, he was probably more in the right than—"

"So long as somebody did it."

"Ah—yes." He switched gears. "Now tell me. What's the situation really like outside?"

"Gran?" Mandy interrupted. "Will your guests be staying here in the house or down at the camp?"

"Oh . . . some in each, I suppose."

"Well, you want to decide, don't you, so we can make up the rooms?"

"First, my dear, I want Colonel Birdsong to give me his report."

"Of course, dear." She smiled, then looked at me, and the smile withered to something like a pinched stare.

"Gran, the country is in very strange space," I began, working from a script that I had been writing mentally ever since we landed in San Francisco. "So much of the opposition to you has been focused on Gordon Pollock, his aura of political power, and his own personal following, that removing him puts the entire Federal movement into a warp. There is no secondary personality, and not much of a structure, to carry on."

"And so?"

"So we have a situation filled with kinetic and emotional energy, but no direction. The inertia of everyday events and institutions is stopped. For a span, perhaps a brief one, we suddenly find ourselves in a situation a lot like the Roman Republic of the first century B.C., in the aftermath of the Civil Wars. Or the French Republic of the 1790s, after the Terror. Or the Weimar Republic in the early 1930s, after the economic collapse. There is confusion, discontent, hope, all mingled. The established order has broken down, and no single engine—no government body, no church doctrine, no invading army—is pushing the pieces back together.

"This is one of those delicate balance points—where one man can move a nation. You cannot do that when there is momentum, because you need a huge amount of force to bend the direction of everyday affairs even slightly. And huge power is not given to any man. But when there is a pause, like now, when the train runs out of track, when the ship of state runs into shallow water, when the pendulum is at the top of its arc, ready to swing in another direction . . ."

"Yes?" Gran prompted.

I shrugged. "If this pause goes on long enough, the country will collapse. It will end as a coherent nation and become instead a swamp of regional interests. The Midwest will barter its corn and cattle. The Rockies will export coal and gas. And California will sell its pele and its wines . . ."

Here I nodded at Mandy, but she just glared at me.

"But there will not be enough common interest to hold it together as a nation," I continued. "That is where we need you, Gran. You could unite them. You could be our Caesar, our Napoleon, our Hitler—"

"Unlucky role models, don't you think?"

"Well, yes. Still, the country needs someone to rally around, to make sense of the confusion. That man should be you—but you have to move fast."

Gran steepled his fingers and sank down in his chair. His eyes focused at a point in the rug eighteen inches from his toes. I had said enough and knew when to shut up.

Mandy sat on the very edge of her chair, the tip of her tongue touching her upper lip, her eyes blazing at him. But she, too, knew when to shut up around Gran.

After a minute or more, his eyes slid over to her. He put out a hand and touched her thigh. He gently rubbed his palm up and down, rucking her skirt up and back across her tanned knees. Gran's face had an expression of longing and sadness. Whatever he was going to say, he knew how it would end.

"I have to go, you know."

"I know," she said evenly.

"You could come with me, even just for a little while. Think of it as a vacation. A kind of honeymoon. Or, well, a camping trip."

"Would we be coming back here to live?"

"Probably not. The country has to be run from its power centers. But we could visit . . ."

"It wouldn't be the same."

"No, it wouldn't. But I would still love you."

"When there was time, when the affairs of state did not need you more." Here she shot a hard look at me.

"Yes, that's true. Still, I could give you—" He paused, calculating. "—a third, or half of my days."

"Not enough, Gran."

"No," he agreed.

"It wouldn't work. Because this is my place. This is my life, what Mother built and left to me. I won't give up this plantation. And just how would it look in Baltimore, if the—what?—President's? Speaker's? The Big Man's wife— mistress? consort?—ran a pot plantation on the side. Junk to pollute the minds of our nation's stalwart youth, right?"

"Something like that." He grinned, but the corners of his mouth were drooping.

"I won't leave," she said.

"And I can't stay."

She lifted his hand off her leg, gave it a squeeze, and put it on the arm of his chair. Then she rose and, back straight, head high, walked out of the room. The queen from her court. I never saw Mandy Holton again.

"Leave me alone now," Gran said. "We will discuss strategy tomorrow."

I left Sanders and half the men invested on the hill and took the yellow truck down to the camp. There I arranged a snap inspection for 1400 hours and came prepared to put the whole five companies on punishment drill if they were slacked off as badly as my first trip through the camp had suggested.

We went down the rows of men and women, giving out a flick here for a frayed cuff, there for a scuffed boot or dirty weapon. I test-fired a thumper and saw the shell fall in the river without exploding: two weeks' duty in the supply depot, counting shells and checking the pins.

We went down the rows of Stompers and Turtles, checking off the crew chiefs for cracked fan sets, leaky gaskets, or battle computers that punched up FFFF instead of 0000. I switched on one of the Stompers and ran her turbines up to red, listening for synch and watching for smoke. She coughed blue at 9,750 rpm: three days assigned in the rotor shop, packing bearings.

Then I took the whole troop, tech specs as well as grunts, out on a little field march. Ten miles through the hills, double time with full packs. On the final leg, I stepped aside and counted off the last hundred grunts—and gave them extra drill.

Every one of those lads and lasses knew that Colonel Birdshit had finally come to California.

The next morning I rolled up to the house in a Turtle with Lieutenants Wong and Gervaise. We met with Gran and Major Sanders in the map room or control center or whatever Mandy kept that big room for. I had brought along a field cyber with projection rig. Its disks were crammed full of demographic stats, situation reps, political vectors, troop concentrations and capabilities, elint summaries—about 900 megs' worth of data on the whole country. I set it up to display on a white wall and began briefing Corbin and the others.

"The political options are largely unchanged from this spring," I began. "The West is mostly ours, adhering to the nucleus of the TENMAC. The East belongs to itself, or to anyone—except anyone named 'Corbin'—who can claim to hold Congress."

I brought up a simple two-color map on the wall, green for us, red for them.

"Now, it is never quite that simple. First, in our own West, allegiance is a sometime thing. Utah, with its Deseret tradition, is talking about a 'closed community.' It would work, too, except their citizens hold the deed on too much ground outside the State, and they are afraid they might lose it."

"They will," Corbin said.

"Nevada wants concessions. What they are, and in return for what, nobody is saying yet. Just 'concessions.' And the Ore-Wash Axis wants a laundry list of environmental miracles out of you, ending with 'stop the rain' and 'bring back the price of timber.' "

I shaded the map while talking, with patches of blue and yellow.

"The Farm Belt wants to see how you stand on farm issues, particularly whether the next government is going to continue meddling in the market. I gave their military envoys assurances, when asked, that I could not think why you would want to do that, but they just hum and haw and suck on their mints. Maybe they want a freer money market, or maybe—who knows?—a war with Canada over exports."

"Not this year," Corbin agreed.

"Finally, there is Rupert the First, by the Grace of God, King of Montana and All the Lands to the Ocean. *Which* ocean, he does not say. Probably both. He is trying to run the country by fiat from Helena. Although he has fanatical supporters in Wyoming and the Dakotas, for the rest of the country his transmissions are just so many free-floating photons."

"Is he insane?" Barney Wong asked.

"Possibly. No matter. We still have to whup him, and he has an army about thirty thousand strong."

"Shit," Gervaise said.

"What about the East?" Corbin asked quietly.

I slid the colors up on the wall.

"The Midatlantic was strong for Pollock, and to them you are still 'the enemy.' That creates a vacuum now being filled with lightweights. Money moguls, mostly. All the real military people chose up sides and came to our war long ago.

"Outside of the Middle States, however, there is no psychological dominant—unless you count aggravated fatigue and the desire to be left alone. New England is still

allied with us, but mostly to annoy their southern neigh-
bors. The Ohio Valley and the Rust Bowl want markets.
That means they are beginning to realize they need the
West, and not just on a contraband basis."

"We'll trade," Corbin affirmed.

"Of course." Next I brought up an orange-and-yellow
patchwork on the map.

"The Deep South would like to sign a nonaggression
pact with you and go their own way. But that turns out to
be about eight ways, because they cannot even agree on
Standard Time. And Florida, of course, is fast becoming a
Caribbean Island."

"Bet Georgia loves that," Pet Gervaise chuckled.

"They *are* talking about a ditch," I nodded. "Big one—
dug with atomics."

"And finally, that leaves us with Old Mexico. . . ."

Their three heads craned forward and studied the map.
They were silent for a couple of minutes, with only their
eyeballs moving.

"Lost them?" Barney Wong asked at last.

"Not quite. The psychometry says the various States
need a northern affiliation more than ever. And opinion
about the General is pretty evenly divided—even inside
some heads. For one thing, he is the GV military officer
who ran the State of Yucatan fairly and progressively. For
another, he is the babykiller who incinerated three cities
in Coahuila. Now, that does not count entirely against us.
Call it the Whipped Dog Syndrome—"

Corbin made a face at that.

"—but just our having the guts to actually *use* The
Bomb impresses a lot of people. Even on this side of the
river. We have been riding that wave for four years."

"What does Mexico *want?*" Corbin asked.

I studied the map myself. This one did not have a single
color or code. The key was not clear. What does any
people want, who once ruled a subcontinent from pyra-
mids of stone, whose land is more bitter than dust and
richer than the Pharaohs' Egypt, who have taken the
bootheel from every European who ever landed there?

What does a woman want, when she has been raped so
often, it is the only love she knows?

"Respect," I said at last. "That man who can show his
understanding for Mexico's heritage and potential, can
rule her."

"Then we'll do film clips and docudramas," Gran said
immediately. "Check our Merida archives—we must
have a couple of thousand feet of children and me
speaking Spanish. And our road system, the new docks at
Progresso. . . . Narration in the vernacular only." He was
giving orders to Pet Gervaise as if she were part of his
video crew, not a fire team leader. And she was nodding
away and pretending to take notes.

After that thought had run out, Corbin looked up at me.

"What else, Billy?"

"Nothing else, except to come up with a plan. Our
strength is on the map." I keyed up the symbols for
various military units: black circles ours, black squares
others. "You only have to move them where you want
them and decide who gets hit first."

"Rupert?" Wong ventured.

"Eventually, but not the first," I said. "Save him for
mop-up."

"What about the politics in Congress?" Corbin asked.

"Ah!" Missed that dimension. I quickly overlaid the
map on the wall with an orange-and-black checkerboard,
which clumped up in some areas.

"Here are the party standings as of 2018, the last valid
election after the start of the war. And here they are
today." I keyed again, and the checkerboard faded. "Nothing, since the Bootheel Election of '20 was disputed and
no candidate took his or her seat in Congress. No one has
a seat now, and the last session adjourned *sine die*. Pri-
maries were spotty this spring, and no one is sure what
will happen."

"So," Corbin concluded, "the man who called for new
elections now would be picking up points for leadership."

"Something like that," I agreed.

"And to do that, I'd have to be somewhere in or near
Baltimore. Which is close to us." He studied the map, its

puddles and swatches of color. The East Coast around the capital was uniformly hostile.

"What about my authority as a member of the last Special Executive?" he asked.

"Good question. And was it invalidated by your breaking the GV charter and bringing troops into the country?"

"It's going to be a question of what people *want* to believe," Corbin said quietly, almost to himself. "Like most things. But they don't know what the stakes are—and don't have a reason to care. Our task, then, is to create a venue, an arena in which they are forced to choose and believe. Just as we did in Houston."

"A victory march?" Pet asked. "Like Napoleon returning from Elba? Slow enough to let people rally to him, but too fast for the opposition to organize itself. Something like that?"

"And when the East closes Baltimore with a ring of steel?" Corbin countered.

"I didn't say we wouldn't take weapons," she purred.

"I don't like leaving Rupert behind us," Barney Wong said. "Feels like a pincers."

"I think we can take care of him later," I said. "From Baltimore."

Corbin looked from one of us to another, then turned to my major, Sanders. He had sat through all these discussions without speaking, following them only with his eyes.

"What do you think, Carl?"

Sanders considered his words for five seconds.

"I think they will lay roses at your feet, General."

"Then let's do it."

The conference turned operational. We discussed troop strengths and how to move them so they would build our "standing wave" of support. We weighed our army along the Mississippi and how it would play into the eastward roll. We gave thought to the western desert, the great barren patch in Nevada and Utah that we would have to cross. We counted satellite uplinks and plotted transmissions that would show the victory march to its best advantage.

After two hours, I looked up and my eye was caught by

a flash of material in one of the doorways. It was a sleeve of red silk. I could guess whose it was. After two or three seconds it disappeared.

By noon we had hammered out the details. We agreed that the five companies camped here should move out as soon as possible, but no later than tomorrow at dawn. I would leave this day to begin arranging the route and our outside troop strengths.

We broke for lunch, which I insisted we all take in the camp. Our aides went out, but Gran hesitated.

"I think I'll stay here for—" he began.

"For what?" I asked sharply. "To say good-bye? To torture yourself? Or to torture *her?*"

Gran turned his head aside, looking toward that door where I had seen the sleeve.

"Your destiny is to rule this country, Gran. You must go to that destiny. And you cannot do that and have her, too. Even if she were willing, she is on the wrong side of the economy. Your alliance would not serve anyone's interest."

"I know." Corbin's shoulders sagged half an inch, his jaw muscles loosened. With one step, one turn of the heel, he seemed to age ten years. It was a man carrying fifty-two winters of hard fighting whom I led out from the house of the arches on that California hilltop.

The rest of our story is in the history books.

While Napoleon may have taken twenty days to march from Cannes to Paris, it took us twenty months. Half the State of Nevada met our armored column coming out of the passes of the Sierra, and they cheered us as we started into the Carson Sink and the great deserts east of Reno. Nevada, like California, had been Granny's home.

Utah had not. They blockaded the main road, old I-80, against us at the State line. The Mormon troops and the Desert Pilgrims were backed up by at least three "legions" of Rupert I's fanatics. They outnumbered the 750 men and women we had in marching order by at least eight to one. Gran could have radioed to his friends at Nellis AFB and had a wing of heavy bombers to cover us in forty minutes. He could have made a strategic strike and reduced Salt Lake City to lath and cinders. But none of those would have done our work of consolidation.

Instead we rolled my yellow truck, the Nuke Wagon, out in front and fired a brace of our star shells high in the air over them. The Pilgrims ran for it. Our Stompers dove on the roadblock itself, blasting it apart with concussion grenades. Only Rupert's men held their ground and kept firing. They were only put down with a bullet each to the head. I had never met this King Rupert, who could inspire such loyalty or fear, but I was beginning to get a feeling he would require our special attention.

Passing through Colorado, Corbin sent a special task group, under Mike Alcott, backed up by reinforcements moved in from our army along the Mississippi, to the Federal Strategic Forces center at Colorado Springs. Alcott was to reason with the "First Strike Fellahs" and get them to acknowledge Corbin as the only viable alternative to a complete power vacuum on a nationwide scale.

The FSF had been indoctrinated in loyalty, not to the extinct Gordon Pollock or any one man, but to the Constitution of the United States and the country's duly elected chief executive. Alcott had no other options except to put the center under blockade and try to starve them out. The pushbutton warriors had enough resources with them under the mountain to survive a thermonuclear war, stay sealed in two years, and come out to plant cesium-reducing hybrid corn and rebuild the American way of life. Alcott made the gesture anyway, but privately he told Corbin to start winning elections.

That was not so easy. Our allies in the various western States may have backed us when it was a shooting war against a single Federal force under Pollock. But now that Corbin had won and wanted to put his own name on the whole enchilada, they got skittish. They had second thoughts. They saw the possibilities of running their own little regional empires, on the model of Rupert in Montana. They wanted their quid-pros.

East of Colorado, the victory march broke down into a hopscotch of private consultations, Corbin and his closest aides meeting with the local honcho and his or her bully boys. When talks broke down, there was usually some military maneuvering, which Corbin won because he had always managed to hold the greatest resources at any point in time. He also had some chits out, of course, and he called them in with a vengeance.

When the opposition gave in, it was more through exhaustion than conversion.

Corbin was finally allowed to approach Baltimore, but only on his way to Annapolis to negotiate with the Maryland legislature, and he could come as only a private citizen—no bodyguards, no honor guard, nothing. He told me later about walking across Rotunda Square in the Capitol Complex. The groundskeepers had maintained it perfectly; even the twenty-four fountains were still spraying.

"But it was empty, so empty," Gran said. "So much white marble and pink granite, cold and stiff, like icing on a cake after they've called the wedding off."

It was not until 2024 that Corbin felt strong enough to call for congressional elections, and he did it from Columbus, Ohio, because the capital was still officially closed to him. However, by that time his popularity with the rest of the country was so great that they fought over where he was to campaign. They were throwing roses at his feet, as Major Sanders had predicted.

Corbin could take his pick from more than fifty-six districts that assured him a landslide if he would only put his name on the ballot. In 232 other districts, the write-in campaign was at least eight points ahead of the nearest official candidate in the polls. However, he could not run for them all himself. So he plotted it carefully, making sure the candidate of his choice was known—and that the man or woman so favored understood it. For his own seat, he ran from his old district in West Texas.

"Purely sentimental reasons," he told the nation with a mock humble smile. And he let it be understood that he meant it as a salute to Texas, which had first welcomed him under the threat of impeachment. Actually, it was for political reasons, as we on the inside knew. By representing only sagebrush and armadillos, Corbin limited the number of strings on himself and could isolate himself from local interests.

When the 117th Congress was called to order in January 2025, the Corbinites held 342 of the 620 seats in the House. Among them was Mike Alcott, who had easily taken his former district in Massachusetts; he was working hard to help heal the breach in the East. Gabriel Ossing, Corbin's nephew, had also won a seat, in Maine. That case was full of loopholes, because the boy was still in his twenties, technically under age for a congressman, and although his mother was an American, he was technically a Canadian citizen. In their enthusiasm, the voters of Maine had waived all that, but one could still question whether local statute should take precedent over constitutional law.

Alcott was totally Corbin's man now, his whip in the House. Alcott shaped up the vote that made Corbin Speaker. Alcott marshalled support for most of Corbin's bills and proposed the extraordinary measure that was to install him as Speaker for a guaranteed term of ten years. Even the most faithful Corbinites hesitated over that one. It was a completely unprecedented law, surely counter to the Constitution, and would certainly be challenged in the Supreme Court. Only the fact that Corbin had just named six new associate justices and the chief justice—the years of civil war and confusion having been hard on an already elderly Court—gave the bill any hope at all.

The measure presumed that Corbin would win the next five elections and keep his district. But considering where he was running from, that was no problem.

There was also the presumption, among the other congressmen and -women, that Corbin would meet any challenge with military force. He had done it once. And they had also seen how quickly, as Speaker, he had signed commissions in the FSF for Alcott and me. I got three stars, Alcott two.

That became a sore point, later, when we finally decided to mop up for Rupert I and bring Montana back into the Union. I had thought the job would be mine.

"Can't spare you, Billy," Corbin said, in what was to be our last interview.

"What?" I was shocked. "Do you know how little I have to do these days? Just fly around the country, inspect bases, review fitness reports, poke my nose into rocket silos, and run a gloved finger across mess-hall griddles. Just personnel and public relations work. All protocol."

"A necessary job, considering our tenuous position," he nodded.

"Tenuous? Well, yes, but the fight against Rupert is going to be the last grand act of the civil war. I have worked for it, Gran. I want it. It should be mine."

"That's not how military decisions are made, and you know it." His eyes never got much higher than my campaign ribbons.

"But, Gran—"

"The decision is made, General."

"May I know who is going to direct the action?"

"That's really no . . . General Alcott." Still he would not meet my eyes.

"Mike! But you need him in Congress, he is—"

"He has done his work in Congress, and now I need him in the field against King Rupert."

"I see."

And suddenly I did. That was Alcott's payoff, the quid-pro for his work as Gran's whip.

My own career, my years of service with Granville James Corbin, somewhere had taken a wrong turn. Maybe I should have run for Congress. Maybe I should have left him in California and marched on Baltimore myself. Maybe I should have been born a white man—a full white.

I asked to be dismissed and left his office. That very afternoon I folded my nice, newly printed commission three different ways, so the corners stuck out, and sent it to Corbin. He never acknowledged it.

All this was years ago.

I went back into the business that I know best—sludge. The technologies had progressed in groundwater reclamation, and there was a steady market for it in Louisiana, where the deepest water wells were bringing up a Hell's broth of refinery chemicals. I took my back pay, bought a small detox outfit, and started in. This was honorable work, helping people living healthier lives. In its way, it was clean.

Granny Corbin, reaching his moment of greatest power, had developed what my people call the Custer sickness. He saw himself as a kind of natural force, a power to move people and shape the Earth itself. He thought his actions and decisions constituted some kind of law. And he did not see consequences.

The best of my people laid down their lives fighting such men. The lesser ones, the weak ones, my ancestors, laid their weapons and lived. It is for them—and for me—that I am ashamed.

Chapter 22

Granville James Corbin: MARCH 14, 2028

[From the WWY-CV Archive]

Take apart with a hammer. Rebuild with tweezers.

That's the instruction manual we have followed in restoring the country, reuniting the eighty-three States into a working nation. The last five or six years have been a real scramble.

Simply getting to the stage where we could hold the 2024 elections, I had to keep a lot of people happy. That meant making promises as fast as I could talk, handing out psychological blank checks by the fistful: concessions, special considerations, rights to levy new local taxes and repeal old ones, Federal licenses and monopolies and charters to issue and rescind, sons and party faithful to favor. We needed a cyber to backtrack the trail of my agreements with State governors, legislators, party bosses, community organizations, business groups, military officers. And sometimes, in keying up the totals, the outgo was maybe more than we had in hand to offer. But I never told a deliberate lie, never gave both A and B the same cookie, when I could help it, and never incurred a debt I had no intention of repaying.

Things went faster after the elections. My friends and followers had enough political clout that we could order the priorities in Congress. However, I very quickly discovered that being the political linchpin in the Federal government didn't mean a whole lot. Not when that government was, in most people's lives, merely an economic inconvenience, a club of political cronies in Baltimore to be paid off with a few user fees, while the separate States operated on wholly libertarian doctrines and held the real power. This still wasn't a nation but a patchwork quilt of regional interests. Civil war had burned over them like a fast prairie fire, scorching the grass but hardly touching the deeply tangled roots.

Luckily, fierce anti-Union feeling still existed in pockets like South Florida, Lousiana Free Port, and the lands of the late King of Montana. During the months immediately before the elections, I had sent our best GV units in to probe their defenses and gauge their war-making capability. But we soon figured out that another series of military victories wouldn't reunify the nation.

So we changed the agenda. By placing stories with the right correspondents and providing some exciting video footage, the final, later-stage mopping-up operations could be made to look more dangerous than they might actually, tactically, have been. A few sponsored editorials, appearing in the media of neighboring States, declaimed against the threat to public safety. And Rupert I and his Aryan Legions did the rest, giving us enough material to carry the whole campaign.

When my agents introduced the "Petition to Ensure Domestic Tranquillity" in forty-four State houses, all in the same week, the emotionally exhausted and now frightened legislators fell on it with glad little cries. The primary purpose of this artfully vague document was contained in the resolution that I be "empowered to form a stronger, more vital Union." Whatever that meant. On my terms.

So I proposed to reorganize the national economy. Those loyalties our hopscotch wars had not been able to bind, the dollar would stitch together with links of steel.

Also, for the first time in a dozen years, we could attend to the country's international trade relations. From the vantage of Baltimore, I could peel back the concessions that foreign traders had demanded from the individual

States, or taken outright, like Colombian oil rights in Louisiana offshore tracts, Asian drug traffic in California, the English coal cartel in Pennsylvania and West Virginia, and Soviet soybean policy in Mississippi. I closed up those proprietary U.S.-Them Trading Associations that had been forced on our soil—and kept those trading rights in the name of the Federal government.

When the local interests protested, I pitched the argument in terms of selfish profiteers who would rather sell their product to foreigners than serve the needs of the nation. And I made sure that our newsats colored the story that way.

Oh yes: After the elections I put the satellite networks directly under Baltimore's control. It was all done quietly, no dramatic changes in staffing or programming, but the people at the top were mine, and so were the budgets.

I reorganized Federal policy on commerce. The former practice had been to fill the treasury in Baltimore by granting sweeping Federal monopolies to existing sectors, trade groups, and companies. That had tended to eliminate competition and confirm the regions' traditional economic strengths: heavy manufacturing in the Northeast and Ohio Valley, bulk farming in the Midwest and Old South, defense contracting and specialty crops in the West, timber in the Northwest.

Instead, I encouraged competition and broke up regional interests by offering attractive licenses and limited monopolies to companies and entrepreneurs who would operate outside each area's sphere of expertise. With the free cash in the Federal coffers, I made sure that the necessary infrastructures could be built—new roads, new energy supplies, technical training, universities, water resources, health care, et cetera, et cetera.

This policy not only revitalized the local economies but also, by the way, just in case you didn't notice, increased their dependence on Federal administration of these programs.

Of course, to keep this new economic structure stable, I also had to reorganize our policies on finance and banking. I set up a series of cross-subsidies. Heavy user fees—and even a new issue of Federal taxes, small ones at first—were settled on the established businesses. And these provided new cash resources that the Federal Reserve loaned out at special low rates to new, multi-state banks and brokerage houses, which in turn could offer attractive loans to the new ventures and buy securities from them with long-extended redemption dates.

It has been my policy never to make these moves compulsory, never to revoke statutory freedoms or civil rights. But I was always clever enough to find the point of leverage that made a deal attractive, voluntary—and unavoidable.

Of course, individuals had to be encouraged to move into these new business sectors. In the wake of the war, and to bleed off our standing GV troops as well as the State militias, I offered a great many federal service contracts. The *quid* in these contracts is payment, for a term, of life maintenance, relocation expenses, individual retraining, and apprentice fees. The *pro quo* is a period of personal service or labor, at or below local wage levels, in the part of the country and at the company that the individual's Federal case officer directs.

There was some grumbling over these contracts. But they were perfectly legal and, considering the chaotic state of the country as I found it . . .

Oh, I would say there have never been more than about seventy million individuals under Federal contract at any one time. That's less—certainly, isn't it?—than the clientele served with entitlements in the later years of the twentieth century.

International relations—I mentioned those, didn't I? Yes. Well, I refurbished Cheyenne Mountain, updated the weapons the FSF would have to work with, put new and more powerful satellites into geosynch, and announced an official foreign policy of "Don't Tread On Me."

Last year, I launched a fleet of 200 hunter-killer submarines to patrol along our coasts, with their electronic senses angled offshore. I have plans to annex Guatemala as a buffer State, despite the political fallout from the Bottom Thirty-Two, as some people now call Old Mexico. Then we will dig an atomic ditch ten kilometers wide across the isthmus, following the borders with Honduras and El Salvador. It's a wide stretch, mountainous, a bad place for a canal. But we have *a lot* of nuclear devices.

After that, we may still trade with Canada. If they're nice about it.

I've already had one opportunity to demonstrate the effectiveness of this foreign policy. The NATO signatories—that grinning, shambling, clanking remnant of the Cold War—protested our withdrawal of troops from Europe at the height of the Civil War. From some archaic, kneejerk impulse, they felt they had to *punish* the United States for *treaty violations.* England and Germany—who were about the only members left—tried to work economic sanctions on us. When those failed, they sent a small expeditionary force of about 5,000 men to land on Fire Island.

Too late for the active phase of our war.

Mike Alcott and the FSF picked them up inside of four hours. And then, will full warnings, I sent two ICBMs—but with warheads of only about five megatons each—against Newcastle and Kiel, small cities on the eastern borders of both countries. Prevailing winds took the clouds away from their main population centers. I could afford to ignore the protests of the Norwegians and East Germans.

The United States doesn't need NATO as a buffer zone anyway, not in Europe, not anymore.

"Don't Tread On Me." For the next twenty years or so, I shall let the Third World rot in the first circle of Economic Hell. Let the little dictators and the flea-bite guerrillas feed on each other. Let the Sov Bloc pick its teeth on Africa and the Middle East. When I am ready to reenter the geopolitical situation, it will be ready for me.

The Second American Civil War caused some 63,000 fatalities, most of them combatants, not civilians. Compared to the population at large, some 430 million, that's an absurdly small casualty count. Most people hardly knew it when the fighting was going on. We conducted the war like a game of *go,* with blocks and traps, instead of pitched battles. Or have I explained this already? Anyway . . . no reason for the media to call me a butcher. We fought a *clean* war.

After a leader reaches a certain level of dominance or prominence, his followers *want* him to succeed and will obey him if he is only halfway credible. After all, as every stage comic learns: The audience wants to laugh. The enemies of that success are not the random grumblers in the audience. No, they are those near-equals, the would-be leaders who stand in the wings and wait to rush onstage. They are the ones any leader must watch for and deal with.

I've had my share. Carlotta would not leave well enough alone. Ever the plotter. Ever the politician. Two years ago she tried to stage a coup with nothing more than a handsome young FSF general. He wasn't even from the winning side.

How to deal with them? Well, one way is, a leader can use the would-be equals as scapegoats—targets to draw the attention of his own grumblers and strengthen loyalty to himself. I found evidence that Carlotta and her champion had sold secrets to Sov Bloc agents. The timing coincided nicely. I hanged them for that.

Another technique is to draw the dissidents' followers to his cause, deflating the competition and using them as a source of converts. It is better to absorb than to defeat . . . I guess that's Takusan Matsu speaking.

Unfortunately, Carlotta didn't have any followers. Or not enough to use. So I hung them all.

Another plot surfaced last year, led by the governor of New York. He tried to persuade the farming States of Vermont and New Hampshire to secede with him. Just like that. Walk out of the Union. He must have been crazy. Now *there* I could appeal to his followers, and to the industrial belt in that northern tier he tried to tempt into sedition. I made even stronger supporters out of them. My nephew, who kept his Maine seat in the '26 elections, was most helpful there.

Yes, Gabriel is shaping up nicely. I send good reports on him to Clary, who has settled in Minnesota, up near Rainy Lake. She likes to be near the border with her beloved Canadians. However, for her own protection, I keep a watch on the house. Who knows what might happen? Especially if there's a raid.

Gabe, as I was saying, is shaping up. He's learning the ropes in Congress. Learning to work the flock. A good sheepdog knows how to keep on its flank: when to nip, when to bark, and when to show his snout.

They *are* sheep, of course. But there are one or two who think they know more than is good for them. Fair faces concealing slippery secrets. You can see it when they rise to speak. Too mush gesture. Too much graciousness toward the Speaker's chair. And then the content of what they say sorts out more like criticism and sedition. Wolves on their bellies, trying to bleat like sheep.

He's in my will, of course, Gabe is. My only kin. I can leave him nothing but money. My military strength, the old Gentlemen Volunteer units, has been disbanded and absorbed into the FSF. And the political power he will have to build for himself; he's already started that. But money will be enough. There would be something like $130 billion, with a B, if I were to die tomorrow. That's enough for any boy.

Tomorrow. At first I accepted the Speakership for ten years. On the installment plan, as it were. But the situation is still too unsettled for that. We need to bind in the weak ones, the waverers, with a gesture. Tomorrow, Mike Alcott will move that Congress vote me the chair for life. A small correction of an earlier mistake, he will say. But they will read the message correctly. Yes, they will.

Alcott troubles me. Because *he* is troubled. He was here this morning.

"Gran, we move too fast," he was saying. "Some of these developmental programs and reforms . . ."

"The nation needs decisive action," I told him. "We are in an era of reconstruction. We must rebuild those economic strengths that pertained in the years before—"

"But the people got used to the laissez-faire, to running things themselves," he interrupted me. He never used to interrupt me, not even in private. "When you tie them to these contracts and monopolies—and now the craft laws—you go too far. They resent it. I hear talk of taking this to the Supreme Court. And Justice Renfrew encourages it."

"My Court will support me."

"Not when you're trying to create guild associations for most of the technical and professional jobs, with regulated entry and hereditary sponsorships. That's—that's medieval!"

"Only as a temporary measure. Until we get the cashflow up to pre-'15 levels. Then we can declare a free state, and let them shift—"

"It's purely un-American, Gran. I can't even keep our hard-core two hundred in line on this. I've got maybe *six* votes in my pocket right now. And I have to tell you frankly, mine is not one of them."

That was too much!

"Traitor! You traitor," I hissed at him.

His face froze up.

And instantly I regretted it.

"Ahhh, Mike . . . And I thought you understood so well—what we were trying to accomplish."

"I understand what you want," he said stiffly. "It's the means we disagree on. May I go now, sir? There are committee meetings to attend."

I should have kept him, soothed him some more. But he seemed anxious to leave, and I let him.

That grumbling, the "resentment" Alcott mentioned . . . The ratings, of course, have been lower than I'd like to see. But when I am Speaker for Life, the little resentments will fade. The people and the Congress will see the sense of what we are doing.

And now, gentlemen—and lady—if you will excuse me, we have a country to run . . . One last question?

I would tell them: A man can't choose the era he's born into, but he can choose how to conduct himself in that era. Look at my own career. Not a promising time, the late twentieth century, and yet I built a personal fortune, obtained political power, fought and won a bitter war— and now will lead a sick nation in its reconstruction.

What century would I have preferred? That's easy. The eighteenth, of course. Revolutionary America. Such a time of creativity. A whole nation being built from scratch, with the whole world of political and moral principles to choose from. I can think of one or two improvements I could have . . .

Well, enough of the personal. Time's wasting.

Epilogue
Michael Alcott: Tu Mortuus

To begin with, it wasn't the normal pattern.

Usually, by 10:30 in the morning, the committees are in session, and if there is to be a debate or vote in the full House, the members move in quickly, most of them late. If they have something to discuss out of session, they gather in the office buildings or bunch up in the tunnels. The New Rotunda, that hideous, cold, deco-marble fishbowl with its stupid fountain, is just for tourists. But this morning they were standing in knots under the glass of the Dome when I crossed. Should have rung bells in my head, but it didn't.

For one thing, the mix was wrong. The Connecticut Kids were there, Jasper Bruce and Caspar Long, talking with a clutch of California congressmen they had been killing in debate since January. Everyone knew they were Corbin's new pets, late converts to the cause. We all assumed they were just trying too hard, going for their legislative spurs when they should have been content to carry spears for a year more. But here they were chatting and laughing. I actually saw one slap a back like old pals. Strange.

Off to one side, standing one foot to the other, was the New York Crowd. This was the closest thing we had to a Loyal Opposition, if you didn't count the Coahuila Cluster. The NYC was muttering among itself and studying the toes of its collective shoes with great interest, when it wasn't stealing glances at the Kids' group. Suspicious.

But I was in too much of a hurry, being late myself, to put all this together. It just shook itself out later, afterwards.

Others were there in twos and threes, a total of about eighty or ninety people in the Rotunda. In that space, it was a mob. I was pushing through from the east doors, actually elbowing my way at one point, when the knot I was pushing against suddenly surged west, opening a way for me. That was when Corbin came in from the other set of doors.

How could I see, if the place was so mobbed? You'd know if you had ever been in the New Rotunda. The floor is dished by a series of shallow steps, concentric rings of them on an awkward spacing of one, two, and a plateau. They make normal walking almost impossible, and you can't do a straight line across the place. The steps force you to angle down toward the huge fountain, that dumb crystal-kink creation that drips and oozes water.

Now, to get to the House chamber, Corbin was crossing diagonally, next to the fountain. And the Connetícut Kids with their newfound friends were waiting for him there.

"Granny!" That's how Bruce greeted Corbin. He wasn't shouting, although I heard it distinctly. The Rotunda was suddenly that quiet.

He raised his hand, as if waving, and then I saw the flash. Light from high in the Dome, reflecting off what was in Bruce's hand.

Of course it was a glass dagger. Nothing else would get through the metal detectors. We should have been doing body pats but, with no incidents, people quickly get tired of the inconvenience.

I don't think Corbin even saw the dagger. He stopped to say something to Jasper Bruce. And for some reason Bruce left his hand up high, kept his big smile long past the moment of greeting, and still did not strike.

That was for Casper Long, who had edged around behind Gran and raised his own glass dagger. He brought it down crookedly, only catching Corbin on the shoulderblade.

I've studied the body with the doctors and seen how shallow that first scratch was.

Corbin did not even turn. By that time he *must* have seen the dagger in Bruce's hand. And Bruce still did not strike for about two more seconds. Enough time for Gran to take him apart.

People say the conspirators rushed him, buried him with their bodies, all stabbing at once. But those people were not there to see. It didn't happen like that.

People say the bit about Corbin being a black belt was all media peep or the figment of a copywriter's imagination. But I had gone through basic training and hand-to-hand with him, back when we first formed the Gentlemen Volunteers. And hadn't I seen him out there on the rooftop at dawn, in Las Vegas and Houston both, doing his karate exercises, the slow moves and the fast? He was a killer with his feet. But here . . . He could have broken a twig like Jasper Bruce without working up a sweat—and then used pieces of him to whip that mob into a corner.

And Corbin wasn't too old, either, like some people say. I had been in the gym with him just two weeks before. Older, yes, and aren't we all? Yet he could still do fifty pushups without gasping. I saw that with my own eyes.

But people are right when they say Corbin did not fight back. Bruce had plenty of time to plant his knife. He must have been going for the neck, something cute with the carotid, but he botched it. The strike went wide and caught Gran on the point of his shoulder. Must have been right on a nerve, because I could see the pain register on his face.

Corbin said something to Bruce. I din't hear what it was, and anyone standing close enough to hear had already fled for his life. But Corbin said it with a look of real sadness. That I could see.

It gave time for Casper Long to put in a really serious blow. Which he did, the one that staggered Corbin, turning his body around one bent knee.

Then the mob moved in. Most of them were unarmed, until someone put a foot through the Rotunda's curtain wall and people began picking up and passing around the glass shards. They must have cut their hands on them, mingling their blood with Granny's when they stabbed.

I stood alone to one side, about the only person there who wasn't part of the conspiracy. Either that, or there were dozens of bystanders who joined in on impulse. I thought they would turn and finish me off, too. But they didn't

Like robots running down, after the first flurry of blows and the blood, they slowed up, stood around, some looking at the body, some looking away. Then they moved out, some running but most walking. Until the Rotunda was almost empty.

Corbin lay on his back, half in the fountain, with the water dripping across his face and his open eyes. It washed away the blood that still seeped from the gashes, and the water got pinker and pinker. I wanted to go and close his eyes, but I could not make my feet move.

They have killed him, killed the General. It was a mob murder, but Bruce and Long clearly started it. I testify to that.

So, why doesn't somebody find them? No one can disappear without a trace. Not anymore. Not with the cybernet checking credits and reservations every time you turn around. So, let's track them down! Bring them back! Punish them for conspiracy and murder!

Or doesn't anyone care?

TRAVIS SHELTON
LIKES BAEN BOOKS
BECAUSE THEY TASTE GOOD

Recently we received this letter from Travis Shelton of Dayton, Texas:

> *I have come to associate Baen Books with Del Monte. Now what is that supposed to mean? Well, if you're in a strange store with a lot of different labels, you pick Del Monte because the product will be consistent and will not disappoint.*
>
> *Something I have noticed about Baen Books is that the stories are always fast-paced, exciting, action-filled and seem to be published because of content instead of who wrote the book. I now find myself glancing to see who published the book instead of reading the back or intro. If it's a Baen Book it's going to be good and exciting and will capture your spare reading moments.*
>
> *Another discovery I have recently made is that I don't have any Baen Books in my unread stacks—and I read four to seven books a week, so that in itself is a meaningful statistic.*

Why do you like Baen Books? Drop us a letter like Travis did. The person who best tells us what we're doing right—and where we could do better—will receive a Baen Books gift certificate worth $100. Entries must be received by December 31, 1987. Send to Baen Books, 260 Fifth Avenue, New York, N.Y. 10001. And ask for our free catalog!